HOCKEY WITH BENEFITS

TIJAN

Edited by: Kay Springsteen
Developmental Editor: Becca Mysoor, www.fairyplotmother.me
Proofread and beta read by: Crystal Solis, Amy English, Paige Maroney, Kara Hildebrand, Serena McDonald, Rochelle Paige, Dominique Laura, Chris O'Neil Parece, and Kimberley Holm
Photographer: Paperback Model (PBM)

1

MARA

I liked hockey. I already knew it, but by the third period, I *really* knew it.

The wine might've been a factor, or the two beers that my roommate bought me, but either way, I was having fun. I had a new appreciation for the sport.

I was also enjoying watching Cruz Styles, the team's star player, zip around the rink like he'd been born on skates and not with two normal feet. He wasn't the only one, though. They were all going so fast, like they were flying on ice. It was exhilarating to watch. It wasn't my first hockey game, but it was my first hockey game at Grant West. Everyone on campus had been raving about the new guy for a while now.

His looks didn't hurt either.

His picture was flashed on the jumbotron so many times over the night that I'd lost count. It was having an effect on the three girls in front of me, and also in my vagina. With the hockey mask on, you could still see his fierce dark blue eyes. His high cheekbones. With the mask off, he had a whole chiseled jawline that wasn't legal. I swear. And those cheekbones were set high and wide, giving the sides of his face an indented look, but it worked on him. Not to mention the messy dark hair on top of his head and how he had the look where he could rifle his hand through it, let it go and he still looked fucking hot. Comb that shit back, put him in a suit, and he'd be giving off 007 vibes.

The guy wasn't just pretty. He was sizzling hot, and right now, he was whipping down the ice, going left, through two defenders, creating an opening to the goal and *bam*–the puck was slapped–*denied*. The goalie thrust his leg out, and the puck went off it, going behind the net.

It was picked up by the other team and sent sailing to the other side of the rink.

Off Cruz went, but he'd be back in two seconds because that'd been the theme of the night.

Grant West was pushing hard the whole night, but Cruz was leading the charge. Over and over again.

I was half winded just watching them.

"Yo." Miles Gaynor moved next to me, his shoulder lightly bumping into mine. "You know Race Ryerson?"

"What?" I was fully in a drunk haze, and I was enjoying it.

Miles had first been a class friend. Then a party friend. Now he was kind of a roommate. A little skinny, floppy brown hair, but where it looked cute on him, and baby fresh cheeks, the guy was a looker. It'd been because of him that I was living in my own little space in the attic of a house where he and his cousin, a guy from the football team, and a couple other girls all lived as well. They were all chill, but I'd only met them twice and hanging out at the hockey game was the second time of those two instances. When my roommate from first semester left college to pursue a job in her family business, I hadn't wanted to stick around and see who else my college chose to be her replacement. Hence, Miles.

He nodded to my left. "He's been staring over here at you almost the whole time. Isn't he with someone?"

I frowned, but looked around, the edges of my vision blurring before I focused and saw the guy Miles was talking about. At my look, he diverted his head, but bent down to his girlfriend, who was cheering for the team.

There went my nice buzz.

Tasmin Shaw and Race Ryerson.

As he talked to her, she stopped cheering, her smile falling as she leaned forward, her eyes searching, searching, and finding me. I frowned, narrowing my eyes, but she only went still before raising a hand up and giving me a slight wave and smile with it.

I scowled, but she barely blinked at that.

Goddamn.

"What's the deal there?"

I jerked forward, my whole body going stiff. "Nothing."

"He's never been a creep before."

"He's not. His girlfriend is next to him. Tasmin Shaw."

"So?"

I shrugged. "Taz is probably just confused why I moved out of the dorms. She lived across from me, that's all." I was lying because while she wasn't from my hometown, she knew people who were, and I was guessing that she'd heard the gossip. Her boyfriend too.

My phone buzzed, and I glanced at the screen.

Kit: OMG! Your mom?! Are you okay?

Dad: Checking on you. Wanted to see how you're doing? I'm so sorry you're going through this. I know you like your space and you don't process like that, but I'm here if you want to talk. Any time, no matter what day or hour. Love you, honey.

Nope. Kit was a friend from back home. Panic burst in my chest, right before everyone and everything began to swim around me. Turning my phone off, I refused to deal with what I knew that text was about, what the gossip that Taz and her boyfriend had heard about me. It'd been the catalyst of why I came to the game tonight. What my mom did earlier, why I panicked, drove three hours home and three hours back wasn't going to be dealt with tonight.

I wanted more to drink, and the sooner the better.

"OH!" His eyes got big, and his shoulders went low. "I didn't even think about that. Good to know. Just thought it was weird, that's all."

I fixed him with a look. "Look. You don't have to do this."

My stomach was swirling, and I wasn't getting a good feeling here. Miles and I partied. Sometimes we shared a table at the library, but that'd been the extent of our friendship. I had rules with friends, no personal questions. There was a reason for it, and it was significant. I was usually able to handle that rule with friends because so far, I picked the party crowd. Deep meaningful conversations weren't the norm. It was mostly drinking, flirting, all that jazz. Sometimes there was a catty comment from another girl, and I had a few run-ins. It happened with me, not because I sought them out but because a guy was hitting on me, and the girl got jealous. Guys liked my face. It was round, but my chin somewhat gave me a heart-shaped face. They also liked how my hazel eyes looked combined with my long cinnamon dark hair. Plus, the fact that I was tiny, petite, but I had a rack and some ass. I also had sex appeal, and the reason for that is because I enjoyed sex. God. With my life, it'd become my coping mechanism, but guys could sense that from me and that's what they were only interested in from me. Beyond that, I wasn't the girl that got the guy.

I knew the deal. The guys knew the deal. It was the other girls who didn't.

I was fine with the deal, not that I partook. That's just what the guys wanted from me, but it gave me space sometimes with people. But what Miles was bordering on was something that felt like what a friend would do for someone.

I didn't want those types of friends. Or, to be more accurate, I couldn't have those types of friends.

"What?"

"You. Me. This." I gestured to the roommates, and the game. "I've got walls. I know this. You know this. They're there for a reason. You don't owe me anything. You don't have to be protective because a guy is looking my way."

He took a step back, his tone coming out cold. "Fine. I just know we watch out for each other at parties. Didn't think it was different here, but cool. Good to know. I won't watch out anymore."

Crap.

He had me because he was right. We did do that.

"Miles," I started.

"I'm out of here." He pushed his hands in his pockets and shouldered through the crowd.

Another roommate came over. Wade Kressup, Miles' cousin. His gaze slid to where Miles had just disappeared before he bent down to me. I was almost a whole foot below him. "Do I ask?"

The buzzer went off, signaling the end of the game, and I shook my head. "Nope."

I sighed, needing to refocus my thoughts. I was off today.

I turned my phone back on long enough to send a text to Miles.

Hey. Some stuff happened earlier today, and it was serious. I don't want to get into it, but it's no excuse. I'm sorry for being a bitch. Thank you for being you.

Everyone was heading out, but I stayed for a beat. I needed to get grounded. Too many emotions I was trying to ignore and thoughts I was trying not to think were creeping in. Add to all that, I'd been a bitch to a friend and yeah... I wasn't doing so well on being a decent human being here.

The whole day had gotten away from me.

My chest felt like it was being sucked out of me.

It took me a little bit before I realized Cruz was down on the ice. He was staring up at me and he half raised one of his gloves up. I gave him a small nod right back. Which, okay, I was down for what he was asking to do. Because that whole gesture was an invitation, but also crap, because that meant I'd have to turn my phone on.

"We're heading out." Wade was still there. The crowd was starting to disperse. I couldn't see where the other roommates were.

"I'm going to find my own way back. Thanks for inviting me out tonight."

He frowned a little but nodded. "Okay. Well. I'll catch up with the rest. See you later."

He headed off, and I went to the bathroom. When I was done, the crowd had lessened significantly. Still. I knew it would be a wait, but I couldn't bring myself to turn my phone back on. Because of that, I went over to the door that the players used and slid down to the floor.

I got comfortable.

I didn't have to wait long.

Fifteen minutes later, still sweaty from the game, Cruz Styles found me in the hallway. He'd changed into his Grant West hockey sweats and hoodie. He also had a ball cap pulled low over his forehead, and both his hands were inside his hoodie.

He tapped my foot with one of his and gave me one of those smiles I'd been seeing on the jumbotron all night. "Need a ride?"

"You're supposed to look intimidating for your team pictures."

He frowned but held out a hand.

I put mine in it, and he pulled me up. "Huh?"

"For your pictures." I motioned behind us to where there

was a six-foot mural picture of just him. He was in his hockey gear, holding his stick and smiling wide for the camera. "That doesn't strike fear in anyone. The opposing team comes through here. They look at that and want to be your friend."

"No, no, no. You got it all wrong." We turned for the door. "That smile gets under their skin. They've already come in hearing about me, and then they see that, and they get confused. Some guys want to wipe that smile off my face and others want to be my friend. Then I leave 'em all in the dust when I make the first goal and by then, wham. They're all sorts of fucked up."

I laughed because it wasn't true at all. Cruz was just being Cruz.

He opened the door and I stepped out, knowing which one was his truck and heading there. "You didn't shower?"

He went to the driver's side as I got in the passenger side, and he smirked my way. "What? And forget how hot and bothered I saw you were up in the stands? Figured we could shower together. You game?"

He sent me a smile as he started the engine, and I couldn't help but smile back because like Miles, Cruz knew the deal. No personal shit.

He knew the rules because he was my not-friend with benefits.

And he was right. Showers with him were the best.

2

MARA

I was crushed against the tile in the shower as Cruz was pumping into me from behind. His arms were wrapped around me, and one hand slid down my stomach, finding my clit. I moaned, pleasure rushing through me as I couldn't even stand anymore. He was holding me up, but I didn't think he was aware of it. Both his legs were planted between mine, and I was just skimming the bottom of the shower floor.

He was rolling over my clit, and I moaned, my head falling back against him.

His mouth dropped to my shoulder.

He kept pumping up into me.

This. God, this.

We'd come a long way from our first time. An impromptu study session in my room. I'd been horny. He asked to massage my ass, and I wasn't about to turn that down. We ended up screwing twice that night. I almost smiled now, remembering how we sixty-nined each other first, but then a wave of pleasure shot through me, almost making me bend in half, or I would've if Cruz wasn't firmly plastered to my back.

"Fuck," he grunted in my ear. "You feel so good."

I felt my climax coming, but I didn't want it. Not yet. He always made me come first and held off for his. I started shaking my head, pushing back from the wall and into him.

He chuckled, that sound in my ear a caress by itself. "No way, babe." He was playing my body, his fingers going slow and smooth, *sooo* slow and smooth over my clit.

Another thrust up, and he held–I screamed, my head hitting his shoulder, and I arched all the way up as I went over the edge. It ripped through me, and I was almost weeping from how good that felt.

I loved sex. There was nothing better in the world.

The sensations were still coursing through me, and I realized in a daze that Cruz was waiting until I was done. He had moved back a little so he was fully holding me up, and then as I let loose a deep sigh, as I could feel the trembling starting to wane, he nipped my ear. "My turn."

I was switched in the air, my legs wrapped around his waist once again, from instinct. My arms came up around his neck, and he carried me out to his bed. I was beyond able to process, but I had the thought we were going to soak his bed when he dropped me down. He didn't break contact, coming right on top of me. He reached over, getting a condom. Then he buried his head into my shoulder, slid in, and he was thrusting all for himself now.

He went hard, growling as he ground in for the last pump.

I held him tight, my legs and arms keeping him to me, and then he let out one last savage roar as he finished.

He lay on me for a moment.

Sometimes I didn't mind this, sometimes I hated it.

Cruz was a nice guy. He could be a dick at times, but generally he was decent, but because of my baggage and the rules, we didn't make a lot of conversation once the sex was done. Earlier had been an exception. I blamed the alcohol in me, or other stuff...

I waited to see what he'd do.

He groaned, rising and separating from me, but he only dropped down to the bed beside me. He had a hand on his stomach, his very ripped stomach, as he was catching his breath.

I still lay there, my mind very blessedly blank. For now.

After another few minutes, he frowned at me. "You want to go again? Usually, you're getting dressed and out the door before I can pull the condom off." He did just that as he was speaking, twisting to toss it into the garbage by his nightstand. He lay back down next to me, his gaze focusing on me.

I knew I should get going. It wasn't good to be here when everything would catch up to me, because that's what I'd been doing since leaving Fallen Crest. Keeping busy, drinking, the game, being around others, and now sex–all to keep the shit from my mom out of my head.

I felt the wall starting to crumble and sat up.

"Hey."

I paused, staring at him.

Still frowning, he studied me a moment before sitting up, his hand going to the inside of my leg. "Stay a bit." His hand moved in, finding my center, but he only teased me, running his fingers around me. "Guys are here. I'll grab some food, and come back for round two?"

We could hear them in the house. Cruz's room was on the back section of the hockey house. He had a decent room considering he was a freshman, with his own bathroom and that was realty gold in the hockey house. The drawback of his room versus my place was that if I didn't want to slip through the house, running into his teammates or who else they invited back tonight, I'd have to slip out through his window and go around to the stairs that are attached on the side of the house.

But I considered his offer and knew better. "You're going to go down there, get food, and the guys will pull you into their party." Which meant, it was time to go. I sat on the edge of his bed, noting how he had the thought to throw down a giant towel before we landed on his mattress. I picked at it. This thing was huge and thick. "Where'd you get this thing?"

He laughed, laying back. "No personal questions, Daniels."

I snorted, reaching for and pulling on my underwear then my bra before I stood and looked for the rest. "I didn't know that was a personal question. My bad."

"It is because my sister made it."

He was right. That was personal.

I saw him grinning at me and couldn't help but grin back. That was his effect, but not just on me. On everyone. Everyone liked Cruz, even if he was being a dick, they still liked Cruz. I blamed whatever star-power charisma he had going for him.

I tugged on my jeans, then my shirt.

"I drove you here. Need a ride back?"

"Uh…" I was looking for my shoes.

He sat up and reached down on his side of the bed. His hand came back up holding my shoes, and he handed them over. "Here."

"Thanks." I took them and sat back on the bed to pull them on.

I felt the mattress depress beneath me and looked over. He was standing, going to his closet.

I sat there, watching as he dressed, pulling on a pair of sweats and sweatshirt, not so much unlike the ones Miles wore earlier to his game. I hadn't given him an answer, but I was seeing that he wasn't giving me an option.

He grabbed a hat, pulling it over his head, before putting his phone and wallet in his pocket. His keys were last.

"Guess I'm getting a ride home?"

His eyebrows shot up in response, but that was it.

This was our norm, bare minimum talking. Once I was ready to go, he held the door for me.

There was an exit at the end of his hallway that went down on the outside of the house, but I was glad not to run into anyone else on this floor. The doors were closed or the few that weren't, the rooms were empty as we passed by.

His roommates knew our deal, but I still tensed.

Cruz followed me in the hallway, out the door, and down the set of stairs to a gravel alley by their house. We passed the rest of the house; all the lights were on, and music could be heard from inside.

"Here."

I would've gone past his truck, but he had parked it so we wouldn't have to go past the front lawn. I could hear people out there so who knew who was all there.

Going around to the other side, I got in, and drew in a breath as I decided it was time to start handling some shit, no matter the time of night. I turned my phone on as he was reversing to the road.

"Hey!"

Cruz paused the truck and rolled down his window. One of his teammates came over, but I focused on my phone though I could hear him grinning as he asked, "Where are you two headed?"

"Dropping her off, then I'm coming back."

"Sweet. We gotta celebrate tonight. Though it looks like you alr–"

"Don't go there."

I paused at hearing Cruz's dark tone, starting to go through the first text that showed up and looked up, seeing AJ Atwater looking me over. Messy blonde hair, a slight curl to it, and wide green eyes. His face was a little long. Tall, and a little gangly, but I knew he wasn't gangly at all on the ice. I could guess what he was going to say and gave him a look. "Don't be a dick, Atwater. You spread shit about me, and there'll be payback. Real easy to tell a few of the right girls you got an STD. You hear me?"

I did not play with this shit. Ever.

Guys were total assholes. Doing their best, coaxing, being all nice for girls to have sex with them. Then when they did, the worst ones ruined the girls' reputation, disrespecting them. I liked sex. I'd been having it for a long time. It's how I handled my life, but I was safe. I picked decent guys, and I liked what Cruz and I had. He got off. I got off. He didn't disrespect me, and I wasn't a girl who wanted to be a girlfriend. It would work until assholes like this started saying shit.

He swallowed hard. "Right. I mean...right."

Cruz said, "Keep your mouth shut. You know the deal."

Atwater stood back, straightening, and he nodded quickly. "Sorry. Honestly. Post-game celebrations got to me. Meant no offense, Daniels, but it'd be fun if you came to a party every now and then. I know you're cool to hang out with."

I relaxed a little and gave him a small grin. "Maybe next time?"

"Cool, cool."

I went back to my phone as he and Cruz had a small conversation. I tuned them out, hearing Atwater ask him something about hockey because that's how these guys were. One was a jackass. Threats were made, then bam, after the apology, back to their normal guy chit chat.

I scrolled through my texts.

My dad.

Kit sent another couple texts.

A few other friends from high school, the girls I hadn't spoken to since graduation.

Then, crap. Tasmin Shaw. I checked the time. She must've texted me after the game, but I scrolled through and didn't see any other surprising texts.

"See you, man."

Cruz and Atwater were finishing up.

I put my phone away, still hearing it buzz from my notifications. I waited till we'd driven a block. "I'm not in the dorm anymore."

He glanced over, but there was no reaction. "Okay."

I gave him directions until we were outside my new place. He leaned forward, scoping it out. "I've been here before."

"Miles Gaynor lives here. There's a place in the attic."

"You're in the attic?"

I nodded before opening the door and sliding out. "It's not that bad. Like a small apartment." I headed off, giving him a wave.

He waited till I got in my door. Once inside, I paused and listened to the house. It was silent. I hadn't noticed any lights on from outside, but I went upstairs. And after taking another shower, I dressed in my pajamas, grabbed a bottle of wine, and curled up on my little couch with it.

I needed more numbing.

3

CRUZ

The party was still raging when I got back. I snuck in through a side door, but as soon as I cleared the doorway, Adam Labrowski was there. Our captain, and also on first line with me. His arm went around my shoulders. "Hey, man. Where'd you head off to?" He looked around me. "You didn't bring any food back with you."

"Styles. What's up, man? Awesome game tonight." Gavin Miller, who was not on the team with us, or even someone who lived in the house, held up a fist. He was from a frat on campus, and enjoyed partying with us. A lot.

"Hey, man." I met his fist with mine, and said to Labrowski, "Is that a standard thing now? Every time we leave the house, we come back with food?"

He cracked a grin, his arm falling from my shoulders. "Nah, but that'd be awesome if we did that."

AJ waved from the table where they were playing beer pong.

I gave him a nod back. "We could convince Atwater."

Labrowski snorted. "Dude. We should."

"What are you guys talking about?" Keys came over,

another player and the third member of our line. A bunch of girls were with him.

Labrowski told him, and Keys was all for it.

"Hi, Cruz." One of the girls switched from Keys's arm to mine. "I was in bio last year with you."

"My bad." Miller held out a hand towards her. "This is Bianca. She hangs out a lot at the house with my brothers."

Bianca smiled. "I went to high school with a couple of his frat brothers, so I know them that way. I was looking for you earlier. Where were you?"

Bianca was a pretty girl. A very pretty girl. Wavy brown hair. Big hazel eyes. Pouty lips, and normally, I'd be interested. Or somewhat interested because it was obvious Bianca was a girl down for a quick ride and nothing after that. Or that's what a lot of them said, but I knew the game. A lot of them lied, which is why I appreciated what I had with Daniels. Unlike other girls, she meant what she said. We started hooking up last semester, and it'd been going well. Smooth. We hooked up a few times a week, and I was either out or she was right afterwards. Today had been a little different, but I knew Daniels by now. I'd not hear from her till next week. Our arrangement was that we screwed each other, not others, and because of that, I gave Bianca a smile, and pulled my arm out from her hold.

Keys and Labrowski were smirking because they knew my deal with Daniels. Miller didn't, and his mouth was almost falling open as he was clutching his beer to his chest.

"I had to give a friend a ride home." I nodded towards Keys. "You been keeping my man company tonight?"

"Oh." But she blinked, and I gave the girl props. She rebounded fast, latching onto Keys's arm. He lifted it, putting his arm around her shoulders, and she sunk into his side. "Marcus has been great."

Her friend added, sultry and her own pouting lips pushed out, "But we're glad you're back."

Labrowski grunted. "Without food, I might add."

I laughed, feeling my phone buzzing in my pocket. "Get over it." I saw the screen and yeah, the party was over for me. "I gotta take this. See you guys."

Winding through the party, giving hellos back to people, it took a little bit before I hit the stairs and got to my room. Once there, the phone had stopped ringing, but it was my mom. I called as soon as I got through my door.

"Mom."

"Titi was hoping to stay up to talk to you, but she zonked out a bit ago." And as her usual self, she was cheerful on her end, which I gave my mom credit because she easily could've not been. She had three children. One was in college, and liked to get beat up in hockey games twice a week. Another was buried. And her third was, well... my little sister would never not be a little girl for the rest of her life.

I grinned, faintly. "How's she doing?"

"Good. Her new worker is working out great. She brings magazines with her, and on her break, they go through them together."

"Are you serious?"

My mom laughed, but there was a twinge of exhaustion in her tone. "They cut out pictures from the magazines and put them on this canvas. It's called a fashion board. I've never seen your sister light up the way she does with this new girl. It's..." She sniffled, her voice coming out a little shaky. "She smiles as much with her as she does during your hockey games."

"Give that girl a raise."

An abrupt laugh came from my mom. "The agency pays her, but I know what you mean. I tell you, if they take her off your sister and put someone else with her, I don't know how I'm going to do it, but I'm hiring her personally. Bank loan or something."

"We'll figure it out, Mom."

"Oh, gosh." She chuckled, but there was a sniffle too. "I called to talk about you, not about my problems. I watched your game. You did great. Titi boasts about you to Dawn, that's the new girl's name. They watch your games together when they're doing the fashion boards. I think Dawn's got a little crush on you."

"She's never met me."

"Like that matters to some of these girls. Titi raves about you, and the girl has eyes. She sees how handsome you are."

"Mom."

"I *get* to tease you. That's my job as your mama."

"I know." I sighed, missing her. Missing Titi.

"Am I hearing music in the background? Are the boys having a party?"

I stretched out on the bed, yawning. "We don't have a game tomorrow so the guys are celebrating."

"And you took a call from your mother." She was back to teasing.

"I gotta make sure Titi is handling you okay."

She chuckled, but I could hear her own tiredness. She managed the local grocery store, and there were staffing problems lately so my mom ended up doing her job *and* theirs. Plus taking care of Titi, and being on our own, she'd be passed out as soon as her head hit the pillow.

"You can go, Mom."

"You just want to go and keep partying. I know my son."

Some of my grin faded. "Yeah. You know me." But we were both not talking about the obvious, how she was probably dead on her feet. "Love you, Mom."

"Love you too," she said softly. "I wanted to hear your voice, tell you what a great game you had tonight."

"Thank you. Give Titi a hug and kiss for me."

"You know it."

4

MARA

"What's up, Daniels?" Gavin Miller dropped into the seat next to me.

New semester meant new classes, and we were in an auditorium for our anthropology class. He dropped his bag at his feet, turned to me, and threw his arm around the back of my seat.

In my head, Gavin was Grant West's version of someone I knew from my hometown.

Both came from wealthy families. Both in fraternities where they were legacies. Both square muscular bodies. The difference between them was that Zeke had blond hair, the guy from my hometown, while Gavin had dark hair, and well, their names obviously.

"Anthropology, huh?"

He chuckled before settling more in his seat. "Needed something easy this semester but that looks good on the reports. My mom's up my ass about last semester's grades. Speaking of last semester, I knew the reason you ghosted our parties then, but not now. What's the deal? Gaynor told me you were pricklier than normal at the hockey game on Friday. We had a bash on Saturday."

Right. The game. There'd been a whole weekend between then and now, and I'd not responded to anyone's texts or party invites.

"Coast is clear, Daniels. Burford backed down. I like having you at parties. You tend to keep the idiots in check. You're good for the party environment."

"I don't do anything."

"That's the point. You take no bullshit, and the girls know that about you."

"You want me to come to a party?"

"I do. A lot."

The beef he was talking about was because of him. He'd been the reason. We were studying in the library. Sabrina Burford was into him. He was into me. She took offense, coughed the cunt word, and bam, there you have it. That was also the same night Cruz and I hooked up for the first time.

"I'm not fucking you, Miller." I leveled him with a look, watching his reaction to that. I wanted to make sure that was crystal clear.

He eased back, but there was no flicker on his face. His lip curved up just slightly. "I know. Word is that you pick a dude for those needs, and you stick with only him but there's no relationship strings attached."

I almost dropped my pen. "Who told you that?"

"I got friends at Cain University. Your buddy Zeke talked. He's a chill guy. I really liked him."

Fucking figures. I slouched down in my seat. "I'm going to murder him."

He held his hands up in surrender, leaning back from me. "He wasn't spreading gossip. He just said you're smart and don't treat you like the rest."

"Right, and that means he needs to spread that shit about me?"

"I've not said anything to anyone. I swear. I'm sharing

because a chick as hot as you, I'm guessing you already got that guy picked out and it's not me. I'm cool with that."

I gave him a hard look.

Gavin snorted, slouching down in his seat too. "Man. You are super distrustful. That's cool, though. I see I got my work cut out for me. I like you, Daniels. That's all. I mean, I'd love to get in your pants, but I'm aware that's not what you're offering so that's fine too. Still want you to come to our shindig this weekend. Guys have an away game, so we're doing a watch thing at the house and then partying all night. Cool if you could come."

I was about to respond, but caught movement behind and looked. Cruz was coming in, along with one of his teammates, Wes Barclay. They went down one of the aisles until a girl held out her hand. Barclay swung in next to her. Cruz saw me, and paused in the aisle, but he only blinked once before taking the empty seat on the other side of his teammate.

"Bianca."

"Huh?"

Gavin flashed me a grin. "That's Bianca. She was all over Cruz at their party Friday night. Turned her down, and I have no idea why." He winked at me. "She's almost as hot as you, Daniels."

I rolled my eyes. "Keep up with that shit and I won't come over this weekend."

He frowned. "What girl *doesn't* want to get compliments?"

I gave him a look.

"Shutting up now."

The professor was coming in so I gave him a nod. "Thank you. And I'll come this weekend."

"Nice." He gave me a wink and then class started.

Me: Stop talking about me to people.

Zeke: What's up, Daniels! How are you? How's it going? Also, you're going to have to be specific. I talk to a lot of people so that's going to be hard to do.

Me: Had a conversation with Gavin Miller about the type of guys I fuck. IT'S NOT YOUR BUSINESS!

Zeke: Oh yeah. Now that makes more sense. My bad. I was rolling and had half a bottle of Jack in me. Sorry about that.

Me: fuck you fuck you fuck you fuck you fuck you fuck you fuck you fuck you

Zeke: I've missed you, Little Daniels.

Five minutes later,

Zeke: Still missing you.

Thirty minutes after that,

Zeke: Also, by the by, I liked Miller. He seemed like a good guy. Felt connected in a bro-way if you get my drift.

Zeke: Text again, Daniels. Once you open that door, you can't close it. It's the text-gate.

Me: That makes no sense.

Zeke: See! Got you. Tag, you're it.

5

MARA

Dad: Do you want to be involved in where your mother goes?

Knock, knock!

I was reading over my dad's last text and well, needless to say, I was happy for the distraction.

I put my phone away and went to the door.

I was guessing it was Miles. He and I went back to being he and I. There were a couple library study sessions, or where I studied and Miles dropped his books there, his bag, and went to socialize. He tended to find a girl, bring her over. She studied with us, and then he'd either go to her place after or she came to ours. But he and I were back to being our surface-only friends, so I opened it, asking before I saw who was on the other side, "Libr–" I stopped. "You aren't Miles."

It was another of our roommates. Skylar. Her and her girlfriend, Zoe, lived on the second floor. While Skylar wore mostly athletic clothes, pale skin, had long blonde hair with a few dreadlocks, Zoe was almost the opposite. She was a dainty artist, wore mostly flowery dresses and the *cutest* shoes, had light brown skin, and kept her hair mostly in braids. Zoe also was a fan of jewelry, with long and short necklaces, bracelets, and different earrings.

Skylar gave me a small grin and half of a wave. "We're having some people over tonight for pizza. That cool with you?"

That was another thing in this house. They liked to make sure everyone signed off if there were going to be a lot of guests. I was guessing it had to do with the noise level since Skylar was on the soccer team. Wade was on the swim team. And Darren, the guy who lived on the first floor, was on the football team. A lot of athletes in the house.

She added, "Also, we're considering doing a whole study event too. You in?"

I nodded. "What time? How much for the pizza?"

"Whenever and whatever you want to chip in for supplies. Zoe's taking a cooking class elective this semester, and she's got the chef bug. You know, if the artist thing doesn't work out." She gave me a wink.

I grinned.

I had needed the weekend alone, but the week of classes made me look forward to a study/pizza night.

"I'll be down in a bit. Thanks for the invite."

Skylar had nodded and started to turn back but paused and gave me a brighter smile. "Of course. See you down there!"

My phone started ringing behind me. Skylar went downstairs and I went to pick it up, shutting the door.

Zeke calling.

I frowned, but answered, "Dude."

He laughed, a baritone voice on his end and sounding hoarse. "Batten down your hatches, Little Daniels. I'm going to violate your rule and, gasp, ask how you're doing! And don't give me the bullshit of not asking because apparently, I'm the only one with balls to wade through your toxic hostile attachment barriers."

I grew up with the guy so I just drew in a breath, knowing Zeke would ignore whatever I said. I settled down on my couch and hit speaker, putting the phone next to me. "I'm fine."

"Bullshit."

"Zeke," I started to warn.

He was unrolling the ball inside me that I'd been able to take all my mom stuff and stuff it in there.

"I'm also calling to let you know that a certain Fallen Crest nurse got sacked."

My stomach clamped right back up. "What?"

"I made some calls, found out what nurse leaked your mom's info, and yeah, she's gone. Finito."

I couldn't talk at first. God. My mom. My dad's text... I'd kept that all locked up in the Mom Drawer in my head. I'd been in the process of shutting it all away after reading what my dad asked, but Zeke yanked the entire drawer back out. It was spilling all over the floor.

"You did that?" My voice was raspy.

"I am all the way connected in Fallen Crest. It was the least I could do for a friend."

I was speechless, my heart pounding hard in my chest.

Then he got quiet. "I looked up what your mom has."

"Zeke." I shot to my feet, but I took the phone with me. My chest was so tight.

"Her stuff seems like a lot."

My throat was closing up. "Zeke, don't do this. Okay?"

"Just calling to say... I don't know, Daniels. You never let us know, and I've known you since kindergarten. You could've shared."

He had no clue. No idea how she could be. To say she could be dramatic was a gross understatement. He had no idea about any of it, but he found out. Along with so many others because of last week, because one nurse gossiped and let it spread how my mom ended up in the hospital.

"And what then? You know our friends, how they can be. They're vicious. I would've been tortured for having the 'psycho mom.'"

"You could've told some of us, all I'm saying."

I let out a sigh because dammit, that felt nice hearing and that I was hearing it from Zeke said *a lot*. "Zeke?"

"What's up, Little Daniels?"

"You and I are not phone friends."

"Maybe that needs to change."

I cocked my head to the side. "You and I don't share feelings."

"I know, but I'm a new man. My dad took away the car and bank cards and I had to get my shit together. But I'm here. There's been some hiccups, but all in all, being Zeke Allen at Cain University is quite fucking amazing."

Some things never changed. Same old Zeke, boasting how great he is. I relaxed a little more. "That's good to hear. Your frat is good?"

"They're...getting better."

"I'm sure."

He laughed. "Okay, Little Daniels. I wanted to share the news about the nurse and to let you know that the Zeke Maestro is thinking of you. Give me a call the next time you're drunk, and we can talk about philosophy."

I barked out a laugh. "Looking forward to it."

We hung up after that. I wasn't going to reflect why that call felt nice, but it did. Half of me was normal because of my dad. Half of me was messed up because of my mom, but Zeke was all the way at Cain, California. He used to be such a douche, but I was tending to believe that he *had* changed. Or at least he had some humility in him now.

Maybe having a phone friend *was* okay?

Changing into some jeans and a tank top, I grabbed a textbook, some cash for the pizza, and rum and mixers on the way out. Then I headed down, using the stairs that led right to the kitchen.

Zoe had a whole spread in the kitchen. She looked up, smiling, some flour on her cheek. "Hi! Welcome to the downstairs lair."

I put my cash on the counter. "For you, for all this."

"Oh my gosh, you didn't have to do that."

I ignored that, giving her an easy smile and moving to grab a cup from the cupboard.

Skylar came in, her hair pulled up into a ponytail since she'd left my place. "You can put your soda in the fridge. There's some room."

"Baby." Zoe said something to her, but I poured myself a drink before putting my soda where Skylar just told me. When I was done, I glanced back to them. Skylar was helping her out, putting the cheese on the pizza.

I asked, "You guys need more help?"

"Nope. I've got a whole system put together." Zoe nodded toward the rest of the house. "Grab a seat at the table if you want to study because fair warning, each of the guys invited a couple friends over. It might turn out to be a party even though we didn't all agree to a party tonight."

I noticed her and Skylar were both eyeing me, a little cautious. It took a second before I realized they were waiting to see if I'd get mad about that.

"Oh!" I waved that off. "Going to be honest, I never care when the parties happen."

Both looked relieved.

They weren't kidding about the party effect. The living room and dining room was full of people.

"Daniels!"

Gavin was just coming in from the front door and walked toward me, his arms in the air. I braced myself, keeping my drink steady as he got to me, pulling me in for a tight hug. "How you doing? Long time no see."

He let me go as I said, "We had class together. Today."

"I know. Too long, too long." His eyes were a little glazed and his cheeks were red.

"Started partying already, huh?"

He laughed and shrugged. "Never too early." He eyed my drink. "Whatcha got in there?"

I moved back, bringing my drink to my chest. "Nope. It's mine. Get your own."

He laughed again, his arm coming down around my shoulders, and scanned the room. He had come in with a few others. I recognized them from his fraternity. They were doing handshakes and shoulder pounding with a few other guys. I looked around, seeing Miles in the corner. He saw me looking and jerked his chin up in a greeting. He was talking to a few girls.

Darren was on the couch, controller in hand. He was playing the new FIFA game with another guy.

Wade was coming down the stairs. Seeing me looking his way, he gave me a chin-lift too. "What's up, Daniels?" He came over, saying hello to who was eyeing him back. "What's up, man?"

"Hey." Gavin's greeting was less enthusiastic, but his arm fell from my shoulders. He was looking from Wade to me, a twinge of suspicion in his gaze, but he just smiled. "I need beer."

Wade laughed, but as soon as Gavin was gone, he moved so his back was to the rest of the room. "How are you?"

Oh, boy. The way he was looking at me, and how he asked that question–he wanted a real answer.

I started to edge back when a girl came over. She linked her elbow with Wade's, her hip bumping his. "Wade! I didn't know you'd be here."

He gave her a slight frown. "I live here, so..."

She laughed, tossing some of her hair behind her shoulder. "That's right. I forgot. How are you?" She placed a hand on his chest, and the maneuver put her closer to him and with her back to me. It was obvious what she wanted.

I looked over her head to him, and he was half smiling at her, but half looking my way.

I moved back, raising my drink in a greeting.

He gave me a small nod back.

From there, I made my way to the dining room table. They had a long one, enough where sixteen people could sit around it. Miles said that it came with the house, and moving into the dining room, the sound was a little quieter in there. The rooms were all sectioned off in the house. There was no big open layout. The living room had a doorway that went into the long dining room, and if you traveled the length of the room, there was a doorway at the opposite end that went to the kitchen. On the other side of the dining room wall connected to where the living room and kitchen had their own doorway. I went in there, dropped my stuff at a seat, and sat down. A few others were in there too, a few girls, and a couple guys.

"Hey. You're Skylar and Zoe's new roommate?" One of the girls pointed to the ceiling with her pen. "The one who has the attic apartment?"

"Yeah. Hi."

She used the pen to point to herself. "Jessica. You're Mara?"

I nodded.

Jessica pointed to the other two girls. "That's Allie and Hawah."

Both nodded and waved.

They were all in sweats and T-shirts, their hair pulled up in messy buns. I was guessing they were upperclassmen, like Skylar and Zoe. It was also in their relaxed attitudes. Freshman girls were different at parties. They were dressed up, or in jeans, and there was an edge of uncertainty, desperation to them or they went the opposite route of being so confident that they came off like know-it-alls. They weren't all like that, but I partied enough to tell. The other two at the table were guys, and both gave me a small nod.

"I'm Derrick."

The other guy waved his pen toward me. "Yo. I'm Martin."

I said hello to both.

Skylar popped her head into the room. "First pizzas are done. You guys want dibs before we let the others know?"

The chairs were pushed back, and the girls went first.

The guys were after that. Martin lingered, asking me, "You want a piece? I can grab you one."

I shook my head. "Not hungry. I'll grab one later."

"You sure?" He jerked a thumb toward the other room. "Darren and the others will eat everything in that kitchen when they're let in. Football players are insatiable." He was smirking at me, and I knew who he was connected to now.

"You're on the team?"

His smile widened. "Yep. Running back."

"Martin," came from the kitchen.

He glanced in and back to me. "Last chance. One slice?"

I laughed but raised my drink. "I'm good for now. Promise."

"Okay." He disappeared inside as one of the girls was coming back, her plate piled high with pizza. She sat down at her spot, putting her drink next to her plate. "Not hungry?"

I shook my head. "Not yet."

She gave me a once-over, what she could see of me, and her top lip curled up. "You don't have an eating disorder, do you?"

I gave her the same once-over, my lip curving up too. "No. Do you?"

It was a cheap shot back at her, but she had a healthy and toned body. I could tell under her shirt and sweats. The truth is that I wished I had more muscle on me and there'd been times I spent lifting weights, but it never seemed to work. I just got more tired and felt washed out. I was envious of her, but no way was she going to know that.

She flushed but picked up a piece of pizza and took a big bite out of it. "So fucking good. Glad *I* enjoy eating."

The other two girls were coming in, and they slowed, hearing their friend, their gazes jumping to me.

I narrowed my eyes, but only leaned forward. "You don't have to be a bitch."

"Hey!" one of the girls cried, but I didn't remember which one. Allie? It wasn't Jessica, who looked resigned to this exchange. She put her plate down, sliding into her seat.

"Allie," she addressed the bitchy one. "Be nice."

Hawah was the other one, and she was slower to sit, taking the other seat by Allie, who was still glaring at me as she kept eating her pizza. She started making noises, all directed at me. "Yum. *So* delicious. I *looove* pizza. I love *food*. So yum–"

I was aware of a loud sudden noise of voices from the living room, but I was up and moving around the table. I halted just before her. She had edged her seat back, her eyes wary but still hostile.

God. I hated girls like this.

"What's your problem with me?"

She rolled her eyes. "My problem? I don't have the problem. You do." She gave me a once-over. "Obviously. I bet you're the type to starve yourself and then eat a biscuit and throw that shit up. Ugh. What your breath must smell like."

I leaned down, slowly, so I was staring her right in the eyes. "Let me say this slow for you, so you can keep up. You and me, we don't know each other, but I know you now. What you threw at me, all that does is give me a window into how you think. How *you* view people because it's what makes sense to your dumbass self. What I know about you, is that you're petty, insecure. And every fucking time you're here, I'm going to come down and make your life hell. Because while I'm not an insecure and petty bitch, I *am* one that likes to draw out my payback. Buckle up, bitch. You just made me an enemy—"

The light switched in her eyes. She went from being mean and mad, to being rageful. The chair was shoved back and she lunged for me.

As her hands touched me, I saw red.

There was yelling, chairs were scraping.

I knew in the back of my head that people were running in and what they would see, but I was so sick of taking shit from other girls. It'd been almost nonstop most of my life. About my size, about who I was sleeping with. I kept all my business quiet, and now this? Because I chose not to eat pizza the very first moment it was offered? Screw. Her.

"Hey–whoa!"

There was a scramble, then two hands gripped me around my waist, and I was being lifted away.

"Shit." A male voice grunted as I was being carried out of the room.

Once we were in the other room, I was let go, but he, whoever he was, wasn't releasing me. I shoved him off. "Let go! She attacked me."

It had been Wade and he kept one of his hands on my waist, or was trying. "What the hell was that about?"

A crowd formed around us, some of the guys from that room–I was frazzled. I couldn't remember their names, though I just talked to them. Gavin and Miles came over too, both frowning, and they moved to stand between me and that room.

"You are such a bitch!" Jessica came to the doorway, trying to get at me.

I laughed, and winced because it sounded ugly. "I just educated you. *You're* the petty, insecure bitch. I'm the bitch who's now your enemy."

She screamed, breaking free.

Miles moved in, catching her. That made her try harder.

I was keeping an eye on the kitchen, and just as I started to look to get a better view, I saw Allie coming around and trying for me that way. I moved, going at her because no fucking way was I going to take this lying down. I hadn't started the fight, but I sure as shit was going to end it.

She was running fast too.

"Wha–OH MY GOD!" Skylar yelled.

I heard another scream. These girls wanted to jump me.

I moved around Wade, taking two steps as Allie got to me. There was a group of guys standing to the side and at our sudden movements, they moved into the hallway.

"Damn."

"Okay then."

Allie lunged for me, I ducked, reached back, and caught her hair. Bracing myself, I yanked her entire body down to the floor. Hard. Once she was down, I kicked at her shoulder, pushing her over so she was on her stomach and then I knelt on her back, a hand pushing her face into the floor. "Going to stop or should we keep going?"

There were more yells behind me. I was hoping someone was holding Jessica back because she was still screaming at me.

Allie was struggling, trying to get up.

I tried to kick out one of her hands so she couldn't use both of them to push herself back up.

"You bitch!"

"You're the one who came at me first."

Her head twisted to the side, but I held it down, locking my elbow in place. "Don't *fuck* with me."

"What the hell?" Skylar shoved in and began pushing at my shoulders. "Get off her."

I was resisting until I felt the fight leave Allie and then I stood back. Skylar got between me and Allie, her eyes wide and bulging out. Zoe was crying in the corner, and Skylar frowned at her before her jaw hardened.

Allie was getting up. She was okay, still glaring at me.

Skylar let out a ragged breath. "What happened?" She turned to me. "These are mine and Zoe's friends. They've been over here multiple times and have never gotten into a physical fight. I know them. I don't know you."

I felt people behind me.

Ignoring them, I said, "Your friend was a colossal bitch to me. Like I'm going to take her taunting me, insinuating that I have an eating disorder." I leaned around her, saying to Allie, "I hope to God you don't actually know someone who does have an eating disorder. You don't mess with that shit and for your knowledge, I don't have one but *fuck you* for trying to shame me."

Skylar's attitude changed drastically at hearing me.

She whipped around to Allie, her mouth almost falling down. "Is she serious? You did that?"

Allie took a step back, running a hand through her hair, but she raised her chin up. "What? Like she doesn't have one–"

Skylar began yelling, "You can't do that."

"Oh, come on–"

"MY LITTLE SISTER HAS AN EATING DISORDER!" Skylar was visibly shaking.

Zoe stopped crying and moved in, touching Skylar's arm. "Baby," she said in a soft tone, moving even closer, her body touching Skylar's.

At the touch, Skylar's eyes closed and she drew in a sharp breath. When she opened them again, she hissed, "I agree with my roommate. Fuck you, Allie. Fuck you. You have no idea the torture that goes with fighting an eating disorder."

Allie quieted. "Katie has one?"

It was clearly the wrong thing to say to Skylar because she drew in another breath. "Get out."

"She–"

"I'll deal with my roommate, but right now, get out before *I* put hands on you. You don't mess with eating disorders. You just don't do that."

Skylar started to turn toward me, but I already had my hands up. "I'll leave. You don't have to kick me out–"

"Stay," her voice was low and guttural. "We can talk later when things are calmer." She pushed through the guys, going down the hallway.

Zoe remained behind, looking from me to Allie, then to the kitchen before hurrying after Skylar.

There was a moment of quiet before Wade moved in. "Okay. Time for you to go." He was talking to Allie, who looked ready for round two, but she clamped her mouth shut and went back to the dining room. A moment later, she reappeared with her backpack on and started toward me.

Hands touched me, moving me to the side. I was shuffled back as Miles and Gavin both stood between me and her. Just as both girls got to the front door, it opened. They fell back a step as a group of guys came in.

"Hey." The first guy, AJ Atwater from the hockey team, had a wide smile. It fell as he took in the girls' expressions and scanned the rest of the room. The music from the video game was still playing in the background, but everyone was either frozen or standing still. "Uh, what's going on?"

He was followed by Marcus Keys.

Wes Barclay.

A fourth guy came last.

It was Cruz.

6

MARA

Pizza/study night turned into pizza/study/video game night.

After everyone settled down, I returned to the table and was studying with Gavin and Miles on either side of me. They'd not left my side the whole night, and the rest of the guys took notice. The girls too, because more girls had come. At this point, it was a free-for-all of who was connected to who. Then again, that's how most parties were. We had football players, mostly still playing FIFA in the living room. Wade knew some guys who turned out to be from the wrestling team. The hockey guys were in the kitchen, eating, because they had their practice number three for the day. Those guys were ravenous.

Skylar and Zoe came back out. Zoe, to finish the pizzas, and Skylar, to have a good time. I heard her laughter from the dining room, but she'd not come in yet. I stayed put for the most part except to venture out a few times when I needed a refill. I'd started to get hungry, but I saw a girl hanging over Cruz and promptly lost my appetite. It shouldn't bother me if he was flirting with another girl, but the rules were that while we had our agreement, if he was going to sleep with someone else, then he and I were not going to keep doing what we were doing.

It was close to midnight, and half the group had left. The guys seemed like they were getting a second wind, but the rum was working in me and I needed to either nap or eat. Either way, I was hitting a wall with the studying and closed my book.

Miles glanced over. "Finally."

I grinned at him.

He held out a closed fist to me. "Gotta hand it to you. Studying and drinking as much as you did, you're a college rockstar."

An abrupt laugh left me as I met his fist with my own, before standing up. "I'm going to bed."

Gavin leaned back in his chair. "That an invite, Little Daniels?"

I turned to him. "Stop talking to Zeke Allen about me."

He only laughed. "We have a budding bromance. Kindred souls, him and me. Speaking of, some of the guys and I are thinking about doing a road trip to Cain. You want to go with us? See your buddy?"

I snorted. "Apparently, you've not talked enough about me to him. He and I do not have a visiting sort of friendship."

"What kind of friendship do you have?"

"A reluctant one," I threw over my shoulder before stepping into the kitchen.

The pizza had been moved to the table and island inside. The hockey guys were crammed around the table. The girls next to them. I could feel Cruz's gaze but avoided it because I didn't want any more attention. I'd had enough for the night.

"Your reputation precedes you, Daniels."

Going past everyone to the door, I glanced back at Atwater. He was grinning widely at me, and he wiggled his eyebrows. "Everyone knows about Burford, but now you took down a junior?" He whistled under his breath. "No one's going to sleep on you."

I sent him a sharp look.

He startled, jerking up as if realizing what he just said. "I mean, you know what I mean. The girls won't mess with you anymore."

Allie was a junior. Lovely.

"Just getting my bearings here," I murmured before scanning the room. Skylar and Zoe were there, leaning against the fridge. Martin was with them, a shoulder propped up against the wall, his arms crossed over his chest. There was a girl with them too. All were watching me.

A wave of shame rose in me because I could hear again Allie's screech.

"I'm sorry," I said it to Skylar, who seemed surprised by my words. "I shouldn't have reacted that way. I should've used my words *better*."

Her eyes grew wary.

I waited, but when she stayed quiet, I opened the door and went upstairs.

I'D JUST HEATED up some food when there was a knock at my door.

At this point, I had no clue who that could be, but I went over and opened it.

Cruz, with a hood pulled low over his head, his jawline half in shadow, but those eyes still piercing me. He raised his chin up toward me, and I stepped back. He came in after me, shutting the door and locking it. He jerked a thumb behind him. "You think you might have more visitors tonight?"

"I hope not." I sat at the table and eyed him as he was considering me.

He let out a sigh, coming over. "The guys will cover me, not that we're keeping this a secret, but you know." He came to the table, and stood there, looking down at me. His eyes were dark, clouded over.

I finished my last bite and tipped my head back as I swallowed. "That girl was all over you downstairs," I said, and as I did, I opened my legs.

His eyes flashed, and he smirked, but moved closer, more between my legs. "That was only Bianca. A lot of girls hang over me, a lot of times. They're called puck bunnies."

"Bianca is a puck bunny?" I reached for him, grabbing his jeans and I pulled him toward me.

"I'm not into her." He came, still watching me, looking down at me. "You got something to say about her? Be easier if you just ask it."

Right. I heaved a breath. "If you want to fuck someone else, you need to let me know."

Now his eyes flashed and his face hardened. "We doing the jealousy thing? Because if we're on that topic, if you're going to fuck Miller or your roommate, you better let me know too. Shit goes both ways."

I moved him even closer, my mouth watering at what I wanted to do, but I glanced up, surprised. "You know Miles and I aren't like that."

He snorted. "Not talking about Miles."

I'd started to reach for his buttons but paused and looked up again. "Who?"

He leaned down, just a little. "The swimmer."

"Wade?"

He nodded. "Word gets out." He raised an eyebrow. "You into him?"

"No." I was done with the conversation.

I undid his jeans and slid the zipper down.

He moaned, his legs moving apart as I slid both his jeans

and his boxer briefs down. His dick was right there and fast hardening, and I reached for it. Another groan left him as my hands wrapped around it, and I looked up. He was watching me, his eyes smoldering and fierce.

I began to move my hand over him, rubbing up and down. Up and down. Feeling it harden all the way and as it did, I bent my head, my mouth closing over the top.

He let out a slight hiss of air. "Fuck me."

I moved down, sucking him into my mouth.

He added, "That feels so good."

I started moving.

I loved doing this, but only for Cruz. I wasn't into this for anyone else, though I had done it in the past, but it wasn't the same. Cruz was different, and I didn't want to think about that, about why he was different. I loved making him hiss and squirm and curse and how his knees shook at times, and then I really loved when he grasped my head and would take over.

He cursed again, but he pulled out.

I looked up, confused, but he shook his head, tapping me behind my elbow. "Not this time. Get up."

I smiled back at him, knowingly, as I stood.

He ducked, his shoulder going to my stomach, and he whisked me up. I was thrown over his shoulder and he carried me to the bedroom. And like the last time, I was tossed onto my bed. Unlike the last time, he turned me over so I was on my knees.

My pants were yanked down.

I felt him run a hand over my ass, slow and savoring. "I really love your ass."

I looked back, half panting. "Hurry up."

His eyes flashed, but his dick was sticking straight up, and he'd been pulling a condom out. "Oh, no. There will be no hurrying now."

I groaned, recognizing that look. He'd torture me, and he'd do it all night if he wanted.

Two could do this.

I sat up and moved around so I was facing him.

He settled back, watching me and as he did, I took off my top, feeling his gaze rake over me.

My bra was next, and his eyes were fully melting again. He licked his lips, taking me in before he reached up, one of his hands cupping my breast. "Have I told you how much I love your tits?" He went all the way down, his hand cupping me, his thumb rubbing over one nipple as his mouth took in the other entire breast. He sucked me in, his teeth grazing my nipple and I almost fell back from the sensation. He went with the movement, and he ran a hand down my back, picking me up and laying me more fully so I wasn't bent at an awkward angle. He moved in, his mouth never leaving my tit until now, until he transferred, taking the other one in his mouth. He smoothed his hand down my stomach, going to my clit, and resting there a moment before his fingers dipped inside.

I closed my eyes as the pleasure was compounding me.

Cruz kept licking, sucking, torturing me as he fingered me. He was leaving hickeys all over my boobs, but I didn't care. I seriously loved how he could bring me to a climax in a few minutes, but when I was about to climax, my legs lifting from the bed, he pulled his fingers out.

"Wha–"

He rose over me, slapping my legs apart for him, and surged inside of me.

God. I was so full.

He braced himself above me, and a soft curse slipped from him before his mouth found my neck. He went back to tasting me and he began moving.

"So tight. I love fucking you," he panted next to my ear.

I loved it too, and I wrapped my legs around his hips, raising up to meet his thrusts.

We were both breathing hard. The sounds of downstairs were there, but muted.

Suddenly there was a hard knock at my door.

He went still. "The fuck?"

I squeezed him, keeping him where he was. I touched his chest. "You locked the door."

"Who the fuck is that?" he grated out.

But he was moving again, and I went with him, looking down at where we were connected.

"Mara!" Another hard knock on the door.

"Why the fuck is Gavin Miller at your door?"

"Come on. Harder." I tuned everything out. I just wanted to make sure Cruz didn't take his dick out of me.

Gavin was knocking again, but I reached up, tugging Cruz down to me.

More. I needed more.

Groaning, Cruz slid a hand around to my back, lifting me up, and then he really started pounding into me. He was taking everything over. I could only hold on, feeling him powering into me, and oh God, it was amazing. I wrapped one hand around his neck, my fingers splaying out over his back, feeling his muscles tensing and moving under my touch as he kept going, until–ohGodohGodohGodohGod–I couldn't contain myself. My head fell back. My vision went blind, and I screamed, my whole body spasming and then falling apart.

Waves crashed through me, literally, but Cruz hadn't finished yet. He was still going. I reached for him, and began moving to meet him. His head fell back. He held still as I rode *him* until he made a choking sound.

He was coming inside me.

"Holy fuck."

His head was still back as his whole body was tense and all

of his muscles were rigid. "That was amazing," he said huskily, his chest heaving as he was catching his breath.

Reality and the room was coming back to me.

The knocking had stopped.

I was still half raised off the mattress, my hips and stomach, but as Cruz disengaged, I rolled upright so I was half sitting on the edge of the bed. He took a step back, taking the condom off, but I reached for him. He paused, his eyes narrowing before he tossed the condom into the garbage by my desk.

I tugged him back. I was still drunk, and I didn't want him to leave.

"What?"

"Stay the night."

His head moved back a little. "We've never done that before."

I nodded, feeling an itch inside of me. I didn't know why it was there, why now, but I recognized it. I'd felt it at other times, just a few and knew I'd want him more than once during the night. I wouldn't be satisfied until early morning.

Wait.

He had a game tomorrow. "No, never mind."

He stiffened, his hand catching my wrist and jerking me up so I was on my knees and eye level with him. "What just happened there?"

I licked my lips, feeling this need for him again even though I knew he couldn't go so soon. But I slid a hand down his chest, going all the way to him. "The mood I'm in, you're not going to get any sleep."

"So?" He was starting to get distracted, watching my hand.

"You have a game tomorrow."

"So?" He was still watching, even more distracted.

"So." I squeezed him, just slightly.

He groaned, raising his head so he could see me.

"You need sleep. You stay, and you won't be getting any."

He raised a hand to my chest and pushed me back so I was lying on the bed again. He crawled over me, his mouth finding mine, and then moving down my throat. "Good news for you, I can sleep on the bus."

My knees bent in the air as his mouth traveled farther down my body.

"Cruz." I had one hand lost in his hair.

"Hmm?" He was at my stomach, and he blew some air there, teasing me. He grinned at me, looking up via my body.

God. He looked so good down there. "Are you sure?"

Another flash in his eyes. "Oh yeah. I'm not quite ready to go yet, but that doesn't mean I can't do other things." And with that, his mouth settled firmly over me.

I was squirming in the next second.

I was exploding a few moments later, and before I could gather my senses again, he was sliding right back inside.

I wanted to do this all night long.

I *needed* to do this all night long.

7

CRUZ

"Dude."

Wes said as he swung into the seat next to me. I'd picked the middle range on purpose. Not in the back where guys tend to play their music or video games, and also not up in front where one of the coaches might see me and pull me in for a chat. They liked to connect with their players when they could, but not today for me. It'd been fucking phenomenal with Mara last night, but she had warned me. I needed sleep, badly. We had a good four-hour ride before our pre-game skate so I was planning on using it.

"Dude, move."

"What? You serious?"

I gave him a nod. Loved the guy. He was my floormate too, but I was meaning business today. Wes liked to chat. I was not into that today.

He studied me a second before sighing and nodding. "I'm seeing what you're putting down, but I'll stay till the rest of the guys sit and then switch."

I gave a nod, holding up my fist.

He met it with his, settling in and pulling his phone out.

I had mine out and put in headphones, slipped on my shades, and sat back to start sleeping asap.

I had a game to rest up for.

8

MARA

"Mara? A word?"

It was the TA for my abnormal psych class. It was typically reserved for upperclassmen, but since I'd done so many AP psych classes at my high school, I was the only freshman in this one. The professor had no problem with me, but the TA was a different matter. She'd been singling me out in class for the last week.

"You want me to wait?" Wade asked.

It'd been a shock when he showed up in class this week, saying he had to transfer in after deciding to drop another class, but it was kinda nice at the same time. I was also learning that Wade was a little bit of a ladies' man. A lot of girls liked him. They liked to say hi and they liked to smile at him, and they really liked to surround him right after class.

I shook my head, putting my stuff in my bag at a slower rate. Then nodded to the girl who was waiting to talk to Wade. "Thinking you got something else going on anyways."

His head jerked at seeing her, but he swung back to me. "You sure?"

I gave a small nod. "See you later."

"See you at home?"

But I didn't answer because the girl called Wade's name and I saw the TA waiting for me, her arms crossed over her chest. I approached, my bag on my back and I was holding onto the straps, letting my elbows swing around. "You wanted to see me?"

"You're a freshman?"

I nodded.

Her eyes narrowed. "I don't know what you did to get in here, but I really recommend that you wait a year before taking this course. We cover all the disorders, and Professor Chandresakaran is having us do field trips to some facilities."

"So? What's that got to do with me?"

"You're a freshman." She spoke as if that sentence, by itself, was an explanation.

"What does me being a freshman have to do with any of this? I've taken my AP psych classes. I'm on level with the coursework."

She looked around the room, and seeing some students standing and talking to each other, she inclined her head. "I'm going to speak frankly here. I don't think you're mature enough for these field trips, or to fully comprehend the coursework that we go over."

I snorted. "And you think me being a sophomore would help 'mature' me better?"

"Don't take this personally. It's not. I check out each student before they're able to attend these field trips. I do this to protect the individuals at those facilities, and you're the one I keep coming back to. There's a question mark by your name and after talking to some people, I'm hearing how you're only known for parties and lately there was a physical altercation you were a part of? That worries me. If I can't clear you to go on these trips, you will fail this class."

"You can't do that."

"We can. I can. We're not state-funded. We're a private university, and I take this work very serious."

"So what? You want me to tell you all the difficulties I've had in life or something?"

"You went to Fallen Crest Academy. That school has a reputation of privilege and wealth."

"You can't judge me on that criteria."

She stared at me. I stared at her.

"Look." She sighed. "We're not to the field trips yet. I do have my concerns, but I'm willing to hear you out. If you're willing to risk it and miss the deadline for changing a course, I'll watch how you do in the upcoming assignments. We have our first quiz next week so that'll be the beginning of it. Sound fair?"

"No."

"Tough. This is what I'm willing to offer you."

The next class was coming in, so I left, hearing my name once I stepped out into the hallway. Wade was there, a few girls with him. Darren was coming down the far hallway. He saw us and jerked up his chin, heading over.

I pointed him out to Wade, who held up his hand once Darren was close enough. The two did a man-shake, clapped each other on the shoulder. They looked so opposite, but also fit at the same time. Darren had dark brown skin, a few inches shorter than Wade, and he was more muscular. He liked to wear a lot of baseball hats. I didn't know what position he played on the team, but someone mentioned lineman. I was guessing he needed a lot of bulk for that position. Wade was taller, leaner, his skin between pale and tan, and he kept his hair trimmed short. Miles told me once it was to help so he could swim faster. Something about how even that little bit of hair could slow a swimmer down. But together, they drew attention. They were striking. I figured it had to do with their athleticism. Cruz had the same power, some innate pull over people.

"What's up, man?"

Darren gave everyone a nod before jerking a thumb over his shoulder. "Had class. Where are you guys coming from?"

Wade indicated our classroom. "Abnormal psych."

"Ah gotcha. I heard that's a good class to get into."

"It is so far." Wade turned to me. "What'd she want to talk to you about?"

I took in who was standing with us. A couple of the girls seemed nice. One did not, but I just shrugged. "It was nothing, but heads-up that we have our first quiz next week."

"What?" one of the girls exclaimed. "It's not on the syllabus."

"That's what she told me, so spread the word."

She groaned, pulling out her phone.

"We should do a study thing." The girl who spoke was staring at Wade.

He flashed a smile. "That sounds good. We can have it at our house."

"Tonight?"

Darren gave her a look like she just informed everyone she had a green toe. "On a Friday night?"

"Oh." She gave him a nervous look, laughing a little. "Yeah. We could get a jumpstart on studying, but the hockey game's on tonight too. Study. Watch hockey. Do whatever afterwards." The sly look sent in Wade's direction gave everyone an indication what she wanted to do afterwards.

He was wearing a faint frown but glanced my way. "How about it? Studying at the house tonight again?"

Darren grunted, folding his arms over his chest. "After last night, should you maybe run it by everyone?" His eyes were on me before he gave Wade a meaningful look. "Just to be safe."

"That's a good idea but it should be okay." Wade asked me again, "You up for it if everyone signs off?"

I shook my head, feeling my phone buzzing. "Can't."

"What? Why not?" Darren shot me a frown.

"Alpha Mu is having a thing. I was going to catch the game with them."

"Really?" one of the other girls squeaked. "You know the Alpha Mu guys?"

"You and Miller seemed friendly last night."

I glanced Wade's way, but replied to the girl, "I've been to a few of their parties."

Her eyes got big.

I hesitated, but... I hoped I wouldn't regret this when I said, "You want to come with?"

Her eyes got even bigger. "You don't think they'd mind?"

"They're frat guys. You're a chick. That's basic math."

"Ohmygodohmygod–"

"But I'm going to say up front that I'll probably dip out at some point. If you and a friend want to come, or maybe two of your friends, that'd be better. Keep to the buddy system."

"I thought you said you're friends with them."

"I'm casual friends with a couple, but they're still a fraternity. Better to be safe."

She was not a freshman. She was also in my abnormal psych class, and here I was, a freshman, giving her a hint on how to party responsibly. Sure. The TA totally was justified in questioning the only freshman in her class for maturity reasons.

"Yes, yes! My friends are going to go nuts."

"Wade, we still on for your place?"

Wade's gaze was locked on me, and Darren's gaze was skirting between us.

"Yeah. I think so. Maybe do tacos tonight?" He glanced in Darren's direction.

My phone kept buzzing, so I pulled it out. *Dad calling.*

My stomach dropped, and my throat went dry, but he was calling, and he wouldn't call unless it was important. I gave everyone a wave, indicating my phone. "See you later at the house." I waited until I ducked down an empty hallway. "Dad?"

"I have news." His voice was strained.

My stomach tightened. "Not good news."

"No. I mean, depends on how you view it. The first one is that she was given an added diagnosis. Do you want to know what it is?"

"No." I was so tired of it, of it all. She'd been given twelve different diagnoses all my life. The one that stuck was the personality disorder. She was always in that realm.

"Okay. The other news is about the conservatorship. It does have limitations and one of those limitations is your mother's current place."

"Meaning?" But I could guess what he was going to tell me.

"Meaning that her current facility was not included under my conservatorship. The date I start is the date when she was supposed to leave her latest center. She was talked into staying by a staff member, so it's been voluntary since her seventy-two-hour hold ended. I've talked to the staff, and your mom decided last night that she won't stay where she is. She's asking to leave."

I laughed abruptly. 'Asking' for my mom was demanding and then screaming if that demand wasn't met quick enough. Unless she gave the staff an indication that she'd be a liability, they'd have to let her go.

"Fuck," I whispered. I stopped and rested against the wall. "Didn't you have her going into another place?"

"Yes, but she was told about the conservatorship yesterday, and she didn't react well."

"Of course she didn't. Who would? Why didn't you wait until she was at the new facility?"

"We were obligated to tell her. She has rights."

This wasn't good. She'd have access to her phone.

"Is she already out?"

"She's being released right now. You still have her blocked on all your devices? Your social media?"

"Yeah, but she just needs to set up a new account from a new phone or a new computer and she'll be able to see where I am. I get tagged in photos."

He was quiet for a little. "Maybe you should delete your accounts? To be safe?"

I couldn't talk, my throat was swelling up.

At this point, it was a trigger response. My body was already shutting down, and I felt cold sweats run down my back. My stomach would start churning as soon as it processed that my mom was out of the hospital. She could totally get a car and head up here.

Then what?

What would I do then? Hide? I was already hiding.

"Oh, God. Dad." I broke, my voice hitching.

"I'm so sorry, Mara. Do you want me to drive up? I can get a hotel room. We can just...hang out?"

I was almost laughing at that because though he and I were teammates in this 'team' against my mom, he and I didn't have that relationship. "No, that's okay. I should go."

"You sure?"

I paused, knowing that a panic attack was inevitable, but I'd never heard this tone from my dad. Almost...hopeful? Was I getting that wrong?

"Dad?"

"Yeah?"

"Are *you* okay?"

"Oh, sweetie, you don't have to worry about me."

That was a rule he always maintained with me. With him, I was not to take care of him. I'd never told him, but I appreciated that line. I was still the 'kid' in some ways, but I was in college. There needed to be some give in that dynamic.

I sighed. "Can you do me a favor?"

"Anything."

"If you meet a woman you're attracted to, ask her on a date." He started making noises, but I said over him, "I mean it. You should find some happy when you can. Thanks for letting me know about Mom. I love you."

He paused, a stark silence from his end before he said quietly, "Love you, Mara."

I hung up, but I couldn't leave. The hallway was empty and for a moment, I needed to stand still. Be still. Not think. Not feel. I leaned fully back against the wall and slowly slid down until I hit the floor, then stretched my legs out.

I don't know why I texted Cruz, but I did.

Me: Hope you were able to sleep on the bus.

It buzzed back a second later,

Cruz: Are we breaking your rule right now?

Me: I feel bad if I'm the reason we lose tonight.

Cruz: I wouldn't let that happen, but I got some good sleep on the bus. All good to go.

I didn't want to wish him good luck. Some hockey guys had serious superstitions, and I didn't know if Cruz was one of them. He didn't seem like it, but I made a note to ask him later.

My phone buzzed again.

Gavin: Party! WHERE ARE YOU?!

I sent Miles a text.

Me: Alpha Mu?

Miles: Already there. Got a drink waiting for you.

Hell yes. I needed that drink.

9

CRUZ

My phone was buzzing when we went back into the locker room after the warm-up skate. Coach didn't want us to check our phones, especially not when we were about to head back out for the game, so I opened my bag to silence it. It was my mom, and she never called this close to a game.

I answered, "Mom?"

"Styles!" Coach barked.

I looked his way, and seeing my face, he quieted.

I asked, "What's wrong?"

Everyone else quieted, hearing me.

She started crying.

"Mom?"

I turned away, taking the call to the back of the locker room. The guys could hear, but I didn't want to risk going to the hallway. There'd be too much sound out there.

"Titi had a bad reaction today."

Oh, God. "What happened?" My voice dropped. "Is she okay now?"

"She's–we're in the hospital. I had to bring her in. She had three seizures in the ambulance."

Jesus.

Some of her crying lessened, but it was still there. Her voice was still broken, and I couldn't do anything to help her. Maybe I should've skipped college? Gone straight to the NHL? This was high school for me. Hockey and helping my mom. Titi needed to be carried so much of the time. It was easier if I did it, but when my mom insisted I go to college, they'd made adjustments. They got onto a better insurance plan, one that helped with more machines in the house, and more staff around the clock. It let my mom get a little bit of a break, but this, this was breaking my heart.

"Did they find out what caused the seizures?"

"A new medication." I could hear the background beeping that only a medical facility had. The nonstop beep of call lights. She must've been near a nurse's desk. "She'll be in the hospital until they get it out of her system, and then we have to introduce a new med. It'll take time, but she's stopped seizing. Cruz," her voice dropped again. "It was so scary."

I folded my head down. "I'm so sorry, Mom. But she's getting better. She'll be better."

"I know. I–I shouldn't have called you. Oh my God! You're supposed to be playing right now. I'm interrupting–why did you answer? I could've left a message."

"Mom."

"Cruz, honey. You have to go. I'm horrified. Your coach–"

And the guy himself stepped around the lockers, giving me space, but making it clear he was there. I gave him a small nod. "I gotta go, Mom. I'll call later tonight unless you're sleeping."

"Okay. Yes. Okay. Love you. Oh, I have other news to tell you, but I'll tell you later."

She hung up, and I didn't address my coach right away. These calls, they happened sometimes. They happened more a year ago, but her progress had plateaued over the summer. God. A medication. They were always adjusting her meds, seeing what helped her better, but the problem was that there were always side effects. Real fucking serious side effects. It was a roulette game about which side effect was easier to live with than the other, and after I got these calls, the pit in my stomach came next.

It was there. Tunneling down.

"Everything okay on the family front?" My coach interrupted the usual hole I went down into, filled with anger and hate.

I nodded, feeling scraped raw inside. "My sister's in the hospital. She was calling to let me know."

He was quiet for a beat. I didn't talk about my family, hardly ever. It was easier not to because for one, it was no one's business, but also because I couldn't hide the loathing that always came up when I told people what happened to my little sister.

I loved her. I worshiped her, and she shouldn't be in that wheelchair.

"You good to play?"

"Yeah," I ground out.

"Get in here then. And, Cruz?"

I looked up, waiting.

He was studying me intensely. "I see your anger. If you're playing tonight, use it."

My gut flared, because fuck yes, I would. It's the only place I channeled that pit inside of me. "I plan to."

"Good."

We went back to the other side. The guys listened to the pre-game talk, though I could feel their gazes on me. I knew some would ask me later what was going on, but tonight, I just wanted to rip someone's head off. Or win the game.

I'd settle for the latter.

10

MARA

The Alpha Mu house was a giant brick building with different sections that led off to other buildings attached. It looked like an odd-shaped brick castle on Grant West's frat row, but to be fair, it wasn't just their house that looked like that. A couple others were similar. But the Alpha Mu's was the biggest.

"Daniels!" Two guys in the doorway threw up their hands at seeing me. "About time you got here."

"Hey, guys." I stepped inside, eyeing both as they shut the door.

One was speaking into a walkie.

"Door duty?"

The other gave me a resigned look, nodding. "Yeah. All night. We kinda messed up with something."

The other one finished on the radio and jumped into the conversation. "It's better than bathroom duty and there's worse than that too."

"I don't think I want to know what those are."

"Good call." He indicated down the hall. "Miller's in the basement."

The place was in full party mode. There were people everywhere. Music was blasting, along with neon lighting inside.

"There's a girl I invited to come with me from my abnormal psych class. It was last minute. I didn't catch her name so she might show up and give my name."

"Right on. We'll ask everyone coming in if they're in abnormal psych."

I couldn't tell if he was serious or not, but I added, "I told her to come with at least one friend."

"The more the merrier."

The doorbell rang so I moved on, hearing them open the door. "Any of you currently in abnormal psychology?"

I glanced back, laughing, and saw they were serious with the question.

"Daniels. What up, woman?" A guy I knew from last semester was in the kitchen, waving me over when I got there.

He was mixing drinks, and handed one over to me. "Drink?"

"Thanks." Normally, I liked to bring my own booze, but I knew this guy. He broke down crying one night about his family. I knew how much he missed his grandpa and how he went home every Sunday night for dinner with his grandma. When I learned how he doted on his sister, that cemented it. He'd go crazy if anyone slipped something in her drink. I held up the cup, glancing around. There were some Kappa girls here, and some...nope, *all* were giving me dark looks. Okay, then. Seemed that whole drama with Burford wasn't in the past. I shouldered through, going into the basement.

Two guys were guarding the doorway. When they saw me, they gave a nod behind them.

I ducked past, seeing a large screen mounted on the wall. It was huge, almost theater size, and was high up on the wall. The game hadn't started. The guys were still in warm-ups, and I paused before anyone knew I was there. Cruz was doing his thing. He liked to bullshit. It was almost part of his pregame ritual. I'd noticed that he'd either try to converse with someone from the opposing team, the ref, or if none of them were available, he'd stand on the red line and talk with a couple of his teammates. Wes Barclay and he were tight, so it was usually Wes, but tonight he was talking to one of the other team's guys.

"What's he doing?" One of the guys gestured to the screen. "He does this every game."

"Who cares? He always dominates."

Someone else said, "He's getting in their heads. Setting them up for later total annihilation."

Gavin laughed. "You all are idiots. You even know Cruz? He's not that type of guy. He's chill, so he's being chill, and when they're all trying to get hyped up for the game, he's interfering with that intensity."

"Soooo, what I just said."

"He's not doing it intentionally. Just him being him."

A girl added, "I heard he's super intense. This is all a facade or something."

A bunch of guys broke out laughing.

I could hear Gavin rolling his eyes. "Girl, why you in here?"

"Dude!" One guy broke into harsh laughter, coughing at the same time.

There were other murmurs, a couple girls, but one shoved through the last guys in the doorway and went past me, hurrying upstairs. I was guessing she was the one who made that comment.

From another girl, "You're such a dick sometimes, Gavin."

"What?" He was laughing. "Did I say something?"

A second girl came through, and I pointed upstairs. "That way."

She was angry, but clipped out, "Thanks," before she went upstairs too.

There was a second room that ran the length of the main

room. Alpha Mu used it as a weight room and at the end a Skee-Ball was set up with an arcade basketball game next to it. It attached to that main room at the end, so I went that route, coming to the doorway and getting a scope of the room before actually stepping into it. The game would start soon, the ice was emptying. There was a large U-shaped couch, which was full of people. Mostly guys. A few girls. There were other guys lounging on beanbags in front of the couch.

A bar was set up in the back where I was standing. Some of the guys saw me, lifted a hand in greeting.

"Hey."

"Daniels!" Miles and Gavin both heard me, looking back from the couch.

Gavin threw his arms in the air, like the guys at the front. "What are you doing back there? Get over here, woman!"

Miles was standing up. He waved me over. "Here. You can sit where I was."

I frowned, going around the couch and sitting in his spot. "Are you sure? Where are you–"

I stopped asking because he took a seat in front of me on the floor, and he moved back, leaning against my legs. He rested one arm over my knee, sipping his drink, but as he did that, he put a little space between me and Gavin. He glanced back, gauging my response. I gave him a little grin in thanks.

He grinned back, hiding it as he took another sip.

Gavin was frowning at him, then poked my arm. "Where'd you disappear to last night?"

"I went to my room. Why?"

He was scanning my face and I waited for him to tell me that he came up, knocking on the door, but he didn't. He shrugged, ducking his head. "No reason. I was just checking on you."

"I was okay."

Miles had stilled, overhearing our conversation.

I elbowed Gavin and indicated the screen. "Didn't know you and Cruz were so tight."

He harrumphed. "What? It's Cruz. He's partied here. He's a good guy."

"Everyone, shut up!" One of the guys stood up, yelling. "Game's starting!"

The guys were back and skating up for the face-off. After that, it was *on*.

IT WAS during the second and third period when I headed back upstairs for a refill. I was hoping the same bartender was in the kitchen still, but as soon as I got to the top of the stairs, a different guy saw me. "Daniels, you got two chicks at the door saying they know you."

I veered that way instead. The door duty guys were still there.

One saw me coming, the walkie in his hand. He waved at me. "They won't say if they're in your class or not, so I'm hoping you can vouch for them?"

I looked at them, not recognizing them. "Who are you?"

The two guys threw their hands in the air again.

"Come on! Seriously?"

I heard the other on the walkie. "We might have a problem here."

One of the girls leaned toward me. "Our friend said we were invited via you. She's in your abnormal psych class."

I was about to wave them in when the walkie guy stepped up behind me, touched my shoulder with the walkie, and gestured inside. "One sec," I said to the girls, following him, and once there, they closed the door.

A cry of protest came from the other side. The other guy was speaking over them, but he was sounding stressed.

"You guys now have standards about who comes in?"

His mouth went flat. "If you vouch for them, you gotta stay with them."

"That's okay."

"The whole time."

That was different.

He read my face, and his eyebrows went up. "Exactly. We got in trouble last semester. A girl got too drunk, and she woke up at her place, no memory of how she got there. She freaked, told her RA, and since she only remembers being at our place, you know the drill."

"Not good."

"*Exactly.*" He was giving me a look like he and I were on the same wavelength. "My advice? If you know them and want to be responsible for them, have at it. We'll wave them in, but if you don't want to play babysitter, let me know. We've been sending people packing all night."

"How fun is that."

He let out a hollow laugh. "Right. It's your call."

I was shaking my head before he even finished. "I don't know them, but I'll go out and let them know the situation."

"Okay with me."

We were going back to the door when my phone started ringing. It was an unknown number.

I...

My stomach dropped and a lump instantly formed at the back of my throat. I shouldn't, but I also didn't want to wonder. I needed to know.

I showed him my phone.

His head moved up and down and he pointed down the hallway. "First door. That's my brother's room. Should be clear." He motioned outside. "I'll be nice to the girls, explain the situation. They'll be pissed. They're *always* pissed, but fuck 'em."

"Thanks."

I hurried down and into the first room, testing the knob. It was open, and I slipped in. He was right. Considering how loud the music was, the room was relatively quiet. They must've soundproofed some of the rooms. Then, feeling a pit in my stomach, I took a breath and counted to five before I answered.

"Mom?"

"This is a collect call from Cain Police Department. Do you accept the charges for a–"

"This is Zeke!"

What?

But there was silence until Zeke said, "Don't leave me hanging, Daniels. I need some help here."

"Uh–yeah. I'll accept the charges."

Zeke let out an audible sigh. "Thank GOD. I was a little nervous."

"Why are you calling me? I'm in Grant West."

He laughed. "Your number is the only one I have memorized. Don't ask me why it's your number, but yeah, could you call my boy and let him know where I am? He'll know the drill."

"Zeke."

"What's up, Buttercup?"

"What did you do to get arrested?"

A louder laugh this time. "Uh, I'm a little fuzzy on the deets myself, but once I piece it all together, I'll fill you in. I'm not even really sure where my phone is, or my clothes."

"You don't have clothes?"

"I'm in one of the jumpsuits you see the criminals wear when they go to county. Guess I was only in my underwear, and they said that wasn't appropriate. Had an extra jumper so here you go. Is it sad that I'm hoping to keep this thing? Maybe wash it twenty times, but this will be an awesome Halloween costume."

"I don't want to hear any more."

"Wait!"

I paused, but he didn't say anything. "What?"

"Uh. How are you? How are things with your mo–"

I hung up, letting loose a curse before I started pulling up my ex's name.

The door opened then, a beam of light flashed over me, and a guy stopped short. "Who the fuck are you?"

The guy was a giant, with long black hair pulled up in a messy man-bun. I repressed a shiver at who was going to tell him it was not working for him. Also, he bore no resemblance to his brother.

"I have to make a call. Your brother told me I could come in here."

He moved more into the room, closing the door and flicking the lights on. Getting a better look at me, he was slowing his roll, giving me a once-over. "Never mind. Make all the calls you want."

I narrowed my eyes, but this shouldn't take long.

I hit call and waited.

Unless my ex, who was Zeke's best friend, was sleeping or fucking, he'd answer my call. And he did a second later, "Mara?"

"Zeke just called me from jail."

"What?"

I paused for a beat. "Do you really need me to repeat that line?"

He snorted. "Why are *you* calling about it?"

"Have that conversation with him. Could you go and get him out?"

"At Grant West?"

"No. He's in Cain. I'm guessing at the police station. He called me collect."

He cursed. "Yeah. I'll get him. Uh..."

Blaise had been my with-benefits guy back in Fallen Crest,

but he never knew about my mom. He knew now, and I felt my chest tightening because his tone went soft. He was going to ask about her, how she was doing, how *I* was doing.

So I got there first, saying softly, "See you, Blaise."

"Oh. Yeah. See you."

I ended the call and waited a second. Sometimes the emptiness would start hitting me right about now... This used to happen on a regular basis back when things ended between him and I. I hadn't handled it the best way, and lashed out a little, but the thing was that he had no idea why I reacted the way I did. And now, considering this call, I was realizing that he may never know.

But the emptiness wasn't hitting me, and well look at that. Progress.

"Cain. Blaise. I heard him call you Mara. Miller talks about a certain Mara so I'm going out on a limb and guessing that you're Mara Daniels?"

Right.

I straightened.

I'd forgotten the guy and that I was in his room. Him and his man-bun.

"Hi. Yes." Wait. I blinked. "What does he say about me?"

The guy smirked, going to his desk and grabbing his wallet. "Just that you're super hot, which I agree with him now, and he wants to bag you. He's almost desperate about it."

"I've told him I'm not going to fuck him."

He grinned faintly, grabbing a hoodie and keys, then going to his door. "That's the thing with guys. Unless he sees you with another guy, he's not going to believe a word you say." He reached for his doorknob but glanced back and gave me another once-over. "Do us all a favor and get a boyfriend. No wonder the guys are jumping over themselves for you. Stay in here a little longer and I've half a mind to tell the guys someone else has to go for a beer run."

Fuck's sake.

I gave him a hard look, heading for him right as he opened the door. He held it for me, watching me pass in front and he murmured, right behind me, "Pleasure to meet you, Daniels. You can use my room anytime you need."

I gave him a tight smile. "Thanks." And decided not to get a refill. I got back to the basement during the third period and right as Cruz shot the puck.

The goalie reached for it, but the light went red.

Everyone went crazy. "GOAL!!!!!"

I GAVE MILES A RIDE HOME. As soon as I pulled up to our house, he jerked up. "What? Another party tonight?"

He looked my way, but I was getting out of the car. "Wade and some girls from class were going to study. I'm not sure if Darren was joining them. I'm guessing the studying turned into drinking."

He let out a curse, getting out too. "Of all nights for me to lose my phone."

"You lost your phone?"

"Yeah. If you see an extra phone around the place, it's probably mine."

He started for the back door, and I went with him until I veered for the door that was my own entrance.

"You're not coming in with me?"

I shook my head. "I'm partied out."

My stomach was still churning a little, but not bad enough where I needed to numb it. I was craving some alone time, and a change of clothes.

"Hey, uh."

I unlocked my door, and opened it, but paused, holding it open.

Miles winced, before closing his eyes. "Fuck it. I'm sorry, but... I'm wading in. You and Gavin..."

"There's no me and Miller."

He was already nodding before I finished. "I'm aware of that. All of the guys in his frat are aware of it, and they were ribbing him before you showed up tonight."

I deflated. Just a little. "They didn't bet him to get in my pants, did they?"

"No. Nothing like that, but you know who Flynn Carrington is?"

I shook my head.

"Senior. One of the head honchos in the frat." He motioned to the back of his head. "Dark man-bun."

"Oh. Yeah. I met him tonight."

"Sorry. I, just, you got your stuff about getting personal, but this is kinda serious."

"It's fine, Miles. I'm sorry for snapping at you that one time. Just can't handle questions about my past, that's all."

He blew out a breath, looking relieved and his head bobbed a little. "I saw Carrington watching you when we were leaving. He didn't like that I was going with you, and it's just a thing. Guys can tell. He–Flynn–he's got a lot of power in the frat. His dad's, like, a senator or something, but the guy's a dick."

"Miles, just say it."

"I'm just saying that I could see a situation where Miller will be talking about you when you're not there, and Carrington's going to hear. And he could be the guy that says something, making it into a whole different thing. Like betting him to get in your pants or something." He stopped talking for a second before his eyes flashed something grim. "I didn't like how he looked at you. You know. I mean, some girls are clueless, but you're not. You *know*. He looked like a predator."

I felt the word in my throat, and it was hard to swallow around it.

Fuck, though. Fuck.

"I'm thinking it's time we both have a break from the Alpha Mu house." I amended, "Another break, in my case."

His grin was sad. "Yeah. And, man. Glad that's done." He gestured to the house. "I'm either going to pass out or get a second wind."

"See you tomorrow."

He gave a wave, going through his door. I went through mine, and stood just inside, digesting what he told me because fuck. Fuck! *Fuck!* Was it me? Did I ooze something that attracted drama?

Was I like my mom?

11

CRUZ

My phone was buzzing when we got to the hotel that night.

I checked my texts, taking a seat in the lobby. As soon as I got up to the room, who knew what I'd be walking into. Taking a call up there sometimes was useless. Atwater ran naked through a bunch of connecting rooms one time. Other times, Wes would already be sleeping.

There were a bunch of texts from my teammates, from classmates. Miles Gaynor. Other guys. Girls, but no Mara. I knew our deal. I'd loved our deal when she presented it at first because I didn't need a girlfriend. Hockey took too much of my time, along with my family. Girls tended to need attention and I didn't have it to give. I got the benefits of sex without the other needy shit. It was a win win, at least for me. I didn't know why Mara was how she was. We'd been doing this thing since the end of September, but man, I kinda wished we could amend it a little so we could be friendly at times. I got her worries. Well... I didn't. She never explained why she didn't want to be friends, but that wasn't a stretch. Friends meant feelings could get involved and with sex already involved, I knew the dangers.

Though, if anyone could pull it off, it was Mara. She had a steel wall around her heart, I swear, but the girl was cool.

Laid back. Funny at times. There was never any grief.

Fuck it. The most she'd do is tell me not to text her.

Me: Hey.

Mara: Hey. Sorry about the L.

Me: We'll get 'em tomorrow.

Mara: Not trying to be mean here, but what are we doing?

I chuckled.

Me: Texting.

Mara: Why, tho?

Me: ?

Mara: Don't mess with me.

Mara: Plz.

I frowned at that. That wasn't like her.

Me: Ok. I was messing with you, but what's with the plz? You okay? For real.

I hit send, and a couple seconds later, my phone came alive.

Mara calling.

Whoa.

I stood, answering it, "Hey."

"What is this?" She sounded hella frustrated before adding, "I'm not trying to be a bitch, but I can't play games right now. What's your endgame with this?"

"With texting you?"

"Yes," she bit out. "And asking if I'm okay. Like, do you actually care? For real? Or is this just some new head game because I really like what we have and if you're starting to change the rules, just...don't. Please."

I was taken aback, and for a moment, I wasn't sure what or how to respond to that. Noticing the front desk worker watching me, I said, "Hold on."

I went outside and moved down a little from the entrance in case anyone recognized me. "Okay. For full transparency here, I just wanted to text you. I thought the worst that would happen is you'd get pissed and tell me not to do it again. As for head games, I don't do that shit. We've been messing around for three months and three weeks, and I don't know. I kinda feel that if any chick in a situation like ours who could handle a little texting would be you."

"You want to be friends?" Her voice got a little quieter. "You want to know random things about me, that I like laundromats? Things like that?"

"Maybe texting buds? I mean, we don't want to get too carried away." A pause. "Laundromats, huh?"

"Fuck off."

But she was laughing as she said it. That made me grin. Talking to girls was like walking a minefield. I wasn't sure where to step. One wrong direction, and kaboom.

"I know your policy on personal questions, but for real–you okay? Something happen tonight?"

I was waiting, bracing, if I said the wrong thing.

She didn't say anything, not for a few seconds and a few more. I was sweating at this point.

Finally, in a quiet tone, "You know Flynn Carrington?"

Gut check.

Red alarms blared, but I kept it restrained. "Uh. Yeah. Why?"

"I was at Alpha Mu tonight, and he saw me. Not a big deal, but Miles warned me about him when we left. Said the look he saw from him was..."

I could guess. Miles was doing her a solid, warning her about him, but all the guys knew.

I still couldn't say the word, not for her. It was guy code, which was fucking odd in this situation.

"What'd he say?"

"He said Carrington was looking at me like a predator."

Fuck to the no, no, no.

"What's your plan on handling him?"

She let out a nervous sound, like an exclamation. "Hell if I know? Gavin's already texted me, asking when I'm going back for their next party. I was planning on avoiding the frat, you know? But Gavin can lay on the pressure."

I wasn't liking hearing that from her, but hell if I could say anything about that.

"Miller's going to lay it down until he's put in his place. He's just built that way."

"I know. I can handle Gavin, but I'm a little worried about Carrington. And I feel stupid saying that because it was a *look* that someone else saw, but I know how guys are. I know how they can be."

"No, man. Chicks are like deer. Some know exactly when a hunter's got you in their scope. Trust that."

"What? You're not going to 'fix' this situation for me? Be a typical guy?" She was teasing or I was hoping she was teasing. There was a bite to her tone, a little bit of one.

"I'm a little worried that would violate the new amendment to our emerging treaty right now so… no?"

She laughed, carefree and I relaxed. Slightly.

"Thanks for that."

"Yeah, no problem." *For what?* I had no clue.

"It's kinda too bad you're four hours away."

"Probably for the best. After our talk, I'd come over and have slow sex with you and we are not slow sex people."

She laughed again.

That kept me smiling.

She said, "No, we aren't. Hot, sensual, and hard sex. The best kind."

"Right."

Another laugh.

I was all the way scoring here. "I should let you go. Got a

feeling if I don't head back to the room, Barclay's going to send out my own hunting party."

"Hey."

"Yeah?"

"Can I–before your games, do you like being told 'good luck'? What's the proper protocol for you?"

"It's like you know some hockey players?" I teased. "Uh, no luck, but I always like a text that says, 'Win, asshole.'"

She burst out laughing. "Are you serious?"

"Yeah. Just nothing that indicates I need luck. I'm not one of those guys."

"Okay. So for tomorrow, win, sucker."

"That's better."

"All right. Bye."

"Bye."

Win, sucker.

I liked that a lot.

My phone buzzed when I was heading inside.

I read the text as I got on the elevator and started laughing.

Mara: Win or be my bitch on Sunday.

Me: That's like a bribe *not* to win. Do better.

Mara: Getting used to the amending treaty here. I'll do better tomorrow.

Me: You better.

Mara: Win, fucker.

I was still laughing when I got to the room.

12

MARA

She started calling Saturday morning.

I didn't recognize the number, but the foreboding feeling in my gut told me it was her.

And it was a little after four in the morning. 4:03.

It kept ringing.

I kept staring at it, curled up in bed, unable to look away and a second later, my phone lit up again.

I should answer. I started the same thoughts I always did. *It might not be her.*

It might be Dad.

Maybe Dad was in an accident?

Maybe she was in an accident?

Maybe it was her and she really did need my help?

Was she bleeding right now? Had she cut herself?

Again?

Was she in the hospital again?

If she was in prison, if she was in Vegas and ran out of money, if a guy just fucked her and she didn't know his name... Those I didn't care about. But there was one question, one that

I hadn't asked anyone because no one could give me the answer–that's the one I answered the call for.

"Mom," I said it quietly, my voice hoarse. "What you were in the hospital for, did you really try to do it?"

She gasped on the other end, and then a hoarse whisper, "Baby. Oh, baby." Her voice started trembling. She began to cry. "Oh, my beautiful baby girl. You answered. I heard you came to the hospital. I'm so happy you did. I'm so sorry your father kept you away. He shouldn't have done that, kept my daughter away from her mama. A girl needs to see her mama. Oh, Mara honey. Beautiful Mara. How are you?"

She wasn't answering.

She went from sad to rushed to angry to frenzied to gushing and she ended with a question that I knew she didn't care about. Because of that, I didn't answer and without waiting for an answer, she rushed forward, "Can you believe this shit your father is trying to pull? Baby. Baby, I need your help. You owe me that. I pushed you out of my pussy, didn't throw you in the trash, not like what your father told me to do." A hard laugh from her. "I bet he's never told you that, but it's true and you know what would've happened if I'd done that? I would've had a life. I wouldn't have gained those six pounds. Six up, six down. My tits are sagging. I was talking to a guy inside. He's in for drugs, but he's a surgeon. He said he could fix my tits and he could tighten my pussy. I think I'm going to do it. Listen, where are you? I wanted to come and take you out for dinner. My friend, Marshall, he's the surgeon, he's getting out in ten days, and he said he'd take me out for a weekend. You want to come with us? I bet he could do something for you too. Fix those cheek lines. Freshen your face up. He could give you some ass." Now she was laughing. "A little fat back there–"

She wasn't going to answer.

"Mom."

She was still going. She hadn't heard me.

Talking about all the features the surgeon could help me with, because she cared, because she was looking out for me, because a daughter represented her, but I couldn't screw him. She chuckled, her voice dropping low, "I mean, if you wanted to, you could. Maybe you should? Get a sugar daddy. But no threesome business. I mean–"

"Mom–"

She ignored me. "You think he might pay for a threesome? Some mother-daughter action–"

I couldn't. Not anymore.

I hung up, and like I did with all the new numbers she called me from, I blocked this new one.

Her old number was already blocked.

I went through all of my media and deleted every single one but goddamn. If she searched my name, it'd still pop up.

Wouldn't it?

I couldn't risk it.

Once I was done, I did a google search for my name and went through every hit that gave any identifying information about me. I searched, found where to have it taken down.

And right after I was done, two hours later, my stomach revolted.

I sprinted from the bed, getting to the toilet just in time to empty whatever had been inside.

I stopped puking after six times; the last four were only bile.

It was later, when I was curled up by the toilet with a blanket over me that I started going over the call with a clearer head and this was the first time I thought the doctors got it right, or one of them did. A new diagnosis was probably correct. She'd escalated.

She was harder.

I STAYED IN ON SATURDAY. Sometimes I sought people out or parties, but it was different on Saturday. I couldn't explain it. I just wanted silence. My own space.

Peace.

I turned my phone off all day, and I studied for that quiz.

Went out for groceries later in the morning, as soon as my stomach felt steadier.

That night, I studied more and ended the night with a movie. I was in bed when I glanced over, considered turning my phone on.

I left it and rolled over.

I TURNED it on for Sunday. Notification after notification began rolling through.

Miles wanted to go to the library.

Gavin wanted me to head over for another party.

A few girls from class, asking if the quiz was truth or rumor?

Zeke thanked me for calling Blaise to get him out of 'the joint.'

Then a few last ones that made me pause.

From Tasmin, who lived across from me in the dorms.

Taz: Party at the hockey house. Want to come with us?

"Us" would be at least her and her boyfriend, Race.

Tasmin and I weren't texters. We didn't invite each other places. I frowned. Why would she start now?

Then there were a couple texts from my dad.

Dad: I was told that she called you. Are you okay?

Dad: Want to talk about it?

I skipped over his and pulled up the last one. It wasn't that I didn't want to talk to my dad, but he was too close to *her*. I always felt like she took entire chunks of skin off my body, leaving me exposed. I needed time away from her, and that meant him too right now.

The last text was from Cruz.

Cruz: Getting back tonight. Want me to 'get back' tonight? ;)

That one made me smile.

Me: Your joke didn't land. Sorry to break it to you.

Cruz: Too early for texting. Come crawl in bed with me. Going back to sleep unless you wake me up.

I wanted to go, so bad, and that terrified me because it wasn't good to want to be around someone as much as I did right now.

But, it was hard to fight against that offer. I wanted it, really, *really* badly.

This.

This was why we shouldn't have done the texting because it made me like him a little bit more. No. Not even that. It made me feel safe with him. A little bit safer.

That was dangerous to someone like me.

Never feel safe. When you did, that's when the world would get pulled out from under you.

That's when you would fall.

I could never get comfortable. I could never feel safe.

I surrounded myself with people I didn't fully like... Or I kept them at bay, the ones that were already in.

I messed up, but fuck it, because if he texted right now, I'd respond. If he called, I'd answer.

I was staring at my phone, knowing what I wanted to do and what I probably would do, but this was a last-ditch effort to distract me from doing it.

I hit call.

She answered after the third ring, and her voice was drowsy which made sense. It was a little after nine and that was like five in the morning for college people.

"Mara?"

I called Tasmin.

"Why did you text me that last night?"

"What?" She yawned. "What time is it?"

"Early enough for church if you're the God-fearing type."

She laughed before catching herself. "I'm so confused. This is Mara Daniels calling me?"

"Why'd you text me that last night? Inviting me to the hockey house?"

"Oh." She yawned again.

I heard a male voice in the background, saying something.

She replied, sounding from a distance, "No, baby. Go back to sleep."

Baby.

That was a nice 'connecting' term. I was jealous, hearing it.

"Why did I invite you to the hockey house? They had a party to celebrate their win yesterday. I actually thought you'd be there. Were you?"

"No."

"Oh."

"That was it? No other reason?"

"Um, no? I mean, no. Wait. Are you talking about Blaise–"

"I know you're aware about my mom."

She got quiet, real quiet, after I said that.

She did. She knew or she would've been like, *'Your mom? What about your mom?"*

A few seconds later, she said, "Your mom? What about your mom?"

I laughed, shaking my head. "You took too long for your response. I know you know."

"I got a call about it, but I didn't know if I should believe it. I actually didn't until just now." She asked, quiet, "Are you oka–"

"Do not ever invite me to another party."

She drew in a sharp breath.

My eyes were stinging but I added, "Do not text me. Do not say hi to me. You see me on campus, and you don't. You don't see me. Got that? Do not pity me."

She didn't respond.

"Do you hear me?"

"Yeah, but Mara–"

I hung up, wishing I didn't give a shit about what I did. That was a lie. Everything was a lie. Tasmin was being nice and not pitying me, but that same part of me knew she did pity me. A little bit, whether she'd ever admit it or not. I remembered her mom. Paid attention even though she didn't go to the same school as me, but I still watched. I observed.

Tasmin had the family I never had, would never have.

Fuck, but also *fuck*.

I could go see Cruz.

I didn't understand it. I didn't want to understand it, but I just knew I could go *now*.

I couldn't have gone before.

13

MARA

My hair was tucked under a baseball cap with a little spillage. Oversized sweatshirt. Leggings. Sneakers. I was hella comfortable and I knew in no way incognito, but the cap was pulled low, and I was sneaking past the cars in their driveway. I went up, and around, going to the little ledge by his main window. I knelt. His curtain was still pulled shut, but I reached for the window and found it unlocked.

I slid it open, moved aside the curtain, and surveyed his room.

The window was directly above his little couch. His bed was to the left, right in front of the door. He was still sleeping, on his side and under his blanket. I moved quietly, stepping down onto his couch and slid the window back in place.

His door wasn't locked. I went over, locked it, and watched him for a second.

He looked so relaxed, I was second guessing if I wanted to wake him.

But no. I had to remind myself we were only fuck buddies, so I took my sweatshirt off, undid my bra, and toed off my shoes. Going to his bed, I lifted the sheet up and slid inside.

"Wha–oh!" Cruz came awake, rearing up. Realizing who I was, he relaxed. His head went back to his pillow, and he drowsily grinned at me. His whole face was soft from sleep. As I finished moving in, laying on my back and still on the edge, his hand went to my stomach, moving under my tank top. "I didn't think you'd come over."

"This okay?"

He nodded, his eyes darkening. He moved in, his mouth touching mine.

I always loved that first touch of our lips. That was my thing. I never told another person, but the first kiss always gave me tingles and warmed me up. But smelling his toothpaste, I pulled back. "You brushed your teeth recently?"

His eyes closed. "Went to the bathroom after we texted, thought just in case." Then his eyes opened, and he grew a lot more focused. His mouth found mine again, this time it was more demanding, and just like always, I was swept up from the rush of his touch.

It wasn't long before he moved over me, his body on mine and we kept kissing.

Closed mouth. Open mouth. With tongue. I loved all of it.

I loved how he peppered kisses down my throat, down my body.

How he bent over me, caressing one breast as he tasted my other one and all the while, rubbing against me as I was moving up and against him just as hard.

I fucking loved this.

He kept kissing me until it was torture.

I was writhing under him, straining for him, but he was taking his time.

I pulled back, gasping and out of breath. "What are you doing?"

He grinned down at me, grinding into me, and I groaned from the sensation. Cradling my head, his hand on the side of my face, he said, "I'm savoring you." He went back to kissing me, his hand cupping my breast, his thumb rubbing over my nipple.

The inferno in me was lit. I wanted more.

I reached down, finding his sweatpants' waistband and started to slide my hand inside, but he caught it and lifted it up, pressing my hand down as he rolled more concretely over me. He was halting any other way I could reach for his cock. But he kept kissing me, his tongue sliding inside and taking ownership of me in that way.

I tried with my other hand.

He caught that one and pinned both down as he kept tasting me.

God. It felt so good.

His mouth, his tongue. He was so good at this. Hours. I could do this for hours with him.

Arching my back, I tried to lift him a little bit, but he only chuckled. His mouth moved over mine again. It never left me as he was doing a slow move up and into my body. I could feel him, his dick was straining, and he was grinding into me through my leggings.

I wanted that last connection. Needing it, I wound my legs tight around his waist, pushing back against him.

He groaned this time, his mouth falling away as he was panting.

"Babe, let me wake up to you. I wanna take my time."

"We're not slow sex people."

His eyes had a dark molten look simmering there and he focused back on my mouth. He murmured, "We are today." He bent down, his mouth catching mine and this time, he wouldn't let go. Not that I was fighting him. I opened right up for him, my neck arching up and into him, and he moved with me. This gave me a small opening between our bodies. I snaked my hand out from under his, found his stomach, and he sucked in a breath at the touch. I slid down, slowly, with purpose, my palm flat against his stomach, under his waistband. He didn't stop my touch this time, and I knew I had him. I found him, wrapping my hand around him, and he gasped, breaking away from my mouth. He fell half down, his mouth rasping against my ear. "I fucking love when you do that."

"Do what? This?" I squeezed lightly.

He moaned.

"Or this?" I began moving up and down.

Another deep and guttural groan from him.

I kept pumping him and he held himself still, feeling me feeling him.

"God, you're so good at that."

I laughed. "The compliments that happen in bed."

He grinned, laughing, and he turned to see me more fully. All the while, I kept working him and the glazed, darkened look in his gaze was my reward. I loved seeing that look from him. "You got a few more before I bury myself in you so deep I'm gonna poke your stomach."

"See. Love the shit you say to me."

He laughed but lifted himself up more so he could see me touching him, sliding up and down over him. "Goddamn," he whispered before his whole body shuddered and he reared up. The blanket was thrown off. His hands caught my hips, jerking me down, and took hold of my leggings, whipping them off me. Leggings normally didn't work that way. They stuck like a second skin. They were pushed down, not whipped off. Not with Cruz. At the sight of my bare legs, he paused, eyeing me, and his tongue touched his lip.

I knew what he had in mind, and I was torn.

I wanted his dick in me, but he bent, peeling my underwear down, this time going slow. He laid me more fully down on the bed, getting comfortable. I closed my eyes, knowing he was going to torture me all over again.

His mouth settled over me, and I almost came right then and there.

He began, and he moaned a second later. "*Fuck*! I love eating you."

I twisted, knowing I was the one with the lidded and glazed look now, but I loved watching him as much as he loved eating me. Sunday breakfast.

I had the thought, before the edges of my vision blurred and I could still think. "Twist up. 69."

He moved around, and my mouth closed over his dick as his returned to my clit.

I was *really* happy that I came this morning.

"WHAT ARE YOUR PLANS TODAY?" Cruz asked as he came from the shower, heading to his closet.

I flipped over in bed. Unlike him, who was getting up to head to the ice rink, I was being lazy. I'd not dressed, and I pulled his blanket more firmly over me.

"Uh. Studying? Probably."

He dropped the towel, and my mouth watered.

It was a crime against hockey players to cover up their hotness with those pads and jerseys. For real. These guys were insane with how many times they went to the rink to practice. There were skill sessions through the day. Weight sessions. Actual cardio sessions and then there was the real practice. Mix in studying, getting all the sleep they needed, and all the fuel, these guys were some of the busiest athletes I knew. But all that work equaled mouthwatering salivating bodies. I was drooling, looking over Cruz's body, his back, as he was reaching for his shirt and all the muscles were shifting together.

Then how the shirt came down over him, hugging and falling over his back perfectly.

Then, God, the sweatshirt. The hoodie. The *hockey* hoodie. His last name on the back. His number, 71. The two crossing hockey sticks on the side, and it was a vintage-looking sweatshirt too. The best kind. *And* I was having a hot flash as he was now pulling on his boxer briefs. He bent down, bringing them up, and his leg muscles. The sweats. How they draped over his lean hips.

Um. Totally thinking I needed to buy Cruz a vibrator, so he had one here for me. Damn sure I was going to replay this later.

It took me a second to realize he was looking at me, looking at him and judging by the smirk, he knew where my thoughts had gone.

I grinned. "No shame here. You're a hot individual."

He laughed, raking a hand through his hair before he went to grab the rest of his stuff. Wallet. Keys. His phone was by me on the nightstand. He came over, grabbed it, but stayed, looking at me.

"Hi."

He moved in closer. "Wanna stay? Or come back? We can do a day of studying and you know. Now that we can text, I think studying is okay. We're in the same class." His knee bumped against the bed suggestively. "Whaddaya say? I'm remembering how we first hooked up. Sex apart, the studying was great."

"You serious?" I sat up, the blanket tucked over my chest.

He nodded, his gaze going to exactly where the blanket was covering. "I can pick up food on the way back."

I was considering it, but that was a whole day in the hockey house. "What about, I go to my place. You come with food. We study there?"

His eyes lit up. "Even better. More privacy."

I nodded. He was picking up what I was putting down.

"Sounds like a plan. I'm down. Anything in particular you want me to pick up?"

I shrugged. "It's up to you."

A door closed down the hallway, and a moment later, there was a thump on his door. "Head out! I'll be in the truck."

That was Barclay.

Cruz headed for the door but looked back. "You good to leave on your own?"

I nodded, laying back down and stretching. I was familiar with how long the Sunday skate usually went. "Might take my time before leaving."

"Alright. See you later."

He left but locked his own door before he did.

Because of that, I closed my eyes...

...his bed was so comfortable.

14

MARA

Male voices. A lock was turning. Then, "Dude, you have a chick in your bed."

I woke up to that.

And, crap.

Cruz came in, dropping his bag and stripping off his hoodie like nothing was happening while Barclay was grinning from the doorway.

He lifted his chin. "'Sup, Daniels?"

I pulled the blanket back over my head and scooted down in the bed, curling into a ball.

"What's going on?" Atwater was joining the conversation. "Did I hear you say Daniels? She in here?"

"Hiding in the bed." Barclay's amusement was heavy.

"Daniels, that's not a great hiding spot. First place we check is the bed."

"Go away!" My voice was muffled from the blanket, but they started laughing.

"Guys." A step creaked under Cruz. He was moving through the room.

"Wait. We'll go, but Daniels, we're trying to talk Cruz into a game of laser tag. He's saying no, but maybe you want to come?"

Laser tag?

I sat up. My head came out of the blanket. Cruz was by the bathroom.

I asked, "The new games place?"

Both nodded. Both wearing eager grins.

I narrowed my eyes. "Not going to take any crap from you guys."

Atwater shook his head while Barclay held his hands up in surrender.

"We know the deal. Mum's the word." Atwater made a show of zipping his lips and tossing the key.

Barclay rolled his eyes, but added, "Cool if you hang out, if you want."

I glanced at Cruz, who was still standing in the bathroom doorway, waiting and listening. Seeing me looking at him, he raised an eyebrow. "I like laser tag, so up to you."

Laser tag or a sex/study session? Or laser tag and *then* a sex/study session?

"I'm in."

"Yes!" Atwater's fists went up in the air and he turned to do a jog down the hall.

Barclay's hand pounded the doorframe, and he pointed at me. "Head out in forty minutes."

Shit.

"I have to change–"

"You're good."

I looked at Cruz. He indicated my clothes. "Those are fine."

Leggings and a sweatshirt? But I shrugged. I could shower here. "Sounds good."

"Sweet. Okay. See you down there." He reached in and pulled the door shut, and I waited, seeing if there'd be some innuendo or a wink, but nothing. I got no teasing and that was refreshing.

Cruz crossed the room, locking the door, and narrowed his eyes at me. "You joining or..." He laughed as I flung the blankets back and led the way, still in my tank top and underwear.

Turning the water on, I leaned in and waited until it was warm enough.

I peeled my shirt off, and dropped my underwear, stepping out of them. Going inside, I wasn't looking, but I could feel Cruz right behind me. His chest was brushing against my back.

We'd showered together before, but it was always sexual. Or it always went sexual.

I took the shampoo, put some in my hand and handed it over my shoulder. I heard his low chuckle as he took it and as I was lathering my hair, he reached around me, putting it back. There were other times when I'd not been in the shower with Cruz, but I had watched him. He always went fast. A brisk scrub through his hair, over his body and after a rinse, he was done. Easy-peasy, so when I felt his hands in my hair, helping me work the shampoo in, I started grinning.

I didn't know if I should be grinning.

He shoved my head back under the showerhead, and I stopped caring.

Cruz was acting like a professional hairdresser. There were no lingering touches or grazes. He washed my hair, rinsed it, and reached around me, stepping in and coming in full contact against my back. Okay, there was some rubbing now, but he took the conditioner and worked it in my hair, repeating the process. I did nothing, letting him do the work. It was nice.

Once he was satisfied, the body wash came out.

He lathered himself up, and as I was washing my body, I felt his hands going over my back. My ass. *In* my ass, and I squealed a little, jumping. Another low chuckle from him before I felt his hands running down my legs. I stopped, just watching as he washed and rinsed my entire bottom half. As he moved his hands up my legs, rotating around to the front, he stood, coming back in contact with me and his hand moved up between my legs.

I held my breath, waiting to see what he'd do.

Now he lingered.

I leaned back against him. His fingers moved through my folds, a very thorough cleaning until one of his fingers slipped inside.

I reached out, pushing against the shower wall as he very suddenly and very drastically changed the feel of the shower. His finger went in. A slow slide at first, going deep, and I groaned, but he readjusted me so I was angled better for him. He began moving in and out. Still slow at first, until I widened my legs, and a second finger moved in. Pretty soon, he had an arm around my waist, cementing me up in the air as his fingers were plunging into me.

He knew my body so well. He knew how many pumps he needed, at what angle, how and where the way to grind against me, how long to hold, and he knew the *exact right moment* for his thumb to start moving over my clit at the same time.

I was almost crawling up the wall as I exploded. He held me upright, waiting until my legs could work again.

I let out a shuddering breath when my feet touched the floor and didn't slide out from under me, laughing shakily when I looked back at him. He was watching me, a dark and lusty look.

"You want?" I motioned to him. His cock was sticking right up against his stomach.

His hand wrapped around himself, giving it a few strokes before he shook his head. He leaned in, crowding me back against the side wall and his head folded down. He murmured, throatily, "Something to look forward to after laser tag."

A zing went through me, and his mouth found mine. That

zing electrified, coursing through my whole body. I was out of breath at the end of the kiss, but he stepped away, moved the showerhead to give himself a last rinse, and winked as he stepped out of the shower.

God.

I turned the other way, giving my back to him because I was shaken.

That felt–different.

This whole day felt different, like we were shifting, and for a moment, fear branded my insides. A shiver went down my spine, and I couldn't breathe. For a minute. A few seconds. It felt like an hour, until–*OFF*–I shut it down. Everything.

Once I did, I gasped, silently, but my lungs seized.

I couldn't bring myself to turn around. The water was raining down on me, and I reached out, the tips of my fingers pressing against the tile. I closed my eyes, counted.

One.

Two.

Three–my fingers started shaking.

Four.

My lungs were closing–five.

I pushed off, and whipped around, but he wasn't there. Thank goodness.

I could do this. I could go to laser tag with Cruz. We could hang out. We were already going to hang out. We were texting. We'd talked on the phone.

The changes didn't mean I had to shut this down.

Yeah. That was it.

Because if it didn't–I couldn't go there.

I still needed this connection.

It was fine.

Fine.

Everything *would* be just fine.

Still, as I grabbed the towel Cruz had left on the counter for me, and began drying my body, I closed myself off to what I was doing. I went in my head, and did something I hadn't done for a few years.

My brain was a house. There were rooms. Doors. Hallways.

I put my mom in one room. My dad in another.

Miles. Gavin.

My roommates all got their own room together.

Tasmin, her boyfriend.

And the last one, Cruz. He got the basement.

Once all the doors were shut, and the hallways were empty, I could function again.

I moved into the bedroom. Cruz wasn't there. He'd made the bed and my clothes were on top, not folded, but laid out. He added one of his hockey hoodies, and I grabbed it. I'd put it away, but after I was done dressing, there was a warning knock before the door opened. He popped his head in and gestured behind him. "Guys are taking off. You want to ride with me or…?"

"No," I choked out, clearing my throat before my voice sounded normal again. "No. I need my car. I'll meet you guys there."

"You good?"

"I'm good."

He jerked his chin up before heading out.

I waited a little. I didn't want to go out his window if I didn't need to, so once the house was quiet and I heard the cars leave, I went out through a side door.

"You good?"

"I'm good."

The thing was…me, my issues, I should've been lying through my teeth with that statement.

I wasn't.

I was still holding his hoodie, too.

15

MARA

I drew up short when I went inside because it was bustling with people. People I didn't expect to be here.

"Daniels!"

Aw, shit. That was Gavin and looking behind him, I was seeing a good portion of Alpha Mu guys with him. Atwater came over at that time, draping an arm around my shoulder as if I were there for him to rest his weight on. "Nah, man. Daniels is with us." He motioned to my sweatshirt, or Cruz's hoodie. "Check the shirt."

Gavin smirked. "Yeah, right. She parties with us. How about it, Daniels? Alpha Mu against the hockey house. You joining?"

"She's here, isn't she?" Atwater's tone was casual, but his body was rigid.

I glanced over, seeing Cruz at the counter, watching what was going on with us. His gaze flickered over the hoodie, but no expression crossed his face.

I needed to draw a boundary. There was no girlfriend/boyfriend ownership here, so I stepped out from under Atwater's arm and motioned to Gavin. "I'll go with Alpha Mu."

"What?"

"YES! First victory."

"Cru–" Atwater started to turn his way but caught himself. "–awp. Crap. Okay." He pretended to leer at me. "Get used to losing, Daniels."

"Little Daniels isn't–"

I turned to glare at Gavin, who had stepped up next to me. "Stop calling me that."

He frowned, his eye twitching a little. "Allen–"

"You're not Zeke Allen. I've not known you since I was in kindergarten. Mara or Daniels, I don't care, but Little Daniels is not your name for me."

"Yeah. You put him in his place." Barclay joined us, his vest on and holding his laser gun in hand.

"Stuff it, Barclay."

Gavin just got a laugh in response, but turned to face me directly, his back to them. He lowered his head, lowering his voice too. "You okay?"

"Yeah, just you're not Zeke. I don't want to have to deal with his annoying ass when he's not even here."

Gavin's head lifted back up and he nodded, a half-grin showing. "Makes sense. Daniels."

"Thanks." Looking around, I said, "I'm going to grab my stuff."

"Make sure to tell them what team you're on."

"The losing team," Atwater added.

They continued to rib each other as I went over to the counter. Cruz stepped up next to me as I was paying. "She's on our team."

I glanced at him, surprised because his tone was firm and authoritative. But he wasn't looking at me, he was watching the doorway, and I saw Flynn Carrington coming in. Cruz didn't give me a choice. He turned back to the girl, who had paused at his command. He motioned to the vest. "Change her team. She's on ours."

She looked my way. I gave a nod.

She made the switch and my vest lit up neon blue instead of green. Cruz took my gun, and I pulled the vest over my head as I followed him back to the group.

"What?" Gavin saw my vest. "She's on our team."

Atwater and Barclay both looked over, but didn't hoot to rub it in. They were quiet, looking Carrington's way before shifting, just slightly so they were standing between Cruz and the rest of the Alpha Mu guys.

"Daniels is with us." Cruz was saying it like that was final.

He handed my gun to me, and as I took it, he touched my arm, urging me behind the rest of the hockey guys. I knew what he was doing, and I got it. He wasn't even eyeing me, seeing if I was going to start balking at the possession he was laying claim to me, but I wasn't going to. I saw the look Carrington gave me when he walked in, and the look had changed slightly at seeing Cruz handle me.

"You going to give me slack for this?" he did ask when we fanned out, putting more space between me and Carrington.

"No."

His head turned to me. "Really?"

"I know what you're doing. Thank you."

He continued to eye me, but I ignored him, getting familiar with my laser gun.

"You know anything about laser tag?"

"I know enough not to shoot my teammates."

The side of his mouth lifted up as the rest of the guys came over. They formed a huddle.

Labrowski took control, going over the rules first, which was basically that you needed to be hit twice before you were considered dead. And when you were, you had to lay where you died. You couldn't return to your team's base and tell them any information. The chips in the vest let us know when we got hit and what team was winning, etc.

That was it.

He ended with, "We cover each other as we fan out just like on the ice." He looked at me. "You up for going high?"

I nodded. I actually preferred that, and well, that was the team meeting. We went to our end and started running inside. The guys worked well together, teams of three worked as they 'cleared' each corner. Cruz moved with me, and I wasn't surprised that Barclay and Atwater were also with us. When we got as close to the middle as possible, they found a ledge, and all three of them formed half of a human ladder for me to climb up. I stepped up on Cruz's shoulder and he hoisted me the last of the way, but I'd been on the dance team in high school. I knew how to tuck my body for being thrown in the air. When I got up, I looked over the edge and saw three guys coming their way.

I leaned over and made a motion to get their attention. They looked and I held up three fingers, pointing in the direction they were coming from. The guys immediately got into hiding spots. I went back over to the other side, laying as flat as I could and setting up my position like I was a sniper, my gun on the ground in front of me.

Pow! Pow! Pow!

"Got you–AGH!"

"You're dead."

There was cursing, and then the guys moved off to the side. I used to play this with Zeke and our group of friends. Kit and the other girls didn't like it as much. They mostly went to flirt with the guys or try and rub up against them in the dark corners. Not me. I actually enjoyed this stuff, so I fully got into character.

I could see a farther corner up ahead, so as they came around it and paused before looking around the next turn, I could take them out. They wouldn't know who shot them.

Two more Alpha Mu guys did just that, and I thumbed off

rapid shots, getting hits so fast they couldn't regroup fast enough. Both were dead.

Two more and I repeated the process, until one guy saw me and dove out of the way. I had to scurry, knowing he'd come for me right away, but as he took two steps my way, Cruz materialized out of the shadows and got his two hits in. The guy growled, but he fell where he was taken out.

Cruz moved back, hiding again, and there was a burst of sounds from the far left. Shouts and curses sounded out, but then out of nowhere, five Alpha Mu guys burst around the corner. I got two. The other three paused, not spotting me, but I couldn't get to them. They were edging along the wall where I was hiding, but they weren't looking up. One turned the first corner, and suddenly a barrage of shooting happened. Atwater and Barclay swept in. Cruz was coming up from behind.

Atwater was dead, but Cruz and Barclay were still good to go. They were making some hand gestures to each other, not speaking. Cruz looked up my way, motioning they were going to move ahead. I nodded to let him know I got the message. It was time to advance now.

They were soon around the corner. For the rest of the game, I picked off any Alpha Mu that got past them. I checked my vest to see how many remained for each team. We had eight guys left, and they had two. Gavin was dead. Carrington wasn't. The other one still going was Leander.

I saw someone going through the maze, but they were too far away. They were going fast and were hunched over so their vest couldn't get hit so easily. Smart.

Another burst of shots rang out and I looked at my vest.

Leander was dead, but he took Labrowski with him.

Carrington was left.

I was waiting when Cruz and Barclay came back. They looked up and I pointed where Flynn had gone.

They kept going. Three more hockey guys were on the

other side of the maze going in the same direction. I kept waiting, expecting to hear a similar sound of shots any second, but it was just quiet.

Then, I felt a ping and rolled more out of instinct than at understanding what just happened.

Someone got me!

I kept moving back, hurrying along the edge of the room. I'd been out on a cut-out section, so I had more room to lay flat, but since I was moving back, it was narrower. There was less room, so I swung my gun around and I started shooting at my equal height. It wasn't until I got to another corner, and moved in, that I was able to stop and scan my surroundings. Flynn had figured out I had a vantage point, and he'd jumped up too somewhere.

I waited, my breath quiet and even, but then looked at my vest.

He was still alive, but so was I. He hadn't gotten his second hit in.

I was toward the end of our side, and I saw Cruz and the rest still alive, looking around, but they were waiting back. As Barclay moved around a corner, he was shot dead.

Middle!

He was in the middle, and that meant he couldn't follow me. He was on a stationary position.

I waved, getting Cruz's attention, and I motioned, giving him three positions. Right. Middle. Left. He nodded, following me, and I held two fingers up, indicating he was in the middle.

Cruz got it, patting two of his teammates and pointed, but to the other side. They helped him up. I almost started laughing, seeing Cruz trying to be inconspicuous so high up. It was small for me, so it was *tiny* for him. But when he motioned at me to move forward, I got his understanding. We were going to flank him, and I began edging out, but trying to keep pace with Cruz, who was moving surprisingly fast and stealth at the same time.

Flynn wasn't looking my way. He was watching beneath him, so we got closer than I thought we could. He saw Cruz first and swung. Cruz began shooting. I joined in.

Ding, ding, ding!

We got him.

My vest lit up, declaring my team the winner.

"We're done!" someone yelled from the back.

"Victory to the hockey gods!"

I watched as Flynn got down, and Cruz jumped right afterwards, coming over toward me. He held his arms up, and I slid down. Once he had me, I let go of the side and he eased me down to the floor. He didn't say anything, neither did I, but Flynn was watching us. His head was tipped to the side, his laser gun raised next to his head too, and he had a slight frown on his face.

Cruz didn't double down. He could've eased me ahead of him, a hand on the small of my back, but we both walked side by side.

"Yessss. Hockey rules." Atwater was going around, fist bumping his teammates. He came to me, holding his fist up and I met it with mine. "Our secret sniper got half those guys for us."

"We playing again?" Flynn had followed us to our end. Some of his Alpha Mu brothers were with him. Gavin was on the end, his gaze locked on me.

Cruz stepped farther away, moving so it looked like I was standing next to Atwater and not him.

If we played again, my secret was out. They'd be looking at the top for me.

"I'm down. Let's switch places. You guys come in from the east."

It was one of the Alpha Mu guys who spoke.

Labrowski jerked his chin up. "We're down." He hollered behind him, "We're switching it up."

I started trailing after them when Flynn spoke up again. "How about another trade?"

They came to a stop, looking where Flynn was looking. At me.

Labrowski's eyebrows went up. "You want Mara?"

Flynn's grin was sly, and his eyes flashed, darkening. "Be nice to have our own little sniper this time. How about it?" His gaze scanned over Labrowski, who was the team captain, but rested on Cruz.

This officially got not-fun.

If I chose the hockey team, I knew rumors would swirl around campus that Cruz and I were a thing. I didn't want that. But if I chose Alpha Mu, I did not want to see what Carrington would do.

When all eyes went to me, I reached up and undid my vest. "How about I take off because I have a quiz tomorrow?"

"What?" Atwater grumbled. "Stay."

A couple other guys tried getting me to stay, but I flashed a grin and waved my gun in the air. "It was fun, folks, but this college girl needs to go."

I headed back through the maze, sidestepping around some of the Alpha Mu guys who were doing the switch. They saw the target was off me, but no one said anything. I headed over to the counter, handed it back, and laid my gun next to it.

The front desk clerk came over, beginning to sterilize it, but her eyes trailed behind me. "Hey." She leaned forward and indicated where I had just come from. "You know Cruz Styles?"

"Yeah."

She bit down on her lip, an almost shy look coming over her. "He single?" Her eyes came back to me, sharpening. "I mean, it didn't seem like you and he were together, but if you are, hands off for me."

My teeth clenched together. "As far as I know, he's not attached."

Her eyes lit up. "Could you put a word in for me? I'm, you know, down for whatever." A sheepish grin showed. "I slipped him my number earlier, but he wasn't making eye contact with me."

"Yeah." My mouth was so dry on that word. "Sure. I can let him know."

"Thanks." She was beaming now. "He's so gorgeous. About wet my pants when the team came in."

I gave her a thumbs-up.

Right.

WHEN I GOT to the house, yelling was coming from inside the house. There were extra cars in front of the house, so I guessed they were having a few more friends over. I headed up, just getting into my apartment when there was a sudden burst of footsteps on the house stairs. They were coming up and coming fast.

I paused, waiting.

The hallway door opened, and it was Wade. He saw me, jerked his chin up as he raked a hand over his head. "Oh, good. Glad I caught you."

I eased the door back but moved so I was in the doorway.

He motioned downstairs. "We've got another study group going on for class tomorrow. Friday was a bust. You wanna join?"

I considered it. I'd been planning on studying by myself until Cruz showed up, but if he was still playing laser tag... I shrugged. "Sure. Thanks for the invite."

His smile widened. "Cool."

He went down, and I shut the door.

I grabbed my stuff before checking my phone.

Me: Studying in the main house with others. If you want to still do S/S today, I'm down. Just let me know.

His text came through before I got to the first floor.

Cruz: I'll come over later.

I didn't respond because we were in uncharted seas now since laser tag. For the normal human, it might be all cool, but to me, I knew better. When you started easing up on the rules, more and more boundaries started lifting and soon we were close to texting like we were "checking in" with each other. If we were friends, totally fine. Normal. But what we were, rules were different.

Going in through the kitchen, I saw Skylar and Zoe.

Zoe had her back pressed against the counter, by the sink. Her hands were on Skylar's elbows while Skylar's were holding onto Zoe's hips. They were kissing, and as I paused, Skylar pulled Zoe closer against her.

They kept going, clearly not knowing I was there.

I started edging backwards, but Skylar's head lifted. "Oh!" Her eyes went wide.

"Sorry. I wasn't sure of the protocol here."

She started laughing.

Zoe eased back, but rested her side to Skylar's front, who wrapped her arms around her. "Everyone is preoccupied. We're not used to remembering you're here too."

"I get that."

Skylar was taking in my bag. "You're here for the study session?"

"They're studying abnormal psych?"

"Yeah. They're in the dining room."

"Thanks." I started to go past when Skylar called my name.

"Yeah?"

Zoe squeezed Skylar's hand, giving her a reassuring smile before heading past me.

Skylar straightened, now a little self-conscious. "Uh." She

ran a hand through her hair, smoothing it out before taking a deep breath. "I'm sorry I've not come up to talk about what happened last weekend."

I shrugged. "It's cool. I mean, I'm the one who got into it with your friend. I apologized, but I meant it."

"No, I know. I was, well, I was surprised when you apologized. I was so mad about the eating disorder comment. Allie was being a bitch, but Allie's been a bitch lately. A lot. No one knows why and Hawah told me later what all Allie was doing. I wanted to clear the air since they were my friends."

"Uh, sure. Yeah. I'm sorry."

Skylar stared at me for a little bit with a funny look before she blinked, clearing it. "I–uh–I heard that you had an altercation with a Kappa girl last semester."

Oooh. I was seeing where she was going now.

Two fights. The apology was cool, but now she was wading in to see if I was a problem roommate.

"Look." Okay. She needed to understand some things. "I'm shorter than other girls. I have good tits, some ass, and I'm petite. Guys like me. I also don't come across as high-maintenance and I'm just keeping it real, but I like sex. Guys know that from looking at me. Girls see that and your friend was the last in a long line of girls trying to take me 'down a notch' or something. I've had some say they wanted to teach me 'a lesson.' I learned the sooner I stop it, and if I go overboard a bit, they actually shut the fuck up. In high school, I became friends with the bitchy girls. I did it on purpose so they wouldn't fuck with me. Not that I'm proud of who I ran with back then. I'm a freshman. New place, new people, and new bullshit until people learn not to mess with me. I'd like to say it won't happen again, but it's just not true. It might. I don't have a problem with food, so your friend didn't trigger me, but just hearing the venom coming from her, no matter what she would've been saying, I probably would've still reacted. *But* I should've tried harder or in a better way because she's your friend. If she's here, or coming here, I can take off if you need?" I shifted back on my feet. "Ball's in your court. You want me to leave?"

I don't know if it was Skylar's job to have this talk with me, but I wasn't holding it against her. I wasn't going to get all 'how dare she' because the truth was that she was being responsible. I'm new. She didn't know me, and she had people here she loved. She was looking out for them too.

"I won't go as far as moving out, but I can keep to myself. I *can* promise that."

That funny look was on her face again until she shook it off, and a rueful grin showed next. "I can't read you. Like, at all."

"I don't care."

She laughed, abruptly. "You're honest, that's for sure."

"Hey–hey!" Wade popped his head into the room, then stepped fully inside. "You're here! I thought you changed your mind." His eyebrows pulled down, and his gaze skirted from Skylar to me and back. "What's going on?"

"I was–" Skylar started.

I heard the apology in her voice, and I stepped in, "I was asking if I should order food or not. Or do you guys already have some?" I checked the clock. I'd not eaten all day and it was nearing four. I moved past her, past him, and saw the same girls who had been talking with Wade the other day. They were spread out at the end of the table with a couple guys in the middle. They stopped talking when they saw me, and I went to the opposite end of the table, putting my bag down. They had snacks on the table. Some fruit. Couple bags of chips. The guys had beer and the girls had plastic cups with drinks, I was guessing mixed drinks or just juice.

I pulled my phone out. "I'm starving. Anyone else want pizza?"

In the kitchen, Skylar smothered a laugh.

The irony was not lost on me either.

16

MARA

It wasn't until after the pizza showed up, and another hour into studying that I needed a break. I headed to my place for the bathroom and when I was coming back, one of the girls was waiting for me in the kitchen.

"Hey."

She was the one I invited to the Alpha Mu house.

"Hey." I paused, waiting to see where this was going.

"I couldn't go to the party because–well, it doesn't matter, but my friends went. They gave your name at the door and said you never vouched for them."

I was trying to remember. "Right. Yeah." I relayed what the door guy had told me.

"So why didn't you vouch for them?"

I narrowed my eyes at her. "You serious? You wanted me to babysit them when I didn't know them?"

"You could've just vouched for them, and not have to babysit them. They're not children."

Okay. Yeah. Because that's how it worked.

"Uh huh." I made to move around her.

Further discussion was pointless. She didn't want to put herself into my shoes. I relayed everything to her, and hoped she'd be like, *"Oh yeah, you were going to leave and my two friends that you don't know just showed up. Makes total sense that you wouldn't claim them considering their new rules."* She didn't do that, and there was no "aha" moment with her. She had a bone to pick with me. And I literally told Skylar hours earlier that I'd try better with confrontations. Though, this girl didn't seem like the type to pick, pick, pick, target, bully, and so on. She seemed just mad that she hadn't gotten into the Alpha Mu party, or in this case, that her friends hadn't gotten in.

I frowned. "Why do you want to go to one of their parties so much?"

"What?"

I repeated my question.

She moved back a step, still frowning.

"Is it some weird fixation with a fraternity? Because if so, there's better frats to party with, safer frats. Some are amazing and great. This one–"

"This one has connections the others don't. They have senators as alumni. Fortune 500 CEOs. Professional athletes."

I could list three other fraternities on campus with better reputations, and which had the same resume, but she seemed dug in on the Alpha Mu fraternity.

"Is there a particular guy you want to bone or something?"

She blinked at me. "What?"

"Your other reason doesn't make sense. So, is there a particular guy you want?"

She continued to stare at me, a look of panic flaring for a brief moment. "No."

Liar. She was so lying.

"Who is it?"

"It's no–"

"Just tell me and maybe I can introduce you–"

She rushed out, "Leander Carrington."

Now I was taken aback. "The door guy?"

"What?"

"The door guy. He's Flynn Carrington's brother? That guy?"

Her mouth pressed closed, and she lifted a shoulder before saying tightly, "I don't know if he was the door guy, but he's a freshman. And Flynn is his older brother."

"Why do you want to be set up with him?"

Her mouth went flat once again.

"I'm not reaching out until you tell me."

She sighed. "You know at orientation, they put us in clubs?"

No. I never went. "Sure. Yeah."

"Well, he was in the club that I was in charge of and..." Her cheeks got red. She lowered her head.

She was being shy. The guy she wanted to meet was the guy her friends had met. But it was fine. He seemed like a nice enough guy. "I can introduce you."

Her head whipped up. "You serious?" Her chest rose, and held... It was still holding.

I frowned, willing her chest to move. "What's your name?"

"Susan."

"What time do you do breakfast on Tuesdays?"

"Breakfast?"

"You want to meet him or not?"

"I can meet you at nine."

"Done. Campus coffee shop. Get there early and grab a table."

"Are you serious?"

It was an easy enough thing to do. "Sure. Yeah."

"Oh!" She began waving her hands in the air. "Thank you, thank you, thank you."

"Don't thank me. My advice, move on to a different guy at a better frat."

Her hands stopped moving, but she held them stationary in the air. "Why do you hang out with them?"

"I'm currently asking myself the same question."

I started to go around her but paused when my phone buzzed in my pocket.

She moved around me, hurrying back to the room.

My phone had either been on silent earlier, or I hadn't had cell service for the last hour. Either way, I was just now seeing an unknown number had called me thirty times.

That wasn't right.

The phone had been by me the whole time. Thirty times was possible, but all without me getting one notification?

I knew I was going to regret it. It was a hunch, but I hit call back.

It rang, and rang, and rang. I let it go, expecting a voice message recording to start but it never did. Then, after the sixteenth ring, it was picked up.

Loud music and voices were heard first before a girl asked, sounding harassed, "Yeah?"

"Who is this?"

"Who is *this*?"

"You called me."

"No, bitch. You called me. I was strolling by, and the phone wouldn't shut up, so what do you want?"

It was Vegas. I hadn't put the area code together till just now.

Vegas.

I knew what Vegas meant.

That bark was back in my throat, and I swallowed over it, needing to speak. "This is on a payphone?"

"Yeah. Listen, your gripe isn't with me. I gotta go."

"No, wait."

"What?"

"Did you see anyone on the phone before you walked past?"

She was quiet. My heart started to thump. Hard.

"There was a woman on it."

"What'd she look like?" Why was I asking? That was the better question. It was my mom. That was certain, and again, why was I asking?

I expected the same irritated response, but instead, the woman's voice grew louder, and also closer to the phone. "I don't think you want me to answer that. You missed the call. Maybe better to leave it alone?"

God. It was my mother.

I whispered, bending over, "What'd she look like?"

"Not good, honey. She was banged up. Someone worked her over."

That made me reel because there was no way. But... there was. *Was* it her?

"Are you serious?"

"Listen, I don't know what's going on here but my advice? Let it go. She's gone. Be like looking for a needle in a haystack."

My mom called and as long as she was standing upright, I let it go. Always. It was my rule with her, but to hear what a stranger was saying? If that'd been her? She got jumped or roughed up by someone?

What should I do? Go there? Look for her?

Call my dad and tell him so he would worry about her too?

I didn't know.

Do nothing and feel this information burn a hole in my gut. That was door number three, and door number three is what I would do, but it would hurt. It'd hurt so much.

She was my mom, end of the day.

"Thank you."

"Listen, if she shows up again and I talk to her, I'll give you a call. What's your number?"

I gave it to her, along with a name, and she ended the call with a soft, "You sound young. Seems late for you to be up worrying about this lady. My advice, head to bed. I'm sure the lady is fine. She seemed like a survivor when I saw her."

I thanked her again, and when the call was done, I saw that Cruz had texted.

Cruz: Heading over. Still studying?

I was going to text him back when Skylar spoke up, "You okay?"

I was a little dazed, staring at her for a second. My head was still reeling. "What?"

Her eyes fell to the phone in my hand. "You look like you saw a ghost. You okay?"

A fist rammed into my chest. "How much did you hear?"

She shrugged a little. "I mean, the whole thing, but just your side. Not enough to know what's going on, but enough to know something's going on." She eyed me. "I mostly heard you and the other girl before. What you offered to do, that was nice of you. Unnecessary, but nice."

Flynn's brother. Leander. The girl. Breakfast.

It was coming back to me. "Uh, okay."

"That guy you're introducing to her, is he a nice guy?"

"He was nice enough, but I had a three-minute conversation with him. Getting him to go to breakfast will be nothing. I'm figuring she can figure it out for herself from there."

"You're going to tell him about her?"

"No."

She frowned. "How are you going to do the introduction then?"

"I'm going to tell him I'll buy him breakfast. He'll show up. We'll sit at her table. I'll leave early."

She blinked, staring at me. Slowly, her eyes closed, and she began shaking her head. "Just when I thought I had you figured out." She began laughing. "That's kinda genius in the most simple way."

The house's doorbell rang just as I said, "Not genius, just easy."

Wade was heading out of the dining room and paused seeing Skylar and me in the kitchen. He shot us a small frown before answering the door. "Oh, hey man. How's it going? You here for Gaynor?"

"Uh..."

Wade stepped back and Cruz stepped in, seeing me right away.

Need flooded me, instantly, and seeing it, but also seeing how I wasn't moving or saying anything, Cruz gestured to me. His backpack was slung over one of his shoulders. "Daniels said you guys had a studying thing going on. We're in anthro together. Mind if I crash?"

Wade's head reared back, and he seemed startled, going from me to Cruz before nodding eagerly. "Yeah, man. The new star of our hockey team? You can crash anytime you want." He laughed slightly as Cruz stepped farther into the house. Some of the other guys came out, hearing Cruz's name and approached. Hands were shook. Shoulders pounded. The guys were doing their "athlete heralding" thing.

And Skylar drew in another deep breath, moving to stand next to me. She said under her breath, "Now I really don't have you figured out."

I wanted to fuck it all, take Cruz's hand and lead him upstairs.

I used sex to hide from life, but there were times when I didn't want it to control me, and this was a moment where I felt it would. It was a fine line that I walked at times, and I didn't want to step over it, letting sex start to replace the very thing my mom liked to take away from me, my life. I was a college student. I had to study, so therefore, I would study. Because of that, even though I was feeling a burning sensation searing in my stomach, I forced myself to return to the table.

To my seat.

I picked up a slice of pizza and ate it.

I never tasted it.

Cruz came in, and the girls' voices went up a notch. Wade who? Who was Wade again?

It was all about Cruz after that.

I studied, and in a way, I wanted to ignore him. Cruz, being Cruz, didn't let that happen. He moved to sit next to me, and as he sat, he pushed his leg up right next to mine.

I closed my eyes, feeling that sensation settling me, just a tiny bit.

But over the next hour, I kept looking at my phone.

That unknown number never called.

TWO HOURS OF STUDYING, and Cruz's leg was pressing so hard against mine, that I was struggling to stay in my seat. It was obvious what he wanted, though he never talked to me. He never looked at me. There were no secretive looks. The others didn't seem to notice anything, and he had moved his bag on the table so it was blocking everyone's view where our legs were.

But I heard the girls flirting with him, or trying.

They weren't getting the 'go ahead' signal from him, so the girl who liked Wade had started flirting with him again. The other two guys might've been more enamored with Cruz than the girls. They competed with them for his attention, asking him about their next hockey game.

"So, Cruz. Can I ask you a question?" Wade spoke up, and everyone quieted.

Cruz shifted, leaning back in his seat. "Yeah, man. What's

up?" One of his hands dropped to his lap. He looked the epitome of cool and calm.

"You're like a shoe-in for the NHL, right?"

One of the girls started giggling.

Cruz lifted up a shoulder. "I mean, you never know, but I hope there's a good chance I'll go there. Why do you ask?"

"Did you ever think of going straight there? Skipping college?"

And that's when his hand moved to my leg.

Heat engulfed me, and tingles shot from that touch.

I moved my leg. His hand moved to the inside of it, and I almost jumped.

The need was back and pulsating inside of me.

He was saying, running his finger up the inside of my leg, "Most guys go to college before the NHL. It's pretty rare to go straight out of high school, and to get to play. It's always been hockey for me. That's been my focus all my life."

His finger was at my core, and waves of desire were spreading through me, like an inferno. Slowly, methodically, he pushed down, and began to rub. Fuck, how was he doing this? His voice was normal. It looked like he was resting his hand on his leg. And he was holding a whole conversation where Wade and the other guys were hanging onto every word he was saying. The girls perked back up, remembering who was sitting at the same table as them.

"Oh, yeah. I get that." Wade was nodding back.

Cruz gave another shrug, as his finger circled around me. "College was a good play for me. With injuries, you just never know."

"But didn't they try to draft you? Or asked you to enter it?"

He didn't respond right away, rubbing me. "I was approached, yeah."

A second finger joined, and he began moving more

intensely, pressing, grinding. Before a moan slipped out of me, my hand grabbed his wrist.

He was still looking at Wade, but I caught a slight twitch at the corner of his mouth. Then he yawned, the *mother fucker* yawned. The pounding was between my legs, right where he was touching, and I could remove his hand. So easily. I could do that. No more tormenting.

But I wasn't.

I pressed his hand harder into me.

He made a strangled sound, and covered it with another yawn. "Sorry. Traveling, and studying. I'm always wiped by Sunday. How about you, man? Do you have plans for swimming after college?"

Wade launched into his spiel about how he found swimming, how it was going on the team, and what he wanted to do after college. I didn't hear a word of it because Cruz went back to rubbing my clit. I sat there, pretending to study with one hand holding my highlighter, and the other was holding onto Cruz's wrist.

God. He was so good at that.

Another sweep, another caress. Then he pressed in again, holding, and ohmyfuckinggod, I was coming at the table. My hand clamped down on his wrist, even as my legs quaked, and when the last of the waves subsided, he turned his hand around, linking with mine briefly before pulling his hand free. Wade was talking to another of the guys. The girls were enraptured, so I shot Cruz a look from the side of my eye. He was looking right at me, and grinned, slowly, but his eyes were dark and piercing.

I opened my mouth, an excuse to leave on the tip of my tongue when the back kitchen door opened.

Plop!

A cupboard was opened and closed. Another cupboard.

The sound of the fridge door being opened.

Things, containers were being placed on the counter.

A bag was crinkled.

More crinkling.

A plate.

The sound of a knife or fork moving over a plate.

The click of something I couldn't decipher.

The fridge was opened again. I was on the end so I could hear everything more easily than the others.

Whoosh! The smell of toast.

I heard more sounds and then the slightest squeak of sneakers against the kitchen tile.

Miles came to the doorway, a plate of toast in hand and was raising a mug to his mouth. He froze, taking everyone in, the mug at his mouth. His eyes went wide. "Ooh–" He choked a little on his coffee before adjusting and waving with the plate, a tiny motion. "Hi, everyone. No clue a whole study thing was happening here."

"Hi, Miles." One of the girls, not the one that liked Wade, waved.

Miles saw Cruz and lit up. "Styles. Man! What's up." He walked around, and I ducked to avoid having coffee or toast spilled on me.

"What's up?" Cruz reached back, giving some space between us from the motion, and his hand met Miles's in a half handshake, half slap.

Miles scanned the table and sat across from Cruz. "Guessing I'm joining the party." He put his things down and went to grab his bag.

I sighed.

THIRTY MINUTES LATER, my phone started lighting up.

I saw an earlier text from Gavin and clicked on it.

Studying with Gaynor at the library. What are you doing?

Me: Just saw your text. I'm in for the night. See you in class on Tuesday.

He responded, but I scrolled through the rest.

Tasmin: Can we talk?

Five minutes later,

Tasmin: You were a bitch to me on the phone, and I'd like to know what I did to piss you off.

Five more minutes later,

Tasmin: I'm not trying to be a bother here, but wth?

Ten minutes after that,

Tasmin: Text me back or I'm telling my brother.

That did it.

I hit *call* and stood from the table, heading up to my place as she picked up.

"Finally," she griped.

"I was a bitch to you because we're not friends. I do not want to set a precedent where you think we're going to be friends. And for you threatening to call your brother on me, fine, but get ready because knowing how he is, he'd chew me out. Threaten me. Then he'd turn right around and tear into you to leave me the fuck alone."

She was quiet for a second. "I wasn't talking about that brother."

Oh. That's right. She had a twin, who was in a crew, and they were known for handling themselves.

"I don't know your twin. Remember? Want a go at me, you should've stuck with the one I used to fuck." I ended the call, annoyed. If Tasmin wasn't connected to people from back home, I might've been friends with her. But she was and that's just how it worked out.

"Who did you used to fuck?"

I cursed under my breath.

I'd left the door open, and Cruz was standing there, my bag in one hand and his in the other.

He came into the room, shutting the door, and put both bags on the couch. He remained standing.

"I grabbed your stuff, told them I'd drop it off on my way home. I'm pretty sure one of those girls is waiting to proposition me when I leave here." He didn't come toward me, instead he put his hands in his sweatshirt, stretching it and getting comfortable.

Or he looked it.

I couldn't read him right now.

I was also remembering that I was still wearing his hoodie.

This was the shit I didn't want to deal with in our arrangement. But I *was* dealing with it because I didn't want to end what we had going, and I didn't want to think any more on that because I should end it, right now, as soon as possible.

I said, "You know Tasmin Shaw?"

He frowned a little, his head cocking to the side. "I think so."

"Ryerson is her boyfriend."

"Oh, yeah. He's a cool guy."

"I used to have the same arrangement with her half-brother that I do with you." My tongue was sticking to the back of my throat. I did not want to talk about Blaise with Cruz. "Except he and I were friends."

His eyes flickered before a long slow nod. "I see. It didn't end well?"

I hated this, *hated* it. But here I was, going personal.

I went to my chair by the couch and scooted back in the corner, bringing my legs up and hugging my knees to my chest. I looked away because I did not want to see Cruz when I said some of this.

"Things are a lot with my home life, and that's all I'm going to ever say about that, but I use sex to cope with it. Blaise fell for someone, called quits on our arrangement, and well; it was during a really hard time at home. I was losing the thing I used to cope with what was going on, and I didn't handle it very well. Not because of him, but because I didn't have another lifeline set in place. If I had, I wouldn't have cared. He didn't know any of that and I'm still embarrassed, even a year later, how I reacted. I can be...a bitch to push people away."

"Blaise DeVroe."

He wasn't speaking like that was a question. He knew who Blaise was. "Yeah. Seems I have a type."

"Your ex is another major athlete." Cruz let out a short laugh. "You acted like you didn't know who I was when we hooked up the first time."

My head whipped to his. "I didn't. I found out in December."

His eyes were narrowed, and there was a coldness that I'd never seen directed at me. Ice went down my spine. "I don't like being targeted or used."

"Fuck you. I did neither."

His jaw clenched. "I don't believe you."

Okay. This was going the route it needed to. "Then leave, Cruz. Our arrangement was for a reason. I didn't lie, ever. I had no clue who you were until your name started popping up in everyone's conversations about the hockey team. The door's that way. No skin off my nose."

His jaw was still clenching, and he looked away, a harshness coming off him. "I didn't want a girlfriend."

"We're *not*. I don't want a boyfriend."

"We're something because I'm pissed thinking you targeted me, and I'm not leaving. I should've walked the second you said your ex's name."

"He wasn't my ex."

He shot back, "He was your ex of *something*."

I couldn't fight against that.

"Goddammit!" He rose from the couch.

I watched him, locking down, waiting for him to walk out that door. It's what he should do. He knew it and I knew it, but I wasn't being a bitch. I wasn't sealing the end of us in place, and that was terrifying me.

My phone started ringing again, but I ignored it.

I was waiting for Cruz to either leave or do what he came here for. He needed to make the decision, and I'd handle the consequences.

He wasn't moving, but he was glaring at me. He was seething, looking like he hated me.

That calmed me for some crazy reason. It did. If he hated me, we could still do this. Hate fucking was sometimes the best kind. Hate fucking. Loathe fucking. Just a good personal barrier in there, between him and me that kept us from getting close because we were already too close. It was too personal. Too dangerous.

Too foolish.

But if he hated me, yeah. I could see it. We could still do this then. He just had to keep hating me.

My phone stopped ringing, and a second later, it started up again.

Cruz cursed, going for the phone. He answered, "What?"

A woman's voice was on the other end.

He blinked, frowning, but handed the phone to me. "Some lady in Vegas?"

I launched off the chair, snatching the phone from him and I went to the bedroom. "Mom?"

"I'm not her."

It wasn't the lady from before. Different voice.

"Who is this?"

She coughed into the phone, her voice coming out hoarse. "I got a call from your mom. I was in the same facility as her. She asked me to give you a message."

Every word she said was searing me. "What's the message?" I didn't want to hear it. It would be bad, so bad.

"She said she knows where you are and if you don't want her to show up and fuck your life up, she wants fifty grand." The lady's tone grew firm but cold. Businesslike. "You've got to the end of the week to get it to her, and she said if you want instructions on how to get it to her, unblock one of her numbers. She'll be waiting for your call."

She ended the call after that.

"Who was that?"

Cruz was still here.

Fifty grand? She was *blackmailing* me?

Blackmailing her daughter?

What was the fifty grand for? Was she in trouble? *Again?*

My walls were rattling. They were threatening to explode, and I tried bringing up the house imagery again. Everyone had their own room. I could walk freely through the hallways, but it wasn't working. I couldn't focus on envisioning a house.

I was so fucked.

My mom was blackmailing me, and if I gave in, she'd keep doing it. "This is payback for ignoring her."

Right? Or was she really in trouble?

My chest was starting to hurt.

"Ignoring who? Who was on the phone?" Cruz was at my side, and he lifted my hand. "Jesus, Mara."

He pulled back my fingers. I saw the blood trickling down. I'd sunk my nails into my skin and hadn't felt a thing.

Huh.

I looked at my other hand, wondering if I'd done the same with that one, but no. It still had the phone.

That's when I lost it, throwing my phone.

A deep and primal scream ripped from me, and I couldn't stop.

"Mara!"

I couldn't.

I couldn't.

I couldn't.

My mother.

I couldn't–

Cruz picked me up and ran.

I was still screaming.

I wanted to puncture my own ears.

Pain. Something. I needed to feel something other than what she was doing to me.

Cruz was fumbling, reaching into my pockets. I didn't know what he was doing. I didn't care. He was searching his own pockets. He tossed something in the corner, and then I was being shoved underwater.

I choked off, the water cascading inside my mouth, but no. That was even better.

I could drown.

Could I drown?

Would that make it stop?

"*Fuck!*"

I turned, starting to fight off whoever was there.

"What–Mara!" Cruz was yelling in my face.

Cruz.

It was Cruz.

I looked down, in a daze, seeing he was soaked, his chest heaving and his eyes *blazing*.

"Baby, stop screaming." He moved in, huddling over me since I was starting to shake from the cold.

I felt that. Why was I cold?

He pushed back some of my hair, cupping and framing my face. His forehead rested on mine. "If you don't shut up, your neighbors are going to call the cops. I have no idea why your roommates aren't up here yet."

Shut up?

Screaming. I'd been screaming.

My throat was hurting.

I whispered, "You hate me."

His eyes flashed. "I don't know about that, but yeah, I'm still pissed."

"I need you to hate me."

He frowned, not saying anything. But the need was too deep, too *now*.

I reached for him.

17

CRUZ

I didn't know who this Mara was, and the thought didn't sit right with me. She was lying on her stomach, stretched out on the bed, and I was moving inside of her from behind. I ran a hand down her back, over her ass, and she curled her back for me. She was always so responsive to me.

I loved that.

Did not love whatever was going on with her, but there was an extra frenzy to her. It was addicting. I felt it in my blood, this voracious need to keep going, keep tasting, keep fucking, just keep keep keep.

I'd only felt this on the ice. The hardest games, when you just inch out the win, get that last score or get past their last line of defense. It was the same feeling. Man, the rush. It was like ecstasy, but you're in the zone.

I was feeling it now, this new demand to dominate her, as if I could fuck myself into her body, get under her skin where she'd never not feel me there. Every guy after, she'd be feeling me and not them.

A growl erupted from me, and I started fucking her harder. "Fuck, Mara."

Leaning down, my body over hers, I reached for the top of the backboard and began ramming into her. "*Fuck*, you're tight."

She went crazy, meeting me just as hard.

Fucking her was like tasting heaven normally. This one was like needing to conquer it or heaven wasn't going to let me in again.

She'd already come for me twice so this time was for me, and I felt myself coming. The pleasure that spilled out.

Goddamn. I had no words.

I had no energy either. We were at midnight and had been going for the last three hours straight. I had an early skate, so I needed to head home.

I waited a little longer, until the last of the rolling eased up before I eased out of her and tossed the condom in the garbage.

I moved to the edge of the bed and sat there a moment. I needed to catch my bearings.

She sat up, the sheets rustling behind me, and skimmed a hand down my back. Coming up, her legs rested on either side of me, and she leaned against my back. I could feel her cheek on my spine and her arms went around me, resting on my stomach.

She could be such a bitch and times like this, so sweet.

That scream earlier. I'd only heard a similar scream once and it gave me nightmares for years. Hearing that coming out of her, my blood went to ice. We'd definitely shifted, but knowing Mara how I did, she'd try to deny it. It was useless. I was addicted to her, and it was becoming more. Same for her or she would've kicked me out in two seconds tonight.

And her ex. Fuck.

That guy. He was already a legend in the soccer world. I followed the sport, it was a nice escape from the pressures of hockey sometimes, but he was the real deal. Jesus. *Fuck*. Fuck! That took me right back to the beginning of what are the chances she sought out two guys on similar paths. The NHL was circling me, but I wanted one more year at least in college. I had hopes to still finish my degree, but no one knew that. Even my mom didn't. So yeah, logically it would not make sense that Mara didn't know who I was, but the thing was, I believed her.

Or I wanted to believe her.

Or *fuck* again because it'd been the perfect timing for that phone call. It worked. I got distracted.

I was still in bed with her.

I needed to go. All the mess happening, that was one thing I knew for certain.

"No more texting."

I tensed but turned to see her. She shifted, bending her knee and bringing her leg back in.

Man, her eyes. So tormented. Now I knew what was in there, or got a glimpse, I couldn't unsee it. She had *serious* ghosts from her past.

"No calls. Nothing. I mean, unless you want to come over for this, but we need to stop the other shit."

She tucked her head down. I could feel her pulling away from me.

Whatever storm had been in her, was still in her, but it was like I fucked it down each time we went a round.

"Okay."

I pushed up from the bed, and I could hear her breathe easier.

Such a mind fuck.

I ignored it, not knowing what to do with her, and began dressing. I was ready to go within minutes and grabbed up my bag and keys. Checking my phone, I cursed because there was a missed call from my mom and a following one from Titi. I'd have to send a text to both in the morning. Titi woke up early so she'd be happy. My mom, I'd like if she could've slept in, but I didn't know what shift she was on with the hospital.

She was quiet in the bedroom. I was reaching for the doorknob but screw it.

I went back and paused in the doorway. "You're going to be okay?"

"We're not–"

"We're beyond that right now. Are you going to be okay? I heard that call. That lady—her voice was loud."

She wouldn't look at me but nodded. She sounded so hollow when she said, "I'll be okay."

I braced. I didn't know why. Maybe my own past history because right now she was reminding me of someone too, but either way, that situation was most certainly not this situation. "I can come over in the evenings."

She looked up, and even her eyes were glassy and empty.

I winced at seeing that. "After practice, before dinner."

"No. Eat dinner. Come after, and then leave after."

She was pushing us back, giving us less time, but I got what she was doing. A routine, a schedule. No texting or calling, but we'd have this.

"See you tomorrow night."

I left, not hearing her say goodbye, but she wasn't like that.

Going down the stairs, I went out the door and headed for my truck.

"So, you're fucking her."

I stopped. It was the swimmer. "It's none of your business."

He had his keys in his hand, and he finished shutting his car door. A bag of food was in his hands. His gaze went up to where her place was and he nodded, slowly, looking resigned. "Guess not."

I waited, but he didn't say anything more.

I got in my truck, and drove home.

18

MARA

I woke the next morning, my body *fully* exhausted from everything, but it was a good exhaustion from Cruz. I could still feel him, deep inside of me. Not thinking about anything else, I grabbed my phone, unblocked one of my mom's numbers and called it.

She answered with a clipped, "About time–"

I shot up in bed. "You are a shit mother. You were a shit wife. You want to blackmail me for fifty grand? Good fucking luck. You want to know what I'll do in return? I'll go to the police. I won't let you threaten me, do you hear me? Do not try me or we really are done. Forever."

She was quiet on her end.

I didn't wait to hear the sobbing because that was her next move. She'd go straight to being the victim, so I hung up and blocked her number before going to get ready for the day.

I had a quiz I needed to ace.

Me: Need to run something by you. Breakfast on me tomorrow morning? 9 am? Campus Coffee Bar?

Leander Carrington: Who is this?

Me: Uh, show up and find out.

Me: Just kidding. This is Mara Daniels. Show up. Free food.

Leander Carrington: What's this about?

Me: Are you serious?

Leander Carrington: No. See you there.

TUESDAY MORNING, Leander was lingering outside the campus coffee bar when I approached. He saw me and came over, his hands in his pockets. "What's this about? Also, was this a secret thing?"

I'd been reaching for the door past him but stopped. "Why?"

He had a sheepish look on his face. "I didn't know if this was a date or something, but Mikey mentioned you asked for my number and yeah, Miller heard and, yeah."

"Did they come with you?"

He winced, motioning inside. "Miller's here."

I cursed, swinging open the door and marched in. Susan was in a back booth, and she perked up when she spotted me. Her hand went up until she saw my face, and she lowered it as I marched over near her, but not to her. I felt Leander trailing behind me. Gavin and two other guys were in a separate booth. I motioned at Gavin. "Out."

He raised an eyebrow. Scooting back, he rested his arm across the back of the booth and motioned to me with his drink in hand. "Good morning to you too."

"Get out."

"Uh, Mara?" I heard Susan behind me. Her voice was so small.

Leander had turned to look at her instead. "Hey, I know you."

"I ran your orientation club."

"Yeah! Sarah, right?"

"Susan."

"Susan. That's right. I'm so happy you remembered me."

"I–"

I could work with this. "Leander."

He frowned at me.

I motioned to Susan. "We were going to have breakfast with Susan this morning, but how about you go on ahead without me?" I gave Gavin a dark look. "I'll handle this guy instead."

"Uh, you said–"

I held up a fifty-dollar bill, and he whisked it out of my hands. "Thank you very much. Susan, what would you like? On me?"

"Oh. I'll go with you."

She moved behind me, pausing just briefly to say under her breath, "Thank you."

I nodded, waiting until they were up at the counter. "Can we at least go somewhere else?"

Gavin was studying me with narrowed eyes before sliding them to where Leander and Susan were, but he nodded, one long up and down motion. "Sure, Daniels. Anything for you." He motioned for the guys. "See you guys."

Both waved as Gavin got up and I felt him following me out of the coffee place. Susan gave me a little grin before moving closer to Leander, which Gavin also caught. He waited until we were outside before saying, "What was that?"

"Nothing."

"Daniel–"

"Leave it alone. My God."

He stopped walking. "You know what? Enough of this shit. You were weird at laser tag. You don't respond to my texts and now you're just snapping all the time. You're not that fun and you used to be fun. I don't think I want to be friends with you anymore."

Oh... I shrugged and kept going. "Okay."

I got three steps before, "Are you kidding me?"

I kept walking. I had an hour before class, and still needed coffee, so I veered toward the food courts.

"Daniels!"

He was following me. I kept walking.

"Come on!"

We were attracting attention, and oddly, I didn't care this time.

"I was–can't we talk about this?"

That made me smile, and I didn't know why. I didn't pause because I really needed some caffeine, but I said over my shoulder, "You're not fucking me, Miller."

"Why is that always your go-to? I thought there was a basic foundation of consideration for friendship."

Well, damn. He had me there.

I was going through the door but paused and stepped aside as a group of students were leaving. I shifted to the side, my arms folded over my chest. "Miller, you don't act like a guy just wanting friendship."

He was more wary, closing the distance between us. He stopped a few feet back. "Yeah. I can see it that way." He gestured behind to where we'd come from. "What was that back there?"

"None of your business."

He was studying me again before he looked into the food court. "What are you getting in there?"

"Coffee."

"Because you didn't get it back there?"

"You're not wrong."

Another long up and down motion of his head. "Because I was there?"

"Again. You're not wrong."

"Because you weren't there to go on a date with Leander Carrington?"

I didn't respond to that one.

"Hey, Mara." Skylar was coming up the sidewalk with a few people. "What's up? Don't usually see you at the food court."

"Coffee."

"Oh yeah." Her gaze skirted from me to Gavin. She said to him, "Hi. Gavin, right?"

"Hey. Yeah."

She stopped walking and shot him a confused look before switching back to me. "Did you hear that screaming the other night?"

I went cold. "No."

"Really? We couldn't figure out where it was coming from. Felt like it was from your place. Were you watching a movie or something?"

"You know, I think I was. After studying, right?"

"Yeah."

"I put on a horror movie, but I fell asleep. That's probably what woke me up."

"Oh." She visibly relaxed. "We got a little scared there. Wasn't sure what to do and we were in bed. I don't think anyone else heard it so for a minute we were even thinking we had a ghost."

"No one else heard it?"

"Wade went to Lindsay's house. Darren didn't say anything. And Miles was stoned."

"Right." Small blessings.

"Okay. Well, see you at home?"

Her friends had gone inside and were waiting. Skylar joined them, and I stared at Gavin.

He stared back, raising his eyebrows.

I rolled my eyes but went in to get some coffee. Gavin followed me, and as I got my coffee, he paid for it. I didn't fight him on it, and then, together, we went to wait outside the building of our morning class.

CRUZ CAME OVER THAT NIGHT.

He came over Wednesday night.

Thursday night.

Friday and Saturday, he was gone for an away game.

He came over Sunday night.

And we repeated the next week, until Thursday.

19

CRUZ

"We gotta party Saturday night."

I shot Atwater a look. "Dude. It's too early to start talking about that shit." I was giving him and Wes a ride to the rink for our six am practice. Wes was yawning. I was pissy, and AJ was bouncing in the truck. Which was making me even pissier.

"He's going to rough you up in practice if you don't stop fucking moving."

"We should. After our game on Saturday. It's been so long since we've had a party. If Adam is game, then we're doing it."

Wes and I shared a look. I was pretty sure it'd not been that long ago when we had a party, but AJ seemed worked up about it.

"I'm going to pitch it to the guys."

I said, "Wait till after practice, and don't let Coach hear you."

Wes grunted his agreement.

"I'm going to invite Daniels too."

Wes started laughing. "Now he's for sure going to rough you up."

AJ didn't seem bothered, glancing my way. "That cool with you? It was fun with her at laser tag."

I just growled because I had nothing else to say. Why he wanted to invite my very much not-friends with benefits chick, I had no clue. But he did. And I was remembering how it felt sliding into her last night. How sweet she felt, clutched around me.

"Why are you inviting Daniels? She's not yours to invite, man. She got a friend you're into or something?"

AJ frowned, his head cocking to the side. "I don't know."

Both Wes and I groaned because that answer was definitely not the one we expected. No one was out driving, but I still hit the turn signal, heading toward the parking lot for our entrance.

"Now you have to tell us the real reason."

I was enjoying that Wes was speaking for me.

AJ shrugged. "She's not partied with us in a while. I think it's time."

"We're in the middle of our season. We can't have a big party." I pointed out, pulling into a parking slot, and turning the engine off.

As we unloaded and began heading in, AJ shrugged again. "Ryerson made a comment. That's why."

I frowned, remembering the connection between Ryerson to his girlfriend, to who her brother was, and to Mara. I paused. "Wait."

Both did.

"What did he say?"

He shrugged again. "Just that Taz was asking how she was doing."

What the fuck? The phone call I overheard between Mara and Race's girlfriend had not ended on a good note. "You need to say more than that. I know a little about Mara's deal with

Ryerson's girlfriend. She won't come if you invite her. I have to be the one to do it."

"She'll come if her friends come."

Maybe. Probably not.

Wes's eyes narrowed. "Atwater, be straight. What are you doing?"

AJ studied us for a beat before his shoulders deflated. "Okay. I'm into one of Taz's friends, and she's too scared to come to our house unless there's other people. I was thinking a *small—*" He emphasized the word because we all knew Labrowski would not be down for a big event, not until after our season was done. "—thing where she'd feel more comfortable. Ryerson's cool, but sometimes his girlfriend doesn't always come. She's always talking about Daniels, so I was thinking we could invite Daniels and her usual crowd. Taz would show up, and then my girl would definitely come."

I had no clue which point to handle first.

"One, your logic is asinine. It's a party, most girls aren't scared to come to the hockey house."

"This girl is."

I ignored him. "Secondly, just ask Race's girlfriend to come. She'll come. She has in the past."

"You think?"

"Third, Mara's usual crowd is Gaynor and Miller. If Miller comes, he might bring some of his brothers and that shit's no longer a small thing anymore."

Atwater stared at me, considering. He switched to Barclay, who held his hands up. "I'm not a part of this. This whole thing has come out of your ass, but I agree with everything Cruz said. Also, you need Labrowski *and* Keys to okay this or our asses are in a sling."

"That girl's been hanging around the house more. The one whose brother died, that was Adam's best friend. I think Labrowski wants her to meet more girls. Make friends."

And Atwater just figured out how to get Labrowski to agree with the party.

If Labrowski said yes, then Keys was more likely to sign on. I shared a look with Wes. We both knew that we were going to be having a party Saturday night.

I sighed. "I'll mention it to Mara."

"Yes!"

"But you and I are doing some one-on-one in practice to pay for it."

He groaned, then coughed. "I mean, bring it on."

SINCE REALIZING Mara was in my same anthropology class, I'd stayed away. It was part of the thing with us, but today I dropped down in the seat on her other side, letting my hand graze her arm. Mara's head had been folded over her book, but she snapped up, her eyes wide as she glanced at her arm. We had a few minutes before Miller would grab the seat on her other side.

"What are you doing?"

I tried to gauge her attitude. She hadn't hissed that question at me, though I was breaking our rules. But she'd been extra hot last night. *Fuck.* We both were. I was starting not to like the no-texting rule between us. Which was an admission of surprise to myself because I liked what we had during the first semester. First semester and the first week, but things started to slide. We were trying to right the course again, but I don't know.

A part of me was enjoying that I had an excuse to sit here.

That I could shift to the side, could run a finger down her leg, loving how it'd make her eyes glaze over, the same look I was rewarded when I was in her honey spot.

That I had an excuse to break our agreement, or bend it.

Bend her...

"Cruz."

Right. "We're doing a party Saturday night. The guys want you to come."

She didn't show any reaction. That wasn't altogether surprising because since her breakdown that night, it's like she caught herself and was making up for her slip of control. She'd been locked down, and the only time she let herself go was in bed with me. Like she gave herself permission, not that I was complaining. My dick was already hard, all the different positions we'd not tried yet playing out in my head.

But last night, man. How I stood, how she turned around, how she backed up—okay. My dick was rock hard. Christ.

"Why?"

I glanced back, seeing Wes staring at us. He raised an eyebrow, indicating the empty chair beside him. I gave him a slight nod, and right then, Bianca tried to drop into my usual seat. He stopped her, nodding my way.

She looked our way, but I focused back on Mara. "Because, I don't know. AJ wants you there and you know how he is when he gets something in his head. Just show up, or he'll pester you all week until you say you'll come."

"Are you serious? But, we have—"

Miller was coming, along with two of his frat brothers.

"It was either me asking or him harassing you all week." I stood up, grabbing my bag, and because I was itching to touch her, my leg brushed against her as I went by. I ignored her small gasp. "Just come, okay?"

Miller's eyebrows pulled together, a small frown on his face as I passed him. "Styles."

"Miller." I kept going, dropping into my seat.

He paused until he went to sit by Mara.

"She coming?"

I shook my head, before I shrugged. "Not a fucking clue."

And now I had to sit through class with a raging hard-on.

20

MARA

My phone buzzed at the same time someone knocked on my door.

I was just finishing dressing for the party, and came out of the bathroom when my door opened. Zoe came inside. I was speechless for a moment. She was in a full black leather suit with no back, just strips that ran over her shoulders, like the front of a halter top. Her whole face was shimmering with light glitter. It mixed perfectly with her skin tone. She had eyelashes on, and instead of the usual jewelry that adorned her during the day, she was naked. No rings. No earrings. No necklaces or bracelets. Nope. One piece of jewelry, a nose ring, and it was the smallest little diamond.

"Holy shit. You look amazing."

She beamed, lacing her fingers together. I had to look, her shoes didn't disappoint. They were black high heels. "It's Skylar's birthday today."

My eyebrows shot up. "I didn't know that. Are the roommates doing anything for her?"

"We could maybe do a roommate dinner tomorrow, but she

didn't want anyone to know. She doesn't like to celebrate in a showy way."

"Oh okay." I was still going to get her a gift. I was weird. If people demanded gifts, I didn't like giving them, but if they were like Skylar, I loved getting them presents. It was out of character for me, but I didn't care. I liked Skylar and Zoe. They weren't in my business, and instead had boundaries that almost rivaled myself. Plus, they were nice. "What's up? What brings you to my door?"

"You're going out?"

I nodded, checking over my outfit. A party at the hockey house was a little nerve wracking, and I rarely got nervous for parties. But Cruz would be there and with how we'd been lately, I wasn't sure what to expect. We might not talk the whole night until at the end or... I didn't know. I didn't know what I wanted either. I'd enjoyed that he sat next to me in class, even if it was just for a bit, and then panicked because that was the whole point of how we needed to stop violating our own rules.

But I'd dressed accordingly, or tried. Black faux-leather leggings with pockets, ripped on some sections of my thighs and knees, and a few rips on the inside of my legs. On top was a simple white shirt, though it was transparent and hugged my entire frame. Under that was a black bra, and I ended it with tiny black shoes that looked like ballet slippers, but weren't. They were ultra comfortable.

I was okay, but not in Zoe's league.

"That's why I came up. I was wondering if I could ask for a favor?"

"Of course."

"Some of us girls in our group, we're doing a party hop for Skylar's birthday. We're not going to be loud and do anything for attention, but we want to go to as many parties as possible and hang in each place. That's it. I don't know if we'll even drink at every place, but I heard there's a hockey party tonight."

I nodded, getting a feel where she was going.

"You're going, right? Miles mentioned it, said you know the team somewhat."

"Yeah." I coughed. "Somewhat."

"Could we crash it? With you? Or you go, and we'll come later, but you'll be our *in* to get in? Would that be okay?"

Her eyes were wide and her own excitement levels were obvious. She was almost standing on her tiptoes.

I nodded. "Of course, but you don't need me to get in there. Just show up. Trust me, they'll let you in."

She laughed, her voice hitching. "I'm not Skylar. She's more extroverted, not shy. I'm the opposite. I get nervous before doing parties. We've had a whole day already. I baked her three of her favorite birthday cakes, and for breakfast, she had her favorite waffles in bed. I even handpicked a whole bouquet of flowers and snuck it in before the guys saw. She didn't want a fuss made over her, but that's what I love to do. Making a fuss over who I love."

"You guys seem really happy together."

"I am. I think she is. I love her, a lot." She gave another beaming smile, her arms stretched out and she wiggled her fingers toward me. "Thank you, thank you, thank you!" She began edging back to the door. "I'll give you a text when we're close to the house."

"You know where it is?"

Her laugh was abrupt. "Everyone knows where the hockey house is, even me." One last wave. "See you later! And you look sexy as hell."

That was nice to hear.

I heard Miles' voice in the stairway and knew I had three seconds before he'd be bursting through my door. I looked around, making sure I had everything I needed. I trusted the guys at the hockey house so I didn't need to take alcohol with me, but cash? Check. Keys? I grabbed them, putting them deep into my pocket. They were pushed down so far, I'd have to dig them out later. They'd be safe. And what else?

The door burst open. Miles threw his hands in the air, his face flushed. "Pre party drinking! Let's do it, roomie."

I was looking around. "What am I forgetting?"

"Phone?"

"Phone!" I snatched it, shoving it into my other pocket and knowing that'd also be work to get out so it was safe for the night. "I'm ready."

His grin was crooked as he came over, throwing an arm around my shoulders. "I'm in the mood to get fucked up tonight."

"Atwater found me yesterday on campus to make sure I was coming today. He said this is supposed to be a small thing?"

He snorted, walking me to the door. "We'll see if that happens."

IT DIDN'T HAPPEN.

The house was overrun when we got there. Bass music was blasting, though more muted than I was expecting. As we walked inside, the whole first floor was filled with people talking, standing around. A bunch had congregated in the kitchen, where as we walked in, we found Atwater busy finicking over food.

He saw us, and did a double take. "Finally! You're here." He threw down a towel that'd been over his shoulder. A red apron was tied around his waist. He snatched up his phone, typing on it. "I've been waiting for you to arrive."

Miles and I shared a look.

He asked, "You've been waiting for us?"

Atwater gestured to me with his phone. "Daniels. You don't

know the lengths I went to get you here, and now you're here, and I'm going to let the person know who wanted you here."

I frowned. Cruz? But that didn't make sense...

"You told me yesterday this was supposed to be a small shindig."

He looked around, half glaring, before blowing a puff of air that dislodged some of his hair. His curls fell back in place. "It was supposed to be. Keys is going nuts. Also, Angela was supposed to meet new friends, but guess who took her under her wing? Bianca. Labrowski is not happy with me, so yeah. Basically my ass is going to get beat every day in practice for the rest of the season."

I had no clue who Angela was, but Gavin came in from another room. Seeing us, he raised his hands in the air. "My people. Finally."

Two of his frat brothers were with him. They circled us in the kitchen, began eating some of the food. Atwater had put out bags of chips. Salsa in a bowl. Three boxes of pizza, and a whole tray of egg rolls. Fast food wrappers were stacked on one of the counters, along with a plethora of alcohol bottles.

"Sorry to say, but you are looking seriously hot, Daniels. In a way where I want to do dirty *dirty* things to you."

I showed my teeth, rounding on Gavin, but it wasn't him that spoke. It was one of his brothers, who I didn't know his name.

I glared instead.

Gavin laughed, touching the guy's forehead and shoving him back. "Down, boy. She ain't like that. You can look, but don't approach. Trust me. She took my balls on more than a few occasions."

The brother was wasted, his eyes almost cross-eyed, but he stared at Gavin. Something mean and dark flashed in his gaze. He opened his mouth, and I wasn't sure if I wanted to hear whatever he was about to say, but Atwater exploded. Again. "Finally!"

He pushed past us, shoving the frat brother back, and Gavin into me.

I was winded from the impact. It took a little before Gavin extricated himself. He was that drunk, which I figured he would be. I figured most would be since everyone started drinking before the game today. They won, but lost yesterday, so there would've been a renewed sense to drink in celebration.

It was then that I saw who Atwater was greeting. A pretty girl. Long dark hair. Hazel eyes. She was tall and slender, and looked a little familiar. She was with another girl, and a guy. Both of their faces were turned away, but they looked at me, and my stomach dropped.

I recognized the girl. She was on the same floor as myself last semester, and the girl with her was Tasmin Shaw. Taz's boyfriend was on her other side.

"Daniels." The same frat brother fell into my side. His bourbon breath wafting over me. "They got a whole dance floor set up downstairs. What do you say? Wanna go and grope each other in the dark?" He belched, but remained smiling at me.

Two things happened after that.

I saw Cruz across the room. He was standing by the wall, talking with a bunch of people. A girl was there. He pushed up one of his arm sleeves, his fingers going through his wet hair. He must've just showered. He was wearing jeans that hung from his lean hips, and a Grant West vintage hockey shirt. His number was in the top left corner, over a pair of crossing hockey sticks. The back would have his last name in big and bold faded print, some parts of it chipping off. It was the design of the shirt, but I had a weakness for those types of clothes.

God. I could feel the press of him against me. How he ran his hands up the inside of my legs, how he spread them.

My body went from cold, to inferno levels, back to cold

because that girl was on him, almost literally. She had a hand on his bicep, and another just above his wrist.

She was tracing his arm.

The air seized out of me. An icy rage had formed in me.

He looked down, his eyes going to hers as her head was tipped up towards him.

She leaned more into him, swaying, giving him a great view of her cleavage. Or hell, if he could see down her shirt.

Pain sliced through me because he wasn't shoving her hand off. His lips were moving. He was talking to her.

Her head tilted back. She was laughing and as she did, she swayed back into him, using the movement so her whole body was almost pressed into his.

It was all happening in slow motion now, and she reached for his neck, and stood up on her toes. Her head angled for his.

The second thing that happened: Tasmin started for me. I noticed it from the periphery of my eyes, and I wanted to look anywhere else, but I couldn't. I was watching a bad dream happening in real life, right in front of me, and I couldn't stop it.

She caught him, her hands going to each side of his face, and she smashed her lips to his.

My stomach dropped to my feet.

I ripped my gaze away.

Taz had started to approach me, but she paused at seeing my face. "Mara?"

My gaze went past her, seeing Flynn Carrington walking into the house with a bunch of his brothers and girls. One girl was hanging on his arm, but he saw me, and a cocky smirk came over him.

Then a body passed between us. It was Cruz.

I wasn't thinking anymore. I shoved past Taz, going for him.

I could feel Carrington's eyes on me, but it was nothing

compared to the burn inside of me from seeing Cruz and that girl.

He noticed me a few steps away. “Mara—”

I took his arm, a tingling already starting from just the one touch, and dragged him down into the basement.

My head was swimming. I didn’t know what I was doing. I just knew I needed to do something. Anything. I needed to get away, but the burn was rising in my body.

His hands found my hips. “Wait.”

He tried halting me, but I kept going, shaking my head. I was digging in here. “No.”

Gavin’s friend had said dancing in the dark, but I hadn’t known what he meant. I knew now. They set up their main living area in the basement as the entire dance floor, but it was almost completely in the dark. Dark shadows could be seen, grinding against each other, as the music was blaring from the corner.

I stopped at the end of the stairs. Did I want to do that? Dance in the dark with him?

Cruz took over, taking my hand, and led the way this time. He wound us through the couples until we were in a far corner. My back was to the wall, and he was in front of me. Over me. His hands went to both sides of me, and he leaned down. His head was bent towards me. He was so close, his hips touching mine. I reached down, touching his sides, intending to push him away.

I pulled him in.

I felt his breath as he asked, “I know you don’t do personal, but it’s obvious something is wrong.”

“Did you kiss her back?”

He went rigid. “What?”

“That girl. I saw her. Did you kiss her back? Do you want to fuck her?”

He didn’t answer.

I expelled a savage curse. "If you do—"

His hand cupped the back of my neck. "What? If I do, then what?" His body pushed further against me. I was pinned against the wall, and he moved one of his legs between me, lifting me up so I was straddling him. "You'll do what?"

Lust was warring with anger. Goddamn him.

That burn was in me, and it was searing me. Like it was tattooing the feeling of watching her kiss him permanently inside of me. I'd never be rid of it.

"You'll do what, Mara?" His voice was like silk, though it wasn't true. He was pissed. It was radiating off of him, but so was I.

I was livid.

"You fuck her, we're done."

He lifted his head, his nostrils flaring, and he stared at me for a minute before he took my hand, and moved me further into the dance floor. There were others around us, others that could see us, but our movements were still shadowed.

The music was covering our conversation, but it went up a whole level so normal conversation, even this close was barely audible. Cruz leaned down, his mouth right at my ear as he grated out, "Rules are that we don't sleep with others. That's it. That's all." His hand went to my hip, his fingers slowly wrapping around me.

He began moving against me, in rhythm with the music.

"What are you doing?"

His mouth moved to my ear, his hand rising up, slipping under my shirt. "You're going to say that shit to me?" His teeth nipped my ear, pulling on my lobe. He yanked me further against him, lifting me a little so I was again almost straddling his leg. His hand slid down to my hip, and he pressed me into him. He began moving me, slow, with purpose, and it was *delicious*.

Heat surged through me.

His breath was caressing me. "Like I don't know our agreement?" His mouth dipped, finding my throat.

Desire spread through me, pushing the other emotions away, overriding them.

His mouth moved to the other side of my throat, and he grasped my throat, moving my head for him. He began kissing me, sucking, and a pounding began to take over inside of me.

"You got how many fuckers hanging around you? Wanting you? *Telling* you they want you? And you go crazy over one girl? A puck bunny?" He lifted his head, but his hand still held my neck captive. His eyes were burning into mine. His nostrils flared again. "You think I like seeing that shit?" He was moving to the music so if anyone was watching, they'd think we were still dancing, but we were barely dancing. His hand spread out over my hip, moving to my ass, and he was lifting me, helping me grind over his leg. His head bent back down. His nose up the side of my chin, my cheek. Tingles spread out in his trail.

The need for him was building. I grasped for his arm, where she had touched him.

Fuck her. Fuck him. But my fingers pressed down, and I used that to help me climb more up him, rubbing against him as I began to take over.

He shifted, almost bouncing me up. Both of his hands were on my ass, and he was walking us somewhere. I was beyond caring, beyond caring who saw us, beyond remembering why I had cared in the first place.

God.

I was riding him and he was helping me, lifting me, until my back hit a wall. We were in a corner. There were still others by us, but I hoped the darkness was covering us because I had slipped past the point of sanity. A frenzy was in me, and I began riding him harder, then slow, and he cursed, his head bending to my neck again. He was tasting me. His leg was digging up into me. I climbed myself more up on him, and he adjusted so I was straddling him, not just his leg now.

We both stilled as we came into contact.

I almost sighed, feeling him where I *needed* him, where it felt right to have him there.

This. Him and me. This was our deal, no one else's. Just him and me.

He pushed me back against the wall, a hand on my shoulder, and he raised his head to glare at me. His eyes were burning right back at me. "You want this?" His other hand went between us, pushing down into my leggings and finding where I was wet. His finger slid inside, and I bit my lip, almost mewling. That felt so fucking *good*.

He thrust in. A slow drag out of me, and back in. He was drawing it out, until I was panting. My chest was lifting up and down. "Cruz," I whispered. I reached for his hand, but I didn't know if I was going to help him or stop him. I did neither, I only held it as he tunneled once more into me. His hand moved and a second finger joined inside of me, shoving deep, and holding. His thumb went to my clit. He could make me come, right here, right now. I was helpless to stop him, my body screaming for him to keep going, but he held.

"Cruz." I reached for his neck with my other hand, my hips moving, trying to ride his fingers. I needed release.

Then he leaned close, kissing my ear before growling, "You didn't watch long enough, babe. She kissed me, and I shoved her off. I was leaving to call *you*. And there you were, but you messed up." His fingers were moving smooth and deep into me, grinding, holding, before continuing. But he paused again, as his voice came out ragged, "I don't like threats, especially when they're not earned. I'm changing the rules. This. What I can do to you?"

I was on the brink of coming. It was right there. A part of me wanted him to hold off, I wanted to draw this out, but the other part of me wanted to finish because I wanted him inside of me. I wanted him over me, filling me, taking me.

Then his fingers were gone, and I quaked in protest. A cry left my lips.

He smashed them, silencing me in a hard and punishing kiss right before he ripped away. "You want me? Tough shit. I own this. It's mine any time I want, *how* I want. I could bury my dick inside you, no matter where we are, and you'd close around me. You'd pump me back because you want to know why?" His fingers slid back in, one smooth push in before pulling out. "Because you're mine, and this ends when *I* say we're done." With that, he dropped me back down, and raised his fingers, and tasted them. He stared hard at me. "But I'm not done with you. Yet."

MY HEAD WAS BACK to swimming, and goddamn, my body was aching. When I went back upstairs, everything was louder. Taz was in the kitchen, with Skylar and Zoe. Some of their other friends. Zoe saw me first, yelling my name. It sounded like she was shouting for me under water.

Then she was in front of me, her hand touching mine. Her eyes grew concerned. "Mara? Are you okay?"

I looked past her.

Gavin was there. Miles. Atwater. Other hockey players, and in the middle, leaning against one of the counters was Cruz. His eyes met mine. The music faded. Everyone else blurred to the background. It was just him and me, and I remembered the feel of him inside of me. How he looked at me, his eyes almost loathing.

"...you're mine, and this ends when I *say we're done."*

He had that same look, the intensity burning my insides.

"Mara?" Zoe's voice got through to me, pulling me back to the room.

I blinked, trying to shed some of my thoughts away. "Sorry. Yeah. I'm okay. Wait." I reached for my phone, pulling it out. "Did you text?"

I heard her answering as I opened my messages, but her voice droned on, falling to a distance again.

I saw the texts.

Zoe: We're here!! Where are you? We're in the kitchen.

There were others, from earlier.

Unknown: Sweetie, honey. I know you said to leave you alone, but I'm in real trouble.

Unknown: You really need to give me the 50k. It's not for me, Mara. It's to save someone's life. I would never lie about that.

21

CRUZ

Christ. Something was wrong. I could see it on her face.

I started for her, but she jerked away from her roommate. Her gaze found me, and I knew I'd be haunted by that look on her face. I had a hand in putting it there. I knew I did, no matter whatever she just read on her phone.

I cursed, going through the crowd for her, but she was gone before I could reach her.

"That was weird."

I glanced to her roommate, who was frowning and looking at me before turning for her girlfriend.

I pulled my phone out, bringing her name up, and I hit call as I headed outside.

The phone rang. And rang. Then, "You've reached the voicemail of—"

I ended the call.

I didn't know if she drove here or got a ride, but she was gone.

Fuuuuck. *Fuck.* Fuck!

I started to head for my room. I'd grab my keys, then look

for her on the way to her place. My phone rang instead, at the same time I got a text alert.

Mom calling.

"Mom? Can I call you back in a minute?"

"Oh yes, but something amazing has happened! Be quick."

I frowned, but read the text.

Mara: I'm fine. I'm going back to my place. If you decide you want me, then text me. (That was sarcasm if you needed it spelled out.)

22

MARA

I was halfway home before the headlights started behind me. It wasn't long after that when his truck pulled up next to me, keeping track with me. The window rolled down. Cruz's voice came next, "Get in the truck."

"I'm fine."

"Just get in." He softened his tone. "Please."

I gave him a look. "*Please?*" My head reared back. "What happened to 'we're done when I say we're done?' When you're being all alpha and an asshole?"

His face was still in stone, but he readjusted his hold on the steering wheel. "I was pissed. You were acting like a jealous girlfriend, which we've both stated we don't want."

I snapped my mouth shut, because damn it, he was right.

I glared. "I don't like threats."

"I didn't threaten you."

I raised an eyebrow. "Need me to give you a play-by-play of the release you denied me on the dance floor?"

He swore under his breath, a hand raking over his face, and through his hair. "Just get in the truck, okay?"

I shouldn't. I had a right to deny a ride, and walk home on my end. It wasn't far. I'd be fine, the walk would be good for me. My mom's newest texts were steaming a hole in my pocket. I hated her. Seriously hated her even when I didn't hate her at all.

She lied. It was a constant with her and the biggest flag was when she said she wasn't lying. Even as I read it, I *knew* it was a lie. That's what she did. Manipulated. Lied. Deceived. The more I ignored her, the higher she'd up the stakes.

What I could do, right here and now, was to get in the truck. I got into his truck. Cruz wasn't my current biggest headache, and he'd been right that I'd been the one doing exactly what both of us didn't want. Still. The image of that girl was etched in my memory.

"I keep seeing that girl, and I keep seeing her all over you."

"Mara." He sat back in his seat.

"*Not* a fan of hers."

"I shoved her off."

I turned my head to hide my sneer. My stomach was still in a knot, but that girl was only part of it. A small part of it.

We drove the rest of the way in silence until he parked, pulling up behind Darren's Jeep. He cut the engine and hit the lights. We both sat, neither one moving to leave. "I'm going to ask because, well, I am so deal with it. Are you okay? Someone sent you something and I saw your face before you lit out of there."

"Honestly? It's par for the course."

"I don't know what that means."

I sighed, relenting a little. "I think that's for the best." I looked back at him, seeing the anger still simmering under his surface. Anger at me because of what I said to him, but it was warring with concern. Normally, I'd panic at that look, but I didn't have it in me. Not tonight.

I was suddenly so extremely exhausted.

Then I swore, remembering my roommates.

To Miles: I got a ride home, sorry to bail.

To Zoe: Sorry. I bailed. I'm home. I hope you guys have a great night.

Zoe: Hi! Yes. Are you okay, though? I know you don't do personal, but I still need to ask. It's my thing. I care about my friends.

I stared at her text for a minute. Friends.

Jesus.

When had that happened?

To Zoe: I'm fine. All good. Promise.

To Skylar: Happy birthday! I hope you have a great rest of the night. Have lots of fun.

Zoe: Okay, but we're here if you need anything. I mean it.

I hit the number from those unknown texts and blocked it. Again. Just like all the others.

I asked Cruz, "You're still pissed at me?"

"Fuck yes."

"Want to come up?"

He stared at me, "What do you think? Also, that was sarcasm if you needed it spelled out for you."

A short laugh escaped me, but I was opening the door. He joined me, and we went up.

WE WENT ONE ROUND. He left after, and the week was a repeat from earlier.

Every night, he came over after dinner. He left when we were done.

There were no lingering touches, no cuddling, nothing soft but we were almost frenzied. Every time.

We ignored each other in class, and if we saw each other on campus. It was like we were strangers.

That continued for two weeks, until Friday night when he had his next home game.

I went to the hockey game.

23

CRUZ

"Hey, sweetie. Are you excited for the game?"

I was suited up and ready to head out for the pregame warm-up when my mom called. Coach gave me special permission for this call. "Yeah. Are you guys here?"

"We are! Titi can't contain herself. And Dawn is with us too. She's helping with the traveling. Sorry we couldn't get here earlier to see you more. It'll be a long night, but it'll be worth it. Titi has wanted to go to one of your games for so long."

"I know. I'm just happy you guys are here."

Coach came through the locker room, saw me, and pointed at me. "Styles! Get on the ice."

"It's that call I talked to you about earlier."

He frowned but looked at his watch and began shaking his head. "Wrap it up. I need you warming up. Put it all aside."

"It's okay. We'll see you afterwards. I'll let you go. Win, baby!"

My chest was bursting with warmth. My mom said to win, so I'd make sure we won. "Thanks, Mom." I was getting choked up.

She was too. "Love you, Cruz. See you after the game."

I headed to the ice after that.

"REMEMBER. Go out there. Keep your lines. Be smart. Play hard, but also, there's a Make-a-Wish kid in the front row, section C. Sweet girl. In a wheelchair. Here with her mom and her worker. Go over, knock on the glass with your stick, give her some attention. And then after that, WIN!"

A cheer went up.

Sticks were hitting the floor, and everyone stood up, putting their gloves in the middle.

A prayer was said, and Labrowski led us in a chant. It was our time to win. So, win we would.

After that, we headed out.

First skate around, Labrowski went first, but I moved to the back. I wanted to be last.

Each of us went over, knocking our stick against the plexiglass in front of the little girl.

I was last, and I circled around, facing her fully.

She was so tiny, tinier than she should've been, but she was cheering and her face was flushed from all the smiling and yelling. She saw me and tried to get out of the wheelchair. Her handler rushed to her side, helping her push up from the chair. She held her up, tipping her forward until she was staring right at me, right through the plexiglass.

She got all serious. All blonde curls and rosy cheeks and tiny hands. She held out her palm, touching the barrier between us, and I took my glove off, touching it with mine on the other side.

Then her eyes opened wide, and the smile was going to break her face, it was so wide.

I looked her right in the eye and mouthed, "I love you, Titi."

She was beaming so much. "LOVE YOU, CRUZZIE!"

I laughed, looking at my mom beside her, who was smiling and wiping away the tears.

I put my glove back on, and hit the plexiglass with my stick. "Love you, Mom."

She couldn't say anything back. She was crying and smiling too much, but she reached out, touching the glass with her hand before I took off.

I joined the team at our bench, and sensing the looks, I said, "The Make-a-Wish kid is my sister."

My coach blinked a few times. He hadn't known that part. "The one that was in the hospital?"

I nodded.

"What's her name?"

"Titi."

He gave a nod before addressing the team, "Win it for Titi."

"FOR TITI!"

Labrowski skated over. "You want the face-off?"

I glanced at Coach, who shrugged. I said, "Oh, fuck yes."

WE WENT HARD. Pushing, pushing, pushing.

The other team was good. They were aggressive but we matched 'em at every turn. I did and my team backed me up. Labrowski was our captain, but tonight, he was sharing it with me.

My mom was here. Titi.

This was for them.

We scored. They scored.

We scored. Them.

It went back and forth until the third period.

Enough.

Coach yelled for line change, and it was first line again. We dropped onto the ice.

I was on with Labrowski and Keys. We went back and forth until I saw an opening, and I went for it, zipping around my guy, the next guy. There was a hole. I pretended to shoot it in, but faked, used my skate to push it forward, just past the goalie on his right and I tapped it in.

Goal!

We were ahead, and now we had to hold them off.

Nah.

I was always taught the best defense was an aggressive offense, so when I hit the ice again, I took it right back to the goal. Their goalie hated me. He saw me swinging his way and I could see him get ready. Good. Fucking good. I wanted in this guy's head.

I repeated this every time my line went out. I pushed, and I pushed hard, until the final horn went off, signaling the end of the game.

We won, 4-2 and I scored two of those goals. I assisted one other.

The team must've planned it because as we went through with the other team, my own team circled around and each one went past me. They hit my shoulder before going to Titi and rattling the glass in front of her. She was going crazy. Tiny arms in the air. Her cheeks were red. Dried tears on her face, but I knew they were from the game, from happiness. That's how she was. She'd also head to bed as soon as the game was done, because this would exhaust her for the next two days.

I was the last one to go over. I pulled my helmet off as I stopped in front of them. My mom stood, pointing to the bench section and back to Titi. I frowned, not sure what she was asking, but nodded. I started back there, and once I saw my mom picking Titi up, her tiny legs dangling helplessly before she tucked them in. I knew what she wanted, what Titi wanted, and my sister's eyes were wide and unblinking. She wasn't looking away from me.

I tried smiling at her but had to turn away.

Jesus.

I was emotional.

My mom carried my sister to me, a blanket over her legs, and at the bench section, I stepped in and took my sister into my arms. I waited, my mom fixing the blankets over her legs until she was fully covered, and Titi tried to wrap her arms around my shoulders.

"Settle in. It's easier to cradle you."

She did, relaxing back, and I held her like she was a baby.

The guys had gone back to the locker room, but I saw Coach waiting. I gestured to the ice, and he gave me a nod.

I stepped out, my sister in my arms.

The people in the stands had started to disperse, but people took forever so there was a decent amount still standing by their seats. I felt their attention.

Titi was crying, and trying to gasp for breath, but she was smiling so hard while she was doing it.

I did a circle and Titi tipped her head back, beaming up at me. "Again."

I went again.

"Again."

I did a third.

By then, the team was back, and they were watching me.

Titi's hands were in the air, her head fully back as I was holding her, and she wiggled. "Again, Cruz. Again!"

I went a fourth time. This time, the team stepped on the ice and skated with us.

She saw the guys and began trying to sit up. She wanted to see them now.

I jerked my chin up at Labrowski, "One second."

I went back to our mom, and she saw what was going on.

She came down and helped me adjust Titi so she was sitting more upright but I could still hold her securely. The blankets were wrapped around her legs again. Before I went back on the ice, she leaned forward and said to Titi, "One last time. That's it."

"But–"

"Your brother is tired."

That quieted Titi, and she leaned back against my shoulder this time.

One last round and the guys went with us. Titi watched the whole time, waving her hand at them. Half the guys were waving back. They didn't know what else to do. That was Titi. She was three feet from someone and waving like they were three miles away, you waved back. You had to. And you were smiling because she was beaming like she just saw the world for the first time.

I took her back when we were done.

Titi wrapped her arms around my neck. "Love you, Cruz."

I hugged her, kissing her forehead. "Love you back, Titster."

She giggled, and I was guessing it was Dawn, her new helper, who stepped in and took her from me. She was put back in her chair and covered all up so she wasn't chilled. I waved a last time as the girl started to push her toward the wheelchair accessible entrance.

My mom held back, wiping tears away from her face.

The guys trailed past me, going to the locker room again.

My coach was last, stopping beside me before giving my mom a nod. "Ma'am."

"Thank you for tonight, Coach."

He grinned faintly. "I'll give you a moment." He said to me, "You got the night off."

"Thanks, Coach."

When he left, my mom stepped closer and gave me a hug.

She squeezed me so hard, whispering to me, "I love you so much."

"Love you too."

My mom sighed, stepping back, "I need to go and help Dawn."

"Titi will be exhausted."

"She'll fight it as hard as she can, but you know how tired she'll get. She'll be zonked until Monday, but it was worth it. No game tomorrow?"

I shook my head "One and done with this team. We'll get them on the next rotation. Thanks for coming."

"Thank your coach for helping make it happen."

"He didn't know Titi was my sister."

"All the more reason to thank him." She gave me a last hug, saying again, "Love you and so proud of you!"

A third hug before she pulled away, hurrying toward where Titi was taken. Normal circumstances, they'd get a hotel and I could see them tonight or in the morning, but not with Titi. They had a two-hour drive back home because she'd need her bed and her specialized equipment. She always slept better in her own bed.

"She's gotten smaller. I didn't know that could happen."

I tensed, not able to believe *she'd* approach me now.

Sabrina Burford, who went to my high school, was standing on the other side of the plexiglass. Her face was ashen, and I saw her blink back some tears before she tried wiping them away.

A rage of fury began rolling through me. "Eat shit, Sabrina."

I headed in, knowing she better not gasp in outrage. She should've been expecting my response, especially after tonight.

She didn't, but I was in a mood.

I wanted to get drunk and fuck the rest of the night. I wanted to forget the reason my sister was how she was.

After getting to the locker room, showering and changing, I texted Mara.

Me: I need a full night.

There'd be parties galore going on tonight, but she responded as if expecting my text.

Mara: I'm at your truck.

24

MARA

He had showered, and he was dressed in a hockey sweatshirt and jeans. He looked edible, but I saw him in there. Saw her. Saw how he loved her, and my chest burned from envy. I had no idea what it was like having a family member love you as much as he loved his sister, or how much she loved him.

And his mom. She was everything my mom wasn't. Giving. Loving. Enduring.

Could see that in two seconds.

I knew he'd need something. His sister was half asleep before she left the arena. The high she had, she'd crash, and he would know that. As he approached me at his truck, I saw it was eating him up.

He blew out a ragged breath, seeing me. He stopped, almost glaring before raking a hand through his hair.

There was tension between us. Had been since he found out about my ex, ramped up the night I got mad about the puck bunny. It was simmering under the surface the whole time. The sex was good, but there was a harder element to it than normal.

An edgier element, like he was punishing me. I got it. I did. A part of me was punishing him, too.

But, I needed him as much as he needed me tonight.

"The guys want to celebrate."

I gave a nod. "You said a full night. I'm yours for the night."

His eyes flashed. That was exactly what he needed to hear, and he stepped up to me. "I need to be with the guys tonight, for a little bit."

But he needed me too. He was looking at me like I was a mirage in the Sahara Desert.

"It's okay, Cruz. I saw how you held her tonight. I get it."

His jaw clenched. "You get what?"

"I get that you need some things tonight. Normal rules don't apply."

"We had a problem the last time they didn't apply."

I stepped to him, pressing a hand to his stomach.

He drew in a breath at my touch, his eyes flashing once again.

"Not tonight. I *saw* her. You have the same smile as she does."

His eyes darkened and in the next second, I was pinned against the truck. His body was against mine. His hands were hoisting me up, holding my thighs in place, and his mouth was devouring mine.

Oh yeah. He had needs tonight.

A sensual shiver wracked through me.

His tongue was rubbing against mine, tasting me before he lifted his head, his eyes still dark, but the sexual need was pulsating from him. He bent his forehead, resting against my shoulder as he started grinding up and into me. Slow. His hands holding my legs firmly apart as he moved up. In. Against me. Around. And he did it again, and again, and again until I was combusting from the need of him being inside me.

He dropped me back to the ground and stepped back, his

chest heaving silently as he stared at me. "We're going to do slow sex. Hard sex. I want you in seventy dirty ways tonight. You got me?"

Jesus.

I got him. I was already a quivering mess.

But I got him.

THE HOCKEY HOUSE was partying it up. The entire place was lit when we pulled up.

"I'm surprised Labrowski and Keys went for another party?"

He jerked his shoulder up, as he parked in the back. "Labrowski's got a friend. He's got a soft spot for her, and if he caves, Keys cave. She wanted a party tonight."

The music was pounding louder than the other night when we got out, but then again, who was going to call the cops of the Grant West hockey team? Especially after tonight's win? It was different. Cruz's sister aside, there was a different feel to the game. It was more primal. Raw. Desperate. And the win had been fought for and won hard. Cruz did that. So, when we got out, everyone wanted a piece of him.

He held my hand, keeping me attached as we went through the backyard before getting to the house.

I saw the looks.

Girls noticed the hands. Guys too.

Once we got into the house, Cruz pulled me against him. My back against his front, and he had an arm around me, his hand sliding into my pocket.

That was noticed as well.

He took us to get alcohol, and he bypassed beer, taking the bottle of bourbon instead.

Atwater offered to mix me a drink, which I accepted. I was not into drinking straight shots tonight. No way. I'd really be messed up, but not Cruz. He took the bottle and walked us to a back room where a bunch of guys were. I'd never been in this room, it looked like a small media room. Three couches, one against each wall, with a bookcase filling up the fourth wall. A TV was in the middle of the bookcase, and two video game controllers were being used as two guys were in chairs on the floor, duking it out on Madden.

"Styles! Sit, my brother." Labrowski was drunk, his head rolling against the back of the couch and his arm resting over the top. A girl was sitting by him, bent over as she was inhaling something that wasn't not drugs. She leaned back, smiling at Cruz. "Hey, baby."

I half expected this to be Bianca, but it wasn't.

Cruz went rigid. "Fuck off."

She froze.

Labrowski started laughing. "Yeah. Take your powder with you."

She turned to him, looking like he kicked her dog.

He narrowed his eyes at her before making a shooing motion. "Get lost. We're not into druggies."

A guy started laughing, coming in and dropping to the couch beside Labrowski.

She glared at him. "Get lost, Brian."

He just giggled, shaking his head. "Even the hockey team doesn't want you. Try the tennis team next, Jennie."

She kept glaring but brushed the rest of the white powder into a container before standing. Seeing as Cruz was sitting down, she turned so her ass was to him when she bent over and licked the table. One long and very sexual lick.

When she looked back, smug at first, she saw that he had pulled me into his lap. He wasn't looking at her and the smug factor fell away.

Labrowski waved his hand, snapping his fingers. Two guys showed up, and he motioned to her. "Get her out of here."

Cruz moved me so I was sitting firmly on his lap. His hands were on my hips, keeping me in place. He leaned in, nuzzling the back of my neck.

I suppressed a shiver, and I couldn't help myself. I leaned back against him, my back resting totally on him and he moved his mouth to the other side of my neck, his tongue beginning to taste me.

"I'm seeing that you're going public?"

I couldn't answer. I was a writhing ball of sensations, but Cruz clamped a hand over my stomach and lifted his head. "Tonight's special."

"Uh huh." Labrowski didn't believe him.

Cruz laughed but gave him the middle finger before going back to me. He slid a hand down my front, pausing at the end of my shirt before slipping up underneath.

I bit my lip, my whole body holding still.

I looked around.

The guys, each and every one, were watching.

Nope. This was not for me. I stood, ignoring Cruz's protest, and took his hand and the bourbon. I waved it, pulling him to his feet. "Come on. I'm not into this much PDA."

"You told me–"

"Let's take this to your room." But it wasn't a question. I took his hand, lacing our fingers, and began leading the way. He must've changed his mind, going with me, because he pushed up behind my back and his arm snaked around me, grabbing the bourbon again. He took a drink, his other hand tucking into the back of my jeans as we weaved through the party.

It was a full house, fuller than I'd ever seen it.

Everyone wanted to talk to Cruz, but he was beyond words already. Whatever emotion he had from his sister, was riding him hard. He was a whole different animal. Other girls, it might scare them, but not me. For maybe the first time I started considering that he could handle my shit? If I laid it all out for someone one day...

We turned the last corner, getting to the stairs as the door opened.

Tasmin was there. Her boyfriend was with her. Both took me in, but right away, they saw Cruz's hand and trailed more fully to him.

I ignored both, pulling Cruz up the stairs and then to his room.

Before I could open his door, he moved, pushing me against it. My front was to the door, and he was behind me, plastered to me.

"You want me to fuck you tonight?"

He ground up into me.

"Huh?" he asked as he did it again.

I opened my mouth, the pleasure taking over now that we were more in private.

"Cruz," I gasped, trying to push back from the door.

He ignored me, grinding up as if we really were having sex through our clothes.

"I want to fuck you all the time," he whispered, his forehead resting against the middle of my back, and he skimmed his hand down my side, going to my pants and hooking over the waistband.

Holy shit. He really was going to peel them down and sink in from behind.

I shoved back from the door, adjusting his hold and was panting as I dropped to my feet. I reached for the doorknob, opening it and we were inside.

I expected to be pinned against the door since that'd been his theme tonight, but nope.

He bent, threw me over his shoulder and I was tossed onto the bed.

He followed me down, but before he could start, I patted his shoulder. "Lock the door."

He growled, stretching out over me, his mouth going to my neck.

I said it again, "The door, Cruz. The party has a weird vibe. I don't trust it tonight."

He pushed up, locked the door in a flash, but made sure the windows were closed, locked, and the curtains pulled shut. A fan was switched on to drown out any sounds, theirs or ours. Total privacy.

After that, he stalked toward me, his eyes glittering with his intention.

My mouth went dry. I was aching for him. Had been since the hockey game.

He let out a sigh, as he fell back to the bed, but catching himself so he didn't land on me. He moved over me, and leaned down, inhaling me. "I want to do so many things to you tonight."

My body started trembling, and I just wanted to wrap my legs around his, bring him into contact against me. I wanted the grinding to come back now that we could finish it, but this was his night. I waited, seeing what he did first.

He was looking me over and his eyes flared. He sat up on his knees, his hands went to my pants. He undid my zipper, then shifting as he pulled them down. My panties were next. Socks. Shoes. I was bare to him from the waist down.

My pulse was pounding. So hard, so loud.

He bent down to my pussy, and I expected him to lick me there, but he didn't. He knelt back up and moved closer toward me. His eyes found mine, and my own widened because I'd never seen that look from him before.

Suddenly, his finger slid inside me, and he lifted me up.

I squeaked, my entire body up in the air from his

momentum until I was sitting upright and against the headboard.

His finger kept thrusting inside me, his thumb rubbing my clit and I was melting. The pleasure was rolling through me, but I was being lifted again in the air. My legs were spread apart, and he moved in, settling me on top of him.

Oooh.

I liked this position.

He bent his head, tasting my neck before sliding up to find my mouth.

God. That meeting.

His mouth to mine.

I sighed, settling even more over him, and as his tongue slipped inside me, I felt him sliding up my shirt.

I had no problem helping with that.

Pulling back, I was tugging at his shirt. I took his off. He took mine off.

My bra was next, sliding down my arms, and as we did all of this, he undid his jeans and his cock sprang free.

I grabbed it, started to stroke it.

He panted into my ear, "I want you. I want to feel you."

I nodded. We had this discussion. Both of us were clean. I was on birth control, so I was lifted up. I reached, finding him, and helped guide him into me as he lowered me over him.

Holy mother of–he felt so good inside me. Damned good.

And then he began moving. I started rolling over him. Every time I thought it was the best with him, until the next time. But right now, *this* was the best I'd had with him.

I hissed as he was pounding up into me, until I growled and pushed him back on the bed. He went down, moving his legs and I climbed back over him, my knees on both sides of him. I sank down once more. Then, a hand to his chest, I rose up and rode him.

He groaned, his head falling back, and his hands clenching

into my ass. He was helping me move over him, but this time was just me. He wasn't thrusting up. It was my turn. All me. Everything was for me right now and I kept going, riding, riding, riding until I almost screamed.

My body jerked. My mouth opened. I would've screamed, but Cruz shot up and covered my mouth with his hand. My teeth sank down, but before I was breaking his skin, his hand moved, and I was being lifted once again into the air. My climax was racing through me, shattering me, and it just kept going.

I was helpless, riding out the waves until they ceased, but in the meantime, Cruz moved me back so I was underneath him. His mouth on mine, and he was thrusting into me for his release now.

We did enjoy a good missionary position, even for all the things he wanted 'to do' to me tonight.

We'd get to those.

I WAS LYING in his bed, and had no idea the time. We'd been going at it for hours, or it seemed like. That'd just been the appetizer for what happened afterwards, but if I didn't move again in my life, I would've been happy. I'd lived a good life, a very sexually satisfied life.

Cruz collapsed next to me, his hand on my stomach. "My dick is worn out."

I looked at it and laughed a little. It was ready to rest too.

The music was still going, the bass pounding through the floorboards. We could hear people talking, some were outside. There was shouting and laughing.

"The party is still going on."

He raised his head, glancing my way. "You want to go down there?"

My stomach growled.

We heard and both of us shared a grin.

I said, "I'm hungry."

He let out a tired sigh, nodding before he closed his eyes and laid his head down again. He ran his hand along my leg, rubbing back and forth. "Thanks for tonight."

"For what?"

He rolled, laying on his side so he could see me. "For–I don't know. I was rough at times."

"We've been screwing long enough you know I like that."

A flash of a grin. "I know. I seriously love fucking you."

I laughed. "Same here." I bit my lip because... I wanted to ask, but I knew the rules. But we'd already violated them so many times. "That was your sister?"

He quieted, falling back down. His hand clenched over my leg before leaving and resting on his own chest. "Yeah."

"Can I ask what happened?"

"She's always been small, like really small, then she... She was in a car accident. Survived, but half paralyzed for the rest of her life. The accident affected some of her growth hormones. I can't really explain it in all the medical terms, but she's only going to get a little bit bigger for the rest of her life."

"How old is she?"

"She's supposed to be in high school, but mentally, she's probably more in fifth grade."

"Who was the girl helping her?"

"I think that was Dawn, her new worker. My mom said she's been a godsend."

"Your mom seems nice."

He looked at me again, a different expression on his face, as if he was studying me for the first time. "She is. She's a really great mom. Our dad left after the accident. We were too much baggage, so he started new. Divorced my mom, divorced us. He moved to Arizona and has a new wife, new kids. Whole new family."

"Does he help with money?"

"Somewhat. My mom sicced lawyers on him. My dad's wealthy, his family was in oil so there was a settlement. He doesn't send the money. It comes straight from the bank, but to be honest, it's not enough. All the medical bills, insurance, my mom uses that money to cover most of that."

"You said your sister used to make that towel blanket thing. She did that before the accident?"

As soon as I asked the question, I knew it was the wrong thing to say. A prickling sensation came over my arm. Bad move. Bad question. Cruz didn't answer, but he sat up and looked my way, rubbing a hand over my stomach again right as it let loose a long and loud growl.

"Want to go down and get food? I can make a pizza."

I nodded, sitting up with him.

We both went and showered first.

A quick brisk washing and cleaning, and I left the shower first, wrapping a towel around my body before taking a second one for my hair. I padded into his room, starting to go through my clothes.

"Hey."

He went past me to his dresser and pulled out a drawer. Some of my clothes were there, folded all nice.

He moved aside, going to his closet. "You left some things here one time, so I washed them. Kept forgetting to bring them with me, but they're clean."

I was relieved. That's all I was going with because my underwear looked like it was done for life. He hadn't realized he'd ripped it in half. I tossed it in the trash and pulled out a clean one. My bra was okay. There was also a pair of black leggings, so I pulled them on.

My shirt was a mess. It reeked of booze and smoke, and I had no clue where the smoke came from. The sweatshirt looked too hot for a party.

"You have a shirt I can wear?"

"Yeah. Come in here."

I went to the closet. He motioned to some hanging and some folded on a shelf. "Pick whatever."

The girl inside of me wanted to wear a shirt that had his name on it, his hockey number on it, but I knew that'd be asking for even more attention than we were already going to get. I grabbed a random shirt that had no correlation to who Cruz was. It was a black plain shirt, no lettering or numbers on it.

It was perfect.

And it was huge. I rolled up the sleeves, but let it hang so my ass was covered up.

"Ready?"

I finished tying my sneakers and nodded. "Yeah."

He led the way.

When we got to the main floor, a lot of people had left.

I caught the time, noting that it was three in the morning so whoever was here were the long-haulers for the party. The kitchen itself was a mess.

Cruz cursed, taking it all in.

Cups were everywhere, liquid seeping over the counter and onto the floor. Pizza had been ordered, but the boxes were soaked. The pizza was picked over, only a few bits here and there remaining, but even those looked nibbled on. A few guys were in the kitchen, but Cruz scowled at them. They scrambled out.

I bypassed him, locating a garbage bag under the kitchen sink, and began going over what was on the counter, tossing everything or most everything into the bag.

Cruz began helping and we worked together until most of the trash was bagged up. After that, he took the bags to their dumpster or wherever their garbage went, and I began taking care of the dishes. Most could go in the dishwasher until that was full. I started a load, and by then, a few guys came in, hearing the sounds.

I started piling the extra dishes in the sink, plugging it and began filling it with warm water. Added soap.

"What are you doing, Daniels?" Atwater was confused, looking around, but he was weaving on his feet.

Cruz came back in, seeing his friend almost toppling over. "Go pass out in your bed, dude."

"Huh? Oh. Yeah. Okay." He headed off, bumping into the wall as he did.

"Daniels." Gavin came around the corner, surprisingly sober. "Didn't know you were here."

Cruz turned on the oven then pulled out a bunch of frozen pizzas from the freezer.

Enough of the counter had been cleared and wiped down so I started washing some of the dishes.

"I'm surprised you are. Your frat didn't do a party tonight?"

"They did, but I heard this one was off the chains so a bunch of us came over. Where were you?" There was a bag of chips and a bowl of cheese. Gavin wasn't as sober as I thought. He began munching on the chips, dipping them in the sauce and not noticing how bad that cheese looked. It must've been sitting out for hours.

I pulled it away from him, dumping it.

"Hey." He reached for it with his chip, but I raised my arm, pushing him back.

"I just saved your life. You can thank me when you're sober."

Cruz had opened the fridge and pulled out a new jar of cheese. He grabbed one of the bowls I washed, rinsed it, dried it a little, and poured the cheese into it. He slid it over to Gavin with the jar still tipped over. "Sit. Let it drip out."

Gavin sat on a stool on the other side of the island. He

stared at the bowl, nodding at what Cruz told him. He kept eating the chips.

I glanced back, seeing Cruz had four pizzas ready to go. The oven was still heating up.

He laid out some towels, moving the dishes I'd cleaned and put them to air dry. Once he was done with that, he touched my hip. "You want something to drink?"

I nodded. "Rum and coke."

"Me too, please." Gavin didn't look up from his eating but held up a finger.

Cruz narrowed his eyes at him before moving into the other room where they had more booze set up. Once he was gone, Gavin raised his head up and gestured in his direction with a chip. "You two a thing now?"

I stopped washing dishes. "What?"

"Know you're fucking. Pictures are all over social media of you two."

"Pictures?"

He indicated the house. "Here. Tonight, I'm guessing. He was all over you and some of you two on a couch. There's one where you're making out against his truck." He focused back on me, but his eyes were slow to center. He was on something; I could see it now. "Could've told me you were fucking him."

"It's no one's business."

He laughed at that, tipping his head back. "You and him? It's everyone's business. You two are hot. Gotta say that. You do a porn, make sure to sell that shit. It'd make you six figures."

"Stop talking."

Pictures. There were pictures and Cruz was the golden boy after last night's game. *Of course* there were pictures. Everyone had a phone. We were getting more and more reckless. Then again, being secret hadn't been the main objection.

I'd known word would get out, but this was faster than I'd thought.

Cruz came back, holding a beer and two other drinks. He put one in front of Gavin and handed me the other before narrowing his eyes. "What's wrong?"

Gavin was fixated on his current chip, but he started laughing.

"Shut up," I hissed.

Cruz looked between us two.

Still staring at his chip, Gavin asked, "You going to tell him or am I?"

I opened my mouth.

He beat me to it, dropping his chip and staring at Cruz with some hostility. "Pictures of you two all over social media. Congrats. If you were fucking in secret, you're not anymore."

Cruz went still, cursing under his breath before his eyes slid my way.

I felt sick to my stomach, but I mean, we both made the decision.

He said softly, "Don't freak out and ghost me."

An unbalanced and a little hysterical laugh left me before I closed my eyes and just shook my head.

Shit, shit, shit.

"Is that her freaking?"

"No. That's her not being happy," Cruz answered Gavin.

"You've seen her freak then?"

They were still talking about me like I wasn't here.

"Yeah. One time there was a bad one. Blood–"

"Blood?"

"Screams."

"Screams too? You were screaming, Daniels? Or wait, screaming from coming?"

"Shut up, both of you." But they were talking casual, maintaining a cool and calm effect and I knew they were both doing it for me, so I didn't flip the fuck out. I wanted to flip the fuck out.

I wanted to do more, but I thought about the real problems in my life. My mom. That put things into perspective for me. There'd be more attention on me. More girls who might pretend to like me, but mostly more girls who'd hate me. It just happened. Jealousy was rampant. And Cruz being Cruz, I was not looking forward to class on Monday.

I asked Gavin, "Are you going to give me attitude about this later?"

He shook his head, going back to his chips. He pulled the cheese jar from the bowl and set it aside. The oven beeped at the same time, and Cruz put two pizzas in as Gavin replied, "Wanna fuck you. Sorry, Styles. I'm keeping it real." He focused back on me, ignoring how Cruz's jaw got hard. "Have since I first saw you, but I didn't get there first, and because I like you as a friend, that's what I'm cool with being." He dipped a chip into the cheese. "I'm really hoping to stay awake until those pizzas are done."

Cruz moved in, touching my hip and jerked his chin toward the stairs. "We should talk."

I nodded, going with him.

He followed, saying over his shoulder, "Watch the pizzas."

"Did you not just hear me? I'm hoping to stay awake. Not a ringing endorsement to keep your house from burning down!"

Cruz ignored him.

We went to his room, but this was pointless.

I grabbed the rest of my stuff.

"What are you doing?"

"I'm going home."

"Hey–whoa." He jumped in front of me, his hands in the air.

Maybe I should've been panicking. I don't know, but I wasn't. I was tired. So very, very exhausted. And I looked up, knowing Cruz was worrying about me freaking out, so I spoke calmly. "Turn the oven off and take me home."

His eyes cleared and he lowered his hands. "You sure?"

"I want to go home, and I want to go to my own bed."

His chest rose. He looked like he had something else to say, but then everything went flat. His eyes. His mouth. His shoulders.

He nodded. "Okay."

I CHECKED my phone before heading to bed.

Blocked calls (7)

One got through to my voicemail, and when I clicked to hear it, it was deep breathing. They didn't say anything.

Of course.

I blocked that number too.

25

MARA

I went on lockdown over the weekend except for a brief roommate dinner. Other than that exception, there'd been no Cruz. No Miles. No Gavin. The only one who got through was Zeke, and that was via the phone before I silenced his alerts. His first text was a picture of Cruz and I holding hands, walking through the hockey house.

Zeke: I rate this hand holding at a 7.5. It emotes, but a bit shy on the passion level.

His second text was a picture of me sitting on Cruz's lap. We were in the back room. I didn't know anyone had a phone there.

Zeke: This is an 8.35379. Bodily contact, but your eyes are closed. What it lacks in angst, it makes up for in passion.

The third was a picture of Cruz crushing me against his truck, his mouth on mine, and my hands in his hair. It was another situation where I didn't remember touching his hair, but I must've because I was holding entire chunks of it in the image.

Zeke: A 10.000000. Well done, Daniels. Not handing out any awards here, but if you were on my Olympics team, you'd be a solid silver.

Me: Fuck you.

Zeke: Trying to make a joke of it cause I know you're freaking. Let me know if you want a road trip out of there, even for a weekend.

I was tempted. That said volumes, but I was. Zeke would be fun, and he'd be protective. He wouldn't hit on me. There'd been one moment I had bad judgment when I was spinning out the end of our senior year, but nothing happened.

I was eternally grateful.

I had other texts over the weekend, but after Zeke's invitation, I decided to do my own 'getting away.' I turned my phone off and spent the weekend alone. There was a trip to the grocery store, a couple to get coffee, and I was in the library most of Saturday. That'd been the best decision. I had no idea how empty the library was on Saturdays.

Sunday was a different story.

I WAS STUDYING at a back table on the second floor when a pair of books landed on the table next to me. Tasmin Shaw was glaring at me, her mouth tight as she swung her bag down on a chair and began unpacking her things.

I straightened in my seat. "What are you doing?"

"You are annoying."

"Excuse me?"

"You're annoying." Her phone. Her computer. A notebook. Two pens. She spread her texts out, and then sat down in the chair across from me with an extra oomph. She glared at me. "You have major baggage. You were so rude to me, and you know it wasn't warranted. I'm nice and you know that too. But I saw the pictures. They're all over social media. You and Cruz Styles? Do you have, like, a self-sabotaging button or something? I know you like to keep things on the down-low, and that's who you end up banging? Anyways, I'm here because you need support and sucks for you, you already unloaded on me. I'm aware of the root of your baggage. You made a mistake when you confided in me in our floor's bathroom last semester, and fuck you, but you made me like you in that moment. So whatever. Even you being a *total* bitch to me, I'm still here." She ended it with a harrumph and snapped open her computer.

I took my phone out and pulled up Zeke's number. I hit dial.

"Daniels! What's the what? More pictures? Wait. I mean, not more pictures? Or no..."

At hearing Zeke's greeting, Tasmin raised her head, her eyes holding mine steadily.

I held hers right back and asked, "Is Blaise with you?"

Zeke got quiet before he started coughing. "Uh. Yeah. Why...you don't want to talk to him, do you?"

I almost smiled at the supreme caution he was having around 'his boy.' "No, but you might want to let him know that his little sister is sitting across from me at the library, and she's informed me that she's going to be my support system. Instead of being a bitch to her again, I'm going to cease fighting it. Let your boy know and if he has a problem with it, he can suck it."

I enjoyed the myriad of emotions that flashed across Tasmin's face. Shock. Horror. Caution. Fear. And then she ducked her head down. I caught the slight grin she was trying to hide from me.

"Well, technically, he doesn't need to 'suck it' anymore, since you know he's super–"

"I don't care. Bye." I ended the call and started a countdown.

Three.

Two.

One–Tasmin's phone started blowing up.

Zeke did his job, but Tasmin just gave me another withering

glare before answering, speaking tightly, "I do not give one fuck what you're going to say."

Now I was the one smiling because I was fully enjoying this. I wasn't hiding my smile, though, and it only grew as I heard her brother's voice over the phone.

She cut him off, "I don't care. I. Don't. Care. You're not listening to me. I am here. You are not." There was a pause as she listened to him, before she huffed out, "You can tell Cross anything you want. When my twin calls me, I will put my foot down. You've not endured me when I put my foot down. Cross has. I'd advise you to ask him what that experience is like, and yes, make sure you use the phrase that I'm putting my foot down." Another pause as she listened to him. "Whatever. Fuck off, Blaise." She rolled her eyes and said quickly, "I mean, I love you, but fuck off about this. You have no say."

She ended her call, putting the phone back down.

It started blowing up right away.

She declined that call. She declined the next, and the next three.

I was almost scared to ask, but, "Are those all Blaise?"

"No. I think he sent out a group text. My boyfriend is probably coming here. My twin is calling. My twin's girlfriend is calling. They're all calling."

I grunted. "Maybe you shouldn't be my friend. It's a lot of work, if you ask me."

She seared me as she upped her glare to a whole new level. "I get you being exhausted because of your mom, but what's your issue with having friends? You had a whole group of them at Fallen Crest."

"They were the mean girls. I just didn't let them be mean to me, and Zeke aside, I've found that if I let someone in, they always hurt me." I leaned over the table. "Always."

She got quiet, blinking a few times. "That sounds harsh and lonely."

She didn't get it. Any of it. "Just leave me alone, Taz. I'm not worth it. Trust me."

A new determined expression came over her. She sat up straight, raising her chin. "Deal with it."

"So, you're going to study with me? Is that your plan?"

She checked her phone. "Until Race finds me. I'm sure one of my brothers called him."

"I don't do good with friends."

She needed to be warned.

She lifted her head again, a softer smile on her face. "Fully aware, Mara."

Shit. Why did her using my first name make me feel soft?

"Mara?"

We both looked up at the sound of another voice. Skylar was coming down our aisle, backpack over her shoulder, and a few other girls with her. A couple guys too. I didn't recognize any of them. She frowned before flashing me a grin. "You've been holed up here studying all day?" She was taking in the somewhat private alcove that I found, and also the very large table we were at. She nodded at the empty space. "Mind if we join?" She gestured behind her. "Just a few of us. The rest are looking for their friends."

I opened my mouth, but Tasmin beat me to it.

She perked up, a bright smile on her face. "Yes! We'd love if you joined!"

Skylar frowned a little, but gave a casual nod before she took the seat next to me. Some of the other girls filed in, spreading out over the end of the table. The guys with them took off, giving the whole table a two-finger salute.

I had to give Tasmin some points because she waited until Skylar was nice and settled in before she started.

"So." She leaned in, her elbows resting on the table. She rested her chin on her hands and gave another closed-mouth smile at Skylar. "Do you remember meeting me? How was the rest of your birthday? Was it amazing? What's it like living with Mara? I've decided that I'm going to be her friend, whether she wants me to be or not. Do you have thoughts on that?"

"Uh… I think that's great." Skylar frowned, glancing at me.

I had a feeling this was the precursor for how the rest of the day would go.

Tasmin Shaw chose her mission: me.

26

MARA

Skylar stayed the whole time until the library closed. Her friends did too, and not only did Tasmin remain the whole time, but her boyfriend joined. When he showed up, they had a silent conversation via looks. It lasted a couple minutes. Everyone noticed, raising their eyebrows except for me, and then, with a sigh, Race moved to take the seat next to his girlfriend. She leaned over, gave him a kiss on the cheek. He shook his head as he pulled out his books to start studying.

We were heading out now and stepped outside the building.

"We're going to take off." Tasmin waved, her hand in Race's. "See you later. Mara, don't block me on your phone. I now know where you live."

I just groaned, refraining from comment as they went off in the opposite direction we were going.

Skylar burst out laughing. "She's...she's something. Yeah."

My phone buzzed.

Cruz: Wanna come over?

"That Styles?"

I jerked my head up at Skylar's question. She said it softly, cautiously. She held up a hand. "Sorry, but I saw the pictures." Her two friends waved, taking off. Skylar returned the gesture before she turned to me again. "Miles also kinda informed us about your deal too."

"Miles knew about Cruz?"

She nodded. "He said he saw you guys one time, but you didn't know. So, you're normally pretty private, right?"

I barked out a laugh. "I—I just like my own privacy, space. And I think something is wrong with me because everything I do has the opposite effect."

"I'm sure there's a reason you keep people at a distance, but you don't have to with us. Your roommates, I mean. We're all cool. For real. You know that. You've hung out with us. Also, you got me an ice cream cake. That solidifies that you're good people in my books."

"I'm ..." God. There was no explanation that didn't make me sound like a crazy person. "Thanks for that."

Her eyes fell back to my phone. "You going to go see him?"

My body did, already heating up, knowing how it felt being in his arms. But I shook my head, tucking my phone back in my pocket. "No. I'm going to go home, maybe hang out with my roommates, and go to bed like the responsible college student I am. I've got morning classes tomorrow."

She laughed. "I'm hoping to have a couple drinks tonight."

"That too."

I gave Skylar a ride home. We separated at the back doors. I went to my place first, telling her I'd join them in a bit, and she went through the main back door.

The light was on, and crossing the living room, I heard the toilet flush.

Then I registered that the bathroom door was closed.

Someone was in my apartment!

I froze.

The water turned on. Off.

I should run—I started for the door when the bathroom door opened, and my mom stepped out. She saw me, her eyes went wide, and she posed. Literally, posed. Hands on hips. She stuck a hip out and she puffed up her chest. She had the same body as mine, but the years hadn't been totally kind to her. She had bags under her eyes, dark shadows, but a part of me wondered if she used make-up for the effect. Her hair had recently been dyed, this time she was going with a bright red color. It looked good on her. Then, a deep breath and, "OH MY GOD! MARA!" She rushed me, catching me before I'd taken two steps and wrapped her arms tight around me. "Oh my gosh. Honey. Sweetie. I have missed you so much. So, so much! It's been forever." She was squeezing me so hard.

I shoved away, backing up a few steps.

She was here.

In my apartment.

Here.

Panic was starting to build, but it was moving slow. The shock was stifling it. I could feel it crawling up my body, and it was painful. "How did you get in here?"

"Your roommates." She gave a harsh laugh, going into my kitchen.

She went to the cupboard where I keep my glasses and pulled out a box of mac and cheese. "Seriously? This is what you're filling your body up with?" She gave me a once-over, half sneering before tossing the box down on the counter. "I raised you to do better than that. Come on."

She was going across the room when it clicked then what just happened.

"Let's go to a bar—"

I tuned her out, opening that cupboard. This morning, it had been full of my glasses, cups, mugs, a couple wine glasses. Right now, all food. Food that I didn't buy, but it was there. The mac and cheese, not what I bought.

I went to the other cupboard, and it was the same thing. My plates and bowls had been there this morning, and now, she had towels and washcloths in there.

"Where's my stuff?"

"Oh yeah." She was going for my bag, taking it to the couch. "I rearranged a few things. If you're going to keep that freshman fifteen off you, you shouldn't even have dishes or cups where it's easy to grab. Food can go anywhere, but the dishes to eat the food, that's the genius of the dieting." She paused, starting to unzip my bag, and looked me over again. "You look good though, not too many extra pounds, but you should still lose those just to be safe. I don't want my daughter getting stuck with a loser. We need to make sure you get a good guy. Reel him in now. You had a good idea with that DeVroe kid. Too bad he wised up, saw through you, and picked that other girl. Her family is *wealthy* too. He wasn't dumb."

She was saying everything I hated, everything I didn't want to hear, and she was doing it while she started going through my bag. She pulled my clutch out, thumbing through it. I was still reeling that she was here, that she talked to my roommates, that she rearranged my entire kitchen, and all the cutting comments within two minutes for me to register what she was doing.

She was taking my money.

"Stop!" I lunged for her, taking my clutch away, my chest was heaving.

Oh no.

I did what she needed me to do. I yelled and I forcibly ripped something from her. I could only stand and quake, waiting to see what she'd do next. Throw a tantrum. Cry? Whatever it was, she'd be the victim.

She was always the victim.

In every scenario.

If I walked into a room, if she was in a mood, she was the victim.

If I opened the dishwasher and forgot to close it, she was the victim.

A guttural sob came from her.

Years and years of this. It was too much. Too exhausting.

She was going to cry. That was her choice of action. She'd be in full meltdown within minutes.

"I can't believe you just did that to me." Another sob. A gasp. Tears actually were sliding down her face.

She'd wail soon.

And me, I did what I learned growing up.

I shut down. I couldn't leave the room. That'd further give her ammunition, that I was abandoning her. That I didn't love her. Etcetera and etcetera and etcetera. It went on and on. There was no reasoning. She didn't want that. Logic. Common sense. No way. It was whatever she could do to get my attention. And if someone else was in the room, to get their attention.

She was an energy pariah, sucking it out of you until you were so drained that you were hollow.

I had nothing in me. Absolutely nothing anymore. I couldn't even bolster the energy to fight her, to kick her out.

"I kept waiting for you to visit me at the hospital, but you never did. I almost died, Mara. Where were you?" More tears. Deep sobs where she had to hiccup around one. "I'm all alone. You don't love me. Your father hates me. He's trying to get me locked up. I wanted to see you, so I came here, and I'm trying to do something nice for you. Gaining weight is a big deal to girls. I struggle with it myself, but not everyone can have my metabolism. But Mara, I was all alone. Do you know what it was like when I woke up in the hospital and I was alone? How those nurses looked at me? How they always look at me? None of them were nice. They *judged* me."

I couldn't.

I just couldn't.

I took my clutch, my bag, my phone–I made sure I had everything of value with me. My keys.

"Mara!" Another deep sob/choke. She was raising her voice. "Where are you going?"

I paused, once. "Bathroom, Mom."

"Oh." Another sob as tears lingered on her cheeks. "Okay." She settled back down on the couch, reached for a pillow and held it over her stomach. Her head went down. Her shoulders slumped. She looked defeated. "I'll stay here. I'll wait for you. Take your time, sweetie."

As soon as I was inside, I locked the door, hit the fan. I slumped down to the floor.

Everything was a tsunami inside of me.

I needed her gone. Now. I could not handle her.

She would destroy everything.

I needed help.

Who could I call?

My roommates? They'd see a daughter kicking her mother out of her apartment, a mother that drove three hours to see her daughter. I'm sure she told them some amazing and fun story so of course it made sense for them to unlock the door for her.

No. I couldn't involve them.

Who?

My dad was three hours away. Three hours was doable, but I wanted her gone now. Immediately.

I had no clue–my phone started ringing.

Cruz calling.

I answered, choking out, strangled, "Hey."

He was silent for a second. "What's wrong?"

"What?"

"What's wrong?"

"I–" I stopped and closed my eyes. What could I do here?

What should I do? Cruz never judged. He wasn't like that. Maybe that's why I heard myself saying, "I need help."

"You're at your place?"

"Mara, honey?"

My insides withered because she'd come to the door. I was taking too long.

I was sure Cruz could hear her, but I said, "Yes."

"I'll be there in a minute. I'm close by."

He ended the call, but I held the phone in my hand for a long time after.

She was my mother. She had been my person for so long. She was the best thing in the world. I was angry at everyone she was mad at. I helped plot against anyone who was trying to hurt her, and that list was long. Never ending. Everyone was talking about her. Everyone didn't like her. Everyone only wanted to use her.

But not me. Not her daughter. Her little cuddle bug.

Her and me. The two of us against the world.

She really didn't see me when she hit me with the car that one time. She was the one crying about it. It was traumatic to her, what she almost did to her little angel girl. And the time she raised a bat to me, slamming it down on my hand, but oh no. She didn't see my hand there, though I knew she looked right at it. It was another night in the ER where half the nursing staff were consoling her. I sat on the table, got my hand taken care of, while she was almost choking on her own crying in the hallway. And after, if she hadn't gotten the looks she wanted from the doctor, or the front desk person, then they hated her. They had a personal vendetta against her. Such evil people. No empathy in them.

I believed it all, and the list went on and on and on until I was eleven.

Knock. One brief, but hard knock.

I tensed, listening, not ready to go back out.

I heard voices. A male one. My mom's, loud and excited.

Then, murmuring and I heard, "*Excuse me?*"

Cruz said something to her.

I needed to go out there. I needed to help him.

He didn't even know the situation. I *really* needed to go out there.

There was more murmuring. His was low, calm. Hers–I was expecting it to be angry. That's how she was when someone tried to enforce boundaries. Boundaries meant her not getting what she wanted.

I had to go.

I forced myself up, opening the door, stepping out.

"Mara!" Her mouth was tight. The beginning stages of a full-blown meltdown was going to ensue soon. "You didn't tell me that this house needs to be evacuated."

I opened my mouth, flicked my eyes to Cruz, who was nodding still so calmly.

He said, "Yep. I just talked to Miles downstairs. Something wrong with the ventilation and everyone's leaving for the night." He nodded to a bag. "Is this your bag, ma'am?"

"Ma'am." Her tone was curt.

He ignored that, picking up her bag and put his arm through the strap. His eyes went to me, giving me a little appraisal before giving me a nod. "You got your stuff ready? I was just telling your mom that you're spending the night at my place, but we're at full capacity so I won't be able to get a bed for her. Last minute and all."

He was saving me. He was giving me time.

I jerked my head in a nod. "Right. Mom, you need to go. I have a full week ahead of me, and I can't slip in any of my classes."

"But–"

"You drove here?" I was praying, Please God, she drove here. Not that she got a ride from someone.

"Yeah, but–"

"Okay. Great. Come on." I grabbed my bag, putting all my things inside and went to my room, grabbing a second set of clothes. A few of my toiletries.

Cruz saw me coming and opened the door. I led the way. My mom came behind at a slower pace. I heard Cruz shutting the door. He would've locked it behind him, or I was hoping, but at this rate, I didn't care. Getting out of here, getting her out of here was all I needed.

I was gasping for it like I was drowning.

Her presence, her demands, her emotional manipulation was starting to come over me like a blanket. The suffocation was real. The more I was around her, the weaker I got until it was easier to give her what she wanted, do what she wanted.

I was barely keeping it together once we got downstairs. Spotting Cruz's truck, I knew I needed to play my part.

I turned, a forced smile on my face. I went over, hugged my mom. She stiffened at first before clasping me back. I tried to pull back, but she wouldn't let me. I heard another sob as she buried her head in my neck. "Oh, Mara, honey. I've missed you so much. I only thought of you when I was in the hospital–"

"Did you call me? Did you call and leave a message, but didn't say anything on it?" I stepped back, keeping my feelings suppressed and my face blank, but I had to know. Everything else needed to be shut down so she couldn't read me. She couldn't use anything she saw or felt to manipulate me or anyone at this rate.

She didn't answer. Her mouth pressed into a line, and she looked up and to the right. That was her tell. She was searching for a lie. She *had* called me.

I shook my head. "Never mind. There's your car. I'll see you, Mom."

"Wha–wait."

"Here you go, ma'am." He put her bag at her feet. Then, we

were walking down the driveway. He was slightly behind me, blocking me a little.

"Mara!"

Her voice broke, and my resolve almost shattered at hearing that anguished emotion from her.

I slowed...

"No." Cruz said it softly, touching the small of my back. "Keep going. You know you have to."

I had no idea how he knew what to do, how to handle her. It was a lifeline and I was grabbing hold of it. My mom was shouting my name, but we kept going to his truck.

I got in the passenger door.

He went around, getting in, and I glanced over once. My mom had stopped at the driveway, her bag in her hand. Her mouth was hanging open. Her hands were in fists, but she looked utterly dejected. Another dent in my wall. She was my mother. I loved her, but I couldn't let her in. If I did, she'd destroy me and get mad when I was broken, because I couldn't give her any more, because she'd been the one to break me.

"Miles?" I looked at the house. The lights were off. "The others?"

"Miles got me upstairs. Had to go through the house, but he asked what was up. I had a feeling."

"But–" My mind was still wheeling. "How did you know any of that?"

"Your voice was shaking. You told me you needed help. Mara, *you* don't ever need anyone. Miles told me about the lady visiting you. I didn't know who was up there, but if you could've got out, you would've. I guessed. I hope I was right?"

I was barely hearing him, still focused that she'd been at my apartment. My safe place.

"I have to move."

"No, you don't. You can't run from someone like that."

"How do you *know*?"

He didn't answer, his jaw clenching. He jerked his head to the side, staring straight ahead as we drove back to the hockey house. "I just do."

Right. No personal shit, except we were so far wading into personal shit.

"What'd you tell my roommates?"

"Told them that woman in your apartment wasn't your mom, that she was a con woman."

"What?"

"Told them we needed to get her out of there asap and I wasn't sure if you wanted the cops called. Skylar was the one who said about the evacuation thing. Said she had a creepy uncle and they needed to pull that excuse a few times to get him out of their house."

I couldn't. I mean, I could, but I couldn't because that was ingenious. What he told them, what Skylar thought of and now my mom had no idea where to go or who to turn to for allies. I groaned, thinking on that, because *she couldn't stay*. I was so scared she'd get a motel room, shack up with a guy, and start stalking me around college. I could not have that. I would not have that.

I needed to let my dad know what happened, but I couldn't call. I'd break down.

Me: Mom is here in Grant West. She was in my apartment, but she's out and I'm staying with a friend. I have no idea what she'll do after. I cannot talk about it or I'm going to lose it. Please do something to get her away from here.

A part of me always wondered when he would decide enough was enough. That I was on my own with her. Every time I sent a text like this, like when I was eleven and bleeding in my room and I had to text the dad who hated me, when I asked for help–I expected him not to respond.

Cruz pulled up to the twenty-four-seven grocery store.

"What are we doing here?"

He shut the engine off and turned to me. "Well. I figure if we go back to the house, you're going to break down and then you're going to hate that you broke down. And I'm hungry, but I know you have a real aversion to anything date-like, so I figured let's take a stroll through the grocery store. I get my food. You won't break down and it's not a date at all. Win, win, and win."

He gave me a smirk, got out of the truck, and started for the store.

My phone buzzed.

Dad: I'll handle it. I do want to talk about this apartment because that's news to me but have a restful night with your friend. We'll talk tomorrow. Love you, honey.

He still replied. He was still helping.

I felt a weight lift from my shoulders.

She hadn't been able to take him from me.

27

MARA

I first woke when Cruz got up for his morning practice. The bed moved. I heard him dressing.

I was back to sleep by the time he went out the door.

The second time I woke was to the shower.

Rolling over, I noted the bathroom door was open a crack. Light was shining out. The water was running.

God.

Everything came back to me, and I was exactly somewhere I never wanted to be, hiding out in my not-friend/friend-with-benefits/now-who-knew-what-we-were's bed because my mom had officially made her appearance back in my life.

It'd been a nice few months off.

My phone was blinking so I reached over, snagged it, and laid on my back as I went through my notifications.

A text from my dad.

Dad: Got her to come back to Fallen Crest. I think she'll leave you alone. We need to have a talk, though. Love you, sweetie.

Me: Thanks, Dad.

The relief was palpable. I had nothing else to give, to say. She did what she always did. She'd ransacked my insides. A part of me wanted to go to her, beg for her forgiveness. Another part knew that was pointless because she'd never stop. Ever. She needed attention and I had no more to give her. Attention, energy, sympathy. I didn't even know if there was a difference, she just needed it.

Now there was the other part, the aftermath part. Where I felt guilty for just being. Being present. Being alive. I didn't understand it, but I felt it. Every time. If someone could've explained why I felt this after seeing her, I'd love to know. I just knew I felt it, and I'd carry it until I could either drink or fuck it out of me.

So far, last night, I had done neither.

I eyed Cruz, who was coming from the bathroom.

He eyed me back, padding barefoot over to the bed. He sat, bending down to pull some socks on. "Hey."

I sighed, not going through the rest of my phone. "Hey."

He glanced to the phone, then to the clock on his nightstand. "Bunch of us are heading to campus for breakfast. Interested in joining?"

I shook my head. "No. Thanks for letting me crash here. I'm going to head back. She left."

He gave a nod before standing up and disappearing into his closet. He came back out, pulling on a hockey sweatshirt. He returned to his spot, pulling his shoes on. "You sure? You can crash here tonight if you want."

"She's gone. I'm fine. I'll be fine."

He hesitated, then nodded and stood up. "Okay. See you later then?"

He didn't wait for an answer, going to the door.

"Hey."

He stopped, looking back.

I scooted up in his bed, pulling the covers with me. "Thank you for last night."

His eyes flickered, a soft frown showed, but he lifted his chin. "Yeah. No problem."

He left, and I rolled out of bed, quickly dressing. Cruz drove me here last night, but his house was only a few blocks away. I could walk it and get home in plenty of time to get ready for class. I was hurrying, this time easing out his window.

I'd just dropped down from the stairs to the alley by their house when my phone started ringing.

I silenced the call and went to the back alley.

I was a block from the house when my phone started again.

I answered, "Hey."

It was Tasmin.

"So." She hesitated, then took in a deep breath. "Okay. I am calling you to give you a heads-up."

Oh no...

She kept on, "My brother just called me. He found out that Zeke's friends with a guy from Alpha Mu here, and yeah... Zeke's coming this weekend for a visit."

I almost dropped the phone. "Zeke is coming?"

"Knowing Zeke, I'm sure he'll have other guys with him, but yeah. I think my brother freaked over what you said to him. He's sending Zeke to make sure you don't hurt me or something like that."

Jesus. My head was pounding.

"Are they staying at the Alpha Mu house?"

"I'm not sure. I don't know why my brother's so worried. You don't actually do anything. Threats, but those are always empty. It's like I know you better than he does."

Right.

I frowned. "Okay. Thanks for the heads-up. I appreciate it."

"Yeah. Um...are you going to be studying again tonight? At the library? Maybe we'll see you there?"

"I don't know what I'm doing tonight, but I'll let you know. Sometimes we study at my house."

"Oh. Yeah! That makes sense. Where you live. I'd study there too if I lived in a house now. You know. Except for the dorms, not that the dorms are bad. We have the lounges and...yeah..."

My headache was getting so bad.

"I gotta go, Taz. Thanks for letting me know."

"Yeah! Sure. Okay. See you later..."

I ended the call and went to unblock Blaise.

I couldn't believe I had to freaking deal with this.

Once he was unblocked, I hit call.

He didn't answer, but I left a voice message. "Jesus Christ, Blaise. If you actually think I'm going to hurt your sister, you never knew me. Taz is nice. The fact you think I *could* hurt her? What's the one thing I avoid like the plague? Drama. Hurting your sister would bring that in copious amounts. You can chill out. I'm not going to do anything to he–BEEEEEP!"

The call cut out.

My mom. Now my ex.

I growled, stuffing my phone back in my pocket, and ignored the buzzes coming in. When I got to the house, I went up to my place, and stopped just inside the door.

She'd been here.

She'd invaded my space. My dishes were moved. Food that wasn't mine was in their place.

She had started to go through my bag.

I hated that she was here. I *hated* that she had violated this sanctuary of mine.

Fuck her. Fuck–just fuck her.

And fuck how I felt guilty at thinking that.

No one would understand the feeling of someone getting under your skin, taking your life as if it's theirs to control, and how much energy it took to fight to get it back. No one would understand unless they were in the same shoes.

My phone buzzed.

Cruz: I forgot I drove you last night. Did you get home already? I can come back and give you a ride.

Me: I'm good.

I was such a liar.

28

CRUZ

I'd texted Miles when I knew Mara was at class, so he met me in front of her door. He was leaning against the wall as I came from the stairs, and shook his head. "If you'd asked for this before the party last Friday, I'd be like hell no. But..." He unlocked her door, and let me in. "Don't fuck anything up, because our girl takes no prisoners."

I dipped my chin towards him. "It'll be fine. I'm just doing something to help her out."

Suspicion flared in his gaze, but he cocked his head to the side. "If she's pissed about whatever you're going to do, I'm throwing Gavin under the bus. I'll tell her that he stole her keys to give to you."

"Dude. Just tell her I stole her keys."

His eyebrows dipped down. "That's a better idea. Anyways." He held up a finger, making a clicking sound. "Have at it. This never happened."

I shut the door.

I saw the look on Mara afterwards. Someone violated her safe place. I got it. I understood.

Garbage bags were pulled out of my backpack, and I got to work.

I hit the kitchen first.

The food her mom had brought was put in the garbage bags.

I found Mara's real food, and put them back where she had them before. Her towels. Washcloths. They were taken and put away. I was guessing a little, but remembered which went to the bathroom, and the others were put in the hallway closet. When I opened that door, I saw I'd been right. There were two giant empty spaces on one of the shelves.

Dishes were put back.

Glasses.

Even the silverware was returned to the original drawer.

Mara might've had no idea that I remembered this shit since most of my time was entering, then exiting her bedroom, but I noticed things. Always had.

Her mom had gotten into her bedroom, with her nicer clothes moved to her closet and some of her mom's clothes put in the drawer. That stuff was put in the garbage bag as well, and I dug in her closet, finding everything to get it back in the spot Mara had designated.

After that, I combed through the place.

The bathroom's toilet paper was switched around. I corrected that.

She had put some of Mara's toiletries under the sink, putting her own things in its place. That was all made right.

The living room. There were some blankets that Mara liked to grab for her lap. She usually kept them on the couch, so she could easily grab one without getting up, but her mom had stuffed them in the back of the closet. Those were put back.

After that, I studied the room, standing, feeling something else was off.

The air.

The place didn't smell like Mara. It reeked of cheap perfume.

Windows were opened. I found a fan and had that going, helping to clear it all out. When that was done, I looked around for the usual spray that Mara liked and did a few sprays.

There. It looked like no one had been in here.

I grabbed my bags, hit the lock, and headed back out.

THE REST OF THE WEEK, I never heard from Mara. I half expected it.

Seeing her mom, hearing her mom, being in the same room as her, I could feel how toxic the lady was. Everything clicked. Mara hadn't been Mara in that room. She was a shadow of herself, and I hated that.

Hated seeing that. Hated feeling that from her.

So, her ghosting me, not wanting to see the person who was a witness to that moment, made sense. She was feeling vulnerable and exposed, and I seriously did get that shit. Fuck. She had no idea how much I got it. That's why I was brief the next morning, giving her space, not pushing anything. Normal people, that's what they'd do. They'd want to know what happened, get all the emotional feelings out. Feel all close to each other and shit.

Her and me? No. We didn't do that shit.

That's the time when you close up and rally and pull away because even while you don't want to do it, you have to so you feel safe again. You don't feel safe being raw and exposed. Which goes against the grain, but again, I *get it*.

"Penny for your thoughts?"

I started to answer Barclay, but Atwater skated next to him and said the same thing. A goofy smile on his face. "Penny for your thoughts?"

"Penny for your thoughts?" That was Labrowski.

Keys was next. "Penny for your thoughts?"

"Penny for your mind?"

The third line was next.

Then the fourth.

They all repeated a variation of the same question, and I scowled, but I was also fighting back a grin. "You guys planned that like some TikTok video?"

They all started laughing.

Atwater shoved one of the third linemen. "Except for this dumbass. Mind? The phrase is thoughts."

He scowled and ducked, skating backwards. "Don't hit me again, dude."

Atwater went right after him. "Oh! What are you going to do about it?"

They moved off, half wrestling and half pretending to have a brawl, but we'd just finished practice so no one cared.

Labrowski moved up in Atwater's place. "Serious, man. You good? You've been spacing all week."

"Can't be about those pictures of you and Daniels up on the hockey blogs." Barclay moved in. "That was a week ago."

"That was a whole week ago?"

They were talking about me as if I wasn't here. And because I was in a mood, I skated away.

"Cruz! Come on."

I headed for the locker room and held up my stick to Barclay. "You guys seem to be having a better conversation about me so have at it. You all figure shit out. Let me know what you've decided."

I stepped over, walking the rest of the way.

Some of the guys followed, their voices filling the locker room.

I went to my area, peeling off my uniform and pads before sitting down and bending over to start unlacing my skates.

Labrowski sat next to me, doing the same. He glanced over a few times before he said, "Listen, I'm known for doing crazy shit, but when it comes to the games, I'm steady. You being melancholy this whole week is fucking the dynamic up. Guys notice. You're not captain, but you set the tone for us, so whatever's going on, get it out of your head. We're playing Minnesota this weekend. They're good. We need you at your best."

"Dude. I'm aware. I've been quiet, that's it. My head's always on straight for the game."

"I know, but...you have influence. Theirs might not be. Just be aware of that."

He was right. I'd been noticing the looks from the guys, but me being quiet wasn't all about Daniels. Wasn't even a third about Daniels. Mom. Titi. Then Sabrina Burford coming up afterwards and mentioning Titi.

Then the whole storm with Mara's mom.

That threw me way, way back, and I'd not been ready or wanting to go to memories of why I could identify Mara's mom's deal or the look in Mara's eyes when she came out of the bathroom.

We were leaving for Minnesota in the morning, so I had one night.

I needed to hash some stuff out with Daniels, and her ghosting me was not going to continue. We were officially in the 'between shit' that she always said she didn't want. We were there. I was making us go there.

I was finishing dressing when Barclay came over. "A bunch of us are going for some pizza. You in?"

I checked my phone. It wasn't even eight yet. "Yeah. I can go for a couple slices."

"Sweet!" He pounded me on the chest before grabbing his bag. "Can I ride with you?"

As soon as we entered Pete's, the guys headed for the back room. It was mostly a bar, known for their pizza and a couple games in the back room, so it wasn't uncommon for some kids to be playing back there if their family was here during normal 'dinner' hours. Labrowski and a few of the other guys were the only ones legal to drink, so they ordered a pitcher. We were in training, and we had a game tomorrow, so it would only be one pitcher. The guys had been here enough and the workers behind the bar were fan-guys. Because of that, it was the place we came whenever we wanted a beer and didn't want to get any shit for it.

DI hockey went a long way around here.

But because it'd gotten out that the team hung out here, a lot of upperclassmen also started coming as well. Which normally wasn't an issue, but I saw a back booth where Carrington was at, along with a few other Alpha Mu brothers.

Barclay sat down next to me, nodded in their direction. "Wonder if Miller is here?"

I glanced over, hearing Mara's roommate. "Over there."

"Sweet. I like the Miles kid too."

They weren't alone.

Miles Gaynor, Gavin Miller, a few other guys were heading in from the other section of the bar and right behind them were a bunch of sorority girls. Burford was there. She was grinning, her head down, her hand lightly touching Miller's back, but when their attention shifted our way, so did hers.

Her hand fell away. Her head jerked up. The grin vanished, and her eyes got real wide. She stumbled in her step before righting herself.

"What's that about?" Labrowski joined us, setting the pitcher down and a pile of plastic cups next to it. He was talking about Burford.

"Nothing. I know her from school."

"College?"

Labrowski stifled a laugh.

I rolled my eyes at Barclay. "High school, dumbfuck."

"Really?"

I nodded.

"You two don't look cool. I thought you were cool? You studied with her when you first hooked up with Daniels."

"How do you know that?"

Labrowski snorted, laughing under his breath.

Barclay winced before also snorting. "You came back reeking of sex. After that, Daniels was the only girl sneaking out of your room. Figured that was the first time. Was I wrong?"

I swore, long and low. "Had no idea you were this observant back then."

Labrowski hooted, hitting the table with his palm. "Observant! Barclay?"

Atwater was coming back to the table, a wide grin on his face and his own pitcher of beer in hand. He set it down, rounding the table to drop down on my other side. "Barclay? Too bad he doesn't use that skill on the ice."

"Hey!"

Labrowski's head tipped back, more laughter came out. "Burn!"

"Dude." Barclay was scowling and he motioned to the second pitcher of beer. "We have a game tomorrow. One pitcher is fine, but two? Everyone has a phone nowadays. What are you thinking?"

Atwater didn't seem to care, shrugging and pouring himself a cup. "If we ask real nice, they won't post. No one wants to get us in trouble."

Labrowski grunted, taking his own pitcher and pouring for himself. "Don't say that around Styles. He found out sometimes they gonna post what they wanna post."

I narrowed my eyes. "Fuck off, all y'all."

"Damn." Atwater shot upright, motioning behind Labrowski. "Watch it. They're coming over."

The rest of the team was heading in, but they weren't alone. Gaynor and Miller joined, along with a couple other Alpha Mu brothers. Burford and her sorority sisters joined too, lingering at the end except for two of the girls. They were eyeing me.

"What's up, everyone?" Gaynor went around the table, fist pumping half the team. I held mine up as he went past. He paused, just briefly, but kept on, rounding and sinking down on the other side of Keys.

Miller joined him, giving everyone a nod hello. "You all going to win tomorrow?"

The guys started to talk, but I was feeling attention from one of Sabrina's friends. Slender. Pretty face. Dark hair. She had mean eyes, the kind that say they know something about you that you don't want them to know. Because of that, I leaned forward. "Who's your friend, Burford?"

The mean-eyed chick just grinned, all knowing and shit. Smug.

Sabrina sighed, looking defeated for one second, which wasn't a typical Sabrina Burford thing. She'd picked up a drink and set it down before motioning to the girl. "She's from a sister sorority." Her mouth closed and it was obvious she had no inclination to say anything more.

The 'friend' didn't care. Her grin widened and she half leaned over the table. "Hi! I'm Kit. Kit Carlson." She gave one pause before the Cheshire smile came out. "We have a friend in common."

I wasn't getting a good feeling here. "Yeah?"

"Yeah."

Sabrina glanced my way, saying quickly and almost rushed, "She's from Fallen Crest."

Fuck.

Miller went still before turning my way. He was real even-keel when he said, "She came in with a friend of mine. Zeke Allen–"

Jesus.

I'd heard enough.

I was up from the table with my phone in the next half second. I was dialing and the line was ringing by the time I got outside.

I hoped she wasn't going to ghost me tonight. I hadn't called all week. She hadn't called either, so I was hoping that was the extent of it, but me actually calling–*fucking pick up, Mara.*

"Hello?"

She sounded tired.

"I'm at Pete's. You got at least one Fallen Crest friend here and judging by the look of her and Miller, I wouldn't be surprised if the guy shows up–"

"Who?"

"Kit Carlson. Hanging with Burford, a Kappa girl. Miller's here, talked about a guy named Zeke Allen."

She was quiet before she swore, low and under her breath. "They're idiots who think they're friends." She swore again. "I'm coming."

"You need a ride?"

"No." But she hesitated before saying that. That told me she somewhat wanted me to come and get her. That said a lot. A whole week. We'd not had sex in a whole week.

"Hey. Uh."

I frowned, hearing the change in her tone. Self-conscious.

"What?"

"Is Zeke alone?"

I cursed but answered. "He ain't even here, yet. There someone you're expecting with Allen?"

"God, I hope not. I'll be there in a second."

"Mara."

"What?"

"Do you need backup?"

She swore a third time. "Funny thing is, both of them are supposed to be my friends. But I have no idea how to answer your question because the sad fact is, I might need support."

We ended the call, but I lingered, leaning against the bricked wall.

Did not like how the one girl was looking at me, and really didn't like how Miller looked away when I called the 'friend' out. He knew. That said everything.

The door opened. Barclay and Atwater came out at the same time a Jeep pulled up. There were shouts, laughs, some curses. A guy who thought he was something special had just pulled into Pete's parking lot.

The driver was muscular. Built, probably five eleven. Blond hair. There were a few other guys with him, but one drew the attention. Blaise DeVroe. I would've recognized him no matter what because his face was splashed over the NCAA soccer news every other day. I did not like how he moved forward. Lean. Muscled. With intention. His eyes were intelligent. As their friends went inside without a second thought, he drew up short.

His gaze was on me.

I saw the spark of recognition.

He knew who I was. He also knew I was fucking his ex.

I gave a small nod before straightening from the wall. "Know you."

Barclay and Atwater shared an uneasy look.

I played hockey. He played soccer. One of those sports leaned heavily on the violence whereas the other didn't.

He raised his chin up. "Not here for you."

"Then why are you here?"

He gestured inside. "You've not met Zeke yet. I have a dumbass friend."

"That doesn't explain why you're here."

"Look, I have no problem throwing down if that's the situation here."

"Is it the situation?" I was facing him square because I also had no problem throwing down. He was registering that, and he was doing it with some surprise.

He nodded, slightly, edging back a step. "Not here for that reason."

"*Also* aware of that."

His eyes flared again.

The subtext was that he just told me he wasn't here to get back into Mara's pants, or to keep someone from not getting in there. I let him know that I was aware. That's what surprised him.

"Not sure of our problem here." His head cocked to the side, a glimmer of a frown there.

"Our problem is that you're here. I don't want you here."

I was mostly an easy-going guy. Mostly. Here was the other side of me. Get me on the ice, and I was a dick of epic proportions. This guy, he was being introduced to the hockey side of me. Mara was already messed up because of her mom, because of me, and now an ex here? It wouldn't help.

A car pulled into the lot, parking in a spot near us.

A second later, Mara was hurrying for the door, but drew up short seeing our situation. She stuffed her hands in her pockets. "Seriously, Blaise?"

He stepped back, his gaze skirting from her to me and back again. He held his hands up. "Not here for you."

She moved so she was standing directly between us, her back to me. Her tone was cold. "I told you that I'm not going to hurt your sister."

His gaze skirted from her to me. "I believe you. Or I believed your message. Again, that's not why I'm here." He kept looking at me, a new assessing look coming over him.

That surprise was still there. He was reassessing me.

"Why are you here then?" Mara asked.

His hands lowered, and a grin appeared. "You *do* know Zeke, right? You were the one who called me when he was arrested in Cain. Can you imagine the shit he'll get into here? End of the day, somehow his jeep will get confiscated and I'm not driving three hours to pick his ass up from jail. I'm here to keep him *out* of trouble and also to see my sister. That's it. Season is over, and I thought why not a road trip?"

She didn't answer right away.

Mara was one of the strongest girls I knew. She could stand alone. I was here anyways, and she knew it. This guy knew it too, and he seemed somewhat transfixed by the undercurrents going on.

Then the door opened. The music from inside blew loud before the door slammed shut again, quieting it.

The muted silence didn't last long.

The driver from the jeep came out, frowning, but that changed the second his eyes fell on Mara. "Daniels!" He took three steps and swooped her up in his arms.

"Agh! Zeke! Put me down."

He went in a circle, his arm clamped around her legs over his shoulder. "Not on your life. Hell yeah, Daniels! Your roommate inside is being all shady, not letting us know where you live. Came out to collect my boy, was going to have him GPS your phone so we could roust you up for some fun tonight, but no need. You're already here!" He was still circling, going a little faster each time.

She pounded on his back. "Put me down."

He kept laughing, until a growl erupted from me.

He stopped, glancing back and did a double take. "Oh, shit. It's the guy you're banging."

That earned a second growl from me.

He put Daniels down, a wide smile on his face, and held his

hand out. "Hey, man, hey! I'm a huge fan. For real, I am. My frat does fantasy hockey, and I snatched you up as soon as you joined the team. Dude. You've made me so much money. You have no idea."

This guy was...interesting.

Mara grinned at me, relaxing a little. "If it helps, I think of him as Cain's equivalent to our Gavin Miller."

I cast her a sideways look. "That doesn't help."

She shrugged, sidling more to the side.

I shook the guy's hand and his grin widened. "Awesome."

Blaise DeVroe moved up. "You should know that Zeke's got a tendency to be borderline stalker when he zeroes in on an idol."

Atwater stifled a snort.

Zeke didn't seem to care, gesturing to his friend. "Yeah. Mason Kade got me through junior high and high school. The guy's a fucking legend. You follow the NFL? Know who Kade is? I keep hearing rumors that he's going to transfer out, but I don't believe it. Not for a bit. Nah, man. He won't go until his last year or two playing. Free agent, and his team will fuck up. They'll let him go. What a bunch of dumbasses, if you ask me."

Mara's eyebrows rose. "Zeke."

"What?" He cast her a frown but shrugged. "I'm a lot of things, but I'm not ashamed of my fanboy idols. Mason Kade is legit. He kept me on the straight and narrow until your ass came back to town." He slapped his friend's chest with the back of his hand.

"Straight and narrow? You were a douchebag bully until your dad handed you your ass this last summer."

Zeke shot his friend a disgruntled frown. "Let's not talk about that. I'm trying to block that out."

Blaise coughed, his head lowering. "Taz told me you were a bitch to her. What's that about?"

Mara's head jerked backwards. She looked like she'd been slapped.

Zeke's eyes closed. His head folded down. "You really need to work on your segue abilities."

Mara was blinking a few times, but she edged back. "I apologized. That's between me and her."

"Taz?" Barclay spoke up.

DeVroe nodded. "My sister." He gestured to Mara.

"Oh yeah! Race Ryerson's girlfriend. She's super nice. That's your sister?"

"Yeah." He said the word slowly, and his voice dropped down, to a whole more warning level.

Barclay caught on, lifting his hand and moving back a step himself. "Ryerson's a friend of the team."

I went back to watching Mara, whose gaze was downcast, but she edged closer to me another step. And she did it again. At the same time, her gaze was skirting to the door... Like she didn't want to go in there.

Or there was someone in there she didn't want to see.

Back to me.

An inch to me.

To the door.

She paused but repeated until I'd had enough.

"Okay." I had my keys, everything on me. I went to her front and bent over. Fitting my shoulder to her stomach, I straightened with Mara slung over me.

She gasped. "Cruz!"

"Right on!"

I ignored the Zeke Allen guy and said to Barclay, "I'll be at Mara's. Can you get a ride back?"

"Oh yeah! I can get a ride back. Don't forget we got a game tomorrow."

I lifted a hand up in a wave.

29

MARA

"Who were you hoping to avoid back there?"

After Cruz deposited me in his truck, we left the lot, but I hadn't said a word. Neither had he. He gave me four blocks.

I appreciated those four blocks.

I let out a sigh and sat up a little bit more in my seat, stuffing my hands into my sweatshirt. I just now noticed it was his. I'd pulled it on as soon as I got home, had been wearing it when I was at my place, and I forgot to switch it out.

"My friend Kit was inside."

"You weren't worried about the guys?"

I shook my head. "They're fine or I think they'll be fine, but they know something about my mom that I don't want out."

"They've met her, huh?"

I gave him a faint grin. "No. You're the only one who's met her, and maybe I'm being dumb. I mean... I don't know. The drama from that night is only half of a percentage of what she's been all my life."

God.

My insides were turned inside and out, and my outsides

were the opposite. One visit from her twisted me all the way up. "I'm so messed up. I–everything made sense in high school. Get through it. You know? No one knew about her back then. I always knew, even when I was little, that my friends couldn't come over. We lived in town so I could walk."

"How'd you keep her away from your school?"

Gah. A sad laugh ripped from me.

He really did understand. So many would have no comprehension.

"The school had her banned from their property. Things were different in elementary school. She'd come in, and you know, your classmates don't see that stuff. We're just focused on recess or hanging out at the cute guy's desk, stuff like that, but my mom kept showing up to the administration office. I don't even know what all she did, but they banned her from their properties. I think she tried taking them to court."

"CPS get called on you when they did that?"

"She always kept her shit together when they came. They kept sending the same worker, and my mom had her snowed. But the school doing that, helped me. I told my friends that there was always fighting and drama at my house, which wasn't really a lie. I had a few friends who got peeved at me because I never let them come over, but guys like Zeke helped. He overheard a couple of our friends giving me shit, and he butted in, giving them shit instead. It happened a few times until they shut up."

"You're not worried about him or your ex?"

I shrugged. "Not anymore. They won't say anything about my mom, but Kit..." A sick feeling started in my gut. "My mom tried to kill herself."

Cruz let out a soft curse and pulled the truck over.

He kept the engine running but turned to me. "I'm really sorry."

A lump was in my throat, and I started to shrug that off, but

I couldn't. I was crumbling, and fuck! I closed my eyes, trying to numb this, but it wasn't coming. Not this time.

I couldn't stop whatever storm was coming over me.

"I was supposed to get a semester off, but to do that, we lied to my mom. She was told I was going to school in Oregon. Then I got the call from a nurse in January about my mom and what she did. I took off. Didn't think about it. The hospital was back home so it's a three-hour drive. I got there and found out that–the nurse and my dad think she did it to find out how far away I actually go to college. The cuts weren't severe, and she got a nurse who knew me to call me. Otherwise there's an order on her file not to contact her daughter.

"A part of me was *pissed* that's what they're saying. An attempt is an attempt, but the other part of me was just as mad because it could be true. I don't know. I've asked my mom, but she won't answer that question. I, just, I want to know. I don't know why, but I do. I can't stop not knowing. The diagnosis she has, they say they're not usually violent or suicidal. That's not true with her. She's been violent in the past. She defied their diagnosis then, who's to say she wouldn't do that now?"

It was all coming out.

All of it.

Every fucking sad and sordid fact.

I never said all of this to anyone.

"She manipulated the nurse. Literally every fucking thing she does is manipulation, but that nurse who called me was also the one who let it out. Fallen Crest isn't that big. Gossip spreads fast, and now everyone back home knows about her. My old friends weren't the greatest people, and one of them is here. Kit's a bitch, but she helped me out with my thing with Burford so she's here expecting me to do what? Come in and kiss her ring? I have to ask her not to say anything and... I never wanted to owe anyone anything. Ever. Learned that when I was six, not to owe anyone. And now you know, and you're hearing me, and you've met her. I feel like my world is imploding and I don't even know why."

Panic. Fear. Anger. All of it was lit up in me. I couldn't hide.

Old Mara would be a bitch. Push him away. Slam the walls down. Protect myself, protect myself, protect myself. That's what it was all about. Keep everything separate, but nothing was separate anymore. And gah. I couldn't bring myself to cut this tie off to him.

I could push everyone else away. But not him. Not Cruz.

"What do you want to do?"

"I have no idea." I looked over, seeing his face in shadow and for some reason that tugged at my heartstrings. He wasn't freaking out. He wasn't making this about him. He was sitting here and being present with me. He was letting me talk. "I don't want to go back. I don't have the energy to pull a wall around me, but going back to my place or your place and having sex feels like hiding." A hard laugh ripped from me. "Can't believe I'm going to say this, but I don't want to hide either."

"You eat?"

"What?"

He reached for the gear shift. "Did you eat yet?"

"No."

"We're getting pizza and heading back to my house. Pizza and a movie. We're not going back, but also not hiding either."

I considered it, and he was right. It was a perfect option.

That's when I said it. "Thank you for the apartment."

He glanced my way, held my gaze, and gave me a slight nod.

That was it. That was perfect.

WE WERE a third of the way into the movie, the pizza half eaten in the box on the coffee table in front of us when the guys came home. They were loud, and as soon as the door opened, we saw why. Gavin and Zeke had come with them.

So had Miles. "Roomie!"

He opened his arms wide, his coat falling off from the motion. He left it where it fell. He half flung himself toward me but must've thought differently because instead of landing on me, he folded in on himself and ended up on the floor right in front of where I was sitting. Cruz and I both had our feet stretched out on the coffee table, the pizza box moved aside, and each of us had our own individual blankets. "Oooh, pizza!"

Gavin scooped up the box, grabbing a piece and handing it over to Zeke, who was coming in right behind him.

"How are you doing tonight, roommate?" Miles had turned his face toward me, blinking his eyes so many times that it was obvious he was two seconds away from passing out.

I reached forward, half shoving his shoulder backwards. "Fine. Go pass out in a room somewhere."

"Hmmm." It was meant as a protest. It came out like he was eating in his sleep.

Gavin dropped the box, taking us in before ending on Miles. "Come on, Gaynor." He went over and half-picked him up by grabbing his arm and yanking him upright.

"Hey..."

He took him to the hallway as Labrowski yelled from the kitchen, "Do we have more pizza?"

AJ wandered in, munching on the last piece from our box. He sank down in one of the lounge chairs and smiled drunkenly at us. "Hey you two. How's it going? Whatcha watching?"

Cruz answered, but I was focused on Zeke, who was still standing, eating his pizza, his gaze focused on me over his slice.

"What?"

Zeke took a big bite and shook his head, but he was still eyeing me.

"Look elsewhere while you eat."

He gave me a brief grin before transferring his gaze to Cruz, and the same thing. He took another big bite.

Cruz wasn't as bothered, instead shifting back. He gave Zeke a chin-lift sort of thing. It was very manly. "You got a girl, Allen?"

Zeke was still chewing and shook his head.

Cruz motioned to me. "You wanting this one?"

I almost choked on how blunt he was being. Zeke paused mid-chew, his eyes narrowing, but then he kept on chewing and shook his head again.

Cruz gave him a faint smile. "You want me then?"

Zeke started laughing, folding his head down and his shoulders were shaking. Cruz asked in a very casual way, but he waited until Zeke swallowed the last of his pizza before shaking his head. "Dude." He was laughing and had to sit down.

He nearly sat on AJ's lap, who shoved him off until he landed in one of the other loungers. He fell in backwards, his legs rising up from the motion. The chair began to tip to the side from the momentum. Zeke was a big guy. He took in some air before he was able to talk. "You–"

Cruz took his arm away from behind me and leaned forward, his arms going to rest on his legs. He pulled his feet down from the coffee table. "Guys openly stare at someone it's either because they want to fuck 'em or they want to fight 'em. I went with the fucking first because I'm not getting the feeling that you want to fight. Am I wrong?"

Zeke was still half laughing as he shook his head. "No. Sorry, man. Nope. Just drunk here."

Cruz settled back, easing down on the couch again and he pulled his blanket back over him. "Then what's with the weird looking shit?"

"It's seeing Daniels all cozied up." Zeke stopped laughing enough to give me a more serious look. "It's nice to see. That's all."

I shifted on the couch, starting to get uncomfortable.

Cruz glanced back, studying me.

I had no doubt he saw how that comment made me feel, but he turned back to Zeke. "How long you guys in town?"

"Till Sunday." His eyes slid my way. "Hoping to hang out?"

I gave a nod. "For sure."

Gavin came back from the hallway, stopped short at seeing the empty pizza box. "No more pizza?"

AJ started laughing, finishing his slice.

Labrowski yelled from the kitchen, "I got more coming!"

"Dudes!" came from top of the stairs. "Some of us are sleeping. We do have to travel for a fucking game tomorrow."

Cruz tipped his head back. He was about to yell when Labrowski came marching in from the kitchen, a towel in hand and another thrown over his shoulder. He went to the bottom of the stairs, took hold of the railing, and let out a holler. "WE'RE MAKING FOOD! IF YOU WANT A SLICE EITHER TONIGHT OR TOMORROW, SHUT THE FUCK UP! You have fans and earplugs for a reason."

He didn't wait for a response. He marched back to the kitchen, and we heard pans being moved around.

Cruz said, "He's making two pizzas now."

Zeke started laughing.

Gavin turned for the kitchen. "Oh, sweet. I'm starving." He went into the kitchen.

Zeke laid his head back against his lounger and rested a hand over his stomach. He heaved a sigh, but gave me a contented smile. "We stopped at Taco Bell on the way home too."

The door burst open again. This time, a guy walked in with a girl attached to him. Her legs were around his waist, her arms around his neck and their mouths were attached. They were trying to eat each other.

Zeke snorted.

Cruz grinned.

The guy turned around. It was Barclay. The girl was... I shot upright, jolted. It was Kit.

"Excuse us, folks." Barclay said around her mouth, holding up two fingers in a salute. "Just gonna take this upstairs."

Kit was laughing as she pulled him back for a kiss, but she skimmed the couch and gasped. Her head went back, stiffening in Barclay's hold. Her gaze collided with mine. "Mara–"

I jumped to my feet.

I didn't want her to say anything about my mom. It wasn't that I was worried about people knowing what she tried to do, it was about her getting to where I went to college. She already got to my high school friends, but here–I was still trying to keep her contained.

Kit frowned. "Mara?" Her voice grew soft, and Barclay let her ease down from his arms. He stood behind her, his gaze taking me in.

"Wha–" Kit shook her head, seeing Zeke and jerking backwards. "Zeke?"

He grinned, slowly and a little mean. "Saw you all up in his space so I figured I'd catch a ride here with the rest of the hockey team. Get a front row seat to this show." His eyes jerked my way. "Sorry. I should've warned you."

Kit had a boyfriend. I was guessing Barclay had no clue.

Kit flushed, straightening her shirt and pants. She glared at Zeke. "I know all about the shit you and your boy have pulled. Don't start turning r–" She clamped her mouth shut, seeing Zeke's face flood with anger.

He leaned forward. "Might want to rethink your position before slinging insults."

"What is going on?" Barclay asked.

"They all went to the same high school."

Barclay nodded to Cruz.

Atwater snorted. "Oh, damn. High school gossip is the best kind. Out with it! What's all the shit?"

Kit pointed at me. "Not one word or I'll spread *your* shit all over the Kappa house."

"What a friend," Cruz clipped out, standing up behind me.

Kit flushed again. Her hand lowered a little, but she was still glowering. "Just–don't say anything, Mara."

"Kit's got a boyfriend."

Barclays' eyes widened and he jerked to the side, away from Kit.

All eyes went to Zeke, who had leaned back in his chair and gave a smug smile. His eyes went to Kit. "You got nothing on me, and if you threaten Daniels again, you got two new enemies at Cain."

Kit's eyebrows dipped together.

He clarified, "You know I'll go hard for her. I've always had Daniels' back. Things will just be extra-enemy-ish between you and me now."

Kit was losing some of her steam, but she turned to Barclay. "My boyfriend cheated on me. We broke up before I came here this weekend, and FYI, he's the reason I came along."

Atwater hooted. "Dude. That means you're the rebound fuck."

Barclay was giving her another assessing look before shrugging. "I'm okay with that." He swooped in, picking her up, and as she gave a little shriek, he took her upstairs. He said to Cruz, "Wake me up thirty minutes before we gotta go for the bus."

Cruz nodded.

Labrowski came out from the kitchen. "First pizza's done." He took in the weirdness of the room. "What'd I miss?"

30

CRUZ

"You sure about this?" I asked Mara as she was waiting to help the guys to their car. Labrowski, who was sober, drove it to our house and she was taking it to the Alpha Mu house. From there, the plan was to get Miles into his car and she would drive *that* back to their place.

"Miles will wake up enough to transfer cars and we'll all be good." She moved a little closer to me, looking up at me. "When does your bus leave tomorrow?"

"We need to be at the arena by ten."

"Thought you guys usually fly in the night before a game?"

"We do. This time's the exception."

She nodded, taking me in, lingering on my mouth.

Things had changed with us, but things had been changing for a while. I wasn't really sure where to go, but I was going to let Mara take the lead, at least for a bit. Her face flickered before clearing up and she stepped backwards, away from me. "Sounds good. Get some rest. Gotta make sure you win tomorrow."

Right. Win tomorrow. That's how she was doing this?

"Yeah. Thanks."

The guys were ready, waving from the car, so Mara took off. Atwater stepped up behind me, eating another slice of pizza before pointing at the car with it. "Thought she'd be staying tonight?"

Yeah...

I knew too much.

I knew about her mom. Had met her mom. Now I knew her friends. Saw her ex in person. Her old life and this life were together, and I saw it all. She was all the way exposed.

Was that right? Was I getting that right?

Most girls would eat this shit up, but Mara was different. She told me earlier she'd usually run from situations like this.

I sighed. "No, man. Not tonight."

He grunted.

Labrowski had shut down the kitchen. All the lights were off. It was just Atwater waiting for me, and he started up the stairs. Everything was locked up.

It was after I came back from the bathroom before the text came through.

Mara: We need to stop, at least for a while.

Mara: I'm not hiding. I'm not running, but this is all new territory for me. I'm really sorry. This doesn't mean I want to stop being friends, but... I need a breather so I don't use sex to hide from life. If that makes sense?

I dropped to my bed, expelling a ragged breath.

Me: That makes sense. Talk later?

Her text came in ten minutes later.

Mara: Talk later.

We were both lying. We wouldn't be talking later, and both of us knew it.

31

MARA

Cruz's team won both games. Friday and Saturday.

Gavin's fraternity threw a rager for one game, and a party for the other. I didn't know the difference, but they reassured there was one. I went, which was easier because Blaise had gone back to Cain on Friday. Zeke stayed for the weekend, and so did Kit, but she hadn't reached out to me. She stayed at the Kappa house except for Saturday. As soon as I saw some of the Kappa girls at Gavin's frat, I took off. Zeke called to find out where I was that night, so he came over. Zeke fit in so well that if I hadn't known better, I would've assumed he knew Skylar from high school. The two bonded in a weird way, that only strengthened when he stayed the night at our house that night. Skylar asked three times when he was leaving on Sunday because she wanted to make sure they exchanged numbers. Zoe had a perplexed look on her face the whole time, but she never said anything to me.

Sunday happened and we all went out for lunch before Zeke was taking off.

My roommates, all of them, and Gavin joined in.

Once we sat down, I glanced at the empty seat by Zeke. He

draped a hand over it. "I'm taking off from here. I told Kit if she wants a ride, she needs to get her ass here."

She came in a few minutes later, her bag in hand with a few other Kappa girls.

She skimmed the restaurant until she saw us. Her face tightened. She said something. The three other girls all looked our way, but there was no more room at our table except for the one seat. I watched as the hostess approached. They gestured to us, and before long, they were being seated at the closest booth to us, which was in the other section of the place.

Kit and one of the other girls came over. Her friend went to the far end of the table, waving at Wade, and Kit slipped into the empty seat by Zeke. "Hey."

He was watching her. "Hey."

The two stared at each other, like they were mentally having a conversation before Kit looked to me. "We didn't talk all weekend."

"You threatened me."

"I told you I broke up with my boyfriend, *and* he cheated on me."

Again. "You threatened me."

"Far be it from me getting involved in chick drama, but–" Zeke stopped talking as Kit and I both looked at him. "What?"

Kit said, "You get involved all the time."

I added, "You start it half the time."

He grinned. "Both good points, but I want to point out that you took away Mara's chance to be a friend by first threatening her. I know your man's been cheating on you for a while, but I also know that you've been aware of it for a long time too. Got a feeling Mara knew too."

Kit's mouth opened as her eyes snapped my way. "Is that true? Did you know?"

I shrugged. "You caught him, like, four times this summer.

Also, I always thought you were in an open relationship until Thursday night."

Her face got red, and her eyes bulged out. She reached for a piece of bread and began shredding it to pieces. "Would've been nice if I knew this was the community outlook on my relationship."

My stomach shifted. "Why was this latest cheating the final straw? *Was* it the final straw?"

"He fucked Ria and Penny. At the same time."

I sucked in my breath. They were both from our high school friend group.

"Damn." That was from Zeke.

Kit shot him a look. "Sorry, Zeke."

He gave a disjointed nod, which made sense. He and Penny weren't in a relationship, but the two slept together a lot. "No. I mean, nah. I never laid claim to her and vice versa."

Kit let go of her bread, putting it on her plate. It was half torn up. "He fucked them both, for an entire weekend. They were there when I called him. Apparently, he put me on speaker so they could hear the conversation."

That was the last straw. Not the sex. He let them hear what I knew Kit would've never shared with them. Our whole friend group was messed up. Sex was nothing to us, but real emotional sharing, that was precious.

"I'm sorry, Kit."

Her eyes filled up with tears, but she brushed her hand over her face. "It's whatever. Done with by now. About time too."

I pulled my phone out.

"What are you doing?"

I hit send, then turned my phone around to show Kit and Zeke.

Me: Brian, a heads-up. Ria fucked Kit's boyfriend with Penny all weekend long. Kit told me. Thought you'd like to know.

"That's very messy of you." Kit grinned.

My phone buzzed back as I shrugged.

Brian: Thanks for the heads-up, but I knew. Got a steady girlfriend now. Not Ria.

I chuckled, showing Kit and Zeke the phone again.

"Right on. Good for my boy."

I asked Kit, "How'd you find out?"

"Saw that they were at his college for the weekend and got suspicious. You're the only one that doesn't keep in touch. Everyone else is hooked in on a group chat and they tell us where they're partying. Also, I'm not counting Blaise because he hated everyone except you two in school. But anyways, I called around, finally got his roommate on the phone and threatened him. His girlfriend is a Kappa, and the roommate spilled the beans. Told me everything. They made a video."

"Wait. What?" I jerked upright.

"His roommate sent it to me." Her shoulders slumped even farther down. "I watched it. He was fucking Penny when I called, and he put me on speaker as he finished. You can see Ria cracking up in the background, but he stuffs a pillow over her mouth."

"Is there sound?"

She shook her head. "One good thing about the whole thing, but no. No sound, just video."

"Um–" Zeke held up a finger.

"I'm not sending it to you."

Zeke pouted.

"I deleted it anyway, all of it. The roommate said it was just the one copy. I don't think Ria and Penny know, but I'm not releasing that. That's just messed up."

"True." Zeke shook his head, sighing. "That sounds hot, though."

"What are you guys talking about down here?" Wade came to our end, pulling an empty chair over from another table and flipping it around. He dropped down, resting his arms over the back as he straddled it.

Kit looked around, but her friend had rejoined their booth.

"Yo, man."

"Yo." Wade gave Zeke a chin-up nod.

"Zeke," Skylar called for his attention, so Zeke tuned in her way.

Kit was saying to Wade, "I was just telling Mara about how I'm newly and really real single now."

Wade's grin was slow as he glanced between us. "What does 'really real' mean versus just being single?"

I snorted a laugh.

Kit shrugged, seemingly appeased by now, "Just a relationship that was on and off and now it's very, very off. Permanently."

"I'm sorry."

"It's whatever. I didn't lose too much on him."

"Ah." Wade's eyes filled with understanding. "One of those types of relationships."

"Yep."

"And you?" His question was directed at me.

I sucked in my breath, knowing these questions would be coming, but I wanted to keep the conversation about Kit. "What about me?"

I'm none of your business. I'm no one's business.

"You and the hockey player? You guys a thing now?"

I frowned, lifting a tight shoulder. "It is what it is." Totally not an answer, but that wasn't a question I had plans to answer.

Wade frowned.

Kit's eyebrows slammed down.

"I knew before the pictures came out."

"What?"

"Saw him leaving your place one night. It was obvious what he'd just done."

I frowned. "He saw you?"

He nodded. "I said something to him."

"What'd you say?"

He shrugged. "It doesn't matter. He told me it's none of my business and he was right, it wasn't. Isn't. But couldn't help picking up on weird tension with you lately. You and him okay?"

Kit started laughing.

Wade threw her a weird look.

"Sorry." Her hands went up, but she couldn't stop laughing. "Mara doesn't do personal. You don't know your roommate if you're asking about who she's fucking. Mara never wants anyone to know anything about her life, which made me feel horrible when I found out about your mo–"

"Stop!" I snapped out, cutting her off.

My heart started pounding.

Confusion flashed over her face. "But–"

"That shit never needs to be talked about."

I felt my mom. It was like she was there, in the room, and *she* was making a scene like she used to when I was a kid.

Wade knew about her, just not that she'd really been my mom. He and the others only asked the next day about the 'con woman,' but that'd been it. I told them it worked, and she went away.

I hadn't enjoyed lying, but it was easier.

Normal moms were precious, and cherished. They were loving.

Not mine.

If she kept coming...

She'd make a scene.

And another scene.

And another.

If she took advantage of them? Tried to sleep with them? Conned one of them? Stole from them?

They would ask me to leave.

She came, and everything went bad.

I sighed, pulling out my wallet. "Sorry, guys. My appetite is gone."

"What?"

I threw some money on the table to cover my food that hadn't come yet.

Kit stood, lifting her arms for a hug. "What just happened?"

"I just need to go. I'm sorry." I hugged her back. "Stay strong. Don't say anything about my mom, and have a safe trip back."

I was totally cutting my losses here, and being a shit friend, but I needed to go. A panic attack was impending. I could feel them by now, knew how long I had, and I needed that time to get away to my place.

Zeke was next. "Thank you for coming."

"You okay, Daniels?" He angled his head to see my face as we hugged.

I nodded, avoiding his gaze. "I'm good. Just–be safe heading back. Don't get arrested too many times."

His grin was rakish. "You know better."

I laughed, but it only made the tightness in my chest get tighter. "I do. You should memorize your boy's number too."

"Nah." He said it so softly. "Maybe I enjoy knowing you'll always be there for me?"

My gaze jumped up, but I saw there was understanding looking back at me.

That made the ball of emotion shove even higher in my throat now. I had to swallow to breathe around it. I grasped his shirt, and said thickly, "Thank you, Zeke."

"Anytime," he whispered back. "I'll cover you here."

I let go but patted his chest. After that, I couldn't get to my car fast enough. I was almost there, crossing the parking lot before I heard my name being called.

Wade was coming after me. "What's your deal?"

I saw Zeke in the doorway, but I held up a hand. He gave me a nod, stepping back.

I frowned. "What's *your* issue?"

He drew up short at that. "What do you mean?"

"You've been told that I don't do personal. There's a reason. Now, you brought up that you knew about me and Cruz before everyone else and you're asking me if he and I are okay? How is that any of your business? And you're following me."

"I'm your friend."

"No, you're not! I don't throw that word around easily. I don't let a lot of those in, and even less since I had one turn his back on me. You're a roommate, and you're an acquaintance, and you're a hangout friend. My real friends, they don't push. Maybe it's too much that I'm asking for that consideration, but I'm not in *your* business. I'm not asking who you're fucking or how you and her or him are doing? I don't do that. I don't wade into people's business unless they've made it known that's what *they* want. I don't do friendship contracts. You want to fuck me? Is that what this is about?"

"If he doesn't, I wouldn't mind a go."

I tensed.

Flynn Carrington was coming from his vehicle. A few other Alpha Mu guys had ridden with him, including his little brother, who was frowning at me.

Wade stepped closer to me. "Carrington."

He didn't pause as he walked past us. "Kressup. You throwing your hat in the ring?"

I growled, but Wade touched my arm, blocking me from the rest of the guys as they passed. "Imagine that. You being a dick. The world spins another day."

His little brother stopped at Flynn's question, glanced my way, back to his brother, before throwing me an inscrutable look.

"Look at that. Dry sarcasm. Good for you." Flynn turned to walk backwards, his smirk a half grin. "By the way, how's your girl? Oh wait..." The grin was gone, and it was just a smirk.

Wade tensed. "You mean Rosa, the girl I liked before she woke up in your bed, naked and no memory how she got there? *That* girl? Who was so devastated after her medical exam that she quit school and moved back home?"

Oh whoa!

I had my own gut instincts, as well as so many others saying something. But to hear it confirmed and from another guy, that was major.

Flynn ground to a halt. "Those are big words to throw around unless you got proof to back it up?"

Wade's face was like cement. "That's the problem, isn't it? You say your place doesn't have cameras. Her friend said she wandered in there alone."

"I was never in my room that night. I'm the one who found her. *Remember*?" His gaze was hard right back. "I never touched your friend." His eyes slid to mine, taking in Wade's hand on my arm. "Funny. I thought she was already spoken for. Look at you, Little Daniels, getting all these guys to line up for you. Guess they're all content to wait for their turn. Just so you know, I'm not a wait-in-line kind of guy."

"You fucking asshole." Wade started for him.

I got in between them, my back to Carrington, and I placed my hands on Wade's chest. "Stop." I said it low and calm, but insistent. "You can't get into a fight with him, not guys like him."

Wade was grinding his teeth.

I dug in. "He's too connected, Wade. Too much money. Too much family influence. Trust me. I know guys like him. How he's acting, he knows he can get away with almost anything right now." As much as I was trying to talk Wade into having a cooler head, my heart ached for that Rosa girl.

His nostrils flared, but Wade stopped pushing.

Carrington laughed as he went inside, "Thanks for having my back, Daniels. I owe you one."

I glared at him, but he was gone. All his brothers too. His little brother stood to the side. Our eyes met, and he flinched, looking away.

"I don't want Miller coming to our house anymore."

I tucked my hands back to my side. "I'm not the one inviting him, and he's not Carrington. He's not a predator."

Wade's eyes were still a little feral. "Aren't they all?"

"No. They aren't."

He growled. "You know what? Your idea to cut and run, good choice after all." He gestured beyond me. "I can't go in there or I'll be leaving in handcuffs, but, God, if I go and study right now, I'll be thinking about him and what he did to Rosa."

"A bar," I said it, not thinking.

His gaze sharpened on me. "What?"

"We should go to a bar. Lots of stimuli. It'll help keep your mind off of Carrington and your friend." I lifted a shoulder, knowing, just knowing I should've kept my mouth shut. "We can study there. Great idea, right?"

It was a horrible idea.

32

MARA

Wade suggested a local bar that didn't look too closely at ID cards. Worked for me.

It was a pub with a whole section for games, with an inside room that was sports heaven. I counted thirty televisions mounted, most with a different sport playing too. Wade grabbed a high top in the corner.

The server was nice. She barely glimpsed my fake, so we ordered water and beer. It was thirty minutes later, after we'd gotten through an entire chapter for abnormal psych when another roomie came in. Darren, and he brought a whole group with him. I was assuming football players judging by their height and weight. Big guys, or most were big.

"What up, roomies?" Darren snagged a chair at a table. A guy slipped into the other seat that Darren introduced as QB1, their starting quarterback. His teammates or friends filled the rest of the spots. Another group of guys showed up, and soon we took up half the section. It wasn't long after that when the girls started coming over.

The first pitcher of beer was gone within five minutes.

"If I knew you were their roommate, the entire team

would've been hanging out at Darren's house all year long. Sorry, but *damn*, are you fine."

"She just moved in this semester," Wade said, reaching for the next pitcher.

"Don't encourage him." Darren shot Wade a look.

Wade shrugged, filling his cup, my cup, and the QB1's cup. Darren wasn't drinking.

"Don't matter. She's taken."

"What?" QB1 spit out his beer, leaning back in his stool. He gave me a once-over. "Say it ain't so."

I frowned at him. "What's your name?"

"Kyle." He leaned in. "What's yours?"

"You already know her name." Darren bent his head into his textbook.

"Tell me again. I want to hear how you say it."

"Call me Daniels."

"Daniels, huh? That a nickname or something? Something only your best buds call you?"

"Yes." I gave him a flat look. "It's special, just for you."

"Daniels!"

"I stand corrected." I straightened in my seat as Gavin came around the side. He threw an arm around my shoulder, giving me a one-sided hug. "What's up? Why are you here?"

"Wade needed a distraction, and I heard studying in a bar was the best type."

"Fuck yeah, it is." He turned for QB1/Kyle. "Hey, man. How's it going?"

"Miller." They gave each other a fist pound.

Of course they were friends.

Gavin did the same with Darren and Wade, then moved to the next table, repeating. None of the guys were surprised at seeing him.

I frowned. "Does Miller ever study?"

Darren snorted, grinning at me. "Not that I've seen."

Kyle was still looking my way. "You got some friends. Wade. Darren here. Now Miller? Who else you know?"

I had no doubt he also knew about Cruz, but I shrugged. "Dude. I'm here to study."

Wade started laughing.

Darren snorted again. "She 'duded' you. Friend-zoned."

"Daniels!" Gavin came back, his backpack slung over one shoulder. "Make room for me. I'm joining you." He had a chair behind him.

"What? No–"

"Yes." He ignored Kyle, clearing the table himself of all the condiments until there was room for his phone. He made it work. The guys scooted in, giving him enough space.

The server came over and frowned at him.

He was side-eyeing her. "Don't give me shit that this is a fire hazard or something. I know you let others do this all the time."

She sighed. "Why are you here, Gavin? You're not twenty-one."

"How do you know that?"

"I'm in your freshman econ class."

"Oh. Yeah."

She rolled her eyes. "You can stay, but if you get me in trouble, I will make your life hell."

She was walking away when he called after her, "Wanna go out?"

She ignored him, shaking her head.

Kyle laughed, shaking his head. "Why the fuck are you at Alpha Mu? You're too cool to be at that house."

Gavin reached for the beer, giving a shrug before he filled his cup. "Connections. And speaking of," his eyes went to mine. "Heard you had a run-in with one of them earlier today."

"What'd you hear?"

"Just that you had a little thing with Flynn."

"Flynn Carrington?" Darren asked.

Wade said, "It was more me that had a run-in with him."

Darren frowned. "Because of Rosa?"

Wade nodded, tight-lipped.

Gavin met my gaze, confused.

He asked, "Rosa?"

"A chick that woke up naked in Carrington's bed and after a medical exam, she found out she'd had sex. She didn't remember a thing."

Gavin tensed. "When did this happen?"

"Last year. Fall semester. Let me guess, no one talks about it?" Wade bit out.

Gavin shook his head. "No one's said a word. You want me to ask around?"

Wade narrowed his eyes at him.

I spoke up, "No."

"What? Why?"

I answered Gavin, "It'll make you a target. Keep your head down."

"The guys who I could ask–"

"Just don't. Guys like that, they always get away with it and everyone else gets hurt. And the girl, it always comes back to haunt her."

I was aware of the guys sharing looks over my head, but I didn't care. Let them think what they want. To be honest, it wouldn't be so far off-base. I didn't know a girl who hadn't had to deal with sexual harassment, and I knew ten who had worse shit happen to them. Being a girl sometimes sucked and that was coming from a girl who enjoyed having sex, but I wasn't supposed to.

I'd slept with three guys in my life, and was considered a slut.

"Damn, Daniels. Sometimes I think you're too jaded to be my friend."

I picked up a fork and threw it at Gavin.

The other guys laughed.

KYLE and I were at the jukebox, picking songs when a commotion sounded.

The hockey team came inside, bypassing the main room. Some went over to our tables, giving their hellos, shoulder pats, fist pounds, etcetera, but kept on into the sports room. They took up the entire length of the long table that ran the middle of that room.

Labrowski. Atwater. Barclay.

It was almost the whole team, minus a few, but then Cruz walked in. The commotion went up a whole notch. They'd just won both games against Minnesota, who was rated second in the nation, so it was a big deal. Cruz led the team in goals, and he opened up a third of the plays for the other players to score.

I hadn't texted him. He hadn't texted me either.

We both knew we were too far gone. It was sex or nothing for us, which I kinda hated, but I meant what I said. I didn't want to sink back into sex and hide from moving forward. I felt for the first time in a long time that I could progress somewhere. Having friends who knew about my shit and *still* wanted to be friends was a big deal to me.

Right now, it was baby steps, but fuck. Cruz looked *good*, and he saw me as he walked past.

He didn't stop.

They must've come from a practice because his hair was still wet from a shower, and he had the rough look in his face that he got from whipping around on the ice. He was wearing Grant West sweats, ones that hung low on his hips, and a Grant West hockey sweatshirt. It had his name and his jersey number on the back.

Girls were already descending on their table.

I tried not to let it bother me when I saw a girl plop down in the seat across from Cruz. I recognized her from hanging out at the hockey house. I didn't know who her friends were, but she was friendly with all the guys.

I didn't like her.

Or I didn't like how she was smiling at Cruz, who was grinning back.

"Wait." Kyle leaned back from the jukebox. "You and Styles. The pictures. I remember now. That's who you're with?"

"I'm not." I turned back to the machine. We needed music, angry, fuck-you, heartbreak in the most toxic and messy way possible. That type of music. I hit a Nine Inch Nails song and then chose a bunch of Eminem ones. Those would do.

Kyle whistled, laughing under his breath at the same time. "I don't know your story, but I am a hundred percent fascinated by you."

"Shut up."

"No, for real, I am. You're cool, Daniels. Why the fuck haven't you been coming to our football parties?"

I chose not to inform him that I had; he just hadn't met me then.

Unknown number calls (15)

Voicemail (15)

33

CRUZ

Angela just left when Atwater took her seat. He'd been socializing, going from table to table instead of studying, which had been the original idea. The guys weren't keen on the library, but I always got too distracted here. The games on the TVs behind us took most of the attention. Then there were the puck bunnies.

"You see Daniels over there with the football team?"

I grunted because I had. Kyle Ruiz had been all over her, or maybe not all over her, but he'd been giving her the look. Every guy recognized the look. Ruiz wanted to bang her.

She hadn't come over to say hi, and I hadn't gone over there either. We were in a contest of wills right now, who would hold out longest. But I caught how she was looking at me. She wanted me. The same went for me, but fuck her whole 'let's stop' bullshit. I mean, it made sense. I should support it, but seriously, my dick had been hard this whole time.

"I'm so confused by you two. What are you doing?"

The question came from Atwater, but I knew every guy within hearing distance perked up.

I shrugged. "She's got some stuff. I don't know how to answer that."

"Bad stuff? Like head shit?" Barclay pointed to his head.

Another shrug. "I wouldn't say that, but it's complicated."

"You're not going to tell us?" Labrowski leaned in.

I shook my head. "I'm not that guy, no."

A few of them nodded, understanding.

Atwater's eyes narrowed. "That's bullshit. I want to know! You guys are not what you were in the beginning. That much is obvious, and you had her over to the house on Thursday in a hang-out capacity. I feel like I might die without having this closure. Give me closure, man."

I frowned at him. "You need to chill."

"Yeah." Labrowski threw a pen at him. "Get your own fuck buddy that's not just a buddy anymore and then you can have your own closure."

"Argh. Not cool."

I flipped him off as I stood, pushing back my chair. "Not my problem."

Angela was coming back, and seeing me standing, she hesitated.

Barclay saw, saying under his breath, "Oh, man. She's got a crush. Run, dude."

Angela went to high school with Labrowski, so she got adopted into the hockey house, but it was a situation where no one touched her. Labrowski had put it out there. Her brother was friends with him, and he'd died. Labrowski didn't talk much about him, but it was known that her brother died from a drug overdose. So, Angela was around the house. She had crushes on a few of us, but none of us went there with her.

She'd been fine in the beginning of the year, but since she'd become friends with Bianca, she'd changed. She was a lot more forward, more aggressive.

Bianca hadn't showed yet, and I was counting that as a blessing.

I circled around the table, cutting behind another section of tables.

Angela was watching me the whole time. When she moved to try and intercept me, Atwater and Barclay both stood up, blocking her vision. Angela was a sweet girl, but she liked attention. If she was getting attention from someone, she'd stay there. I headed into the main bar section, glancing back once. The guys had blocked her off, so I was good for a while.

I headed for the bathrooms.

"Styles, my man." It was Ruiz. He held up a hand, half turned to me. He was moving in, his eyes glazed. He looked a little rough. "How's it going?"

"Hey." I stopped.

He stepped in, our hands meeting as he pounded me on the shoulder. A little more forceful than was needed, athlete to athlete. Grant West was usually known for its basketball team. They had a player in the past that was phenomenal, a guy named Hunt. But this year hockey was the big sport. Football never had been, and I knew Ruiz had hopes of getting drafted. We were a DI school, but I hadn't heard of any recruiters coming to visit him. That stuff gets shared, even if you're on a different sport. There was no rivalry between teams at Grant West so having crossover friends was common.

We all used the same weight room.

"How's it going?"

"It's good. You?"

"Good, man. Good." He shifted, turning so he was facing where I'd just left. "That chick with your team. Gotta ask, are you hitting that?"

Fuck's sakes. "Nah, man."

"But someone is?"

I frowned. "Angela?"

"Yeah! Angela. That's her name. She was over, being all sweet to Darren. He didn't seem into her, but Wade was a different matter. I usually see her around the hockey team and another girl, Bianca or something. What's her story?"

"Bianca?"

"Nah, man. Angela."

"Labrowski knows her."

"He banging her?"

I stepped back, not liking how he was talking about Angela, but also not liking how he wasn't over here about her. "Why don't you cut the shit and ask about who you really want to know about?"

He stopped. His eyes were having a hard time focusing so he squinted.

He let out an ugly laugh, and I could almost name the beer he was drinking. His grin was lopsided, his body a little unsteady. "You're a straight shooter. I like that about you, and you're right." He leaned in again. "I'm regretting not hanging out at Darren's place more this semester. I heard you're hitting that. Is she good?"

I shifted, my back to the bar.

Ruiz craned his head to the side so he could see Mara, but me, I was looking around for cameras. I was probably screwed either way, but if he kept going, I was going to knock his teeth back in his throat.

"You wanna run that by me again?"

"Yeah, man." He shifted closer. "She's got a tight body. Petite. Small. How I like 'em, and normally they don't have good tits, but she does. You can tell. What's it like? Doggie style, am I right? The shit I'd like to do to her. Stuffing my cock down her—"

BAM!

He was on the floor in the next second and I was standing

over him. I'd hit him so fast, and I didn't give a damn. I wanted to do it again.

He touched his chin. Then his head twisted, and a snarl formed before he jumped up and swung.

I ducked, grabbed his arm, pinned him against the wall, and punched from the left. I could shoot from both hands; I could punch the same. "Right-handed, huh?" I hissed. "Sucks to be you."

There was a stampede behind us. Then hands were pulling me back.

I strained to land another punch.

He was yelling at me, but I wasn't paying attention.

"You fucker! I'll have your scholarship taken. I'll destroy you–"

"Keep girls' names out of your mouth next time."

"What the hell, man?"

Blood dripped down his face. He was yanked up by a couple of his teammates, but he growled, lunging for me. "I'm going to fuck you up!" He was too fast for them, and I was held back and immobile. I couldn't lift my arms to defend myself.

He got a hit in.

"Stop!" Labrowski was there, wading in. He grabbed Ruiz's arm, shoving him against the wall again. "That was a cheap shot, Ruiz!"

"He start–"

I strained to get free, wanting to go back at him, but goddamn. Who was holding me back?

Darren, Atwater, and Barclay. All three. Wade stood behind, pulling his weight too. Four guys. Ruiz had two.

"Hey!" Labrowski turned to me. "Stop it."

Ruiz snarled, "I'm going to mess up that pretty face of yours–"

I twisted, and this time half my body got free, but Labrowski cut me off, stepping into me.

Ruiz's gaze cut to the side. "The shit I'm going to do to your girl now. You think I was motivated before? Try me now. She's going to be panting for me."

"Like fuck you are." Mara took two steps. "Let him go."

As they did, she grabbed his shoulders, and rammed her knee up into him.

He doubled over.

She glared down at him. "I heard everything you said, and I also recorded it. Make a move against Cruz and I will unleash that shit onto the web. The NFL hates scandals. It'd be *unfortunate* if that was released during recruitment."

His face paled. "You wouldn't."

"Try me. You think you're the first guy to be a pain in my ass?"

Two guys scooped Ruiz up and took him somewhere. My guys stepped away, letting me go.

Mara held my gaze.

I took a step closer to her. "You heard what he said?"

She was looking me over, lingering on my face where his punch had landed. "I was coming out of the bathroom when I heard your voices." Her fingers grazed my cheek. "You should get some ice on that."

"You want to get out of here?"

Her eyes darkened and her hand moved to my mouth. "No."

I moved in again, touching the back of her waist, pulling her against me. "Why not?"

Her eyes closed. "You know why. I can't do that right now."

Right.

She didn't want to hide.

In sex.

With me.

Well, this was *still* a confusing place to be in.

"Let's do something else."

Her eyes opened. I saw the need in her eyes, swimming there on the surface. "Like what?"

"A movie?"

She grinned, her hand dropping back to her side. "You really do need ice. He got you once, but it was a solid hit."

"Let's go somewhere," I said it again, my hand falling to graze against hers.

Her body shook a little. "I can't. No matter where we go, you know what will end up happening. I–I just can't right now."

Her pinkie turned, and I hooked it with mine.

I said, "We can talk on the phone, how about?"

"Yeah. We can do that." Her voice dropped to a whisper.

"I'll call you tonight."

My pinkie tightened around hers.

"Okay."

Our conversation was done. We had a plan.

Neither of us moved away.

34

MARA

Tasmin showed up that night.

She hadn't called. Texted. She showed up, and as soon as I let her in, "Why wasn't I invited?"

I frowned. "Here?"

She dropped her bag on the couch, and waved her phone in the air. "This is what that's for. To call me. To invite me. You're going to a bar? You call a friend."

Oh.

"Today wasn't about you."

"Friends, Mara. Friends. Do I need to spell it out to you? You're going somewhere for a social activity, you call your other friends and let them know. Wanna know where I was? Taking care of Race because he's sick. Guess where I would've loved to have gone?"

"To the bar?"

Her hands went wide and moved in an arch. "Yes! You're getting it now."

I shut the door. "You want me to invite you the next time I go to the bar without your boyfriend?"

"No, but let me know. I'm fun. I'm game for anything. Literally. Or, well maybe not literally anything, but for a lot. And if you'd known Race was sick, then I could've told you how he's been a baby all day long." She went to my kitchen, and opened the fridge. "He swears it's food poisoning, but between you and me and everyone else, he's hungover. He and his roommate went out with some guys from one of his classes."

"Good to know." I watched as she helped herself to my juice, then my rum, and held it up to me.

She asked, "You want a drink?"

I had to smile, a little. "I'm good."

"Good." She brought it over and plopped down on the couch. "Okay. I heard Cruz beat the shit out of Kyle Ruiz, and it was over you. Tell me the truth and I'll tell you the rumors going around. Some of them are a doozy, but that's why you have me now. I'll weed out the truly insane ones, like the fact that you and Ruiz have a secret child that your mother kidnapped, and Cruz thinks it's his."

"I could see why he'd be upset."

She snorted, sipping her drink. "Me too, but you don't need to hear that one. Sit, Daniels. Spill. We're besties and it's time you start accepting it."

I sat. I spilled. I did not spill everything, but it felt good. I had to admit that.

Then, when she was leaving, she offered, "I can go downstairs and let Sky and Z know the truth, if you want? You're prime gossip channel material, and trust me, you're going to need a few of us on your side. If we know the deets, we can shut down the absolutely crazy pants ones."

"I'm okay."

My phone began ringing after that, and Taz gave a wave before leaving. "Okay. Offer's always there. Fair warning. I'm going to text you tomorrow. You will have to respond to it. Also what friends do. They text about just general stuff. Rarely are threats involved. Real threats. Take note."

I was answering as she shut the door. "Hey."

It was Cruz. "You got back okay?"

I settled back down on my couch, a blanket over my lap. My computer was still next to me, but since Taz's arrival, I hadn't reopened it. "I did. How's your head?"

"All fine."

"That's good."

"Yeah…"

I had to laugh. "We suck at phone calls."

He laughed. "I was just thinking that. Why are we doing this again?"

"You know why." My stomach clenched, and my phone dropped.

"We're doing the actual friend route? Like the kind where we talk and share how our day went? Shit like that?"

I was playing with the edge of my blanket. "I guess. Taz was just here and said kinda the same thing, but I don't really do this with anyone. I typically don't trust anyone for this stuff."

He was quiet. "That's kinda messed up."

I sighed, sinking lower in the couch. "I know. I blame my mom." That was half of a joke, half not.

"Has she reached out again?"

"No. I mean, yeah, but she's blocked. A weird number started calling this last week. They won't leave a message. I mean, they do, but it's just heavy breathing."

"That's creepy. Could be her other friend?"

"Could be anyone." I went back to playing with the edge of my blanket. "How's your sister? Your mom?"

"Uh, they're good." A brief pause. "Sorry, not used to being asked about them either."

"Is this new for both of us?"

"I think so. I mean, I never had a girlfriend in high school. If I had sex, it was just that, you know. And my friends, we talk about hockey or stupid shit. Sometimes they ask about you, but not in a nosey way. They aren't like that."

"I know. I appreciated how they all were quiet about me coming over. That doesn't always happen."

"A lot of girls like sex. Guys too. No one should be judging."

"You saying that is probably part of the reason you and I were doing what we were doing."

"Were?"

My breath halted in the middle of my chest. "I mean... You know what I mean."

"Right." He didn't sound like he did.

I sat up. "Look, with my mom how she is, I lived life keeping two worlds separate. My home life and my social life. That shattered in January, and now there's a weird mix where people in one world know about the other and I can't change that. I'd run like hell in the past if that had happened, but I'm not this time. I can't, but I also don't want to. I think, I *think* I need to do this."

"Mara." He said my name quietly.

"I just don't want to go back to bad habits, and you know, it's new to me and I want to be cautious. I know it doesn't make sense, but you know about my mom. You've met her. Zeke knows about her. He has my back. Taz, which is new. You. This is a big step for me. I feel weird even trying to explain this."

"You don't have to."

"I know, but–"

"For real. You don't have to. I get it."

I was almost shredding my blanket, picking at it. "The original agreement was that if we're having sex with each other, neither of us has sex with anyone else. I'm changing that so if you want to, you know. You can. With someone else."

Please don't.

He got quiet, again.

I clamped my eyes shut, so tight. Waiting.

"I have no plans for that, but... Thank you. I guess?"

He guessed?

Okay. We weren't a couple. That had never been on the table, so I got it. I understood. He was keeping his options open. That's what he was doing. Totally made sense.

"Right." From me.

"Yeah." From him. Still quiet.

"Okay. I'm going to go. Study. I wouldn't be surprised if we had a surprise quiz in abnormal psych tomorrow."

"Me too."

I stared at my phone, holding it.

I didn't end the call. I stared at my phone.

Twenty seconds later, he ended it from his side.

There was that.

35

CRUZ

I was smashed up against the plexiglass, and threw an elbow back, pushing the guy off me. He grunted. "You're toast, Styles. We gonna burn your ass up." The ref hit his whistle, skating over, waving to the penalty box.

It was a good call, but the crowd booed.

"Whatever."

"Penalty!" The ref went over to identify the actual call, but the guy, number 25, was already heading to the box.

Labrowski came over. "You okay?"

"Yeah." I turned to glare. It was our opposing team's enforcer who'd come after me. He'd been going at me hard all night long, ever since Atwater went after their team's lead scorer. Tit for tat, but I was getting sick of it.

"You good?" The ref came back, and I nodded, my ego more bruised than anything. He gave a nod and headed back to where he'd drop the puck. "Let's play then."

Labrowski patted my shoulder pad, nodding to the bench. "Line change."

Fuck. It was early, but we headed over, jumping in as the others climbed over the wall and got onto the ice. The game was going a few seconds later. “Styles.” Atwater tossed me a water. I caught it as I sat down, squeezing the bottle, the water spraying through the cage and into my mouth.

The coach came over, leaning down. “How are you doing?”

I eyed him, giving him a quick nod. “I’m fine.”

“He’s been going at you all night.”

I was aware. “I’m good, Coach.”

He gave another brisk nod before moving on, hitting me briefly on the shoulder with his coach’s tablet. Atwater sat in the space he just cleared out of and bent forward. “Don’t worry. Keys’ got your back.”

Our enforcer and his enforcer. They’d been trading their targets all night long. Sometimes we didn’t use our enforcer, but tonight was a different matter. The whole game was worse than the others, but Sacramento’s team was living up to their reputation. They were rough and *liked* to fight dirty.

Rules were stricter in college than in the NHL, but these refs didn’t seem aware of that. They were letting too much go.

We were in our third period. They were trying to go hard on me this first game, tire me out for the second game. I gritted my teeth, knowing I couldn’t let it work.

“Go!” It was time for another line change.

The third line went out. We had the fourth still, and then it’d be my turn.

A few minutes later, we were on the ice.

I didn’t wait around.

Skating over, I stole the puck and off I went. The harder they went at me, the harder I played. I needed to remind them of that fact.

Keys went to the left wing so I used his shield, moved around to their center. Around their center. Their defense was coming up, and I zipped around one, back through, and there was an opening.

Labrowski was behind me.

I deflected, hoping he'd catch this fast enough.

I feigned with my stick, but tapped the puck back with my skate, right to Labrowski, and GOAL!

He saw my pass, having seen it eighteen other times this season.

The goalie had moved with me, so the goal was wide open.

The light lit up, and as I was circling behind the net, their enforcer was glaring at me.

I glared right back.

Two minutes later, the end of the game sounded.

We'd won, by our teeth.

MY PHONE RANG as I was walking into the hotel. I'd stayed late for an extra soak and rubdown. I needed it. The coach told me to head in earlier the next morning for another one. I'd need that too, though the most I needed right now was sleep.

Still, I answered, going to the corner and sinking down in a chair. "Hey, Mom."

"How are you feeling?" She was chirpy, but concerned.

I winced. "My body feels like a lump of blue cheese, all curdled up into one big bruise."

"Blue cheese?"

I sank lower in my chair. "Blue cheese."

"He really went after you tonight."

"We're nearing playoffs. It's expected."

"I watch your games, Cruz. The other teams aren't like this one."

I was just so tired. My head felt heavy, and I rested back, closing my eyes. "I know, but I can't do anything except not let them win."

"They're trying to slow you down for tomorrow's game."

"Yeah."

She was quiet on her end for a beat. "I can't give you any advice, so I'm just going to tell you that I love you, Cruz. I have your back. Titi too."

"Thanks, Mom. I love you too. How's Titi?"

She was quiet again.

I sat up, some of the tiredness starting to fade. "Mom?"

"Oh." She laughed, a little abruptly and cut herself off. "Sorry. I–I wasn't sure if I should even tell you or when to tell you, but–"

I sat farther up. "Mom? What's going on with Titi?"

"Nothing like that. She's–she's perfect. She's fine. But Sabrina Burford reached out."

"What?" I clipped out. "She has no reason to be reaching out."

"Well, that's not totally true, Cruz." My mom was speaking in her mom-voice, all authoritative. "She expressed that she wants to make amends to Titi."

"She's got no–" I growled.

"She does, Cruz. She was in the car too–"

I shoved up from my chair and began pacing. "Yeah. She was in the car. She didn't stop–"

"You know how Sissy could be."

"I don't like this, Mom. I don't want Burford anywhere near Titi. She–"

"Titi's asked about her."

I stopped dead in my tracks. "What?"

This shit, right here.

I kept it separate. No one knew. Burford hadn't talked when she came to college, but why would she? It wasn't exactly a shining moment of glory for her, and the only other guy from our school was a science nerd but we'd never crossed paths. We didn't come from a large town, though I knew there were others who might've known. If I got into the NHL, one day this would get out, but when they saw Titi, I hoped the sight of her would stop any reporter from going forward with the story.

"She saw her at your game, and she asked about Sissy's friend. I..." A sob slipped out from her, her voice choking up. "I don't have it in me to lie to her. No matter anything that's happened, Titi still adores her big sister."

My other sister. The reason Titi was in her wheelchair.

"Mom." I sank back down to my chair, sitting on the edge. "I told Sabrina to stay away from both of you. She shouldn't have reached out."

"That's not your place."

"Mom–"

"Listen."

I knew my mom. I didn't need to see her to know that she was wiping the tears from her face as she forced out her take-charge Mom tone, a whole resolved look coming over her. What she said meant business, and I needed to pay attention.

She said further, "I've decided to let Titi see her, or let Sabrina see Titi. I talked to her on the phone. She is apologetic, but she always was back then. We–me–I couldn't handle hearing her out back then. Not that I had any anger or blame for her, but the pain was too much to go through at the time. I've come a long ways now, and Titi is asking. I wanted you to know so you weren't blindsided, but she's driving here tomorrow. She's going to have lunch with us."

"Mom, don't do this."

"I think she just needs to apologize to Titi herself. The girl sounded tortured on the phone. I–I don't want anyone to be like that."

"Don't–"

"Enough, Cruz. I've made up my mind." She added quickly, softening, "I love you, honey. You played a great game tonight. I know you'll do just as amazing tomorrow."

"Mom–"

She ended the call. Goddammit.

Fucking Burford. I told her to stay away.

I went through my phone and hit Burford's number.

It rang, then went straight to voicemail.

She'd declined my call.

A text came through a second later.

Burford: I know why you're calling, but I'm going to see her. I want to do what I can to make things right.

Me: Stay the fuck away from my sister and my mom. They don't need those doors opened back up. They don't need to be hurt more. Stay the fuck away, Burford.

Burford: Your mom agreed. I'm going.

I tried sending another text, but she'd blocked me.

Fuuuuuck.

I couldn't drive there myself.

I expelled a ragged breath and hit dial on Mara's name.

She answered a second later, loud music blasting from her side. "Hey!"

God. She sounded happy.

"Hey."

"Hold on. I can't hear you. Let me find somewhere–one second." She was at some party. Then, it went quiet and her voice came back louder. "Hey. Hi. Sorry. My roommates had people over to watch your game tonight. Please tell me you're going to beat the shit out of that guy from their team? I wanted to knee him in the balls. Taz has been offering to call in favors from people she knows. Don't ever ask her about those people. She'll go on and on about them for hours."

"You know–"

What was I doing here? *Christ.*

"Hey, what is it? You never call like this. What's going on?"

"It's nothing. For real. I'm–How are you?"

She didn't answer right away. "I'm good, but are you sure you're okay?"

"Yeah. It's nothing. Do you want to study on Sunday?"

"Sure." She said it slowly. "We can do that."

"Awesome. Talk to you then."

I hung up before I said anything more. Mara *wasn't* my girlfriend. I'd been about to treat her like she was. She had her own stuff, and I'd been about to lay even more on her.

Damn.

36

MARA

I had no clue what that phone call was about from Cruz, but the rest of the weekend was surreal.

In a good way.

Taz and Race hung out at my house Friday and Saturday night. Taz was chummy with Skylar and Zoe while Race was becoming buddy-buddy with Darren. Wade surprised everyone when he brought a girl over Friday. She was the same girl I recognized from hanging out with the hockey team. Angela. Seeing her and Wade together, I was wondering if maybe I'd been too hasty in my judgment call. She seemed nice, sweet. She was tiny, with long luscious black hair. Her and Zoe also knew each other from an art class, but she stuck with Wade the whole time.

They were super cute, holding hands. She blushed a lot.

Miles was the one most flabbergasted by her, or the image of Wade with her. He kept staring at them the whole weekend until Wade finally said something. The two had a private conversation, and Miles was all forced smiles when they came back.

Angela looked ready to die from mortification, but Taz decided to take her under her wing. Big shock there.

Now it was Sunday.

Cruz was supposed to come over to study. They won their Saturday game, but it'd been just as close as the first one. Everyone had watched at the house, though so many were distracted, but I noticed that Cruz played harder than he had the first night. When they won, words were exchanged between a couple of the opposing teams' guys and Cruz. They went at him first, and his teammates backed him up. No fists were thrown, just words. The refs got involved right away, but it looked intense. I wanted to ask him about it, but I was also a mess at just him coming over.

I was nervous and confused, and I had no idea what was going to happen today.

Knock, knock.

It was soft, but I recognized Cruz. Maybe it was the air. It settled over me before I went, opened the door.

He was there, a slight crooked grin on his face, his backpack over one shoulder. Jeans and a Grant West hockey T-shirt. His ballcap was pulled low over his face, and damn, I was always such a sucker for that look on him. His prominent jawline so square and rough-shaven.

"Hey."

"Hey."

I stepped back, feeling the room shrink in size as he came in behind me, his hand grazing mine as he went to set his bag on the couch.

My stomach fluttered.

He was glancing around, a restlessness to him, as he stretched.

I frowned. "You okay?"

"Yeah." He barely skimmed a look at me before going to the bathroom. "One sec."

My frown just deepened.

Cruz was being weird. I'd never gotten this vibe from him. Like he was distracted, and on edge. I didn't know what that was about, but hearing the toilet flush, my sink run, he came out a beat later. Still, barely a look at me.

He gestured to the kitchen area. "Mind if I make a drink?"

I held my hand out, giving him the go-ahead. "Help yourself." But he was already going for it, opening the fridge, grabbing one of my juices, putting it on the counter. He took a glass, poured himself a healthy dose of pineapple juice, then filled the rest with my vodka.

My eyes almost popped out. It was nearly half and half.

"Cruz." I took the vodka from him, and put the cap on it. "What's going on with you?"

"Nothing." He took his glass, going back to the living room and sinking down. "Let's study."

Oh no, no, no.

I went over, took his glass, and put it on the stand by the couch. Then I pushed him back. A part of me wanted to sink down, straddle him. The old me would've, but this was a new me. The real me, or the one I was trying to let out. And because I didn't want to go back to my old ways, I forced myself to perch on the side of the couch.

"Does this have to do with your game yesterday?"

"What?" Understanding dawned. "No. That's just hockey."

"Then what's going on?"

He raked a hand through his hair. "Nothing." Hunching forward, his arms moved ahead, his shirt tightening over his broad shoulders and back.

"Hey." I poked him in his biceps, his very sculpted biceps. "It's me here. I got that phone call from you on Friday. Remember? Remember who I am? You're the one person who's seen my dark shit. Share. What's going on with you?"

"I don't want to talk about it, Mara. Let's study." Then a

different look came over him, sensual and dark, and I could feel the air in the room shift. It was more sizzling, electrifying as he focused on me. He leaned back, raking his eyes over all of me, and going slow. Purposeful. My clit was contracting from the perusal, and I shifted, but he clocked my reaction, saw how I started to move my legs. A measured grin spread over his face. He leaned over, his hand going to my knee.

I jumped from the touch, even though it was just my knee, but my knee was close to my vagina and he knew he only had to move his hand north a little, following the path. He'd know I was already wet.

His thumb rubbed over my knee, holding still for the moment.

Tingles spread behind his caress.

"Unless you want to spend the day doing something else?" He knew how his touch was affecting me. "You still on the no sex thing with us? Holding firm?"

I gritted my teeth because it was like pushing through wet cement, but I reached for his hand and lifted it off me. I pushed up from the couch. "You're an ass." I stalked off to the kitchen.

"I was just asking."

He knew better. That was the point. He *so* knew better.

My chest was rising, heaving, and my pulse was racing. Goddamn him, I was pissed. I went back, my arms hugging myself something tight, more to keep myself in check. "Fuck you."

"That was the point." But he didn't sound mad. He was resigned as he got up and began reaching for his bag.

He was going to leave.

"Hey." I went over, grabbing it out of his hand. I held it behind me. "What was the point of that? Having you over is a big deal. We're friends now, right? Aren't we?"

He was standing, his hands in his jeans pockets, and his head fell back. "Yeah. I guess."

My nostrils flared. "You *guess*?"

"Yes. We're friends." His head jerked up, and his own nostrils flared. He was all intense. "We're more than friends. I'm not the one hiding from that."

I moved back a step but stopped.

His words were a punch, and I felt it.

"You don't get it." I was shaking my head.

"Then explain it."

"I have! This is new to me. You and me, we have sex today and I'll go back to my old ways."

"What's the old way? Fucking and running?"

I sucked in my breath. That was another hit from him, right to my sternum.

"That's right. That's what you do. You screw me and what? Don't take my calls for another week? Two this time? Cut me off? You fucking someone else, Mara? You're trying the friend route with me, but I know you. I know you need sex. You're not using me for that need so who you using? Miller? He finally get in there? Maybe your roommate. The swimmer. Saw him this morning at the campus coffee place. He looked like he got laid last night, he was all beaming and shit. That from you?"

"Shut up."

His eyes narrowed. "Make me."

This was the dick side of Cruz. Why was it coming out? Why now...? That Friday call.

"Why did you call me Friday?"

"Maybe I wanted a screw."

"You weren't here."

"Maybe I thought I could get you to drive to see me."

His words. So biting. They were clipped out. He was on edge, and he was pushing for a reaction.

It hit me. He was doing a Mara. He was trying to push me away. And when it all connected, a calmness settled through me, anchoring me. I wasn't going anywhere.

"I don't think this is about me. Did something happen with your family?"

He cursed, low and long, his head folding down.

"Your sister? Mom?" I moved closer.

He was shaking his head. "I don't want to talk about it. I– don't push this."

My throat swelled up. "*Is* it your sister?"

He let out a ragged breath. "Seriously, Mara. Don't."

I took a step toward him, but only one. "Cruz."

"Let's–" He was looking around, lingering on his bookbag, then his gaze went to my bedroom. He cursed under his breath again before looking up, pinning me with his gaze. They were so haunted. "Let's get out of here. How far's the beach? Let's go to the beach."

"The beach?"

"There's one an hour away. Let's go there."

He was talking about a beach that a lot of Grant West students used. Chances were high we'd see others there. "You sure?"

"Yeah." He nodded to his bag. "You and me. Let's just get out of here. Clear our heads. What do you say?" He glanced back to me. The haunted look hadn't left. It increased. He needed to clear his head. Not me, but... We were friends. I felt myself nodding. "Sure. Yeah. You and me."

He expelled a sudden burst of air. "Thanks. Uh, how long till you can go?"

I motioned to my room. "Ten minutes?"

"I want to run and grab something. I'll be back. Ten minutes?"

He took off right after, and I–well, okay then.

This is what friends did. We went to the beach when one of us needed to clear his head.

On the drive out, riding shotgun with the windows open and some Phillip Phillips on the radio, I was enjoying this. I was feeling a sort of contentment that I never knew I could feel. While I acknowledged that, there was a small, the tiniest, feeling of fear kickstarting inside of me, but the contentment was so massive.

I was leaning toward the good feeling.

I was going to lean all the way into it and stay there. I was going to enjoy the day because no matter how I sliced it, the beach was going to be awesome. Booyah.

Cruz didn't talk the whole way there, which was fine with me. I wasn't in the mood to talk either. I was riding the wave of feeling my 'positive and not panicky' feelings.

We were heading to Outpost Breakaway, a locals' place, and one of those locals was a guy in the Alpha Mu fraternity. Word got around the party group about this particular place, but I was hoping not many would be there when we showed up.

After stopping for food and booze, we pulled into the parking area. It wasn't overloaded with cars. A few trucks. My hope came true.

"I grabbed chairs and a blanket."

I was getting out, my backpack in hand. Cruz reached into the back of his truck for the groceries.

"You did?"

He nodded, hefting the cooler up and out. "And tossed a thing of wood back there if you wanted to stay for a bonfire."

He didn't wait around for my response, just grabbed two bags of groceries with his free hand and went down the trail.

Well, then. A beach bonfire was the best.

I loaded up my arms, going after him. Once we got to the beach, he picked a spot a bit away from the steps. Enough where people could pass by and we wouldn't hear their conversation, but they'd still see us.

He tossed everything down, going back, so I began

spreading out the blanket. The chairs were put up, and by then, he'd brought everything else. I was on the blanket, my abnormal psych book out, and I glanced up as he placed his book bag next to me. He was staring off at the water, that same haunted look on his face. I could see the shadows going over his face as he tightened his mouth, his jaw clenched.

I sat back, my arms circling my knees. "You sure you don't want to talk about it?"

His gaze met mine as he sat down, and such sadness looked back at me, taking my breath. He shook his head, blinking, and looking away. "No. I just want to forget all about it."

He settled down, pulling out his own textbook.

My phone began buzzing as texts rolled in.

Miles: Where are you? Library?

Gavin: Beers tonight! Where are you?

Wade: That quiz you thought we were having last week, it's happening tomorrow. Want to do a study sesh?

Taz: I'm at the library with Skylar and Zoe. Darren is here too. Where are you?

Miles: You're not with our roommates. I just found them. Headed to the hockey house. You there?

I had more texts coming through, but felt Cruz's attention.

I moved to silence my phone, but as I did, my screen flashed. One last text.

Dad: How are you, sweetie? I'm coming through Grant West this week. Give me a call. Let's do dinner.

A sudden knot formed in my throat. My dad coming through where I go to college? This didn't happen. It wasn't how our relationship worked. I didn't believe in coincidences. He wasn't phrasing it that he was coming to visit me, but dinner. Something was happening. Something Mom-related.

I changed my mind. I turned off my phone.

THREE HOURS LATER, our sandwiches were out and a bag of chips was between us. Cruz had mixed both of us some drinks. I'd also crammed for another abnormal psych quiz. Cruz, I didn't know what he was studying, but he was quiet the whole time.

It felt nice. The whole day. The sounds of the waves.

"We should talk."

I jumped, spilling my drink, then laughed.

"What?"

I shook my head, dabbing at my legs. "I was just thinking that I liked that we hadn't been talking."

"Oh." He frowned, his knees bent, spread out. His book sat between them, but he was lounging forward, his arms loosely resting on his knees. "I mean, we're doing the friends thing, right? Friends talk. We should talk."

I closed my textbook, and leaned back, my drink in hand. "You talk."

He glanced up to me, his eyebrows pinching down.

"Friends tell each other what's going on with them." I took a sip, giving him a *pointed* look.

He snorted, fighting a grin before looking back to his textbook. "Real subtle, Daniels."

"Last names." I whistled. "Have we progressed or regressed with that?"

He laughed again, before letting out a soft sigh. "Friends. Right."

I took another sip. "Friends."

"You asked about my towels, long time ago. You remember?"

I frowned. "Yeah?"

"Where'd you get this thing?"

He laughed, laying back. "No personal questions, Daniels."

"I didn't know that was a personal question. My bad."

"It is because my sister made it."

I remembered, giving the blanket another glance. It looked like the towel that day. "What–that was a towel. This is a blanket?"

"They're the same. This is just the bigger size. They're called beach towkets." He grinned, looking out at the ocean. "That was her word for them. We went to the beach a lot. Our family. She started making them one summer, and fuck, if I should hate them, but I don't. It's the one thing from her that I can't bring myself to hate."

I frowned. "Your little sister used to make these?"

He shook his head, leaning back and putting his hands behind him. He stretched his legs out. He never stopped looking at the ocean. "Not that sister."

Two sisters? I was still frowning, but I also shut up. This was his moment, his time to talk.

"Her name was Sarah. She was best friends with Burford. Titi called her Sissy, calls her Sissy."

I almost twitched from my reaction. Sabrina? The same girl I had a smackdown with in the library? The first time I'd met Cruz?

He laughed to himself, looking down. "I hate that girl, but that day, Miles invited me to your table. You were there. Gavin. And her. I walked up, saw her, and started to turn around, and then you spoke, and fuck, man. *Fuck.* Just your voice made me hard." He flashed me a grin, a wry look in his eyes, but he stared at me steadily. "I stayed because of you that day. Burford didn't call you a cunt because Miller was flirting with you that day. She was pissed because she could tell *I* wanted you."

"Are you serious?"

He nodded, going back to staring at the ocean. "All cards on the table, I figured I should fess up to that part."

"She wanted you?"

He shook his head. "No. She wanted my attention. Since..." He looked down, swallowing again before lifting his chin once more. "I seriously hate that girl, but it's not even because of her. It's because of what she was a part of that day. She was in the car. Sarah was driving. Titi was in the back. Titi–she was obsessed with Sarah and Sabrina. Obsessed. I know I should blame Sarah, but..." A harrowed expression crossed his face. "If it hadn't been for Burford, Titi wouldn't have been in the car. I... How fucked up is it that I'm more mad Titi lives how she lives because of that accident and not that I lost my other sister? Sarah died. She... She was messed up. Burford and her were best friends. I have no idea how they met. Sarah was a year younger, but they were. Sarah wasn't the queen bee, but she kinda was at the same time. Not that I give a fuck about that shit, but just laying it all out. Sarah was popular, but she was such a bitch. Normally she didn't give Titi two fucks. She'd just ignore her and go on about her selfish life. Not that day. Sabrina was nice to Titi when she was around and it's because of Sabrina that Titi was in that car. Only goddamn reason Sarah pretended to be okay with it. That car accident." He cursed, low and savagely, shaking his head and his hands balled up into fists. "Sarah died, and Titi lost her chance at a normal life."

I was aching, wanting to go to him.

"You asked me how I knew how to handle your mom?" He looked my way now, his whole face twisted up. "It's because that's how Sarah was."

I was bowled over, but I wasn't at the same time.

"I know I should miss my sister, and I know she was sick. They gave her so many fucking diagnoses, but man," his voice grew hoarse, "here's the worst shit ever. I'm glad she's gone." He looked my way, that same stricken look coming over him. Bitterness flashed in his eyes before he turned away again. "I can't remember a time when life was fine at the house. No peace. No quietness. Just always fucking Sarah, and her problems, and whatever she decided to hate the second she got up for the day. She was never happy. She was never–and she was vengeful. If I had a good day, and she didn't, she'd break something in the house and blame it on me. Mom was scared of her. Titi doesn't remember her the way she was.

"To Titi, Sarah was loving and the best big sister ever. Every time she says something, Mom and I just give each other a look and don't say anything. I mean, fuck. My God. She's been gone a year and four months and I still can't bring myself to remember the good times. Swear to fucking God, I don't remember any. I've tried. I hate that I feel this way, that I still loathe her, even when she's gone. I think there was one Christmas where she was nice, one fucking holiday. And by her being nice, she didn't throw a temper tantrum that the whole day wasn't about her. I hate my sister. She's dead. I *should* be mourning her. I was told that when someone dies, you automatically remember the good because that's what we should remember. Not the bad. The bad doesn't matter anymore. Just the good, but not me. Not for her. I can't remember shit, and I get mad about that, that I can't because fuck me.

"There should be something. Right? She couldn't have been bad all the time. What kind of brother am I, that I'm unable to do that? Everyone thinks I'm this easy-going guy. Jokes on them. I think of her and I'm relieved she's gone. That's the twisted shit inside me. And Burford went to see Titi yesterday."

Now it made sense.

Now the dots were connecting.

Now I knew what we were doing here.

I reached over, my hand sliding into his.

"I have no idea how the visit went. I can't bring myself to call and ask. I don't want to hear that it went well. That Titi lit up, seeing Burford because of course she would. She'd be so happy, not having any clue that Burford's the reason she's half paralyzed. And I know, in my head, I know that's wrong to think. Sarah crashed the car, for whatever fucking reason, and trust me, some switch flipped in her. Burford's account, the eyewitness accounts. Even a cop saw it. It was on camera. My sister was driving along. Everything was fine, and you can see in the car that Burford is smiling, laughing at something. She turns around to say something to Titi, and Sarah got this look. She got all hard and vengeful. I know that look. Seen it all my life, almost every day, and she yanked the wheel. She drove head on into a semi. Swear to this day. I can't shake the feeling that she wanted to kill Burford or Titi that day, but she didn't realize she might go too. I can't shake it. Burford walked away with barely a scratch. Semi tried to turn, save them, but because he did, he hit Sarah head-on, and Titi was right behind her."

He drew in a breath.

"I can't figure out what I'm pissed about, that Burford wants to make amends? That Titi will love that? Or fuck, because I think that in some way, of both of them making amends, that Sarah's going to be let off the hook? She did that. She wanted to hurt herself, or Burford, or Titi. They'll heal and move on and what? No more blame put on Sarah? Fuck that. I know that's what they'll do. Burford blames herself, feels bad about the whole thing, but she never knew Sarah for who she really was. Not really. Titi, she's all good. Sarah was all bad." He turned my way, his whole face so hard. "I knew how to handle your mom because I grew up handling someone just like her. My own sister got off easy by dying. How fucked am I, that I think that? This is the guy you chose to fuck." He shook his head, shoving up to his feet. "I can't–I need some time." He took off, heading down to the beach.

I let him go, because I understood.

I let out a small sigh and reached for my phone, turning it on.

More texts buzzed through, but I went to my dad's and hit call.

He picked up right away. "Hey, honey. How are you?"

"If you're coming to town because something new has happened with Mom, I don't want to hear it."

He was quiet on his end, and that told me he *was* coming because of her.

I'd made my decision. "I'm done, Dad. I'm done with her."

"Honey. Mara. She's your mother–"

"No. She's never been my mother. I have no idea what it's like to have a mother, but I do know what it was like having a father. I wanted to call and thank you for that."

"Mara, this doesn't sound like you. Are you okay? Did something happen?"

I closed my eyes. It'd been so long where it was about me, not her. I smiled to myself, looking down at the towket with a tear in my eye. "Thank you, Dad. But I don't want to hear about whatever new is going on with her. I'm done."

I ended the call.

Turned the phone off.

And sat there, watching the ocean waves, waiting for Cruz to come back.

37

CRUZ

My phone was ringing. All my roommates knew I'd taken a beach day, so it wouldn't be them. Then I looked and had to laugh. "Hey, Mom."

She was quiet for a second. "You sound upset."

I didn't deny it. I didn't confirm it either.

I gripped the phone tighter. "You sound happy."

She sniffled. "I am. It was–it was a good day, yesterday. You won both games and..."

I looked down, saying gruffly, "I don't want to hear about it."

Her voice got quiet. "Titi was over the moon. I videoed some of it, but she wouldn't stop smiling when Sabrina came over. She was still beaming this morning. She crashed last night. She was just exhausted, but it was a good day."

"Mom..."

She kept on, her voice getting a little louder, "Sabrina told me how you've been treating her."

"Mom–"

"That's not the son I raised. You don't tell people to leave others the '*expletive*' alone. You don't glare at them or treat them rudely. Do you hear me?"

"Mom."

"I said, 'Do you hear me?' You know how I raised you. I need to hear that you know how I raised you."

Like a general giving her orders. I almost smiled at that. "I hear you, Mom. You didn't raise me to be like that."

"If you see Sabrina, I'm not saying you need to be friends with her, but don't be mean. She is not the one who caused the accident. You can't be angry at her for being kind, for making Titi laugh. She's not a bad girl."

I grunted. "She called a friend of mine a cunt."

She was quiet for a beat. "Again, I'm not saying you need to be friends with her. Everyone has some faults, but you, Cruz Corinthos Styles, you shine even brighter."

"I still hate her, Mom." Those words ripped out of me.

She drew in a sob from her end. "Don't say that. She's–"

"I hate her. And I'm tired of feeling guilty about hating her. She wasn't good."

"Everyone has good in them. She had struggles–"

"She tried to kill Titi. She wanted to hurt Burford. She thought she'd be the one to walk free–"

"Maybe she did." My mom's voice was wrangled, and I heard another low sob.

"What?" I stilled.

"Maybe she did, walk free. Maybe she did."

"What are you talking about?"

"I know some don't believe in them, but I saw a medium."

I let out a curse. "What?"

"Yeah, but listen, Cruz. Your sister came through, and she's sorry for what she did. The medium, and I believe her because she brought up specifics that even you don't know about. Sissy talked about how in that moment, she was angry and she reacted. She didn't think it through, but she said it all worked out how it was supposed to."

"Titi was supposed to be paralyzed from the waist down?

I'm sure Sarah would say that that was supposed to happen that way. Of course. I believe the medium too. That's total typical Sarah right there."

"Cruz." Her voice dipped low. "That's not what I'm saying."

I wanted to hurl this phone into the ocean. Maybe it was karmic timing for Mara to be going through her healing process, but dammit. I would've loved to lose myself in her for an entire week. Stop the thoughts, stop the hurting. Stop the ghost of one particularly selfish bitch.

"It's why I let Sabrina see Titi. The medium said that she was struggling, needed closure, and she was right." She began sniffling again. I heard the sob through her voice. "Sabrina walked in, and she looked so wrecked. I could see it in her. It's… It's what I see in you too."

"Mom, do not push me to go see some psychic. I don't believe in that shit."

"You don't curse at your mother."

My head jerked upright, from where I had folded down. "Sorry."

"I'm not saying you need to see a medium, though I believe her, but it was very healing to connect to Sissy. She's on the other side. The medium said that when the soul leaves the body, all the emotions and struggles we go through here, are left *here*. The soul goes to the other side and it's in its most pure state. Sissy said she didn't mean to hurt Titi, but she reacted and in that moment, she was tired of feeling and thinking all the negative and hateful things she did. She was explaining that it was like she was trapped in her own body. She didn't want to think or do the things she did, but it's like she couldn't stop herself. She felt paralyzed inside herself at times. That's what was coming through the medium, and–" She let out a deep sob. "I believe her, Cruz. I–my God, I do. Sissy would do something mean and I'd see a flash of remorse right after, but then her face would go blank. When you said she thought she'd walk free, how do we know that's not what happened in the end? She's free now. She's still my baby. Maybe you hearing this, you can let go of some of your anger too?"

God. I felt so fucking raw. My voice grated out, "She hurt Titi. I can never forgive her for that."

"Oh, baby. You carry so much anger, and I know. I *know* you. You tuck all that down, bury it, and go and you keep shining on the ice. I know you might not want to hear this, but Sarah had a message for you. Do you want to hear it? I won't push it on you if you don't want to hear it."

A message? Through a medium? From my *dead* sister?

"I don't think so, Mom."

"When you're ready then. I have it written down. Maybe I can mail it and you can open it when you want to? How about that?"

I didn't answer. I had nothing good to say right now.

She murmured, "If I send it, you need to promise not to throw it away or tear it up. I want that promise right now."

I was still silent. Nothing good to say, nothing at all. I kept my mouth shut.

She sighed. "You'd be doing it for me. I brought her into this world, and I couldn't help her. You think about that? I've got one gone that I couldn't save, another with storms tearing himself up, and another that's a beacon of joy though she was hurt the most. You promising not to throw away or tear up this message would go a long way for appeasing your mother's guilt. When you hurt, I hurt."

"Jesus, Mom."

"Don't swear."

Her reply was so automatic and instant. It was reflex. I had to grin at that. "Yeah. Send it. I promise to keep it. I won't promise to read it, but I won't destroy it."

"All I need, honey. I love you so much. You know that, right? Titi too."

"Titi the mostest."

She laughed. "The mostest of the hostess. We'll call later in the week. Titi is going to Skate World so we should have some good pictures for you. Maybe we can video call you when we're there."

"I'd like that. I'll clear it with Coach if I'm at practice."

We ended the call, but I took a moment. The ocean was in front of me, but I wasn't seeing it. I was back there, with my mom, knowing she was probably going over to hug Titi right about now. Titi, man. She was the best of all of us.

And Sarah hurt her.

38

MARA

Cruz came back, dropping down to lay back on the blanket. The air around him felt different. He rolled his head, looking up to the sky. His one knee went up, his other leg extended out. “How long are you going to do this friends with no benefits stuff?” He flashed me a wolfish grin. “Because, gotta say, I’m missing the fuck out of you. Pun intended.”

And just like that, my body was an inferno.

I scowled at him, moving away, though my body wanted to do the opposite. “Dude.”

“God. Don’t ‘dude’ me. Barclay dudes me. Atwater dudes me. My teammates, yes. My brothers, but not you. I’m not a ‘dude’ to you.” He got quiet. “I’d like to be your man. That’s what I’d like to be.”

My gaze shot back to him, and my tongue got heavy. Real heavy.

My heart started pounding.

A whole different feeling slammed into me. Yearning. A desperation. I wanted that too, and my mouth opened.

I was leaning toward him—“*Please* tell me we’re in time to see live porn.”

The voice was abrupt, jarring, and not wanted.

I blinked, dazed, still in the trance Cruz's statement brought over me. It took another second before it clicked who was heading our way.

Cruz stood up, his own scowl in place. "Shut the fuck up, Carrington. Keep it moving."

"What's your problem, Styles?"

My stomach fell, as I stood.

"Angela. What are you doing with them?"

Flynn Carrington was here, and he wasn't alone. Angela, Wade's Angela, was with them, along with three more guys. Flynn was wasted. Stumbling. His hair was all messed. His eyes were dilated, and enlarged, and his clothes were in disarray. His shirt was wrinkled, a corner torn off. His board shorts were dirtied with grass stains, and he was swinging around a bourbon bottle that still had a third left to go.

He stopped, his body swaying forward, and he held up his hands, the liquor swishing around in the bottle from the motion. "She's with us. We're hanging out. Having fun. What, Styles? You think you're too good for us? You think you're too good to hang out with us." His eyes got mean and narrowed. They slid to me. "I was serious about the public porn."

I didn't look at Cruz, but I *felt* him.

Carrington's friends also took notice of him, moving back an inch.

I held my breath.

A whole new stillness came over Cruz, his eyes were locked on the target. Every inch of him was rigid and alert. He was primed, seeing his prey stumbling around in front of him. Waves of danger were rolling off him. The hairs on the back of my neck stood up, and I was tempted to take a step back myself.

"You wanna rethink what you just said, you piece of privileged frat brother shit?"

Cruz wasn't wasting time.

Flynn blinked, that mean look just doubling. He whipped his bottle at Cruz, who stepped aside. It hit the rocks behind us. Flynn's head bobbed back before he spat out at the same time, starting for us, his arm raised, "No. Fuck you, Styles! You're nothing, but a–"

He didn't even get to say his insult.

I jumped as Cruz was on him, and by on him, he was *on him*. He went at him, his hand going to Flynn's throat. He hit him in the back of his leg. As Flynn toppled, Cruz went with him, but he wasn't choking him. Cruz took Flynn's arm. He flipped over, bringing Flynn with him, and tossed his body across the beach.

Cruz was after him once again.

He was moving so fast. Flynn's friends stared, their mouths open.

I cursed but rushed forward and grabbed Angela. I pulled her away, just as Flynn tried to fight back. He threw a punch, but Cruz laughed. He *laughed*, as he dodged, grabbing Flynn's arm and he did a whole-body twist again, sending Flynn in the complete opposite direction.

I got it then, what he was doing.

He was using the beach and the motion to fuck Flynn up, but he wasn't hitting him. There was no physical normal confrontation where his friends would've instinctually moved in to pull him off and then it'd be four against one, or two because I would've waded in no matter my size or gender. This way, the guys didn't know what to do and Cruz was landing punches, but he was doing it in a way where no one knew how to handle him.

He knew what he was doing.

I let out a breath, some relief lightening my chest as Cruz grabbed Flynn and lifted him up. They were by a cliff wall, and he slammed Flynn against it. They were far enough away so we couldn't hear what was being said, but Flynn was struggling, trying to get free.

Cruz was still again, eerily almost frozen like a statue until slowly, inch by inch, he leaned in, his face next to Flynn's. He was saying something, and whatever it was, Flynn stopped fighting.

Cruz waited, another beat, until he stepped back.

Flynn dropped to the sand, a hand rubbing at his throat, as he lifted his head to look at Cruz.

Cruz said one more thing. I strained to hear but couldn't. The crashing waves seemed perfectly timed. He looked toward me, his head jerking, and he took a full step backwards, dragging in a breath. He started for me.

Flynn's friends didn't run to him. They seemed frozen until Cruz got closer. They stumbled back a step. One went running to Flynn.

Cruz stared at me, his chest heaving. He was fighting for control. I saw the rage simmering in his gaze, and moved into action. I began putting our things away, as fast as possible. Cruz didn't move. His hands were in fists, pressed tight against his legs, and he was staring at me.

I paused, holding his gaze.

I was his lifeline right now.

I approached, slowly, a hand up. "Cruz," I murmured.

"I want to fucking—" His voice grated out. "One look from him. One–I want to turn around and *end* him."

I'd seen Cruz fight on the ice. He never fought in a clear and obvious way. You couldn't in college hockey, but he still did. The other teams felt it and especially when he was pissed off. He turned into another being in the rink, and I saw him go after Ruiz at the bar, but this guy, *this* Cruz was another beast entirely.

Angela was sniffling next to us.

"What are you doing here?" I asked her.

"I didn't know. I didn't–I wasn't thinking."

Dread lined my insides.

Flynn turned to walk backwards, his smirk a half grin. "You should know that more than anyone, Kressup. How's your girl? Oh wait..." The grin was gone, and it was just a smirk in its place.

Wade tensed. "You mean Rosa, the girl I liked before she woke up in your bed, naked and no memory how she got there? That girl? Who was so devastated after her medical exam that she quit school and moved back home?"

He picked her on purpose.

I looked at her more closely, but Cruz, he couldn't. His eyes were only on me, like he couldn't... A different foreboding sensation began to flood me. Cruz saw something I hadn't. He was pissed, but he snapped and–I turned, more fully, taking in Angela in a whole different light.

She was still crying, but there were old tears dried on her face.

Her shirt was torn. Grass stains on her shorts and on her legs.

Her hair was a wreck.

There was blood at her mouth. Swollen eye. Bruised cheek.

Horror filled me.

She had one nail chipped. One nail was missing. The side of her entire hand was swelling up even as I looked at it, and it was bright red.

She had one sandal, one. The other was gone.

There was more. More scrapes. More bruises.

And she kept sobbing during my perusal.

"Babe," Cruz choked out.

I swung my head to him.

His mouth was white around his lips. "I need to get the fuck out of here."

I jumped, grabbing what I could in a mad dash. Books. Bags. Phones. Keys. Wallets. Then I heard myself repeating, my heart now pounding in the bottom of my throat, "Truck. Get to your truck. Now."

"Styles!" Flynn shouted from farther down the beach. His friends had moved him in the opposite direction, which was smart of them. "I'm going to fuck you up, Styles! You are done. You hear me? DONE!"

Thoughts flashed through me. College. Flynn. His frat. His power. His father. And Cruz. His mother. Titi. What he told me about his other sister. He was the hockey star, but careers could be sidelined before the spotlight found them.

Flynn would do that. I had no doubt in my mind. He would do everything he was now saying he was going to do.

No.

I couldn't let that happen.

I dropped everything. They landed back on the sand with a thud. "Cruz, go to the truck." I tossed the keys his way.

He caught them. "What are you doing?"

"Go to the truck." I was watching Carrington now, not fully knowing what I was going to do, but knowing I had to do something. "Go. Please. Just, go."

"I'm not leaving you here. No–"

"Cruz!"

"No," he repeated it, but he said it quietly.

He was more under control, but not me. I was starting to lose it.

"STYLES!"

My heart contracted, once. How Flynn was screaming, if he got loose, he would try to murder him. He was straining against his friends, trying to get free. They were holding him, all three of them, but Flynn wasn't feeling anything. He wasn't getting tired. Whatever was in him, was making him merciless.

Angela had both of her fists pressed to her mouth, tears sliding down her face. Her entire body was shaking. And then I went back to Cruz, who was still only watching me. His jaw clenched, and his eyes narrowed. "What are you thinking?"

"He'll get away with it." I spared Angela another look. "They always get away with it."

I looked back at Cruz, who frowned. "What are you thinking?"

"I have no idea." But I was reaching for my phone, pulling it out of my pocket. I just knew that this would be covered up. He had three friends. Four to our two? I wasn't counting Angela because who knew what headspace she was in.

"Mara." Cruz moved toward me.

I moved back, switching to video, and I hit record.

A part of me hated myself, that I was doing this, but the other part–he couldn't get away with it. He just couldn't.

"Angela," I spoke up, quietly.

Flynn was still screaming in the background.

"Wha–what?" She hiccupped, focusing on me.

I motioned to my phone. "Can I record you?"

She frowned, blanching. "Why?"

"So there's proof."

She held my gaze, thinking.

She knew what I said was true. She knew it, but I waited, holding my breath.

Her head jerked forward. "Yeah."

I knelt beside her, and hit the light on so I could really see her. "Who did this to you tonight?"

The question burst a dam. Her tears tripled and she folded over.

I swung the camera around, spotlighting Flynn, who was still screaming before I moved it back to her. I sat down, crossed my legs. "You have to say it. Say it once."

She was nodding, but she couldn't talk. She was gasping around the sobbing.

"Mara, maybe–"

"No." I seared him with a look, keeping my camera on Angela. He didn't get it. He just didn't. She was still in it. She wasn't out of it. Right now. Her words were the most powerful right now. And maybe, just maybe, she could use this later.

Maybe.

"Angela–" I started to prompt her, but she cut me off.

She bent over, but her words came out. She told her story.

39

CRUZ

My hand was hurting, but it was worth it. We were at a local police station. Angela was talking to a detective. It hadn't been what I'd initially thought. I was thinking the worst, but as Mara recorded, Angela told a story about how Flynn had been aggressive, though he stopped when she said no. He just hadn't stopped soon enough. They'd been at a party at someone's nearby house, another Alpha Mu brother, and she lost her phone. She went with Flynn because he'd been charming and she thought he was sweet, despite his reputation.

They were making out, and he got too rough. She said no, he pushed. She said no again, he pushed again. He hit her. That's when she began screaming no, and *then* he yielded. After that, she didn't know what to do and they met up with his friends. She thought she'd be safe since his friends were there, but instead of going back to Grant West, they went to the beach.

She said, "We were leaving, but he got a text from someone. Then he said we were going to the beach. I didn't know what to do. I don't know this area."

Mara heard that, and her whole face went flat. We were

thinking the same thing. Carrington was told we were at the beach.

She came over to me now. "She called her roommate. She's coming to pick her up."

I settled more firmly against the wall behind me. "She hangs out at the house. Labrowski was best friends with her brother. And now this? I stopped myself, but Labrowski, he won't."

She moved closer to me, her hand resting on my chest, falling to my pants and her fingers tucked in. Holding on. It appeased me a bit. But the thought of what he did? And the worst part: "He's going to get away with it."

She moved, turning her back to the police station. It was just the two of us in our corner. I rested a hand on her hip, drawing her closer. I needed to touch her. My head folded down. Hers lifted, and she said softly, "Don't say that."

"It's true, and you know it. His dad is a senator. He's going to get special treatment, and he'll have some fancy lawyer come in and then what?"

She held her phone up, her eyes looking almost dead. "Then I leak this."

My hand tensed over her hip. "I thought the police wanted that."

"They do. I'm supposed to send it to them, but I'm keeping a copy. I don't care if it's wrong."

"That's Angela's recording more than yours."

"I know." Some of the dead look lifted, just slightly. Some humanity came back to her. "I won't do anything without her blessing. I'm not like that, but Cruz, I did this for you too. He's going to target us. You know that. You and me. He was screaming how he was going to end you. Him? I take that seriously."

"Cops know that too. It's documented, and we have proof."

"Yeah." She turned and leaned her whole side into me, both

of us watching Angela. I moved my hand up, my arm curling around her shoulders and I held her tight.

Then we waited.

HER ROOMMATE SHOWED up a little over an hour later. There wasn't a lot of conversation after that. Mara went over. She talked a little with the roommate before they left.

The detective had come over earlier too, filling us in on what he could. It wasn't our case, we couldn't know everything. He did promise that they had already been speaking to Flynn. He sounded genuine so we'd see what the fallout would be, if there was any.

That's when they questioned me, saying Flynn was claiming I attacked him on the beach. I gave them a full rendition, and they asked, "He threw a bottle at you first? Threatened you and raised his arm, coming at you?"

"He started for me first."

That went a long way, and they said with the bottle, threat, and bodily movement coming at me, that he incited the violence first. Once I heard those words, a cement truck of stress lifted off me. Then I remembered Angela and it came right back down.

We were free to go after that. Once in my truck, I reached for my phone, bringing up Labrowski's number.

"What are you doing?"

"I'm calling Labrowski. He needs to know."

"No. That has to be her decision–"

"Mara." The emotions about my sister, the phone call with my mom, being with Mara and not being able to touch her, and then Flynn, Angela... I sighed. "I get your loyalty is to her in this situation, but I'm telling Labrowski. I'm on his team. We live in the same house. He's my boy. If it were you, I would never forgive the roommate and teammate who knew and didn't tell me."

She let out her own sigh. "Just–don't tell him the specifics."

"Trust me." I didn't wait. I hit the call button.

After three rings, he picked up, sounding groggy, "What the fuck, Styles? You better not be calling from jail. You know what time–"

"Shut up for a second."

He went silent. Then, rustling sounds came over, and he asked, way less groggy now, "What is it? You okay?"

"Listen." I was staring at Mara as I spoke, "Daniels and I are at a police station, but not in Grant West–" He started to talk. I said over him, "We're fine. I'm fine, but man, Angela."

"Angela was there?"

"Listen to me right now, I can't be the one to tell you, but I'm letting you know, she's probably almost back to Grant West by now. You need to go to her. Okay? You hearing me?"

"Fuck! Fuck! Yeah. Jesus. Okay. You're okay?"

"I'm okay."

"It's *late*. Where are you?"

"Don't worry about us. Call Angela. Okay?"

"Okay. Jesus, okay. Let me know when you're back."

I was so tired and sore. My body had stiffened up from waiting at the station.

Mara said, "There might be a small inn here. We could stay here and go back in the morning?"

I gave her a look. "You really think either of us could get any sleep in an inn around here?"

Her mouth flattened, and her shoulders dropped dramatically. "We'll need coffee then."

I drove to a nearby gas station, filling up the tank. Mara went inside, but came out and met me as I was going in. She had a bag of food hanging from her arm and her hands were filled with two coffee cups. She raised one. "For you."

I nodded. "Thank you. I'm going to take a quick piss."

"I got water as well. Gatorade."

"Thanks. Here." I turned and hit the unlock button.

"Thanks."

I moved past but turned and walked backwards. She did the same, watching me and for a moment, both of us paused. There was no one else here, except one gas attendant inside. We were in the middle of fucking nowhere, had gone through what we went through, and she never broke down. Not once. She stayed and she fought for me. She'd been my anchor when every part of me wanted to go back and finish the job with Carrington. Then she took care of me, thinking ahead, fighting back in her way, and she was there for Angela. She stayed for Angela, the whole time when we went to the police station.

Mara was the one who talked Angela into pressing charges now, not later.

She did that, and even though Mara was saying she did that for me and for Angela, there'd been something about her, like she was too familiar with the whole process.

The thought hadn't fully formed in my head until now, but it'd been there. In the back of my mind, ruminating. Now I couldn't let it go.

She saw the question in my eyes. Her chin lifted. Her face cleared of all exhaustion. She knew something was coming from me, and my God, but she wasn't even flinching. She was facing it head-on.

"That ever happen to you? What he did to Angela, or what I thought he'd done to her?"

She blinked, once. A stricken look flashed in her gaze, but then it was gone after she blinked a second time. "Once, yeah. When I was too young to know anything."

Everything in my body clenched up. She'd been hurt, and I hadn't known her then. It was still there. It still hung over her. She was still carrying it.

"What happened?"

She lowered her head, shaking it, slowly. Her fingers tightened around the coffee cups, but then she looked back up, and a whole different expression was there. It looked deep, tortured. "I don't carry emotional scars from what the guy did. I went to therapy, worked that out of me, but it's what my mom did that hurt the worst."

"What'd she do?"

"She made it about her. It's what she always does." She rolled her eyes, before looking away. "Can you hit the unlock button again?"

She started walking back, and I hit the button. I waited until she got inside.

Until she got comfortable, turned to face me, and I hit the lock button back again.

People were precious and Mara, I was realizing how precious she was.

Maybe more than she wanted to know.

40

MARA

We got to Cruz's house so late. Or hella early in the morning.

After he parked, I got out, my bag in hand and circled the truck, but he took it from me. We gave each other a long look, but no words were shared. He carried both our bags inside.

Atwater, Barclay, and a couple other guys were up, all sitting on the couch and doing nothing.

Cruz had opened the door for me. I went in first, but he came around me, his hand touching the small of my back. "What are you guys doing?"

Atwater had bags under his eyes. His hair looked as if he'd been running his hand through it. "Waiting on Labrowski. He was supposed to let us know if everything was okay."

Barclay was on his phone. "And we're supposed to let him know when you got here."

Atwater asked, "What's going on? I've never seen Labrowski act like he did this morning. He let out a yell or something, woke half of us up. Tore out of here and yelled that we needed to let him know when you got back. That's it. Radio silence until you just walked in. You've been at the beach until *now*?"

Cruz's mouth tightened, and he started to shake his head. His hand rested more firmly on my back, urging me forward a little bit. "Give him some time. If he comes back, he's not going to want to talk to anyone, but guys, he might not come back till later today. Best thing, go to bed."

"What the fuck!" Barclay shot up to his feet, staring at his phone before he showed his screen. "Carrington was arrested by Outpost. It's–"

One of the other guys shoved up too. "It's all over my social media. It's saying sexual assault."

The other guy stood with him, looking at his phone too. "Does it say against who?"

Atwater and Barclay both looked at us, gazes pondering before slowly moving to me.

I held up my hands. "It wasn't me."

"Labrowski..." Barclay was putting the pieces together. "That's where you guys were. Only one person I know who'd Labrowski would light out of here for. Say it wasn't Angela, man. Say it!"

Cruz didn't say it. "Let it go."

"Fuck! Fuck, Cruz! Where's he at? Fucking Alpha Mu–"

"Stop!" I held a hand up and everyone went silent. All eyes went to me. This was getting out so fast. Who would've released that already? I doubted it was Carrington or his friends. Angela, no way. Labrowski? I doubted that. The only others who knew– except her roommate. It wasn't Cruz or I, but her roommate would've known or might've known, depending on what Angela told her.

I said, "It's so late. Trust me, everything that needed to happen, happened. If it's not out who it was, leave it alone for now. Okay? Just, trust me. You want to help? The best thing to do is wait and let Labrowski know you're there for him when he gets back." I reached for Cruz's hand, locking our fingers. "I'm tired, and I have a quiz in a few hours. I *need* to get some sleep."

We both went up, silent, and by unspoken agreement, we put our bags away, went to the bathroom. He turned the shower on while I started stripping. He came back, helping me with my clothes and I helped him with his. For a moment, he rested his forehead to my shoulder, and I reached up, my hand cupping the back of his head.

A wave of warmth and tenderness rose within me. The small things.

Him waiting for me to get inside his truck before locking it. Him carrying my bags. Him coming to help with my mom, putting my apartment back in order because *she* had violated it, how he held his little sister, how he cared, how he didn't hesitate for a second with Flynn, how he stared at me, needing me to keep him from doing worse to Flynn... All that rose inside me.

How he looked at me right before everything. *"I'd like to be your man. That's what I'd like to be."*

I threaded my fingers through his hair but turned to him. My lips grazed his ear, his cheek as he lifted his head to look at me.

I said, my voice breaking, "I want to be your woman. That's what I'd like to be too."

His eyes starting shining, a fierce expression looking back at me, and then his mouth was on mine, and I sagged into his arms. A wall exploded inside me. I was done. This moment, him and me, I was changed because he was in. He was so inside me that I hadn't realized how inside he was, but now I was seeing him and feeling him, and he was mine.

He was my man.

He dipped, lifting me up.

I wound my legs around his waist, and he carried me into the shower.

It was an easy adjustment once he pushed me against the wall, and he slid inside. Up into me.

We both paused at the connection before he began moving, going slow. So achingly, fuckingly slow. A tornado of new emotions swirled in me, feelings that I'd never experienced before.

I'd never made love before. I'd never had someone make love to me, but the gentleness, the tenderness, how he savored touching me, kissing, tasting, this was what that was like.

He was my first.

The softness. How he stared deep into my eyes and I felt it all the way to my heart, my chest overflowing. How I gasped, my fingers holding onto him tightly back as he moved inside me.

God.

We were moving together, but I felt him in every inch of my body, and my feelings, my emotions. It was like he'd always been there, always would be there. I broke, my entire body jerking at my climax, and I gasped, because this was so much. Almost too much. Like I'd been given a window to another world, and I could only stare in befuddlement.

It was magic.

I was seeing, sensing, feeling, breathing magic in physical touch.

I'd never be the same again.

I DIDN'T WANT to look at what time it was when we were about to fall asleep, but I set my phone alarm. Cruz curled around me, his arm over my waist, our hands linked. I lifted a leg, and he slid one of his between mine.

We went to sleep like that.

Just. Like. That.

The calls started after that.

Blocked calls (19)

41

CRUZ

Practice sucked ass. I dragged. Most of the guys dragged. Labrowski didn't show up, which Coach was going to tear into him for why the captain was a no-show, but it was done. Think I got an hour of sleep? I didn't even know, but when we got back to the house, I went upstairs.

"Yo." Barclay had bags under his eyes too. "Breakfast?"

I grunted, heading for the stairs. "Sleep."

He rubbed at his eyes, yawning. "Sounds good to me."

The usual routine was practice, back to the house, shower, get ready for morning classes, and a bunch of us would head to campus for breakfast. After that we dispersed, some staying on campus for early classes and others heading back to the house. Or going to the weight room to lift. This morning, I meant what I said.

I got to my room, opened the door, and stopped short.

A part of me had expected her to be gone. Like normal times. Before, she hardly ever slept over. There'd been the few occasions, but normal Mara. She'd be gone. Giving me her body, nothing else. I'd gotten used to it. Hell. I loved it in the beginning, but it changed. Started changing more this semester, and now here I was. Here she was, still sleeping in my bed.

And I stood just inside my door, watching her sleep.

She was curled in a ball, toward the wall. Some of her hair was peaking out of the blanket, and I could see her form breathing. Slow. Peaceful. I didn't want to wake her up. What happened last night, no one should deal with that. Her. Angela. Other girls. No one. But seeing how she handled Angela. Hearing how she spoke to her, the knowing in Mara's eyes.

"You might not feel it now. Every part of you is probably screaming at you to run and hide. You will regret that. There will be a day where you wished you had the strength you'll have later, that you had rallied it today so you can tell the police what happened to you. It's today. It's not later. You don't have the strength? Take mine. Take Cruz's. You are not alone today, but you will feel alone for so many days after this. I can't take that away from you, and trust me, I would love to do that. I can't. But today, right now, trust me. I don't want you to feel the regret later."

Then later, when I asked, *"That ever happen to you?..."*

"Once. When I was too young to know anything."

I knew it then, knew it when she said those words, and I was sliced from the inside out.

I loved her.

I don't know when it happened. Hadn't expected this to happen, but it was there.

All the times she pushed people away, when I knew there was more inside. Could feel the pain behind her exterior, knew there was so much sweetness behind her cold walls. Knew it. Had tasted it. She gave me that of her, that side of her she didn't give to anyone, and I was learning that she had never given to anyone before.

Warmth. Heaven. Sunlight. That's what she gave me, and things had changed.

A part of me had been bracing for walking into an empty

room, feeling that coldness after she left because it'd always been there. I just hadn't noticed. I hadn't cared because it worked with me. Not wanting what we had now, but now having it, and knowing I never wanted to go without it again.

She rolled over in bed, the covers shifting, and her face was poking out. Enough for some oxygen.

I moved closer, brushing a strand of her dark hair to the side. It was a whole myriad of dark red, chestnut, and a few blonde mixed in. Looked fucking gorgeous on her. I loved her hair. Could grab a handful and you never know what part of the rainbow you'd get, then you could tug on it and you'd get a whole different reaction from her.

I went to the bathroom, closed the door, and did a quick shower. After that, throwing on some clothes, I went back to bed and slid inside, loving the warmth that was her own cocoon. Loving how that cocoon smelled of her, just waiting to greet me back as I reached for her and gently pulled her to my side.

She nestled into me, one of her legs slipping between mine, and I turned to her. Kissed her forehead. My head went to the pillow as I breathed her in, and I pulled her even closer, her front fitting to mine and my hand rested on her ass.

Oh yeah, I thought as I went to sleep. A whole wall had shifted inside of me, shifted to let something in that I never had before either. She did that. She shifted the wall.

I'd never let her put it back.

42

MARA

We did our quiz first thing in class, but it wasn't until after when the TA called my name.

I looked up. My bag was packed, and I was ready to go. "Yeah?"

She motioned for me to come to the front of the class. The professor had already left. "Come here. I want to talk a bit."

I frowned but went over. I was getting As and Bs on everything so far, on the quizzes, on the test, on the papers due.

"Mara."

I looked at the door. Wade was there with a question in his gaze, but I remembered Angela and waved at him. "You can head out. I'll be fine. You don't have to wait for me." I didn't know if that's what he was asking, but I didn't want to risk the topic of Angela. I didn't want to bold-face lie to my roommate, not if I didn't have to.

He nodded before heading out.

"Mara." The TA gave me a tight smile, putting her own laptop away in her bag. She set it on her desk and inclined her head toward me. "Field trips are coming up."

This again? "I've been doing well on all my stuff."

"You have. Yes, but being book smart isn't always the same as being world smart. Look, I'm not trying to ride you or anything. We had another freshman in the class and when we did our field trips, it ended in disaster. I said it before, but there's a reason this is an upperclassmen course."

"You're judging me because I'm a freshman."

"Yes. That's the criteria for this course."

"What do you want from me? I'm doing everything right in the class."

"We're going to the facilities next week. I'm just stressing again how important it is for you to act respectful. The patients there are people. They're mothers and fathers and daughters and sons and brothers and sisters. Just remember that. You never know someone's circumstances. You could end up there one day. I could end up there one day. People just, have struggles and sometimes we're clueless about it. I guess that's all I'm stressing. The opportunity that Dr. Chandresakaran gives the students means a great deal to me."

I was seriously so tired of this. I could open myself up, give her my entire life's resume about how aware I was of what she's talking about, but I didn't. That was not her business, no matter what she was pushing on me. "I'll be fine."

"You're doing presentations when you get back on what you learned. I'll be looking forward to what you learned."

I almost laughed, because going to that facility wasn't going to teach me anything I didn't already know. "Yeah. Me too. Can I go?"

She nodded, a half-smile but also a half-frown on her face. Her problem wasn't mine, and I wasn't going to take it on. But as soon as I was in the hallway, I checked my phone and saw a text.

Angela: Could you come over?

This. This I would take on.

Me: Leaving class right now. What dorm and room?

My phone buzzed again.

Kit: I don't know where your mom is, but word is getting spread around town. My cousin told me that your mom is saying mad shit about you. Saying you came onto her boyfriend when you were like 12. She's saying crazy stuff.

I stared at the phone, everything beginning to circle around me, until I shut it down.

I couldn't focus on this crisis today.

WORD SPREAD FAST. Everyone at Grant West knew about Carrington. They knew he'd been arrested for a sexual assault and no story or rumor was spread about me, about Cruz, or a fight at the beach. It was not spread about who the girl was, and *everyone* was asking.

Gavin slipped into his seat, and I expected him to ask about the rumors, but before he could, a shadow fell over us. We both looked up, and my mouth might've dropped. Cruz fell into the seat on the other side of me. Barclay took the seat on his other side.

"What are you doing here?"

He had a coffee in his hand, and put that on my desk before bending down to dig into his bag. He nodded toward the front. "Class."

"You don't usually sit with us."

He stopped digging in his bag, and turned his head to me. "Saw you earlier on campus and you looked wiped. Don't be a girl and take offense to that. You're still hot even when you look like you're dragging." His gaze fell to the coffee. "Brought that for you, and this." He pulled out a bagel, putting that on my desk too.

Barclay leaned forward. "If you don't want either, I'll take 'em off your hand. Practice was brutal this morning."

I reached for the bagel. "No. I—" My hand closed over it before pulling it out of the bag. I reached for the coffee too, taking a sip. And almost *died* because it was so good. "How'd you know I love matcha lattes?"

The professor was coming in. He leaned back and gave me a slow smile. "I have ways."

Barclay started laughing, until Cruz's hand whipped out. He started coughing after that.

My phone buzzed five minutes later, so I silenced it.

Gavin: You know anything about what happened with Carrington?

Mara: No. The guys aren't talking in your frat?

Cruz: What's Gavin saying?

Gavin: They're a vault. You guys were out there that day. Did you see anything?

To Cruz: Asking about Carrington, if we know anything. Not that I'm complaining, but why are you sitting with us today?

To Gavin: We didn't get back till super late, or super early Monday morning.

It was a vague answer, but I didn't want to lie. Not unless I had to.

Cruz: Just time. You're my girl.

His girl. I stared at the screen, knowing I couldn't hide a smile or ignore the flutter in my tummy. I glanced up, seeing he was watching me, his eyes soft.

I typed back.

I'll expect a matcha latte every day now.

He read his phone, and the side of his mouth lifted up.

Cruz: Not a problem.

A shadow flashed over his gaze.

Cruz: You okay? For real. I wasn't lying when I said you looked wiped this morning.

I could tell him about Kit's text, but a stubborn part of me wanted to deny it, block it out. That was my mom doing her thing, trying to get to me. Boundaries. I refused to give her a rise about whatever bullshit she was saying regarding me.

Mara: I was at Angela's all night. Sure I'll be there tonight too.

Cruz: I'm sorry. That's heavy.

Another shadow flickered over his face, but the professor began calling on us. We needed to pay attention.

WADE APPROACHED me later in the week.

I was leaving the kitchen and heading upstairs to meet Cruz when he called my name.

Zoe was the only one in the kitchen. She grabbed her soup and gave me a little smile before leaving.

"Hey, uh." He raked a hand through his hair, his head shifting around. "Angela's not been returning anything from me. I called her Sunday, but she sent me a text saying she was heading out of town with some friends. That's been it. She did a post on Insta yesterday about studying for the week, but it was a vague post. I know she hangs out at the hockey house, and I don't know the current status of you and Styles, but have you heard anything?"

Angela had called every day this week, and a lot of those calls were me listening to her cry. I'd been at her dorm room both Tuesday and Wednesday nights, late. I hadn't talked to Labrowski. I didn't know what he knew or if he was being there for her. Cruz and I hadn't talked a whole lot this week except for class where he and Barclay were now sitting by us. It was a permanent change. Cruz brought me another matcha latte, but with a breakfast sandwich instead. No bagel. And after class, he grabbed my bag before I could. He also took off, before I could take it back. He waited for me outside, and refused to hand it back, carrying it to my next class.

My throat tightened up, but, "I don't know. I saw Cruz in class, but he's been busy. We've not really talked much."

He eased back, nodding, but his shoulders slumped. "Yeah. Yeah. But, if you do hear something, could you let me know? If she's giving me the draft, then it is what it is. You know?" He tried to smile, but it fell flat.

"You really like her."

His head jerked up and down in a stiff nod. "I do. I wasn't expecting it, but she's nice. She's not what I thought she was, knowing she hangs at the hockey house so much."

"I thought she was a party girl at first."

"She's kinda the opposite. Shy and I don't know. She was different. Is different."

My throat tightened up all over again because I hoped *hoped* he'd still think that if he found out what happened to her, because what happened to her *wasn't* on her. Everyone is foolish and naive in their lives. I touched his arm. "If I see her, I'll let her know you're thinking about her."

"Thanks. Yeah. That'd be nice."

I headed upstairs and was just going inside when my phone buzzed.

Thinking, hoping it would be Cruz, I pulled it out.

It wasn't.

Leander: My bro's on a tear. Watch your back.

Me: What do you mean?

Leander: I know what happened. He ain't going after Styles. Too big of a hockey god. He's going after you. He got drunk last night and started talking. Half the house hates you. Half says to leave you alone. He said you gave the police a video or something. I don't know what was on that video and don't want to know, but he's pissed about it.

Me: Why are you letting me know?

Leander: Because I figure I owe you. You intro-ed me to Susan.

Me: Thanks for the heads-up.

He didn't reply after that, but my phone lit up again.

Gavin Miller calling.

I answered. "Hey."

"What the fuck, Daniels?"

My heart sank. "What do you know?"

"I know Flynn is saying Cruz threw a couple punches at him, and then you made up some recording, saying that a chick was accusing him of touching her or something?"

I was not surprised that's how Flynn was twisting it. "I can't tell you what's on the video because it's not for me to tell, but yes, a girl is on it telling about what he did. And yes, the police saw it and I'm guessing that helped with him being charged."

"He's saying you orchestrated all of this. That you got Cruz worked up, said Flynn touched you too."

"No. I had nothing to do with that."

My door opened, and Cruz walked in. It took one look at me before his face got tight, real tight. He clipped out, "Who are you talking to?"

"Miller."

He came over and took the phone from me. "I just walked in, but I heard enough that you're getting seriously twisted information if you're blaming Mara for any of this shit. I don't know what your *brother* is saying, but he showed up and he started throwing insults as his greeting. Yes. I wasn't having it, so we had words, but it was only words until he threw a bottle at me and threatened me. I saw the chick with them, saw the state she was in, and he and I had a different sort of exchange. Your boy's all the way in the wrong here, and I'm telling you right now, right here, that if he doesn't shut his fucking mouth, the *entire* hockey house knows what really happened. He should be a lot more scared, if you get my drift. Do you get my drift, Miller?"

I couldn't hear what Gavin was saying, but Cruz ended the call a few seconds later.

He looked my way, bags under his eyes before he gave me my phone back.

He sat down on the couch, leaning back and closed his eyes.

My heart was aching again, for him this time. "Angela told Labrowski?"

He nodded, not looking at me. His mouth went flat. "She told him everything, and he got her permission to tell the rest of the guys. They won't say anything, but it's a line of defense. His story should change when he finds that out." He looked wiped out before his eyes slid my way. "I kept thinking all week about you."

"About me?"

"About when you said you had your thing, and your mom made it about her. What'd you mean by that?"

There was a pinching sensation in my chest. "I don't really want to talk about it. I mean, I don't need to. I had therapy for that, but..." God. My mom. I felt my throat starting to close up and tried to clear it. "Her and Dad had divorced by then, and the guy who touched me, he was the latest my mom moved in."

"She didn't believe you?"

"No, she did, but it was like she didn't care. She made a whole dramatic thing about it, calling the police. She was sobbing when they showed up, wearing basically nothing, and they had EMS come for her. They thought she was having a heart attack or that he'd hit her. She was screeching, like hysterically screaming. Bloodcurdling screams. The guy was put in a squad car, and I was in the corner of the couch, balled up because I knew I couldn't leave, but I wanted to just disappear. It took three hours, and a trip to the hospital before they found out the real reason the police were called. One detective asked if I felt safe in the house. I wanted to tell the truth so bad, but I couldn't. If I did, then she'd be the victim again and it was always my fault. *Everything* was my fault."

The memories were coming back.

I said, "One time she asked for forgiveness, for bringing that guy into the house, but she did it in such a way where–" I shook my head, moving down, slumping and curling in on myself. "She took a butcher knife and held it to her wrist, and said I needed to forgive her because if I didn't, she wanted to die right then and there. That was the one time she asked for forgiveness, like she'd done something wrong, but in how she was doing it, I wished she hadn't. The rest of the time, it was my fault. My fault for wanting food, for leaving my room, for making myself vulnerable to him, for going to the bathroom, for not having a lock on my door or–"

"Figure it out! You're a dumb shit so much, but you can be a resourceful little brat. Move your desk in front of the door or something. And it's not like you even really need food. You could stand to lose a few pounds."

I quieted, feeling the well opening up inside me.

"What's happening right now? What are you thinking?"

I shook my head, pushed down the burning in my throat, and hugged my knees to my chest. "I can't talk about her because there's no resolution. She'll never be the mother I want, and it's stupid to even think like that. She will never change. Ever." I looked for Cruz. He was on the couch, but giving me space. "After you told me about your sister, I had this moment of clarity. I've been struggling coming here, not being with her because… It's so dumb, but it's like if I was there, I'd be blamed for everything, but I could handle it or something. Being away, needing to be away, I'm not in control of anything, but I never was. I never am. It's always her. I can't explain it. I just–I called my dad on the beach and told him I was officially done with her."

Cruz cursed under his breath but moved, scooping me up off the couch. He held me to him. I burrowed into his shoulder and neck. He was moving. I closed my eyes, letting myself be carried this time.

I heard the door being locked. The lights went off. He bent, and bent again, and then we were in my bedroom. He moved onto the bed, settling back against the bed's headboard. One of his arms reached over. I heard a small clinking sound. His arm came back under me, and hoisted me higher in his arms, turning me.

I sank down, straddling him. I clambered up, holding him back like a koala.

His whole body shuddered, right before he rested his head next to mine, his cheek to mine. He murmured, "I don't know if this is something you need to hear, but just because she's the mom you got, that doesn't mean she's the mother you deserve."

I inhaled and froze.

Was that what I thought?

Yes. Maybe.

I sat back, looking at him.

He reached up, and ran a hand down the side of my face, to my chin, my lips, and down to my throat. "You deserve everything in the world, Mara. That's what I think."

Things were moving inside me, a wall was opening. Cruz was already inside me, but he was creating a bigger opening, and a bunch of fear began to rush up. I clamped that down because he was right. I, at the very least, deserved some healing.

I'd accept that much, for now. But it was a start.

I whispered, "This, you and me, it's scary as shit to me."

He started to nod.

I stopped him. "I don't let myself get close to anyone. But you, you changed the game. I don't really know what all I'm saying here, but I'm just trying to say thank you and also warning you I'm a mess, but–"

He started smiling during my impromptu speech but leaned in, his mouth touched mine. "Shut up, and *same*."

I laughed, my mouth still to his. Nothing else mattered that night.

It was all, just, perfect.

For the moment.

Unknown number: I'm going to kill your mom if you don't give her what she needs.

Unknown number: Ur a horrible daughter.

Unknown number: U should doe.

Unknown number: Die.

Unknown number: I'll do your mom and then I'll come do you.

Blocked calls (21)

43

MARA

I was in a vehicle, with people.

Tasmin, her boyfriend, Miles, Skylar, Zoe, and I were all squished in Tasmin's SUV.

Friends. Laughing.

I was in the twilight zone.

We were on a road trip heading to Cain. The hockey teams were playing. And since Cain was almost ground zero for Tasmin's entire family, well; we were going for the weekend.

I was also hiding in the back.

But still. Twilight zone.

"So, are you and Cruz officially out?" Tasmin asked from the driver's seat, looking at me in the rearview mirror.

I gave her a look. "What are you talking about?"

"Oh my God!" Skylar erupted while Zoe dissolved in laughter. They were in the back seat. Skylar added, "He slept over last night. By the way, you and he are *not* that quiet."

"What?" I was mortified.

Zoe couldn't stop laughing, and she shook her head at the same time, waving her hand in the air. "We've known for a while, but we didn't say anything because you've made it clear you wanted to keep it quiet."

Skylar snorted. "Until this morning. I was going for a run this morning and saw the two of you seriously making out next to his truck."

Oh. God. I'd gone down with him to say goodbye. We were going to either hop into his truck or go back upstairs. His coach calling him stopped us.

I slouched down in my seat, ignoring Miles laughing next to me. "You and Cruzzie. You two a thingie."

"Finally!" Zoe was grinning from ear to ear. "Also, that's his sweatshirt, right? You wear it *all* the time."

I glanced down. She was right. It was one of his hoodies, I'd forgotten it was his. "I didn't know you could tell it's his."

"It has his number on the back."

Oh. My cheeks got hot because I'd really forgotten about that.

I was just shaking my head because there wasn't anything I could say. Look at me, and how I've progressed. Tasmin, in a car with my roommates, and they're all teasing me about my boyfriend... Or I was assuming he was my boyfriend? We'd not had that actual talk, but no, we were. He said he wanted to be my man. I was his woman. The officialness of this all was new to me.

"Just shut up, you guys."

They all howled after that.

"You're making me regret acknowledging you as friends."

"Never!" Tasmin was beaming at me via the rearview mirror. "Consider me locked on like a zebra mussel. Where you go, I go and you're never getting rid of me."

"Look at you, knowing your different types of mussels." That was Miles.

Tasmin just gave him a smile.

My phone buzzed, and I tensed.

But it was Skylar.

Skylar: Are you freaking out? You can be honest. No judgment from my end.

Me: I'm just not used to people knowing my shit, telling me they know my shit, and me not cutting them off. I got trust issues.

Skylar: You're in good hands. For real. Everyone is happy for you, even Wade.

Wade, who still hadn't heard from Angela, and I was the only one who knew why besides the hockey house. I shifted in my seat, feeling a little constricted.

Me: Thanks. I mean it and I'm working on accepting it.

Skylar: GOOD!!!!!!

Zoe: The hoodie looks adorbs on you. I never said anything before, but now I can and you are the cutest hockey girlfriend.

Me: Omg! Thank you.

I laughed, giving her a look over my shoulder, then switching to Skylar.

"Wait. Are you two texting too?" Zoe grabbed Skylar's hand, pulling it down so she could read her screen.

"What, what, what? Who's texting and not sharing?" Tasmin wanted to know.

Skylar was fast, but not fast enough. Zoe plucked her phone out of her girlfriend's hands and read through, then sighed. "Oh. It's nothing. They're talking about where they want to eat tonight."

She handed the phone back to Skylar, the two squeezing each other's hands before Zoe mouthed to me, "So sorry."

I texted back.

It's okay.

Skylar showed her, and Zoe's smile softened. Zoe shared her screen, and Skylar pumped her head up and down at me, agreeing.

Having friends felt nice, but I double-checked my seatbelt was secured.

Just in case.

Another text came through. Unknown number.

I didn't let myself read it. I just blocked it, and yeah.

Friends.

All was good.

BLOCKED calls (38)

44

MARA

"Daniels!"

We'd walked into a restaurant/pub eatery that Tasmin recommended. It was close to the Cain University campus, and we were greeted with that yell as soon as we walked inside. I froze, for a second, until Zeke Allen came walking from a back section. He was wearing all Grant West clothes, and on the front the words embroidered read, "Cruz Styles' #1 Fan." He came over, saw I was reading his shirt and wiggled his eyebrows. "Nice, huh?" He gestured to the back with his thumb. "Get a load of this." He turned around and the words embroidered there were, 'Mara Daniels' Boyfriend's Fan Club, Charter Captain.'

"Oh, God." I sank down into a squat right there and then. My butt rested on the back of my heels. My head in my hands.

"It's awesome. How awesome is this? And get this, I wear this to all of Blaise's soccer games." He was laughing as he tugged on my elbow and pulled me back up. "Come in here." His arms went around me in a big bear hug.

Greetings were happening around us as I stepped back, and saw Blaise was there, giving his sister a hug. Race was next, getting a half-side man-hug. Seeing me notice him, he gave me a slight chin-lift. "Hey, Daniels."

Daniels.

I mirrored his chin-lift. "DeVroe."

Zeke threw his arm around my shoulder, yanking me to his side. "I call dibs on Daniels' friendship. You're so low on that list now."

Blaise scowled at him before rolling his eyes. "You're a moron."

"Sure am. After all the shit you do, I'm still your best friend."

Tasmin and Race headed farther inside the restaurant, and Skylar, Zoe, and Miles moved in a different direction. They went over to where Grant West people were, including the rest of our roommates. And they weren't alone. Seeing me, Kyle Ruiz stood up from their table, a wince flashing over his face before he made his way toward where I was standing.

"Hey, uh." He raked his hand through his hair.

Before he could say anything, Zeke said, with a bite, "Who are you?"

Kyle frowned at him, lingering on Zeke's arm still around my shoulders. "Uh, a friend of–"

"Really?" I cut in, raising an eyebrow.

He grimaced again. "Look, uh, I'm sorry–"

"For what?" from Zeke.

"I'm sorry, but who are you?"

"Someone who'd like to know why you're apologizing to Daniels."

Now Ruiz raised his own eyebrow. "I'm Grant West's quarterback."

Zeke shook his head. "That don't mean shit to me." He gestured to Blaise with a head nod. "This guy here has turned down soccer clubs from Europe to stay in college. He doesn't go around giving his resume and social media followers before issuing apologies. You know who does that? Douchebags."

I cursed, stiffening under Zeke's arm.

He only tightened it around me, his chest puffing up.

Blaise started laughing. "I might start now."

Zeke threw him a grin. "Do it. I'd pay money to see the next time you fuck up and go that route apologizing to–"

"Who are these guys?" Ruiz asked me, jerking a thumb in Zeke's direction.

Zeke went back to scowling. "We're her friends, and we know who you are. We know what you did too." He lifted his other arm. "Are you not reading my shirt? I don't just have Mara's back, but I have Styles's back. He makes my friend have great orgasms so I'm going to support him as long as he puts that dreamy little pep in Daniels' step that I witnessed when she *came* in here, and pun *totally* meant because that's the type of douchebag *I* am."

Blaise groaned. "I'm out. I can't get into any more fights today."

Zeke called after him, "I'm going to let Styles know you deserted him in his time of need right now. Let's hope he doesn't hold grudges." Zeke focused back on Ruiz, upping his scowl. "Let your apology commence. I'm her friend, if you need to know my qualifications. I'm also Charter Captain of her Boyfriend's Fan Club."

"Okay." Kyle shook his head, raking his hand over his face. "I'm sorry for being a dumbass at the bar. I was a dick. I'm sorry."

"Thanks, Ruiz, but apologize to Cruz too."

He nodded. "I know. Trust me. Eating humble pie here. He's the big man this weekend."

"You're right." Zeke jerked his thumb toward his own shirt. "That's my boi!"

When we went in, Darren gave me a small wave. "I'm going to go sit with my roommates."

Zeke rubbed at his chest. "I don't like this. I don't like being pulled in two different directions."

"Says the guy who goes to Cain University and is wearing a Styles fan shirt."

"That's different. My love for Cruz Styles transcends university alumni donation stipends."

I hid a smile because it really was nice to see Zeke. "We're going to hang out this weekend."

"Damn straight we are. My fraternity is having a party Saturday night. We know the coach is letting your hockey team head back on their own, so we're hoping they'll be our guests of honor."

"I don't want to know how you pulled that off."

"A lot of blackmail." He gave me two thumbs-up. "And threats. They go a long way here."

I held my hands up, beginning to back away. Zeke was being Zeke. I just needed to go with it by now.

Going over and sinking down in the chair across from Darren, he gave me a tight smile before flipping his phone around and pointing to a screen. "You see this?"

Word's out! Cruz Styles is officially off the market until his latest squeeze sleeps with someone else, and word on the street is that could be anyone at any second!

I jerked up. "What is this?"

Zoe said, "It's a campus blog. She covers all the big athletes, but Cruz has been her main focus for the last month. You didn't know?"

"I had no idea."

"That's why we were teasing you. This was posted this morning. We thought you were just being quiet about it."

"How did this get out?"

Zoe shook her head. The rest of the table didn't have an

answer.

Darren pulled his phone back. "You okay?"

I held up a hand, shrugging, and leaning back in my seat. I'd lost my appetite, but... "I'll be fine." But fuck. Fuck, fuck, fuck. We were out in a big, huge way if a blogger was posting about it. And in a seriously insulting way too. "She's implying I'm a slut."

Darren frowned. "Click bait. I'm pretty sure she sells information."

"What's that mean?"

"You could give her twenty dollars, and she'll share her source."

"Are you serious?"

"We deal with her too. Cruz has been her target since hockey started, but she likes to write about football players as well."

"I'm sorry."

He shrugged, hunching over his plate. "I'm pretending it's practice for when we get to the NFL."

That blog stung. And I knew more attention was coming. It was inevitable now.

"Eat. We'll plan retribution later." Darren gestured behind me, right as the server came over.

Retribution. Too bad I couldn't order *that* off the menu.

KIT: I got a weird DM about you. You never called me back so I'm not eager to wade into your stuff, but call me back. I'll send you the SS. Could this be from your mom?

Kit: *image sent.*

I deleted it. I owed Kit a call, but my mom was getting to me through her. I didn't need to see whatever it said to know what it was. My mom being my mom.

45

MARA

After we ate, Tasmin rejoined us and pulled me outside.

"What?" I laughed as she brought out a gift-wrapped piece of clothing. It was big and bulky, and wrapped in brown tissue paper, a light pink ribbon tied around it. "What is this?"

"Something I special ordered for here because I couldn't get it to arrive earlier than today. I fully planned to squirrel it away until the day you and Cruz finally went official, and I'm so giddy that it finally happened."

"What's going on?" That was Zeke, joining our circle. He had a large plastic mug, and a full beer can open inside it. A bunch of guys I didn't know joined him, so I was guessing they were some of his fraternity brothers. The rest of the circle were my roommates.

I ignored him, unwrapping the gift, and when the tissue paper fell away, I was speechless. A full old school hockey sweater with Cruz's number and in Grant West's colors. Purple and white. 71.

My mouth was on the floor.

"Look at the back." Tasmin was gushing.

I turned it, shock spreading through me, and I saw the

words embroidered in big and purple lettering was his last name, his number, two small hockey sticks crossing over each other, and beneath in smaller print was, "Property of Girlfriend."

A choked sound came out of me.

I'd never... I covered my mouth with my hand.

This was a serious gift. She put thought and money into this, and planning, and now hearing she was going to hold onto it until we were official... "I can't believe this," I whispered, my voice hoarse.

She–no one had any idea, but with my mom, how she was, I wasn't celebrated. Gifts were not something that happened in my life.

"Thank you so much, Taz." She had no idea how much this meant to me.

But maybe she did because she was blinking back tears. "I just–with your mom and what you've been through–" Her cheeks were pinking. "I wanted you to know that I appreciate our friendship and yeah. You're stuck with me."

If I were a guy, I would've been on the floor in pain from the karmic kick in the balls. I shook my head, still whispering because I couldn't get anything else out right now, "I'm so sorry for being such a bitch. I–I don't deserve this jersey. I don't deserve–"

"Oh, my gawd, shut up." She hurled herself at me, hugging me tight. She whispered for just me to hear, "I'm happy you let Cruz in, and I'm happy you're starting to let me in. Just know that people do care, and they don't judge, and we're here for you, and you're wrong. You do deserve kindness."

She was wrong. I didn't. I really didn't, but I hugged her so long.

BLOCKED *calls (119)*

WE WERE IN THE AISLE. The Cain students were in the section next to us. Zeke was smack dab front and center, and he enjoyed plastering himself against the plexiglass every time Cruz skated by, which was a lot. I'd gotten more than my normal amount of attention as we walked in, but this time it was mostly from girls. I'm sure some came from the jersey, but I was also sure some came from the blog article. I had no idea how popular that blogger was at our university.

Watching Cruz play was always fun. He scored right away, which set the rhythm for the rest of the game. Atwater scored the second goal. There were a lot of missed shots and back and forth in the second period, but the third is when Cruz got another goal, and he made an opening for Labrowski to sink in for their fourth.

Cain never got on the scoreboard, but judging by how loud Zeke was cheering for Cruz, I didn't think they expected to win this game.

That night, I checked into a local hotel with Skylar and Zoe. The guys were in the next room.

Taz and Race were staying at her brother's, and while they invited us to go there since they were having a small party, I elected to stay close to the hotel. It was the same one the hockey team was using, and since it was Friday night, they were given time off with a strict curfew.

Cruz: What room are you in?

Me: 807

Cruz: Heading up.

Skylar was in the bathroom. Zoe was in the other room, and I was suddenly hit with nerves. Like this was the first time seeing my boyfriend. Like I was sixteen, going on my first date.

My phone buzzed again, and I tensed but it wasn't *her*.

Zeke: Daniels! Where are you? What are you doing?

Me: At the hotel. The team can't leave tonight.

Zeke: For real? Okay. Let's do breakfast? Or lunch. Where's Miller? Noticed no Alpha Mu brothers came over.

I sighed, right as there was a knock on the door. When I opened it, Cruz was on the other side, and his eyes went big, upon seeing me, or maybe seeing the jersey. Until he noticed my expression. "What's wrong?" He moved in, shutting the door behind him, but before I answered, he pulled me into his arms and gave me a tight hug. I was fast melting. He'd just showered, and his eyes had that fun and mischievous spark, which combined with his little knowing look because he knew what I wanted to do.

He still held me against him, his hand moving to my ass. He murmured against my neck, "I like your sweater. Looks hot on you."

I moaned, pressing back against him, right as the bathroom door opened behind me.

"Oh, God. Oh–sorry!" Skylar came out.

Cruz cursed, but reacted in an instant, pulling me out into the hallway. I got a glimpse of a white towel before he was saying through the cracked door, "Take your time. Sorry about that."

Skylar was laughing from inside, and I heard another click and then Zoe's voice before Cruz pulled the door shut behind us. He moved down the hall, leaning against the wall. He spread his legs and pulled me to stand between them. His hands went back to my hips, playing with the bottom of my jersey. "You had this made?"

The nerves came back. I gave him a rueful grin. "No. Tasmin gave it to me as a gift. Surprised me with it when we got here."

"You serious?" His hands went to the front of my hips, and

he lifted me back just a little so he could see the front better. "That's good material too. This is amazing." He turned me around and whistled under his breath when he read the back. He tugged on the bottom of it. "I like this, *a lot*. You're sleeping in this tomorrow night. No. Sleep in it tonight, and tomorrow so it smells more like you."

My phone buzzed again, and feeling it, he took it out of my hands, flipping around to see the screen. He snorted, handing it back. "That Allen guy. He's an odd friend of yours, huh?"

"You saw his sweatshirt?"

"Everyone saw his sweatshirt. He was on the news. I got so many clips sent to me already. Fucking hilarious, though. He's a *true* friend?"

I nodded, somewhat distracted as I read his most recent text.

Zeke: Whoa. I just called Miller and he told me to fuck off. Wth? You guys have a falling out?

I showed Cruz the text.

He leaned back, his hands returning to my hips, and he shrugged. "He doesn't have to know."

"You don't know Zeke." And as if on command, my phone began ringing. I declined his first call, and knew I had ten seconds before he'd be calling again. My voice message was a click, that was it. I didn't have a message for people to wait through. "He is like a starving dog after a bone. He knows something is up and he won't leave it until he knows. He'll either get our version or he'll go to Gavin and get his. Then he'll come back and badger me until he finds out the truth."

And again, on cue, my phone lit up.

Cruz took it, answering it. "She can't talk about what's happening with Miller. It involves his entire frat and some other shit. I'm included in it." A pause. "Hi, Zeke. Yes. This is Cruz." Another pause, longer. "Listen, stay out of this. I mean it. This can get serious–" He frowned, moving to stare at me as he listened to whatever Zeke was saying. "I can't say anything, and do not badger Mara about this. *Trust* me on this." He was listening again before rolling his eyes upwards. "Then think of it as she's in the middle between me and one of Miller's fraternity brothers." He nodded, quiet again. "Exactly. Okay. It's nice to hear you're hashtag teamcruz on this one." His top lip twitched, curving up. "I'll tell her. Yeah, yeah. No. The team does our own meals and things until after the game. Then we're set free tomorrow."

He ended the call and handed the phone back over. "Your friend made sure to tell you that if push comes to shove, he's got your back, my back, and anyone else who stands with us. And he said to remind you that it's not just him, but the entire Cain crew. He said you'd know what that meant, something about a crew from back home."

I slid the phone into my pocket and moved so I was the one leaning against the wall. "In the neighboring town, they had a 'crew' system. That's all he means. Taz's twin and his friends."

"Well, he sounded serious when he said it."

His eyes grew dark, serious, and he stood in front of me, almost over me. He leaned one hand against the wall beside me, rested his other on the other side of my head. Then, leaning in, he paused right before me and murmured, "You look delicious as hell wearing that jersey."

I smiled, reaching up for him and cupped the side of his face. "Shut up, and kiss me, Styles."

He did just that.

TWO HOURS LATER, we were in my room, on my bed. The roommates had headed out, and Cruz was spending too much time on a certain part of my boob. I lifted my head to look, then moved his head off me. "Hey! What are you doing? A hickey?"

He peeled over, laughing. "Took you long enough to notice."

I sighed, inspecting it more. We had sex in the shower, ordered food, and after we ate, we'd been lounging on the bed and messing around. A hockey game was on the television, but Cruz was paying more attention to me and I'd been enjoying the touches, caresses, and kisses. Now I was seeing that he was trying to put a hickey on my breast that looked the size of Texas.

"Seriously?"

He rose back up, kneeling over me, and touched my forehead, pushing me down. "It's like my signature. Let me finish." He bent back down, but I put a finger to his forehead and lifted his head up. "Your signature?" I narrowed my eyes. "How many other girls have you done this to?"

He shrugged, biting back a grin. "A few, but none since you."

Well, that felt nice to hear. When he started 'working' again, I let him. I was kinda savoring the attention. And when I looked again, he'd somehow turned it into a lopsided crown. It was Texas, but with little points at the top.

I loved it.

He gave me a grin, his eyes soft, and smoothed his hand down to my hip. "You like?"

I hated to say it, but nodded.

His grin widened. "Score."

His phone began buzzing after that, and he groaned after checking the screen. His forehead went to my stomach. His hands were on my hips. "I have to go."

I raked a hand through his hair. "Stay."

His hands tightened on my hips, and he said against my tummy, "I can't. Curfew." He lifted his head, the struggle evident in his eyes. He was gazing at my mouth. "Fuck. I'd like to stay. When do your roommates come back?"

"They're partying."

"Where?"

I shrugged. "Other hotel rooms? I'm sure there's a ton on campus, or they could've gone to a bar too."

"And you stayed with me?" His eyes sparked, mischievous.

My eyes narrowed again, but I knew they looked soft cause that's how I was feeling. All warm, and soft, and happy. Another day and that feeling might've sent me running. Not this day. "Like I'm going to turn down a night of messing around with my boyfriend."

"That's right. Your boyfriend." He rose back up, his knees settling on either side of my legs, and he stared down at me. His gaze was going dark, serious. Lust-filled. He glanced at his phone. "You think your roommates will be gone for the next twenty minutes?"

I was already reaching for his neck as I murmured, "Only twenty?"

His mouth met mine. "Make that thirty. I'm going to take *real* good care of my girl."

His girl. My boyfriend. That had my pulse soaring.

IT WAS LATER, after I was in bed, and after Cruz left, that I remembered.

I forgot to mention the blog article.

And I forgot to look earlier, but heaved a sigh of relief. There were no new texts from an unknown number. I checked my calls.

Blocked calls (0)

46

CRUZ

At the team breakfast, Atwater asked Labrowski, "How's Angela doing?"

He'd been going over to her place every day, and sometimes not coming back until the next morning. He'd shower, change, and head back out for practice or classes, or whatever we were doing. He dropped down in the seat across from me with his plate of food, bags under his eyes. He looked haggard, and he shook his head, propping his elbow on the table and raking a hand through his hair.

His hand left his hair, lifting in a frustrated motion. "I have no clue. She's wrecked and I think–" He glanced my way quick. "She's remembering other stuff. She just texted me that she wants to call that same detective because she has more she wants to tell him."

"Man. I'm sorry."

"That sucks." Atwater leaned over his own plate.

The rest of the guys were filtering in. We had our own eating area set up in the hotel, away from everyone else. Less distraction. More team focus time, or that's what Coach always said.

"Please. Tell me about it." Labrowski glared at Atwater, whose head reared back.

"Dude. I'm just saying."

Labrowski's glare doubled. "What are you saying? Enlighten me. You have experience going through this, hearing what another guy did–" He stopped himself, but briskly shook his head. "Just, lay off. This isn't easy shit."

"Hey." I leaned forward, making sure Labrowski had eyes on me. "*We've* got your back."

He visibly relaxed, enough where the glares were more frowns. "I know. I know and thank you. I know it's not you guys that I'm mad at, but Carrington. Guys like him make the rest of us–just, fuck him." He looked back my way and I knew. I'd heard. I'd been there when Mara asked her those questions. His jaw clenched and he looked away. "I'd love to rip into him, just once."

Barclay had been quiet, listening. He leaned forward now, hunching over the table. "So maybe we make that happen."

All of us looked his way.

He lifted a shoulder, inclining his head to the side. "I bet that wouldn't be too hard. Find out when he's alone. No phones. No cameras. No way anyone could record anything. We'd vouch for each other, and yeah. Let's have a man-to-man chat with him. I'm down." At Labrowski's lingering look, he added, "Angela's too sweet for something like that to happen to her. She made cupcakes post-game days. I loved those cupcakes."

Labrowski cracked a grin. "Yeah. She did. Too fucking sweet."

"So." Barclay was looking around. "Let's make it happen." He put his fist on the table, waiting.

Atwater put a fist on the table.

Me too.

Labrowski was the last one.

At one, we raised them up and hit the table at the same time. After that, each of us went to eating.

We had a game to win that day.

47

MARA

I slept in the jersey, per Cruz's request, but I didn't wear it to his second game. Instead, a scarf, a sweater, and Zeke snuck in some beer so that's what was keeping me warm. At the beginning of the game, he was in his section, but it was obvious during the warm-up that there was something extra going on with Cruz and the guys. Mainly Cruz, Labrowski, Atwater, and Barclay. The four were intense, and the rest of the guys picked up the vibe.

The first period, I had no words. It was score after score. Cain didn't know what hit them.

I felt bad. This hadn't been the Grant West team they played just the day before. These guys were on a tear. Shot after shot. They scored three in the first period. Two in the second, and by the third, Zeke was in our section and squeezing between me and Skylar. Tasmin was behind him, along with Race and a couple other girls I didn't know.

"What are you doing here?" I asked Zeke.

He began cheering for Cruz immediately, wearing the same sweatshirt he'd worn at yesterday's game. He wrapped an arm around my shoulder, leaning on me. "Our school's not known for hockey. Football, yes. Soccer, this year, but hockey? Not our thing." He motioned toward the other Cain people, and I noted a good third had dispersed. "They're heading out for the parties already. And by the way," he squeezed me close to him, looking down at me. "Everyone is heading to my frat. You ready for that? OH MY GOD! HELL YEAH, CRUZ. I'LL HAVE YOUR BABIES!"

The red light lit up from his goal, and Cruz skated around, his teammates closing in on him. He skated past our section, looking for me, and as he did, he hit the plexiglass with his stick. The section went crazy. We were higher up, choosing to do seats this time. I saw so many girls watching him, so many taking pics, and so many going straight to their social media.

"You got nothing to worry about." Zeke had been observing me. "You know that, right?"

I nodded, but there was still a ball of worry in my tummy. It would be there for a long time. It was how I was made.

Cruz hit the bench, and the second line was skating out. They'd drop the puck again so for a second, we had a breather.

"So, you two. You guys are good? Official?"

"You saw the blog?"

He frowned. "It got sent to me, yeah."

I shrugged. "Taz offered to help me find out who gave her that information, why it was written how it was."

"Inferring you're a whore?" He smirked at me, amusement in his gaze.

"I'm used to it, but yeah. I'd like to know if she has a personal agenda against me."

"Reading that article, I got the vibe it's because you're with Cruz."

"Still might have to have a talk with her."

"Well." He bumped his shoulder into mine. "I'm here for that, but can I bring up the other elephant in the room? Cruz said to leave it, but would you let me know if something serious pops off with this thing you have going on with Miller? Reason I'm asking is because some of their frat brothers reached out. They know I'm firmly hashtag teamcruz and hashtag teamdaniels if that's the case, but they're saying some shit. Our frats aren't affiliated, but we're friendly, and you know how that can be in the Greek system."

Yeah. That knot was back in play. "Whatever he's saying is a lie. Trust me. Cops were involved, and I really can't say anything else."

Zeke was watching me hard core now, all serious. "And if I told you that the cops dropped the charges against him?"

The bottom of my gut opened. "What?"

He held up his hands, palms toward me. "Just so you know, I'm not believing anything. I know how that shit works. I mean, look at me, but they called, saying we shouldn't let you in and telling my brothers that they should start questioning me."

I swore.

"They're putting pressure on them, to put on me, so I'd put on you, so I kinda really do have to push this. What do you have on him? They're not questioning me about Styles. They're saying you specifically."

I cursed, again. "He's a fucking bitch."

The end of the game sounded, and everyone was cheering. "The cops dropped the charges?"

"That's what they said to my frat brother."

The cops wouldn't drop the charges unless Angela recanted her statement.

"I gotta go." I shoved past him, heading up the stairs to leave the arena. As fast as possible, that's what I needed. I had to get out of there, but I wasn't running. I was fighting because fuck this. No one fought for me at times, so I wouldn't let that stand this time. I'd fight for Angela because no way was this guy going to get away with what he did to her.

I dialed Angela's number first.

She didn't pick up. I waited and dialed again once I was outside and I dodged to the side, trying to find some privacy. My phone was blowing up with text after text, but that would all have to wait.

I called her again. She declined this time.

And again.

My persistence paid off.

"Mara, hey." She'd been crying. "I–what are–are you at the game?"

"Did you take back your statement?"

She was quiet on her end, until a hiccup. "Why–how do–what have you heard?"

Was she serious? A group of people were walking by, so I moved off the sidewalk, finding a corner by the building and I hunched down. My butt was resting on the back of my heels and I put a finger into one ear, trying to hear her better. "I got a heads-up that Carrington isn't going after Cruz. He's going after me. I was warned to watch my back. Now I'm hearing that he's calling a fraternity here in Cain and telling them not to let me in the party."

"What?" she whispered.

"I know someone in that frat and he's asking me about it, saying the cops dropped the charges against Flynn."

"WHAT?"

"The only way they'd do that is if you recanted. Did you? Did you do that?" I heard her starting to cry, and my heart broke. I gentled my voice, "Listen. I'm not trying–" Screw it. If I was going to burn for this, I guess that I was going to burn for this. "I won't get mad. I'm not coming at you that way, but I'm getting ready to fight Carrington on my own and I need to know what I'm fighting for. You or myself. If it's too much and you're taking a step back, that's fine. I mean it, but I have to know. Different strategy, you know?" I tried to laugh, but God. If she was going to let me hang out to dry, then, well, I guess that's what was going to happen.

Who was I kidding? I got a glimpse into a normal life, and it'd been good. It'd been fun, but that wasn't me.

"You know, never mind. I'm sorry. I–uh–I got this. Don't worry about anything. You, you just take care of yourself."

"Mara–"

I ended the call, but dammit, dammit, *dammit*. Flynn wanted to destroy me. Well, good luck because I'd endured worse than him.

My phone was continuously buzzing, so I started going through them. I began responding to the first few until I clicked on one from... Kit?

Kit: Did you see this? This is INSANE! Link.

Dread was already inside of me, but it grew razors and I felt them starting to sink into my insides. This wasn't going to be good.

I clicked on the link.

It went to another article, by the same writer, at the same blog, but this time the headline said,

In My Time of Need, My Daughter Wasn't There For Me:

A story about a mother in need and her daughter abandoned her.

48

CRUZ

We were in the locker room. My phone was blowing up, but I wanted to shower and change before heading out. Coach had given us the congratulations talk and a reminder that we'd all signed off, saying we weren't the university's responsibility tonight.

"What the fuck?" Labrowski was reading his phone before he hit a button and put it next to his face. Whoever he was calling, they answered and he said, "What happened?" He listened for a second before looking right at me. "Hold on." He dropped the phone, saying to me, "Mara called Angela, said something about her recanting her statement."

"What?"

He shook his head. "But she didn't. She broke down crying to her roommate and mentioned that she might do that. But she didn't mean it, it was a thing where she was saying she just wanted everything to go away. Then Mara called her a little bit ago, asking about if she was taking back her statement. Something about a fraternity asking about her too."

Atwater exclaimed, standing by his locker, "Holy shit! Daniels' mom tried to off herself?"

I twisted around to him. "What?"

He held his phone up, showing me the screen. "That's what that blogger is saying."

I took two steps and ripped the phone from him. "What the fuck?" I skimmed it, cursing by the end because there was a video of Mara's mother. I wasn't even wondering how the fuck that happened. Carrington. That's how it happened. Only he would have the motivation to set all of this up.

The fucker had been busy.

I tossed Atwater his phone and started to grab my things. A shower would have to wait.

"What are you doing?" Atwater asked.

Labrowski yelled, "You going somewhere?"

Barclay came out of the shower, a towel wrapped around himself. "What's going on?"

"Heads are going to roll." I hit the button to call Mara, but it went straight to voice message. That meant her phone was off. That was *not* good. I growled, calling Miles first. He picked up right away. "Hey! We're at the hotel and freaking out. Have you heard from Mara?"

"That's why I'm calling you." I dressed quickly, aware of the guys hurrying around me. "Where is she?"

"We don't know. She took off right before the end of the game. Her and Allen were in some convo, and yeah. She just zapped out of there. Her phone's off."

"What'd she and Allen talk about?"

"I don't know. He took off too, linked up with some of his boys and they're looking for her."

I grabbed whatever I needed. Shoved my wallet in my pocket. My bag had everything else, and the rest was at the hotel. Grant West wasn't paying for our rooms tonight, so my bag and a lot of the guys' were checked at the hotel. The plan had been to get another room, one on the same floor as Mara and her roommates. We just hadn't checked in yet.

I slammed my locker shut and began heading out.

Three other lockers shut right behind me, and I glanced back, seeing Atwater, Labrowski, and Barclay trailing behind me. Labrowski was on his phone. Atwater and Barclay were solely focused on me.

I asked Miles, "Are Tasmin and her boyfriend with Allen?"

"Yeah. They took off with him."

Solid. I had Race's number. "Thanks, Miles."

"Wait. What are you going to do?"

"Find Mara."

"Cruz, another article came out today..."

"Another one?" I stopped abruptly, right outside the locker room. There were a lot of people around, a lot of eyes on me. I ignored them. "A second one?"

"Yeah. This one was saying something about Mara's mom–"

"Wait. That was the second one? What was the first one?"

"The one about you and her being official, and there were definite slut shaming themes in it."

"About me?"

"About Daniels."

Fucking hell. "Same writer?"

"Yeah. The one who's obsessed with you."

Christ. I'd need to deal with her, but first things first. "You got a question about the mom one?"

"It's saying her mom is that con woman who showed up, and she–"

I knew what it said. I didn't need to read it to know exactly what was inside the story, based on Atwater's reaction. "Listen, Gaynor. Don't believe shit from that article."

"But that woman is the same woman who came–"

"Then think about that. Think about how we had to concoct a whole lie to get that woman out of Mara's place. Think about the look on Mara's face when we left, when that woman was following us out. Think on that shit, and while you're doing that, I'll be looking for Mara."

"But if her mom really tried to kill herself–"

I wanted to tear out of there, and rip some literal heads off their shoulders. But I couldn't because what was alleged, via Atwater's reaction and what I was hearing from Miles, this was a serious issue. "Article says her mom tried to kill herself?"

"Yeah. And that Mara wasn't there for her."

"That's a lie. Mara was there. She drove three hours to be there, and when she got there—" Crap. I stopped myself because I was spilling Mara's personal life. "You need to hold off judgment and wait to talk to Mara if you really want answers. The only thing I can say is to do that."

"Okay. Regardless, I'm here for her."

"Good. Then tell *her* after I find her."

"We'll look for her too. Skylar already mentioned grabbing the vehicle and driving around, see if we see her walking somewhere."

"Thanks. That'd be helpful." I hung up, started walking out to the parking lot, and I dialed Race Ryerson's number. He picked up after one ring, and I said in lieu of his greeting, "Tell me you know where Mara is?"

"We don't. She doesn't know Cain, and we know people who know people who find people. Taz is wondering if she should loop them in. They could probably find her."

I needed to think about this.

It was Cain. Her phone was off, so she wasn't using a car service to get anywhere. Miles was at the hotel, and she wasn't there. She wasn't with Allen and their group, so she was on her own and walking, and I started looking around, seeing what was in the nearby area here.

I saw it.

A laundromat was tucked away on the corner across the giant intersection before people turned into the hockey arena.

"I think I know where she is."

"Where is she?"

"I'll call you later." I motioned to my guys. "I gotta go over there."

"You need to clean some clothes?" Atwater scratched his forehead, frowning.

Labrowski was back on the phone.

I asked him, "That Angela?"

He nodded to me. "She didn't know Carrington threatened Mara, and she's livid. Not at Mara, at Flynn. She also thinks it was Bianca and her roommate who let everything leak about Flynn first being arrested and now this. She found out that Bianca has been talking to Flynn all week. Confronted her and the roommate folded, told her everything and showed her all the emails, DMs, and texts. Apparently Flynn was using Bianca to get close to Angela's roommate. Angela hadn't been talking to B since this happened, so she buddied up to the roommate. There's a lot of bad shit Flynn was saying about Angela. I have to go back. Angela's going to move in with us until we can figure out a new rooming situation for her."

"Score. Cupcakes every day!" Atwater pumped his fist in the air.

Labrowski shot him a grin, but added, "I'm sorry, Cruz. I–" He motioned to his phone. "I gotta go."

I nodded. "That's fine."

"Here." Barclay tossed him his keys.

"What are these for?" Labrowski caught them before tucking them into his pocket.

That was our way home. One of his buddies drove it here, and we were going to drive it back.

Barclay waved at him, nonchalantly. "So many people drove here. We'll figure a way home tomorrow and if not, we'll rent a vehicle. Take it. Go back and help your girl move."

Labrowski stilled, hearing that terminology.

He only blinked a few times before jerking his head up. "Thanks, man. I appreciate it." He indicated the parking lot. "Is it here?"

"It's at the hotel. Shit. I didn't think about that."

"It's okay." Labrowski started moving toward some student we knew. "I'll get a ride. Go." He waved at me. "Go and get *your* girl. I'll be good."

"Fill up the tank of gas!" Barclay yelled at him.

Labrowski held a hand up in acknowledgement, taking off.

Atwater raised an eyebrow at me. "One crisis fixed. Another on deck. Let's go and take care of Daniels."

Shit just got heavy, real heavy, but I led the way to the sidewalk, then the intersection. We waited to cross. I kept waving as vehicles were leaving, saying congratulations to us, and to me. A few paused to see if we needed a ride somewhere. Atwater took care of them, and then our walking light went on. We hurried across and had to wait one more time. The same thing happened on this way, but it was more Cain people. I was guessing this street led to the student housing. But then the walking light went on again, and we crossed.

Going into the laundromat, I saw one woman in the corner putting clothes into a washer. Another woman was reading a book behind a plexiglass and in a back office. She looked up our way, stared at me, before pointing in the far corner.

I looked but didn't see anything.

I walked forward, holding a hand back to Atwater and Barclay to wait by the door.

I kept going until I could see a mat was in the corner. There was a tiny section between the wall and dryers. It wasn't enough room for them to fit in another set of dryers, so it was left, but on that mat, was Mara.

She was slouched down. The top of her back was resting against the dryer. Her butt and half her leg was on the mat, and she had a foot wedged up against the wall. She was staring ahead, because there was a narrow window by the corner of her wall and next to a washer. The window ran all the way to the floor and to the ceiling, and she was gazing out, a set and distant expression on her face.

I dropped down next to her.

She didn't look at me. I didn't know if she knew I was there.

There was no reaction on her face, or body. Nothing. It was like she was a statue.

I murmured, "Mara."

49

MARA

I remembered that day.

I'd been standing in front of the Fallen Crest hospital, not knowing if I was ready to go in or not.

The doors slid open, and a cop exited the hospital doors.

He'd been raising a white foam cup, steaming, to his mouth for a sip, but seeing me, he paused. Lowering it, he came the rest of the way. I knew him, recognizing him from so many other "mother" moments. As cops went in Fallen Crest, this one was kind. "Mara," he said, drawing close enough for him to study my face, and since he was a cop, he was seeing everything. They were trained that way. He gave a small frown and extended his cup. "They weren't supposed to call you."

I nodded, feeling dazed but also not sure why I was dazed by this anymore. "It's on the file."

He grunted. "They're trained to protect the patient against anyone trying to get to them. Not the other way around."

"Yeah." I knew this. And again, not surprised anymore. I glanced at him, noting some extra tired lines around his eyes. "You got called in for her?"

"I did. Hospital called, but since I'm familiar with you and her,

and the situation, I can tell you it doesn't look like a real attempt. Two cuts on her wrists, horizontal and shallow. Looked scary, I'm sure, and I can also tell you that was probably the motivating factor for why the nurse contacted you the way she did."

I was nodding, also knowing all of this.

I'm sure she looked at my mom's file, saw my number was not there, and didn't read where it said not to contact her daughter. And the nurse knew me from school even though she was a few years older, she'd been in the party crowd. She got my number from someone else who didn't know the situation and there you have it. I got an alarmed not-really-friend from high school calling me to tell me about my mom's suicide attempt.

Hearing what Officer Pullen just told me, my mouth went dry.

"My dad in there?"

His eyes narrowed, just for a brief moment before an impassive look came back over him. "You didn't reach out?"

I shook my head. He knew the deal. If I had, my dad would've told me not to come. I hadn't wanted to hear it.

"He's in there."

A NURSE CAME OUT.

She had a shawl over her shoulders, and she wrapped it around her before her hands went in her scrub's front pockets. I heard keys jangling from the motion. "I know a part of you is worried and I can tell you that your mom's going to be just fine."

I gestured to Officer Pullen. "He said they were shallow cuts."

"They were. Your mom knows. She knew how to make it look."

MY DAD LOOKED AT ME, a deep determination and resignation filling his gaze. "I'm going to talk to a lawyer, see if I can get a temporary conservatorship over her, make her stay in a hospital for a while."

My whole chest tightened up.

He raked a hand through his hair. "She's done enough damage to herself and you."

He wasn't including himself, but he was so very much included.

I gave him a look. "It won't work."

He gave me a look right back. "I have to try."

"You've been trying since before I was born."

CRUZ WAS HERE. I saw him, felt him, heard him, and just sensed him.

"Did you read the article?"

He hunkered down, getting comfortable, but I was angled one way, and he was facing me. After a second, he moved so he was leaning against the dryer, so both our backs were to the same machine. His hand reached for mine, and he entwined our pinkies.

I could handle that. A pinkie touch.

"I just heard about it and heard what it implies."

"She did an interview with a guy."

His pinkie tensed. "The writer is a girl."

I shook my head, even though he couldn't see me. "There's a video linked to the interview. The writer wrote up the article from that video, but the person who was interviewing her in that video was male. I can tell. She was flirting. She's dressed in almost nothing. A bikini top and boy shorts. And she was attracted to the guy, whoever he was, because her make-up wasn't over the top. She dresses for who she's trying to get attention from. She wanted to fuck him. My guess is that the guy was attractive or had money.

And he was younger than her. I could tell that too, by her eyes. She was excited, really excited. And she was biting down on her lip. She only does that if she's a little nervous, if it's someone she doesn't think she can 'get.' She usually hates doing that. Says it's too much of a risk because you could get lipstick on your teeth. That ruins any illusion she's trying to enact."

"I think it's Carrington."

My gut was gone. There was no more dropping for it, and it made sense. Total and complete sense.

"He would've looked into you, found her, and went to her." He added, "Angela never recanted her statement."

I frowned. "What?"

"She's on your side. After your call, she realized it was her roommate and Bianca who leaked the first story about Carrington. She'd been talking to Flynn the whole week too. My guess is that he contacted her after the first story came out. Angela made a comment to her today that she was overwhelmed, something to the effect that she just wanted to take it back and make it all go away. The roommate ran with that and there you go. Angela's moving out right now, but she never recanted her story."

Hope. The bare minimum spurred inside of me. "Flynn still thinks she's recanting?"

"Probably. I doubt the roommate's going to call him and make sure he's on the up-and-up of her mistake."

A little bit more hope. It hadn't all been for nothing then. But still. "The damage is done about my mom. They don't understand how she's so manipulative, and how she twists things. They won't get it. Mothers aren't supposed to be like that."

"I think some will get it."

Most won't. And that's what he wasn't saying.

He added, "Her story wasn't true, and she'll have to take it down. We've had her fined for some of the shit she writes about us because it hurts people."

He didn't get it, or well, maybe he did. All areas of my life were now connected, and I was once again living under her shadow. She'd invaded my sanctuary. People would know, but it wasn't even about my friends, or going to a party and knowing people will judge me. It wasn't about that, none of this was. It was about her, violating my boundaries.

She was in my college life.

I was hiding out in a laundromat because of her.

Cruz tugged on my hand until he wasn't just holding my pinkie, or my hand. He reached over, lifted me up so I was on his lap. He wrapped his arms around me, propping his chin on my shoulder. "It'll be okay."

Maybe. Probably not, though.

"I hate when she would say she was going to kill herself. I hated it so much." A last wall broke in me, and the tears started. I looked down, unable to see him seeing me because it was too real. Too raw. I was too exposed. Those tears were slow. I'd been through so much because of her that it was hard for her to make me cry, but this, in regard to this subject, I'd cry all day long.

"That's real. That's a tragedy. If someone says it, you believe them. You just do. You don't *ever* mess with that, but she did. It's the one go-to she *can* use that I will respond every time. I have to, because if I don't, what if she's not twisting it? Her doctors and her psychologists and her therapists, and her psychiatrists tell me that typically with her disorder, she won't go through with it, but when's the line? There's not a line with that, not that. Someone says it, they get believed. It's my rule. Because if you don't... If you don't believe it one time... When does her one disorder converge into another and *that* one, they do this. She does this. When's that call coming? And I can't do anything, like anything. I go to her, and she uses me up, over and over again until I'm the one who–" I stopped myself, choking back a sob. "Until I'm the one who's thinking about it. But I'm the bad guy. I am. I can't get away, and I can't give enough. It's never enough. It's never–and I'm trapped and here she is, in this life now. This was mine. Just mine, and she got in here. *Again*." I looked up, half seeing him through the tears. "But I love her, and I wish I didn't, and I wish I could just not care. But I do. I do, and no matter how much I try to convince myself otherwise, I *never* want to get the call that she's gone because then she's gone and she's the only mother I have."

"Baby." I heard the tenderness in his tone, but I couldn't see it. I looked down, my eyes swimming, and he pressed a hand to my temple, pulling me close to him. He kissed my forehead, smoothing my hair down, and held me. "I'm sorry, Mara. I'm so sorry."

He held me, and right then, that was enough. There was nothing to say.

Him talking shit about my mom? I didn't need that. I thought enough shit about her. He understood. He got it, and that was the takeaway here for me.

I got him. I got someone who understood.

We stayed like that for a while until Cruz asked, "Let me do some things for you."

"Like what?" I looked up to see him now.

Man, oh man. His hair was messed up, and I frowned. "Didn't you shower?"

He laughed, but in a whoosh, he stood up, lifting me with him. He held me for a moment until I got my bearings, then set me down. He smoothed my hair down once more, his eyes all serious, and he held up a hand. "I'd like to be the one to call your dad about your mom's latest thing. I can tell him about the blogger, and exactly the channels we have to go through to get her stuff removed."

"He's going to know you're my boyfriend."

He grinned, slowly. "Is that a bad thing?"

I swallowed over a knot. "Uh, that's meeting the parents. That's a big thing. A big commitment deal."

"I think it'll be fine."

"What are some of the other things you mentioned?"

"I need to let some people know that I found you and that you're okay. A whole bunch of people were looking for you."

"Oh, no. I didn't–I didn't mean for that to happen, for them to worry about me."

He traced a tender hand down the side of my face, smoothing my hair down again, and drew me back to his chest. "I know, but despite your efforts to keep people at bay, you've failed horribly, and people care. I also don't think you need to worry about people judging you about your mom."

I started to shrug, but he stopped me, his hand resting on my shoulder.

He added, "I mean it. You have people, and some are louder than others. It'll get blasted that the whole interview was a setup. Your mom's truth doesn't need to come out, but we'll change the narrative. Let me do that for you."

I'd had my dad in my corner, as much as he could be, as much as I would let him when I was a kid and when she had custody over me. Then I had a nurse from Fallen Crest and a cop. Now I had Cruz.

A softness came over me. "Yes. I'd really, really, really like that."

"Good." He leaned down, his lips finding mine. He was kissing me tenderly, delicately, gently.

"Gotta warn you also, we've had an audience the whole time." He indicated the door.

Atwater and Barclay were there, both grinning and both waving.

Atwater said, "Heya, Mara. The tear-stricken look agrees with you. You can cry more around us, you know."

I shook my head. "Shut up." Atwater enveloped me in a big hug right away, lifting me off my feet.

Barclay was next, and he added, more quieter during our hug, "We got your back. Angela has your back. All your friends have your back. I'm sure your boy told you, but it's going to be okay."

He let me go, and Cruz stepped up, his arm going around my shoulders.

Maybe it would.

50

CRUZ

There was something interesting about a kid who threw a party for the rival hockey team, who stomped *his* team, at his fraternity and that the party was overflowing to the street. But that's what Zeke Allen did. Once we let him know Mara was found, and okay, and being taken care of, he promptly said he was back to party hosting duties. We were given instructions and a timeframe when to show up, and well; we did. Most of the hockey team came with us, but that'd been after we took her to the hotel, got into our room, and she had a moment with her roommates.

I told Barclay and Atwater enough about her mom's situation where they understood there was some serious "other" shit involved. They, in turn, took it upon themselves to start spreading the word that whatever that blogger wrote, she didn't know shit about anything. Atwater knew a few of the bigger gossips from school, and he got on the phone asap with them. When we got to the party, I wasn't surprised to see that some were studying Mara differently, more curious and less judgy.

It was working.

"She okay?" Zeke found me in the kitchen. I'd been

watching Mara through the patio windows, to where she was sitting with some of her roommates. Tasmin and her whole group were also out there.

I gave him a nod. "She is."

"Everything handled about the mom?"

I gave him a sharper look. "You're aware?"

He nodded, folding his arms over his chest. "Came out earlier. Mara kept quiet about her mom almost our whole lives. I remember weird shit when we were in elementary school, but what kid remembers stuff from before fifth grade? You know? But yeah. It got out among our group back in January. The ones who care have let her know."

I gave a slow nod. That said a lot right there. "Thank you."

He laughed, shaking his head. "No way. I mean, you're part of the reason she's even letting us as close as we've gotten. She didn't let us in last year. Though, I have to admit that I've changed a lot over the summer and fall. I don't take my relationships for granted anymore. Daniels, she's a good one. She's sweet inside even when she wants the world to think she's a bitch."

"I'm aware."

"Take care of her. You hear me?" He stood up, holding his hand out. All the other times I'd been around this kid, he'd been crazy or obnoxious or funny. This time, he was all serious.

I shook his hand back. "Keep being a good friend to her."

He gave me a cocky smirk and saluted me with two fingers. "Planning on it. By the way, her and me, we never went there. There was a short time last year when she was a little messed up, but I didn't go there. Felt like a sister." He gazed at her, that cocky smirk getting even cockier. "I regret that somedays."

I scowled. "I used to think you were okay. Not great, or good, but okay. Strange. A little odd, but okay. You want that shit to go away?"

He barked out a laugh, half hitting me in the chest. "I'm just joking." He shrugged, winking before leaving. "Kinda."

Yeah. Strange kid. Very strange.

Atwater headed over, breaking away from a couple girls. He held up his phone to me. "Angela's all moved in."

"Good."

"Angela?"

Atwater cringed because just in the doorway, coming in was Wade. Miles and Darren were with him. "Where's Angela moving?"

Atwater kept grimacing.

Miles was frowning, moving between us. A few Cain people were taking notice.

Wade asked, "You going to answer me?"

More Cain people came over, and there was movement outside. People were coming in from the back.

Zeke returned, his head angling around the corner until he saw something was happening, then he came the rest of the way. One of his fraternity brothers was next to him. They both pushed their way until they were just on the fringe.

"Atwater. What the fuck?" Wade's voice went up a notch.

"Whoa, man." Darren touched his chest.

Miles moved toward me, sipping his drink, but he gestured with his elbow to Wade. "Something up there?"

Wade was still giving Atwater a look, but at Miles' question, all eyes came my way.

Zeke moved in, right beside me, and I glanced up, seeing Mara standing on a picnic table outside. She was leaning down to get a better look. At seeing me, at seeing Wade and his expression, her eyes got big, and she hopped down.

"Jesus, Kressup. You don't think she's got enough on her plate?"

"What?"

I lifted my chin toward the back, but I knew it was too late.

Mara would be in here in two seconds. "You could've asked Atwater in private, not where there's a scene."

"What are you talking about?"

"Hey." But Mara was here and settling in front of me.

Wade's gaze went to her, then me, then Atwater. His eyebrows were pushed low. "What the fuck is going on?" He pointed at Atwater, then swung his hand to me. "He was talking to him about Angela. She's moving in. Where's she moving? Why's everyone all concerned about this?" He asked the last part as he was noticing the crowd that had gathered.

Miles frowned at my direction, Mara's, and Atwater's before his gaze dropped to Atwater's phone. "Angela hangs out with the hockey house. She said she was gone that Sunday, out of town. You two were at the beach. That's where Carrington was arrested. Angela's gone MIA, and you both have been tightlipped about what happened that day—" His eyes suddenly narrowed. "—about who he assaulted."

Mara moved farther back into me.

Miles looked like he'd been hit. "You serious?"

"What's going on?" Wade was looking between all of us. "Is someone going to tell me what's going on? I mean, Jesus Christ. We're already playing the game where we're not talking about the real elephant in the room."

I started forward. "Don't go there."

He ignored me, gesturing to Mara. "You did a whole Houdini act today, and that article about your mom? What the fuck, Mara? What kind of–" There was growling behind me, but I was already there.

I took three steps to him. "You were already told that article was fake information. Why do you need to bring that up now?"

There was more movement happening behind me, but I wasn't paying attention. Then I felt people lining up behind me. I knew they were Atwater, Barclay, and more of my team.

"What the fuck–why are you in my space?"

"Because you were already told about that article. You're her roommate, and you're bringing it up tonight, at a party, with an audience, when you're starting to think that a girl you're into maybe isn't into you. That's why, and I'm taking offense because if your pride is hurt, and this is how you react, then that makes me feel a certain way with you sharing the same house as my girl. That's why I'm in your space. Now. What's your real issue here?"

He swallowed, before rolling his eyes. "Nothing. It's nothing."

I began easing back.

Wade smoothed a hand down his shirt. "It's very obvious Angela's not into me. Noted." He caught on Mara again, as she moved closer to me, and his mouth tightened. "Seems I fall for girls into hockey guys. That's all."

Mara's hand slid into my back pocket, and she stood next to me.

Wade shoved through the crowd.

Darren lingered before jerking his head toward Miles. "We gotta go with him."

"But." Miles glanced my way.

"We're his boys. Let's go." He held his fist out to me. I met it with one of mine, and then to Mara. She did the same, giving him the cutest smile. He grinned back. "We'll see you tomorrow maybe?"

She nodded. "Make sure he doesn't do anything stupid."

Darren ran a hand over the top of his head. "Nah. He ain't like that. He's just...hurting."

Miles remained, his eyes hard on Mara. "Was it you?"

She tensed, her hand pressing against me. She hesitated, then shook her head. "It wasn't me."

Relief cleared in his gaze, and his head dipped in one firm nod before he finished his beer. He handed his empty glass to Mara. "Then, what Darren said."

They left, and the crowd was starting to disperse, when suddenly there was a screech of brakes. Then another, and another.

"Oh." A guy called out, running inside. "We have incoming." He went straight to the kitchen, finding Zeke. "Alpha Mu guys. I'm thinking they drove here."

Zeke spared me a look. "You know what this is about?"

Mara growled, stepping in front of me. "Me."

51

MARA

Carrington led the way.

He was followed by a bunch of his brothers, and at the same time a lot of Zeke's own fraternity brothers pushed to the forefront too.

Flynn gave Cruz a measured look, which was returned. Then, his eyes found me and all niceties vanished.

God. I gulped.

He came *straight* for me, shoving people aside so he landed smack dab in front of me, or he would've. His finger was up, he was pointing it right at me, until Cruz stepped in. As fast as Flynn had been coming at me, Cruz was walking him backwards, saying, "Step back, man."

Flynn went. He didn't fight it. It happened so quick.

Atwater, Barclay, and the other guys from his team swarmed right after him.

They weren't alone. Zeke got in front of me, and I looked, seeing the rest of my roommates. Skylar. Zoe. Kit and Burford too, a bunch of other Kappa girls. Leander, Flynn's brother was in the mix as well, but in the middle. Not like Gavin, who stood at the back. Leander had his hands out, like he wanted to keep the peace. He was looking between everyone, but seeing me seeing him, he gave me a sad smile.

That was all I needed.

I mirrored him.

Flynn saw it, screaming, "DON'T FUCKING SMILE AT MY BROTHER!" He lunged for me.

Cruz met him, shoving him back, and growled. "I told you to step back."

He hit his arm down, growling right back. "I don't need to fucking—" He didn't finish because he swung on Cruz. Who ducked, and who punched back. Flynn didn't duck.

All hell broke loose after that.

Alpha Mu guys were fighting the Grant West hockey team.

Zeke's frat was in the mix.

There was shoving.

Two guys started trading hits, migrating toward me. An arm came around my waist. I was lifted, carried out of there.

"Hey! Stop. Put me down." I twisted, saw Gavin, and shoved back at him. "Let go of me."

He did, in the doorway and out of the kitchen. Skylar, Zoe, and Tasmin surrounded us.

I was trying to watch the fight, but snapped at Gavin, "Nice of you to fucking show up. I thought we were friends."

"We are." He snapped back, then added, with less of a bite, "I thought so too."

"Your leader in there is trying to ruin my life."

"I didn't know he was going to do that. I didn't. I–" He twisted his head to see what was going on, then cursed. "Screw it. Did he actually hurt her or not? What Flynn is saying makes no sense. Leander tried to tell me there's more to the story."

"Of course there's more to the story, like the fact that there's really a girl that he hurt. How about that? And no, Gavin. I'm not spilling who it is. That's a really shitty thing to do to someone. As your friend, I shouldn't have to tell you that. You should just know by knowing me."

"But do I?" He flung his hands out. "You don't let anyone in."

"You got in!" I shoved at his chest. "Cruz got in. And you're not paying attention." I motioned around. "I've got friends. I let them in, and thanks to your asshole brother in there, everyone has an idea how messed up my home life is."

"What are you talking about?"

I started laughing, hard, brutal, and ugly. These weren't happy laughs. "Are you kidding me?"

"What?"

"Miller." Skylar handed over her phone. I was guessing it was the blog.

He took it, his eyes going wide, but he went still.

"WHERE IS SHE? WHERE IS SHE?" Flynn was screaming from the kitchen.

He was being held back by a bunch of guys. Cruz was bleeding from his face, but he was still standing, and he wasn't being held back. Zeke and a couple hockey guys were in front of him, making sure he couldn't get past them to Flynn.

A bunch of guys were shouting back and forth.

"Shut the fuck up," Atwater snapped.

That sent off another surge. One of Flynn's frat brothers launched at him, and the hockey team, whoever was there, waded in.

"This is—" Gavin had to stop, giving Skylar her phone back. "That's insane. Your mom tried to do that. What are you doing here?"

"Let me ask you something and be honest. Where was Flynn today?"

"At the house."

"Then where was he yesterday?"

He shrugged. "I don't know. Gone. A lot of guys leave for the day."

"The day?"

"Yeah. Why?"

I took Skylar's phone and brought up the video, hitting play. My mom's voice came through, and she was laughing. A whole seductive and sultry laugh. I pointed at the phone. "Because this is how she sounds when she wants to fuck someone. She wants attention from whoever is holding this recording device, and she's eating it up. All the attention this guy is giving her." My mom bent forward, letting one of her tits show. "Her make-up was on point."

"I'm thinking that's a normal thing for women. They know how to do make-up."

"Not her."

He went still, so did my roommates, and so did some people in the kitchen.

The music cut, and I'd be told later that my voice carried as I kept on, clipping out, "Ever dealt with someone who has a chronic personality disorder? Know what it's like? You feel like you want to hit your head against the wall. Imagine that feeling every day of your life. Imagine your mom wanting to sleep with all of your teachers, your friends, your bosses, your co-workers. Jesus. I'm just getting started. That's what she does. Her. She drains you and drains everyone, and you get nothing back. When you're not giving her what she wants, she moves onto the next, and everything is about her. *Everything.* The few times you got a birthday party, they're about her. The few times. If it doesn't fit into her schedule to get you a Christmas gift, you're not getting one. 'Tough shit, you little shit.' I heard that when I six, seven, and eight. Then I stopped asking. When you need to get picked up after school when you're in third grade. Not going to happen, not unless it fits into her schedule." I shoved that phone at him, even knowing it wasn't his, but I was beyond caring. He had no idea. None. "And yeah. Six days ago, your fraternity brother showed up at a beach with a girl and three other guys. He insulted me, threatened me, and Cruz laid him out. Guess what your other brothers did? Nothing. They watched it happen. They didn't do a damned thing. Think on that, Gavin. Your fraternity brother is getting pummeled, and you stand back. It was just me there. No one else. They could've pulled him off in a heartbeat and they didn't. They had time to figure it out, to see what was going on. They stood there, just stood there. I noticed *her*, and the state she was in, and the state Flynn was in, and I started asking questions."

"The fuck you did! You set me up!"

I whirled, seeing so many eyes on me. They'd turned my way, facing me, but I shoved through them. A line opened, letting me pass until I broke through the circle.

Flynn was being held back by the two brothers that'd been there that day.

I started laughing, seeing them. "This is classic. These guys." I addressed them, "You're showing up now?"

One gave me a nasty look.

I raised my middle finger at him. "Where were you then? Huh? Before he did what he did to her?"

"We didn't–" The other guy hit him in the arm. He didn't notice, hissing without thinking, "We didn't know he was going to hurt her! They were kissing, then suddenly she's yelling for him to get off her. And he wouldn't." He shoved back, pushing Flynn into the door as he did. He held his hands up, backing away. "I'm not this kind of guy, Carrington. I'm not down with this shit."

"Dude!" The first guy grabbed him, shoving him backwards. "Shut. Up!"

"I don't care. I'm not down with it."

"It's true?" Gavin had followed me.

My voice almost broke as I said, "Like I said, you know me. You know him. You should know better."

"You fucking bit–"

"My mother." My voice did break. I circled around to see Flynn better. More one on one, though three guys stepped between us, partially blocking my view. Cruz moved up behind me, his hand went to the side of my hip. "You went to my mom?"

"I didn't–"

"You did!" I started for him, but Cruz's hand held me back. "Just admit it. You threatened me five days ago. I got texts warning me that you were coming after me four days ago. Miller said you were at the house today, so that leaves yesterday. My mom's supposed to be in a facility. Where did you find her?"

His face was red. His mouth was clamped shut. He wanted to tell me. He *wanted* to hurt me.

I started nodding, knowing why he was doing it, but man. "My mom? Really?"

Whatever was holding him back broke. He started laughing, a harsh sound. "Yeah, she's fucked up. Offered to blow me and my buddy if we did her. She wasn't in a facility. Went to her place, but she wasn't there. We reached out over her social media. She responded within three seconds. Told us right away where to meet her, and she loved talking about you. She told us all about you, how messed up you are, how you were introduced to sex too early in life. She *loved* telling us that story. You came on to–"

I knew it then. He was just going to go on, and on, and on.

He was going to rub the whole meeting in my face.

He was going to say and do anything to hurt me.

There was no point to this anymore.

"Enough." Cruz moved before anyone could stop him. He wrapped his arm around Flynn's neck, yanked him down, locked his arm with his other one, and applied pressure. "Time to go to sleep, buddy."

Flynn was bent down, struggling. His face filled with color and as he gasped, he slowly, just, went to sleep. He tried hitting on Cruz's arm, but no one helped him.

That said everything.

When he was out, Cruz dropped him. His frat brother knelt, feeling for his pulse, and stood back. "He's fine. He's just unconscious."

Cruz was coming for me. "Party's over."

I nodded, feeling him pick me up. I was just fine with that.

I said to Gavin as Cruz carried me past him, "Hope your trip was worth it."

52

MARA

I was in bed with Cruz when my phone woke me up.

Reaching down to the floor, I grabbed it and brought it up, but Cruz's arm was around my waist. He was spooning me from behind, and no way was I moving away.

Skylar: We're heading back. Wade called Angela and she wanted to talk to him. How are you doing?

Me: Good. Tired. Emotional hangover.

Skylar: I can only imagine. I'm sorry about your mom. I didn't know. We didn't know.

Me: I know. It's... a little weird, to be honest. I'm not used to people knowing.

Skylar: My mom suffers from chronic anxiety and depression. And he told me last night that I could tell you that Miles' brother suffers from schizophrenia.

Me: I didn't know that.

Skylar: It's not something we lead with, but my mom has her good days and bad. It's an up and down thing. Miles can tell you about his brother, but we wanted you to know that we understand.

My whole body sighed. It went from my toes to the top of

my head. I even felt myself sinking lower into the mattress, getting more comfortable than I already had been. I was feeling it at a soul sorta level.

Me: Thank you for letting me know.

Skylar: No problem. Taz texted to tell me she's getting a ride back with someone else. Her and Race. She said to let you know. You're going back with Cruz?

Me: I think so. That's the plan.

Skylar: We'll see you back at the house! Safe travels.

I went through my texts after, seeing a couple from everyone. Most were sharing their support. There was one from Miles, saying the same that Skylar just shared. Then at the bottom, I clicked on it.

Gavin: Can we talk sometime? I've been an ass.

Me: Yeah. Let's do a library study sesh. You can buy me coffee before.

He didn't reply, but another just popped in before I was going to put the phone away.

Blaise: Hey—happy for you and Styles. I never knew about your mom, but it makes sense. You don't need to text back. I just wanted to send a small note to you. Anytime you need something, know that Zeke and I will always back you up. Just saying. Have a good one, Mara.

I frowned, then got a little emotional, but I replied back.

Thank you. You too, Blaise.

Blaise: thumbs-up emoji

Cruz's arm tightened, and he turned, rolling to his back. He brought me with him, and I squawked right as my phone fell onto his chest.

He grinned, his eyes soft from sleep and there were sleep lines still around his mouth. Picking up my phone, he murmured, "Who's texting my woman?"

I rested my head on his chest, loving how his arm swept to brush my hair back and smooth down my back. That hand went under my panties and rested over my ass, cupping one cheek.

"Read the last text."

He did, his thumb moving over my screen. "Well, that's unexpected."

I moved my head so I could see him better. "The one from Blaise?"

He shook his head, the slightest motion from right to left. "No, the one from Miller. If he's buying you coffee, I want to go too. He can buy me coffee as well."

I grinned.

My phone buzzed again, and Cruz's eyes found mine. I gave him a faint nod.

He clicked on the latest text, then chuckled. "Zeke says he wants to grab lunch before we take off."

I stretched over him, sliding one of my legs between his.

He lifted his head, his mouth finding mine, and the swirl of lust started.

I loved it. Every time. Like a warm blanket spreading through me, lined with pleasure. That was just the start-up.

A groan came from the bed next to us. "Oh, Good God! Do not start having sex. We're in here too."

Another thump and curse came from the floor, at the end of the bed where Barclay was on the floor. "Uh. I've got a situation here. Cruz, no disrespect. Mara, you might not want to look while I go to the bathroom."

Cruz's arm tightened around me, but his chest was shaking from laughter.

I frowned, burrowing even closer to Cruz if that was a possibility.

A second later Atwater's laughter ripped through the room. "Morning wood!"

53

MARA

It was a little over a week later, and I was nervous.

My stomach was churning, but I had to do this. We'd had our field trip over the weekend, and today was when we were presenting on what we learned. Wade just finished, so it was my turn.

She looked up. "Mara?"

I stood, smoothing a hand down my shirt as I walked to the front of the class.

I hated speeches. I hated how forced things came across. The use of visual aids. I just hated all of it, maybe because I tuned out unless someone was speaking about something they knew, not just what they learned to get the grade or what they put together based on what they thought the professor wanted to hear.

Maybe that was in the back of my mind because I hadn't prepared for this presentation at all. The professor took a seat in one of the student desks, and I felt the attention from her TA.

I got to the front of the class and brought up a picture of my mom.

A small murmur went through the room. A few people were pulling up their phones, no doubt looking for the article about my mother that we got pulled within a day of it going up.

I gestured to the picture. "This is my mom." I glanced in the TA's direction before addressing the rest of the class. "I was asked earlier this semester if I was mature enough for this class. It's for upperclassmen, and me being a freshman, the TA didn't think I was ready."

I ignored how her eyes narrowed or how the professor's head snapped in her direction. I just told my story. "The truth is that I've been preparing for this class all my life. My mom was diagnosed with histrionic personality disorder, and recently they've attached a couple other diagnoses with it. I can't tell you when I knew, but I've known all my life that my mother was different. We've studied the disorder in here. You guys know the DSM requirements, but the point of this presentation isn't about my mom or how I grew up, it's about what we learned from our field trip. And what I learned from that trip is that I could've done this presentation before the trip. I didn't need to go to a facility because I've been going to those facilities on and off, half my life. I'm tired of it. I've visited my mom there. Sometimes with my dad. Sometimes with a social worker. Sometimes with a child protective service staff member. You name it, we've run the gamut.

"And I can tell you the symptomology of chronic depression, anxiety, borderline, schizophrenia, and Jesus, so many. I know the symptoms. I've seen the symptoms. That's not the point of these presentations. I'm supposed to stand here and tell you how people who have struggles with mental illness are people, and that's true. They are. I'm sure I could go in and get a diagnosis myself. For sure anxiety. With my mom having what she has, I've got severe trust issues. I'm always waiting for the 'shoe to drop.' When my dad calls, I prepare myself every time for the newest crisis because with my mom, the world is ending every day. I've had to teach myself that it's not true. That the world is not after her. The neighbor who looked at her isn't plotting to get her money or her husband or her daughter. That she doesn't have cancer even though she constantly says she does.

"When I came to college, I wanted a break. And I got it. I did, but I've learned other things, like how I can have friends, how they can know about my mom, and they aren't going to judge me. Or look down on me because of her or look down on her because at the end of the day, she's my mom." My voice broke, just one break. "This disease or disorder took her from me. It took her daughter from her. I might not be able to have a relationship with my mom, at least not right now, but I love her. And maybe that's what I need to present about. That no matter the diagnosis or the symptoms or how exhausting and hard life can be, that person is a person.

"They're someone's mother, sister, daughter, loved one, father, brother, son, uncle, aunt, grandmother, grandfather. There's ups and downs, or dips and valleys, and sometimes they'll get help and sometimes they won't, and sometimes they'll get on a new medication and it'll work, and sometimes it'll stop working so there'll be a new medication, and to each their own.

"I can tell you that some therapy works, some don't, some therapists are great, and others aren't a great fit. I can tell you that there are some people who work in that field who shouldn't, but there are some who were born to do it, and I swear, it's their life purpose. There's good and bad. There's heavy and light. So, wrapping up my presentation, which I made it mostly about me, ironically, is that there's ebbs and flows. Some have harder struggles than others. Some can get on one med and they're 'fixed' and others take a lifetime, but it's life. I don't think I did what the presentation was supposed to be about, but I couldn't because I didn't learn anything new going to those two facilities. What I am learning this whole year is that healing can be achieved for some of us who didn't think it was possible, and I'm hopeful that maybe one day, I *can* have a relationship with her. Because I love her, because she's my mom."

I felt weird, and awkward as I headed for my seat. Exposed. But it was a whole different outlook to go from keeping friends at a distance where I was almost living two separate lives to suddenly having people who knew me. Who I could go to, talk to, not have to be vague about the normal and easy questions, and not having to avoid people because my battery for life was already in the red. It was new and uncomfortable, but whatever.

I almost laughed at myself. Look at me, being hopeful.

THE PROFESSOR CALLED ME OVER, with the TA standing to the side. "Mara, I had no idea Torrance was questioning if you should be here or not. I, personally, had approved your place here because I read your application essay. Please accept my apology for any stress you endured from Torrance's doubt. It was not her place to question my decision. I am very sorry."

That was surprising, and then she gave the TA a stern look.

Torrance cleared her throat. She tucked her hands behind her back and squared her shoulders. She didn't totally look me in the eye, but she was looking at me. Probably my forehead so the effect was the same. "I had no idea about your background, and I apologize. It wasn't my place."

Right. I gave each a nod, not used to adults acting, well; adult-like.

When I went out into the hallway, Wade was waiting for me. He flashed me a sad smile. "Things make more sense. I heard about your mom, and read the article."

I nodded, but there wasn't anything to say. I lifted a shoulder. "Uh. Yeah."

A cloud came over him, his eyebrows dipping low. "Can I–uh–I'm sorry if I was a dick that day. At the Cain fraternity party. I–"

"You really liked Angela."

His mouth closed, tightly and he nodded. "Yeah. I did." He laughed, abruptly, and raked a hand through his hair. "I feel like a dumbass because you gave this whole speech and made yourself vulnerable, and I just want to ask you about Angela. She told me she's not in a place to date anyone."

"Did she say why?"

His head lowered. "Said something serious happened. That was it, but how's she doing?"

I didn't have a response for him.

His eyes locked on mine, and he sighed. "I have to let her go, huh?"

"I don't know. Honestly."

"Okay. Okay!" A crooked grin tugged at the corner of his mouth, and he put an arm around my shoulder as we both began for the door. "Roomie to roomie, I could go for a drink."

I held up a fist. "I'm down."

He laughed, meeting his fist to mine. "At the house or the pub?"

I considered it, then knew. "At the pub."

54

CRUZ

I was heading into the bar because Mara texted, said she'd been there since noon drinking with her roommates. It was after practice and the other guys were with me. They headed inside, but I held back when my phone buzzed.

Mom: *picture.*

It was a picture of Titi all smiles. They were at a party, or I was guessing from the balloons and the rainbow painted on Titi's cheek.

Me: She looks good. Happy.

Mom: She is! Things are good, honey. I know we talk often, but I felt like sending that message again today. We're good. Titi's good. You're good. I know you worry, but you don't need to. I love you, sweetheart. So very much. We're going to visit Sissy tomorrow in the cemetery. Would you like us to FaceTime you when we're there?

I stared at my phone, but I couldn't give her the response she wanted. Or maybe she needed. I just couldn't.

"Cruz?"

I looked up, and instantly scowled. Sabrina Burford was coming out of the bar, a tentative look on her face. Then, her chin firmed, and she came closer. "I saw the guys and noticed you were still out here." Her eyes went to my phone. A small frown came over her face. She folded her head, some of her hair falling forward. "I know you didn't want me to go see your mom and sister, but I had to. I'm sorry. I'm not sorry for going, but I'm sorry that I went when you didn't want me to go. That doesn't make sense." She looked away, a sad expression coming over her. "I knew your sister was... I'm trying to say that I knew Sarah was different. But I liked her. Sometimes she could be mean. I saw that side of her, but I also saw times when she seemed tortured. I didn't understand, and I don't know if I ever will, but I know Titi was in the car because of me. I've not been perfect. I'm a bitch, stuck-up, you know. But I am who I am. And I just wanted you to know that I was always kind when I was around Titi. My mom only had me, and I always wanted a little sister. With Titi, it felt like I had a little sister.

"Look, I'm not here asking for your permission, but your mom is okay with me continuing to visit. I'd like to do that." Her eyes flashed at me. Determined. "I'm going to do that. Sarah would want me to do that."

"You don't know what Sarah would want."

She shook her head. "You're wrong. Sarah wasn't always mean with me. We had fun times, and sometimes I think I know her in ways you never will. And I do think she'd want me to continue seeing Titi. She'd want me to do it because she can't, just like when she was alive. She knew I was the sister that she couldn't be. It's half the reason I spent so much time with Titi. Your sister cared, in her way."

"My sister is dead. I don't think she gives two fucks about us."

"You're wrong. I know you think she didn't care about you, but she did. She wasn't nice to you all the time. I know she was jealous of you, but she was also proud in her way. There's a drawer in her room where she printed off every article there was written about you. Ask your mom about it sometime. She knows it's there." She held up a hand, heading back for the door. "I'll see you inside, or not, if that's what you want."

I gave her a look, but I didn't respond. No matter what she said or what she did, Burford and I wouldn't be buddy-buddy. But maybe I didn't need to hate her as much as I did.

I texted my mom.

I'm not ready to FaceTime when you're there, but could you take a flower for her from me?

Mom: Of course! Titi will hold it the whole way there.

55

MARA

The hockey guys came in. Burford went out. Then, Burford came in again, fighting back tears, and I was starting to slide off my stool when my phone buzzed.

Dad: Hey, honey. We've not talked in a bit. I'd love to come see you. I have new things to tell you about.

I frowned, heading outside.

Cruz was just coming in, but pulled back, a frown on his face at seeing me.

I held up a finger and motioned farther over in the parking lot for some privacy. I hit dial and held the phone up to my ear.

My dad picked up right away. "Mara!"

"What's going on?" The alarm was real and tight in my stomach, though he sounded happy.

"Oh, Mara. No. It's all good." He laughed. "I was calling to let you know that I took your advice. I'm attending this support group. I don't think I told you that part, but I met a woman there. She was attending with her sister, who comes regularly, but the woman and I hit it off. Her name is Gabriela and, uh, we've been dating. For a couple weeks now. She's wonderful, Mara."

"I–" I was stunned. "You're dating?"

"Yeah." Another laugh from him, more relieved. "Can you believe it? I really like her."

"You haven't dated since you divorced Mom."

"I know!"

God. He was happy.

I pressed back against the building, feeling Cruz move in closer.

I reached out, touching his chest, and he lifted his hand, taking mine in his. His thumb rubbed over the back of my hand while I choked up.

I said, my voice hoarse, "I'm happy to hear that, Dad. You sound happy."

"I am. I really am, and listen, I'm handling things on this end with your mom. You don't need to worry about anything. Okay? I really want you to know that. I know things are a mess with your mom. They always will be, but at the end of the day, your mom is never going to leave you. I'm never going to leave you. I'm only saying that because sometimes I think you worry I'll go away. I won't. I never was. Right now, you go to college and focus on yourself. Be happy yourself. Be a kid, Mara. Within reason, of course. Don't drink or drink and drive. Don't have sex. Don't get an STD. Don't cheat. You know, the normal things a dad is going to worry about their daughter doing in college. I just want you to be a kid right now."

"Thanks, Dad." A pressure lifted off my shoulders.

"Let me know when is a good time to visit you. I'd love to bring Gabby up with me."

"Maybe next week?"

"Sure. Next week! We'll come for the weekend, and I can meet your boyfriend. He plays hockey, right?"

I smiled, remembering how Cruz had handled everything for me, calling my dad, telling him what my mom did. "Yes. He has a hockey game here. I'll get us tickets."

"Don't worry about that. I'll get us tickets. You just tell me what day. I'll handle all of that."

We ended the call not long after, and Cruz pulled me closer to him. He rested his chin on the top of my head. "Your dad's got a new woman?"

"You heard?"

"Hard not to. He sounded happy."

"He did."

He did. He really did, and standing, half resting against Cruz, I went down the checklist and realized something.

Life was good. I turned in to Cruz, my arms sliding behind his back as I hugged him. I held him as tight as I could, and after a beat, his arms went around me too. Both of his arms.

We stayed there, just like that for a bit.

Life was *really* good.

"Cruz," I murmured, my heart pausing because did I want to say this? Did I want to push this and risk going too far? But I was feeling it, and I was done with holding back. I'd held so much back all my life. I looked up at him.

He gazed down at me. "What?"

I held my breath and then said, "I love you."

His eyes softened. His smile turned tender, and he touched a finger under my chin. "I think I've always loved you." Then his lips touched mine.

So, this was what love felt like.

EPILOGUE

MARA

"Babe!"

I hated skating. Hated it. I was horrible at it, but you know who loved it? My man. And because of that, because it was our four-year anniversary, because we'd been through hills and valleys and we were still shining, hell yes, I was about to put on some skates and slowly move around the rink with Cruz.

He was already out there. I was taking my time, because hello, the definition of the word stall. I was doing it. The less time on ice, the better for my safety.

But at Cruz's shout, the procrastination needed to end. I sighed, stood from the bench, and went over to step onto the ice. After that, wobbly knees, legs, and lots of prayers were being said. But I was out there, and Cruz whipped around me, until he was in front of me, and moving backwards. "You're doing good."

I growled, giving him a look.

He just grinned. "You're cute when you're growly."

I did it again because his eyes got *that look*, and yeah, I'd rather be doing what we were doing in the bed before we got up to do this mid-morning skate.

He chuckled, but turned and knelt down. He patted his back. "Hop on. I'll show you how I move."

I frowned. "On your back?"

"Yep. Come on." He gave me another nod, and with a deep breath, I climbed on, but I didn't need to worry. He reached back, grabbed my legs, and hoisted me up himself, moving me so I bounced higher up. He clamped me to him, bending forward a little, and then we were off.

He was easily holding me in place, and I stopped worrying, wrapping my arms around him so I wouldn't accidentally choke him if I got scared. He was whipping around the ice, and I got it. This was fast, and fun. Racing. My heart was pounding. I felt like I was flying, but I was being held on my man's back, a back that had gotten a little harder as he joined the pros. He was in way better shape than college, and I thought he'd been in amazing shape back then. It was nothing since he joined the Arizona Javalina team.

And that's where we were, moving down here after last year's graduation. The party had been epic with all of Cruz's hockey teammates and roommates. Except Labrowski. He went pro a year earlier, but Cruz waited until he graduated. My roommates were there, with Wade and Darren coming back. They both moved to New York City for different jobs, sharing a tiny apartment. Gavin came as well, and he'd come with his arm around Sabrina Burford. I didn't know how I felt about that relationship. It was new at the time. He'd changed over the last two years once Flynn Carrington was found guilty on criminal charges for assaulting Angela. He pled out, and paid mostly a fine with community service for a year, but it was the civil suit she filed against him that really hurt. The rumor that he paid her was of a significant sum. I had no idea if it was true or not, but he had to attend intensive counseling. He also lost his fraternity and was expelled from Grant West. Ironically, his brother stepped into his shoes, and Leander had them volunteering at a local shelter. I stopped partying at the Alpha Mu house, but I heard once Leander had them doing that volunteering, it changed a lot of the other guys.

But Gavin, his attitude never changed. He apologized, but that'd been it. He stepped back once it was confirmed I'd been telling the truth about Carrington, not that it ever needed to go there, but he made it go there. He chose his fraternity brother, and never chose my friendship again. We still partied at times, though it was a random large house party or at the bar, but those times were rare. I stuck with my roommates and the hockey house.

Zeke also came for the graduation party, bringing an entire sprinter van of some of his friends that had become friends with Cruz's friends. Tasmin and Race. All of Taz's siblings came, and all their friends too. Epic. It'd just been epic, and my body was sore the next day from laughing so hard.

My dad came with his new wife.

Cruz's mother and sister came.

It'd been a whole celebration, and I never would've imagined that I could've been as happy as I had been that night. But I was just as happy today. I got happier every day with Cruz, and he kept zipping around the ice.

They'd opened up the rink to the public for the day. I thought Cruz would've wanted to steer clear, but nope. Not my man. When I asked what he wanted to do, skating with me was his immediate answer. It was his first year on the team, so he didn't get recognized that much in public. Being on the ice was a different matter. I knew he'd be signing autographs once we slowed down. People were eying him as soon as we showed up, gazes skirting to where I'd been on the bench when he was waiting for me, and now I saw a handful of phones aimed at us.

Those videos would end up on social media. Cruz was getting more and more attention in the hockey and sports world.

We stayed on the ice for another thirty minutes, with the last ten skating next to each other. Or I was skating. Cruz held my hand, my elbow, my hip, my ass as he did circles around me, but he loved this shared time together.

Once we were done, a few teenagers came up, asking for his signature. That started the wave of fans approaching him. Little boys. Little girls getting autographs for their older and "too cool" brothers. Teenage girls. Older people. A few parents came over to share their support and thanks that he joined The Javalina.

I waited by the concessions, within eyesight of Cruz, because that was important to him whenever these situations happened, and I was enjoying the hot chocolate I got. He stayed until someone from the rink's staff approached, and after that, the worker was herding people away. Cruz came over, his head ducking, and an adorable grin on his face as he dropped down next to me, except he didn't face the table. He faced me, pulling me into his chest, his arms wrapped around me. He leaned in, nuzzling my neck. "I love you." One of his hands moved up to my face, touching my chin and turning me his way as he lifted his head.

I melted. He sounded so carefree, and I reached up, my hand covering his before I leaned in. My lips found his, and right there. Insta love. Insta lust. Insta warmth. Insta fuzzies. I was totally gone for him. "I love you too."

"Hmmm." He went back to kissing me before lifting his head a little. He gave me a pat on the ass. "It's our day. What do you want to do?"

The team had been given a very rare day off, so we were taking advantage of it.

What did I want to do? I gave him a look, and he started laughing. "What?" he asked.

I just wanted to stay in bed with him. That's what I wanted

to do, but Cruz knew those were my comfort days. I shrugged. "I don't know."

"Okay." His hand took mine, his fingers sliding against mine as he linked our hands and he stood, pulling me up with him. "How about I plan something for tonight?"

I almost stopped, but he only laughed and tugged me after him again.

He pulled me to his side, his arm wrapping around me, sliding into my back pocket, and he took my hot chocolate. It was almost gone so he wagged it back and forth. I nodded, letting him know he could finish it. He did, tipping his head back before tossing it into the recycling as we walked past.

"Let me plan something for tonight." He brought it up again once we were outside and heading for his truck.

I narrowed my eyes at him, suspicion lurking. "You already have something planned, don't you?"

His eyes cut away. He was fighting back a grin. "Maybe."

Maybe my ass. He totally had something in the works.

He did. Once we walked inside our house, I walked into the kitchen and it was full of pink and cream balloons. Pink roses, peonies, baby's breath, and orchids filled the room. I gaped. "Wha–" I walked farther in, seeing them in the dining room.

The living room.

"Oh my God, Cruz. Who did this?" They were in the second living room.

The hallway.

The front entryway.

I went up to the bedroom, and they were in there.

I went through the whole house. Every inch was covered.

"This must've cost a fortune." I was walking back, still in a daze, when I braked because it took a second for me to fully register what I was seeing.

He was kneeling down, holding out a box toward me.

"Cruz," I whispered, feeling tears in my throat.

He opened the box, and a ring. A diamond ring. A *sparkling* diamond ring was there that he was now holding to me. He took a breath, his eyes shining, but a little clouded over. "We've been through a lot. You put up with me with all the intense pressure that comes with my job, the blogs, puck bunnies–"

Oh. I wanted him to stop.

He kept on, his voice dipping, "—when my mom had her accident, and you helped take care of Titi during our holidays."

None of that had been a hardship. I loved his mother. I loved his sister. They took one look at me, and both started crying as they wrapped their arms around me. It'd been an emotional night for the first introduction.

"When Labrowski almost quit school that one time. When Barclay was arrested and went through his dark shit. When Keys got hurt. When Atwater messed with those bikers. I mean, my guys weren't the easiest to put up with, and I'm saying that as one of their brothers. But you were there. Every day. You took care of us, of them. And now this, moving here with me. I know some girls would want to start on their career, but you came with me." He blinked a few times, his eyes shining. "You think you're one way, but babe, you're not. You're another way. You love and you support, and you do all the shit in the background so no one notices. I noticed. I notice. I'm fucking lucky to have you, and I don't want to wait another day before telling you that I want to wake up every morning with you beside me. I want to hold your hand during movies for the rest of my life. I want to smell you, hear you laugh, get texts when you tell me to win or you won't jerk me off anymore." He laughed. "But I just want you, Mara. Will you be my wife?"

I blinked away some tears, using the back of my hand to

clear them off my face, and I nodded, almost running to him. I couldn't see the ring anymore. I didn't care about the ring. He put it on my finger, and after that, I was in his arms. We were kissing, my legs were wrapped around his waist, and he stood, his hands holding my ass.

He pulled back. "Is that a yes?"

"God, YES! I want to be your wife too." All those things he said, it went both ways. Of him helping with my mom. Of him fighting on my behalf against Carrington, taking care of the blogs so they stopped publishing lies about me, or truths about my mom. He worked with my dad to have an intervention with my mom where it was outlined what she could do with me, and firmly what she couldn't. If she didn't adhere to any of the boundaries, our relationship was done.

It hadn't worked. The intent was there, and it did help my mom to hear it clearly and articulately outlined what she was doing to me. She already knew. I'd told her so many times, but somehow being told firmly by two males, who were standing shoulder to shoulder blocking her view of me, the whole experience was a message to her.

She backed off, and big time over the last few years because ironically, the farther I got from her, the more support I received, the easier it was to handle her.

I knew she'd always be a part of my life. I'd always want my mom to be a mom, and I wouldn't get that from her. I'd get hurt, and we'd go round and round, but sometimes I liked checking on her. Right now, she had a new boyfriend and he called a month earlier for advice. He was steady and strong. Not much seemed to bother him, so in a way, maybe he was perfect for her.

I knew what the realistic result would be, but listening to him, feeling my own happiness, I was letting myself be hopeful that one day my mom would get the happiness she never seemed able to find.

Until then, Cruz was carrying me to our bedroom, still kissing me, and laid me on the bed.

His eyes were heated. "We got a fancy dinner tonight. And a heads-up, but we got people coming to the house."

"What? When?" I started to sit up. A party?

He laughed, pushing me back down, and coming with me this time. "Oh, no way. You're mine until then, and we are going to be celebrating our engagement our way." He wiggled his eyebrows. "You know what I mean."

His very hard-on gave me an indication if I hadn't. I grinned, reaching down and finding his dick, pushing his pants down until I could wrap my hand completely around him. "You remember our first hook-up?"

His eyes flashed. "69. Hell yes. You...?" But he was groaning because I twisted in the bed, my mouth closing around him. It wasn't long after before my pants were pulled away and his own mouth found me right back.

I *loved* this guy.

We were currently on the kitchen table, because we went downstairs for something until Cruz hauled me up, laid me on the table, and was between my legs within seconds. He paused, mid-thrust, and gave me an almost startled look. "You're not a big wedding girl, are you?"

I laughed, dazed because I'd been right there, but–"What are you talking about?"

"The wedding." He began moving again, sliding deep and holding, grinding. "I was wondering earlier about if we'd have a big one, and how big, and how many of my teammates you'd be willing to let stand up for me, and it just hit me that you'd probably be good with going to the court place. You would, wouldn't you?"

My body was feeling like an inferno because he was going at me hard now, worked up about what he was thinking, and my brain couldn't follow him. "Huh?"

"The wedding. Big or small?"

I groaned, lifting up, grabbing his ass, and I yanked him in, then raised myself up and ground back on him. "I don't care right now."

"Oh, right." He reached down, falling so his face was just above mine, and he was going right with me. His eyes were focused back on me, only me, and they were darkening in just the way where I knew he was making sure I was going to release first.

"Cruz." I groaned again.

"What?" He bent his head, finding my throat, tasting me there. His other hand lifted to my breast and he held me there, his thumb rubbing over my nipple, going slow, leisurely. Delicious. Tingles wracked through my body.

I lay back down, gasping, and my hands held tight to his biceps now. "Together."

"Hmmm, nope." He chuckled into my neck, lifting his head and finding my mouth. His tongue slid in and *God*, this guy could kiss. "You first, baby. Always you first." And with that, his hand went to my clit. He pressed, rolled, rubbed. He thrust in a last time, and I exploded.

My back arched off the table as I couldn't move, just holding on as the waves crashed through me. Once I was done, or almost as I was done, Cruz began moving again. Harder. Faster. Until he reached up, grabbed hold of the table, and he was *pounding* me.

I held onto his back, and as I began to feel another swirl, a buildup, I had a thought before it happened.

We're going to break the table.

Creak!

It broke in half, right as a second climax hit me, and right as Cruz growled his own. Right as the table gave out underneath us, he grabbed under me and held me up, lifting and backing away. My arms were shaking, weak, but I managed to move to his shoulders, my legs half wound around him as I looked back.

There, in a heap, with two of the legs broken off, was our table.

Cruz snorted in laughter, slowly setting me down on my feet. "Thinking this is a bad time to tell you we got caterers coming in ten minutes."

"Ten minutes?" I whipped to him.

But he was still laughing.

I stepped away from him. "Ten minutes? Really?"

He nodded, containing some of his laughter, though some still slipped out. "Fancy dinner is going to be here, and after, we got everyone coming." He'd said people were coming, but I gaped at him, my legs still a little unsteady.

"Who is everyone?"

He was watching me, gauging my reaction. "Everyone. Labrowski's bringing Angela, now that they had their little girl. He told me to prepare you that she's going to want some serious champagne tonight. Taz and Race. Zeke. Your whole Fallen Crest crew is coming. My Grant West teammates. Some of the guys from the Javs."

"Skylar and Zoe?"

He nodded. "Wade and Darren. Miles."

I checked the time. I had seven minutes left. I squealed, running for the stairs. "Caterers are your thing?"

"I got 'em. Yeah," he called after me. "Oh, uh..."

I paused at the top, and I wasn't going to worry that it was going to be so obvious he'd just pounded me when those caterers got here because he didn't look in any hurry to change that. He was slowly pulling his shirt on, and his pants weren't buttoned. He was barefoot.

He grimaced, just slightly. "I might've told everyone they could stay here."

"What?"

Everything went so fast once we moved to Arizona. He had early team meetings. Buying a house. Deciding *to* buy a house together, because that was important to me. Moving. And then he started training in September. By that time, I'd began my application process for graduate school for family therapy. Call me crazy, but I had a feeling I might have some insight. But all in all, we'd not had time to fully furnish the place, and to unpack everything that we had moved in. Our house wasn't big. We were both just starting out, though Cruz was able to get more money in the last year from early sponsorship deals. I had some from my father that he'd been waiting until I graduated from college before letting me know about. It wasn't much, but it was for this purpose of funding a future home or helping to pay off school debts.

"I know, but–" He raked a hand through his hair, right as the doorbell rang. "Oh, shit." He started for the door.

I yelled, "Button your pants."

"Right." Then I heard the door open, and voices as he was greeting the caterers.

I slipped into the shower, but as I was in there, I was doing it with a smile on my face. I had no idea what kind of ring Cruz got me, but it was gorgeous. There were hints of green in the stone. And the dinner. We had family and friends coming, because no doubt everyone meant my dad and stepmother, her two daughters who were now my stepsisters, and Cruz's mother and sister.

I'd wear the hockey sweater that Taz gifted me so long ago. She would love that, and it got washed yesterday because I wore it a lot.

And smiling at *that* thought, the shower door opened. Cruz stepped inside.

"What about–" I started to ask, but he shook his head, stepping in, his hands finding my hips, and he murmured right before his mouth found mine, "All is good. They're doing their thing. I just want to be with you."

That made two of us, and I had a fleeting thought if we'd always be like this.

I hoped so.

I knew so.

And I also knew, I got my happily ever after.

If you enjoyed Hockey With Benefits, please leave a review!
They truly help so much.

Also, if you'd like to read more stories like Mara and Cruz,
check out:

Enemies (football)
Teardrop Shot (basketball)
Hate To Love You (football)
The Not-Outcast (hockey)
Rich Prick (soccer)
Ryan's Bed (basketball)
Fallen Crest High (football)
Nate (ballet)

Plus, there's so many more!
www.tijansbooks.com

ACKNOWLEDGMENTS

Mara first appeared in Rich Prick (Blaise's book), and she was a surprise to me. At that time, I didn't know her full background story. She kept intriguing me so I wrote a short story of when her and Cruz first met for an anthology that's no longer available. After that, I was hooked. Readers could go and check out more of Mara in Rich Prick, but I don't feel that book gives her the due she deserves. I feel Hockey With Benefits is the perfect introduction to Mara and the struggles she goes through. Also, Cruz.

So, in a way, I want to thank Mara for sticking with me. Cruz's story was also a surprise because in the short story, he came to me first as this easygoing guy. He was friendly. Chill. Just wanted to hook up. Then, I began digging deeper into him and whoa, were there layers in him. And deep layers too.

I fell in love with both of them! And I truly hope you enjoyed them as well.

Thank you to Crystal, Amy, Tanasia, Kelsey, all my proofreaders, beta readers, editors. Thank you to all the ladies in the reader group. I say it every time, but you ladies have no idea how your support and enthusiasm gives me energy to keep writing. Thank you thank you thank you.

And of course, to my pup. Bailey. His happiness and love is truly a blessing. And cuddles.

24/7 help is provided from The Lifeline, giving free and confidential support for those in need or in distress. You can go there for crisis or prevention resources for yourself or loved ones.

https://988lifeline.org/
Or call 988.

THE NOT-OUTCAST

CHAPTER ONE

I was lit, weak, and horny.

That was not a good combination for me. Usually my willpower was strong, like industrial-strength super-latexed condom strong, but not tonight. Tonight, the combination of the booze and cocktails had melded together and taken down my last holdouts of willpower. I was gonzo and then I got this text.

Dean: Mustang party! Now! Where r u???

Dean was my colleague, but let's forget about why he would be texting me because we are not 'texting' colleagues. Kansas City Mustangs. That was the important part of that text, and it was getting all of my attention.

Dear God. I could hear the whistle of the impending bomb right before it hit.

That was the professional hockey team that *he* played on.

Party.

Did I mention the *he* that was him? He, as in the only rookie drafted for Kansas City's newer team? He signed his contract after he had one year at Silvard.

The *he* that the team's owners were hoping could be grown into one of the NHL's newest stars, but that'd been a three-year plan. Nope. *He* had different ideas because once he hit the ice in their first debut game, he scored a hat trick in the first period. First. Period. Playing against five to ten-year veterans, and that had not gone unnoticed. By everyone. After that *he* exploded into the NHL scene and in a big fucking way.

They started calling him Reaper Ryder after that.

It was the same *he* that I perved on during a brief stint in high school, and then again during that one year in college before he got whisked away to superstardom. Though, he didn't know any of that 411 about my perving habits.

The second text from Dean gave us the address where to go, and the whistle got louder, target hit...direct implosion.

It was two blocks away.

He was two blocks away, and there went my restraint because I'd kept away from him for the last four years when I moved to the same city he was living in—of course he didn't know that—but this city was totally amazeballs by the way.

I was doomed. I might as well start digging my own bunker at this rate because I was already downtown partaking in some celebratory boozetails, so here we were. Here I was, well *we* because I wasn't alone. My main girl since Silvard days, Sasha, was on my right, and Melanie on my left. Melanie came after Silvard, but that didn't matter. She was one of my girls. The three of us. We were awesomesauce, and we were walking into this building that looked like a downtown loft, one that was probably the humble abode to someone not so humble, but someone with old-money wealth who enjoyed partaking in their own boozetails as well.

I already felt a whole kemosabe camaraderie with whoever owned this joint.

"This place is *fucking* awesome."

That was Melanie. She enjoyed coffee, girls, and she was an

amazing barista at Dino's Beans.

"Girl."

That was Sasha. She owned a strip club, told everyone she was an angry Russian, even though there wasn't one Russian strand of DNA in her body, and she enjoyed using one word for everything. That's not to say she didn't speak more than one-word answers, but those were her go-to for speaking.

"Whoa." That was me.

Melanie had jet-black hair. Sasha had ice-queen white hair, and me—I was the in between. My hair was usually a dusty blonde color, but today it looked a bit more lighter than dusty blonde. I still enjoyed it, and I also had super chill electric-blue eyes. The other two both had dark eyes so I figured I was still the 'in between' for the eyes, too.

When we entered that party, all eyes turned to us, and not one of us was fazed. We were used to it. Where we went, we got attention. Guys loved us (sometimes), girls hated us (usually), and we didn't care (ever). We weren't going to tone down our awesomeness because of their insecurities.

But we were all works in progress, or at least I was.

I was known to have entire conversations and whole other worlds and every version of apocalypses in my head. That was just me. You'll understand the more you get to know me, but trust me when I say that I'm a lot better than I used to be. Meds, therapy, and a dead junkie mother will do that to you.

But enough about me.

Melanie was the shit, and she really loved the word 'fuck.' A-*fucking*-lot.

Then there was Sasha, she'd been my roommate from college, and here we were, three years out of graduation (well, four for me since I graduated early, and don't ask me how that happened because it still shocked the hell out of me) and going strong. But we were on a mission.

That mission was more boozetails.

There were people everywhere. Stuffy people. One woman who had a tiara on her head. There were guys in suits, some in hella expensive suits, and tuxedos, too.

Whoa.

This wasn't just a party party. This was like a whole shindig party.

Fake Stanley Cups were placed all around with mucho dinero inside.

Crap.

I started to mentally shift through the emails—easier said than done when one was halfway to boozeopolis—that I liked to avoid and I was remembering some of the subject lines of those that I had skipped. There'd been a bunch from Dean lately, though, and one was about some 'Celebrity PR for Come Our Way' and I needed to double down on the crapattitude because I had a feeling we just waltzed into a fundraiser.

"Cheyenne!"

Dean rushed over to us, holding a boozetail in one hand, and his eyes glazed over. He was medium height with a more squat build that he easily could buff up more, but I didn't think Dean went to the gym. He was always at work and because of that, I usually saw him with his hair all messed up. That's how it was now, and his eyes glazed over.

My dude coworker was lit.

I started smiling, but then no. Not good. What corporate espionage was he up to by telling me to come here?

"Where's the bar, Deano?" Melanie.

I was impressed she hadn't used her favorite word.

"There." Directions from Sasha and like that, both my buds moved away.

I settled back, knowing they'd have my back. They'd be bringing the boozetails to me—even better—so I had the time to grin at Dean. "What's happening, hot stuff?"

He never got my quotes. Or jokes.

He didn't react and he grabbed my arm. "Have you read my emails?" Then he looked at me, his head moving back an inch. "What are you wearing?"

Nothing appropriate for a work event, that's for sure.

But I only upped my grin wattage. "I was going for a Daenerys theme. Felt like wanting to tame some dragons tonight." Except I took my own liberty with the outfit. Instead of her flowing robes and dresses, I was wearing a leather, almost corset-like top, one that wrapped around my neck and hung off one of my shoulders. The bottom was more Daenerys theme, a chiffon skirt with a slit up one thigh. And high heels strapped to my feet.

It shouldn't work, but it did. It so totally did, and I had woven colored threads in my hair so they were swinging free, free and lit.

He took another step back, looking me up and down again.

"You are," a pause, "something."

I scowled. "Dude. Insulting."

He had to blink a few times because he hadn't realized I spoke again, then he refocused. "Wait. You're downtown. There's no way you could've gotten here this fast, even if you were at the shelter, but I know you weren't at the shelter. And your place is an hour out."

Case in point, my outfit.

He was right.

Come Our Way. The name of our kitchen had been a marketing and genius ploy, one put in place by Deano himself, because while I wrote the grant that got us five million (not a common thing to happen for a start-up) and got us going, his job was actually to work on marketing and promotions to keep the money, spotlight, and volunteers streaming to our little kitchen. I maintained our grant, and I helped with literally everything else. I was the final say-so on all executive decisions, except for matters that we needed the board to oversee. We had another full-time staff member, but she liked to Netflix and chill (and really Netflix and chill with wine, not the other Netflix and chill) on her evenings. But all three of us manned our little kitchen that fed a lot of the downtown homeless in our corner in Kansas City.

And Dean knew I wasn't known for one to partake in alcoholic libations, but we were here, and I was thirsty.

It was my last day on my medication vacation. I was taking advantage of it.

It was a thing that happened to help cut down on build-up immunity. Sometimes I enjoyed it, but it was usually a whole struggle to get back on and make sure everything was smooth running.

But that wasn't something I was going to think about tonight, though my brain was already starting to go there. Tomorrow I'd go back to living almost like a saint.

Where were my girls with my drinkaloo?

Also, I was firmly not letting myself think of the *he* and that took mundo restraint because he had been a big major part of my daydreams since my junior year in high school through now—especially now since I've been living in the city where he was hockey royalty.

I didn't answer Dean, but spying another Stanley Cup filled with cash, I asked instead, "What's the funding for?"

"Oh!" He perked up, throwing his head back and finishing his drink. A waitress walked by with a tray loaded with fully filled champagne flutes. He snagged two, for himself. "That's why I'm here. I got the final acceptance that the Mustangs are going to dedicate an entire two days to Come Our Way. Two days, Cheyenne. Two days? Can you believe that?" He leaned in, excited, and I could smell how excited he was.

Booze breath. It's a thing.

I edged back a step. "Totally."

So not totally.

"That's awesome."

Really so not awesome.

It was a great PR day for the kitchen and for the team, I was sure that's why they agreed to do it. It wasn't uncommon for Come Our Way to have local celebrities pop in for a day or an hour to volunteer, but the media that followed them was always too much for me. I either stayed in the back kitchen, or I took a personal day. Media days were something *extra* extra. Flashing cameras. Razor-sharp reporters. Sometimes you got a good one who just wanted to spread good news about our mission, but sometimes you got the reporters who wanted to swing things to a more controversial article for the click-baits.

I wasn't down for that poundage.

Plus, the extra buzz in the entire building was like hay fever for my meds. I couldn't handle it, and therapy had taught me to avoid those types of situations, so hence why I usually disappeared—and if the entire team was coming for two days, it'd be insane. I was already not looking forward to it, and yes, I wasn't letting myself think of *him* being in my place of business. At all.

I thought he'd known me in high school, but that turned out to be a result of some slight delusions from my undiagnosed hyper disorder, so that was embarrassing, and then when college rolled around, I intentionally stayed in the background. But if he was going to be at my place for two days—forty-eight hours—there's no way he wouldn't see me, and that information was already bumbling through my head like an intoxicated bee hooked on coke and champagne. It just didn't know what to do or where to sting. Super painful.

Dean was still talking. "...and that's why I'm here. They reciprocated with an invite here, and by the way, it's so on-the-down-low that there's no security outside. Did you see that? To even get in here, you had to know about it."

That made no sense.

Dean didn't care. "And I've already met half the team. Oh!"

His eyes were bouncing around just like my intoxicated inner bee. "I got tickets to their game on Sunday. They rocked preseason, did you see?" He kept edging closer and closer to me the more he talked, something that was so un-Dean-like that I was having a hard time processing all this newness of what was happening around me.

Dean was around the same age as me, a few years older. Coming straight from grad school with a masters in reinvigorating the world to give a fuck about homeless and runaways, he had an axe to grind and an agenda to save the world. He liked to cut loose. You had to in our profession because burnout had the highest success rate, but seeing him this tricked out had that bee flying sideways. He didn't know if he was in my bonnet or my hair braids.

Then I remembered; Dean was a hockey fan.

I was, too, but I kept my undying adoration on the downlow like a lot of things.

Not Dean. He was out of the closet and loud and proud about his love for the Kansas City Mustangs. He also turned traitor and was a Cans fan, as well as the Polars (boo, hiss), but both those teams weren't in this current building or city. So yeah, it made sense now. He was geeking out on the full freakout reader.

That, and I was wondering how much champagne he had already consumed because he just downed both those two flutes in front of me. He was so drunk that my own lit meter was heading down into the empty zone. Not cool. Not cool, indeed, and where were my girls?

Just then, I saw one of them.

And my lit meter skyrocketed right into the red zone.

The crowd parted. I had a clear view right smack to the bar, and there she was. And she wasn't alone.

Sasha had her sultry and seductive pose out, clearly liking what she saw, gazing up at *him*.

Keep reading for the rest of The Not-Outcast!

ALSO BY TIJAN

Sports Romance Standalones:

Enemies

Teardrop Shot

Hate To Love You

The Not-Outcast

Rich Prick

Latest books:

A Dirty Business (Mafia, Kings of New York Series)

A Cruel Arrangement (Mafia, Kings of New York Series)

Aveke (Fallen Crest novella, standalone)

Fallen Crest and Crew Universe

Fallen Crest/Roussou Universe

Fallen Crest Series

Crew Series

The Boy I Grew Up With (standalone)

Rich Prick (standalone)

Frisco

Series:

Broken and Screwed Series (YA/NA)

Jaded Series (YA/NA suspense)

Davy Harwood Series (paranormal)

Carter Reed Series (mafia)

The Insiders

Mafia Standalones:

Cole

Bennett Mafia

Jonah Bennett

Canary

Paranormal Standalones and Series:

Evil

Micaela's Big Bad

The Tracker

Davy Harwood Series (paranormal)

Young Adult Standalones:

Ryan's Bed

A Whole New Crowd

Brady Remington Landed Me in Jail

College Standalones:

Antistepbrother

Kian

Enemies

Contemporary Romances:

Bad Boy Brody

Home Tears

Fighter

Rockstar Romance Standalone:

Sustain

More books to come!